"[A] SPA...
AN EAGE...

D0253927

"FUN AND SEXY, A
KNOCK-YOUR-
SOCKS-OFF RIDE."
Susan Andersen

"RICHARD AND
SAMANTHA MAKE AN
EXPLOSIVE COMBINATION.
DON'T MISS
FLIRTING WITH DANGER!"
Kasey Michaels

"ONE OF MY VERY
FAVORITE AUTHORS."
Julia Quinn

"So you'll make sure I don't get accused of murder."

"I'll do my utmost."

"And you'll make phone calls and whatever else necessary to get me out of this?"

"Whatever else necessary," he agreed.

"And you won't turn me in for theft."

"You didn't actually steal anything from me." He studied her face as her lips twitched. "Did you?"

"Not if you haven't noticed."

Her rather macabre sense of humor again, even if he wasn't particularly amused. "You need to trust me," he offered, "and I need to be able to trust you. When this is over, nothing additional will be missing from my home. Is that clear, Miss Smith?"

For the first time that afternoon, she looked him full in the face. "Samantha," she said in a near whisper. "Sam. You get my last name after I decide I can trust you."

By Suzanne Enoch

FLIRTING WITH DANGER
SIN AND SENSIBILITY
ENGLAND'S PERFECT HERO
LONDON'S PERFECT SCOUNDREL
THE RAKE
A MATTER OF SCANDAL
MEET ME AT MIDNIGHT
REFORMING A RAKE
TAMING RAFE
BY LOVE UNDONE
STOLEN KISSES
LADY ROGUE

SUZANNE ENOCH

Flirting with DANGER

AVON BOOKS
An Imprint of HarperCollinsPublishers

This is a work of fiction. Names, characters, places, and incidents are products of the author's imagination or are used fictitiously and are not to be construed as real. Any resemblance to actual events, locales, organizations, or persons, living or dead, is entirely coincidental.

AVON BOOKS
An Imprint of HarperCollins*Publishers*
10 East 53rd Street
New York, New York 10022-5299

Copyright © 2005 by Suzanne Enoch
Excerpts from *Just Like a Man* copyright © 2005 by Elizabeth Bevarly; *The Trouble With Valentine's Day* copyright © 2005 by Rachel Gibson; *Flirting With Danger* copyright © 2005 by Suzanne Enoch; *Lady in Red* copyright © 2005 by Karen Hawkins
ISBN: 0-06-059363-6
www.avonromance.com

First Avon Books paperback printing: March 2005

Avon Trademark Reg. U.S. Pat. Off. and in Other Countries, Marca Registrada, Hecho en U.S.A.
HarperCollins® is a registered trademark of HarperCollins Publishers Inc.

Printed in the U.S.A.

10 9 8 7 6 5 4 3 2 1

For my agent, Nancy Yost,
who didn't laugh when I said
I had this great idea
for a different kind of story.

And for my editor, Erika Tsang,
who did laugh,
but in all the right places.

One

Samantha Jellicoe wondered who, precisely, had written the rule that thieves breaking into anything larger than a paper bag must always scale walls. Everyone knew it. Everyone counted on it, from prisons to castles to the movies to theme parks to the impressive east Florida estate sprawling before her. Stone walls, electric fences, cameras, motion detectors, security guards, all for the purpose of preventing an enterprising lawbreaker from climbing over the walls into the sanctity of private space beyond.

She looked from the stone wall in front of her to the wrought-iron double gate at the front of sprawling Solano Dorado House and gave a small smile. Some lawbreakers were more enterprising than others. So much for the rules.

Drawing in a slow breath to steady her heartbeat, she unslung the weapon from her shoulder, sank deeper into the shadows outside the gate, aimed at the camera mounted atop the fifteen-foot-high stone wall to the left of it, and fired. With a small puff of air, a paint ball splatted hard against the side of the casing, tilting it crazily up toward the treetops and streaking the lens with white paint. An owl, disturbed by the motion, hooted and launched from a branch of the overhanging sycamore, one wing passing right in front of the redirected camera.

Nice touch, she thought, slinging the paint gun back over her shoulder. Her horoscope had said that today would be her lucky day. Normally she didn't put much stock in astrology, but ten percent of one-and-a-half million for an evening's work seemed lucky enough to qualify. She scooted forward, sliding a pair of long-handled mirrors into place on either side of the heavy gates to deflect the sensors into themselves. That done, it only took a second to bypass the circuitry in the control box and shove one of the gates open far enough for her to slip through.

She'd spent all day memorizing the location of the remainder of the cameras and the three motion detectors she needed to pass, and in two minutes she'd crossed through the trees and landscaped garden to sink into a crouch at the base of a red stone staircase. Thanks to blueprints and schematics, she knew the location of every window and door, and the make and model of every lock and wiring connection. What the drawings hadn't done was tell her color and scope, and she took a second while she caught her breath to admire the sprawl of decadence.

Solano Dorado had been built in the 1920s before the stock market crash, and each successive owner had added rooms and floors—and increasingly sophisticated security. Its current incarnation was probably the most attractive so far, all whitewashed and red-tile-roofed and massive, surrounded by palms and old sycamores, with a hockey-rink-sized fishpond in the front. At the back of the house where she crouched, two tennis courts lay beyond an Olympic-sized swimming pool. The actual tidal pools at the edge of the actual ocean gurgled and sighed only a hundred yards away, but that was for public consumption.

The estate was private and protected, and created to suit the whims of man rather than nature. After eighty years of tasteful modifications and expansion, it was now the house of someone with a massive pocketbook and an equally massive ego. Someone whose horoscope read the opposite of hers and who happened to be out of the country at the moment.

Doors and window casings would be wired to within an inch of their lives, but sometimes the old, simple tricks were best. As *Star Trek*'s Mr. Scott had once said, the more elaborate the plumbing, the easier it was to plug up the drain. With a check of her watch to confirm her timing, she pulled out a roll of gray duct tape. Samantha taped down a rough, three-foot circle low on the patio window, then pulled a suction cup and glass cutter from her pack. The glass was thick and heavy, the pop and squeak when she jerked the cut round piece free louder than she would have liked. Wincing, she set the circle into the flower bed and returned to the opening she'd made.

Swiftly she ran down the list of anyone who might have heard the glass separate. Not the security guard downstairs in the video bank, but at least two more guards patrolled the inside of the house while the owner wasn't in residence. She waited a moment, listening, then, with a deep breath and the customary adrenaline flowing into her system, she slipped inside.

Two more pieces of duct tape kept the curtains in place over the hole. No sense in revealing her exit to the first guard who wandered by. Next came the stairs, a genuine Picasso hanging from the wall at the first landing. Sam passed it with barely a glance. Another would be hanging in an upstairs conference room, both wired with sensors and worth millions. She knew about them already, and tempting as they were, they weren't the reason she was there.

Samantha paused at the third-floor landing, crouching on the stairs and leaning around to view the dim, long, gallery hall. Even as she reflected that she'd seen lesser collections of arms and armament in museums, she checked for any sign of movement or sensors newer than her blueprints and scowled at the number of shadowed places a guard could be standing, where she'd never see anything until she was right on top of him.

Her target was in the middle of the hallway, through a door on the left. Sam didn't bother glancing at her watch again; she knew how long she'd been in the house, and how much longer she was likely to have before an outside patrol discovered either the hole in the glass patio door or the small mirrors at the front gate. With another deep, silent breath she pushed off.

Keeping low, she made for the nearest of the motionless knights, pausing in its shadow to listen again before she slipped forward once more. It was going to be close; she needed to be through that side door before the next patrol came by. And because of the razor-sharp timing this was her favorite part—not so much gadgetry as pure nerves and skill. Anyone could purchase the former, but the latter was what separated the women from the girls.

Ten feet from her destination she stopped short. A thin, dim glint of moonlight ran straight across the hallway, two feet above the floor and three inches from her left leg. A wire. No one ran a wire across the middle of a hallway. It was stupid, not to mention primitive and dangerous to the residents. Of course no one was *in* residence, but surely the security guards would occasionally forget the damned thing and either fall on their faces or set off the alarms—or both.

Scowling, she edged closer to the wall to see how the idiotic thing was anchored. What she should do was step over it, get what she'd come for, and leave, but its presence was just so . . . wrong. High-tech security everywhere, and here a damned steel wire.

A damned copper wire, she amended, looking closer. Wire set into small, flat black panels on either wall, stretched tight and not precisely parallel to the floor. Close, but not exactly. Yes, the house's owner was famously fanatical about his privacy, but trip wires seemed a bit much. Nor had she seen any clue that he was less than fastidious about the mansion's craftsmanship. Her frown deepened.

"Freeze!"

Sam froze, crouched behind the wire. *Shit*. The guard was early. Thirty feet in front of her, on the far side of the door, a shadow stepped out from between two gleaming silver knights.

"Don't move a muscle!"

"I'm not," she said calmly. He belonged there; she didn't. And he had a big gun held not quite steadily in both hands. "I'm not armed," she continued in the same cool voice, eyeing the shaking weapon and silently urging him not to panic.

"What's that over your shoulder, then?" he snapped, edging closer. A drip of sweat slid down his forehead.

Be calm; make him feel calm. She knew how to work this—she'd done it before. "It's a paint gun."

"Put it down. And the bag over your other shoulder."

At least he hadn't already begun squeezing off rounds in her direction. Young, but with some training, thank God. She hated amateurs. Sam put her things on the floor, easing them onto the tasteful Persian carpet runner. "You don't have anything to worry about. We're on the same team."

"Like hell." Freeing his left hand from the butt of the pistol, he reached for his shoulder. "Clark? I have an intruder. Third floor, gallery."

"No shit?" came over the radio.

"No shit. Dispatch police."

Taking a heartbeat to be grateful that the owner liked his privacy enough to keep cameras out of the main house, Sam produced a loud, suffering sigh. "That really isn't necessary. Your boss hired me, to test security."

"Like I've never heard that before," he retorted, his sarcasm blistering even in the cool darkness. "No one told me, so you can tell it to the cops. Stand up."

Slowly she straightened, keeping her hands well away from her sides as her adrenaline pumped up another notch. Just in case, she took one long step back, away from the wire. "If you knew about it, it wouldn't be a test. Come on, I could have had the Picasso downstairs, or the Matisse in the drawing room, or anything else I wanted. I was supposed to test the central security. Turn on the lights, and I'll show you my ID."

The lights went on, quick and bright enough to make her jump. *What the hell?* There wasn't any of that voice command shit in here—and the guard looked startled, too, the gun twitching alarmingly. "Easy there," she urged smoothly. She bent her knees a little, getting ready to run.

His blinking gaze, though, was beyond her shoulder, toward the stairs. "Mr. Addison. I found—"

"So I see."

Sam fought the surge of annoyance, and the damned curiosity to see the rich and rarely photographed. If she got out of there, which was beginning to look dicey, she was absolutely going to kill Stoney. *No one in residence, my ass.* "Richard Addison, I presume," she muttered over her shoulder, relaxing her stance again.

"I thought he hired you," the guard said, more confident now beneath the overhead lights and with backup.

"Not him," she returned, deciding to keep up the game. "The security firm. Myerson-Schmidt. *Your* boss."

"Doubtful," the low voice murmured from closer behind, just loud enough for her to hear. For a rich guy, he moved pretty quietly. "She's not armed, Prentiss," Addison continued at a more normal level, cultured and slightly faded Brit in his voice. "Lower your weapon before someone gets hurt, and we'll sort this out downstairs."

Prentiss hesitated, then holstered his pistol. "Yes, sir."

"Now, why don't we have a look at you, Miss . . ."

"Smith," she supplied.

"How unexpected."

Sam wasn't listening. She was watching Prentiss snap the holster closed over his gun, watching him stride forward, obviously pleased to be able to show off for the big boss. Watching him not even glance down. "Stop!" she ordered, abrupt panic making the command shrill and tight.

"Like h—"

"Jesus." Sam whipped around, angling for the stairs and plowing at a dead run into Addison, registering no more than a glimpse of bare chest, startled gray eyes, and tousled black hair as she took him down to the floor with her. With a pop and flash at her back the hallway exploded. Heat slammed into her even pressed against Addison on the floor. The house shook, glass shattering. Drawing in its breath, the gallery roared even more thunderously, and the lights went out again.

Two

Tuesday, 2:46 a.m.

Richard Addison came to with an EMT holding open his eyelid and flashing a light in his left eye. "Get the bloody hell off me," he growled, shoving as he struggled upright.

"Lie down, Mr. Addison. You may have internal inj—"

"Shit," he rasped, lying back again as pain shot through the back of his skull. On top of that, his ribs felt like someone had caved them in with a baseball bat. He tried to draw in a breath, hacking at both the pain and the sharp, acrid scent of smoke. With a rush everything came back—the explosion, the guard. The girl. "Where is she?"

"Don't worry, sir," another voice said, and a second EMT blurred into his line of vision. "We've contacted your physician to meet you at the hospital."

"No, where is the woman?" He didn't need to ask about Prentiss. He'd felt the heat of the flames, the burning debris smacking into his face.

"We're not sure about anything, sir. The bomb squad, homicide, forensics are all here, but they have to wait for the fire department to finish. Did you see the device?"

Richard coughed again, wincing. "I didn't see a bloody thing."

"Are you sure about that?" a third voice asked, and he refocused.

Plain clothes, with a cheap but tasteful tie. Homicide, from what the tech had said. "And you are?" he asked anyway.

"Castillo. Homicide," the detective affirmed. "Your guard downstairs called in about an explosion and an intruder. That would be the woman you're talking about, I assume?"

He nodded. "I assume."

"Well, she sure wanted you dead. Bad enough to take herself and your security guard out with you. You were lucky you made it down the stairs. Can you describe her?"

For the first time, Richard glanced at his surroundings. He was on the second floor, just off the landing, and the back of his head continued to throb where he'd slammed it against the floor. The fire crew hadn't dragged him down the stairs, or Castillo wouldn't have made the comment about his being lucky. And he damned well hadn't done it on his own.

"She said her name was Smith," he said slowly, pushing upright again. "Slim, petite, black clothes. Her back was to me, and she wore a baseball cap. I'm afraid I didn't get much else. Green eyes," he added, remembering the glimpse of her face as she'd launched herself into his rib cage. As she'd saved his life.

"It's not much, but we'll do a search of local hospitals. Even if she had armor on, I doubt she made it out of here without a scratch." The detective ran a finger across his thick, graying moustache. "Let's get you to the hospital, and I'll catch up with you there."

Wonderful. The press would love that. He shook his head gingerly. "I'm not going."

"Yes, you are, Mr. Addison. If you die now, I get fired."

Two hours later, hearing the chatter of media and the glint of camera lights down the narrow, echoing hall of white plaster and linoleum, he was wishing he'd held his ground and stayed at the estate. Of course the press had found out. And

God knew what a spectacle they'd try to make of his stay in a hospital. He told his doctor as much while they sewed closed a four-inch gash across his chest.

"You're taking this well, actually," Dr. Klemm said, taping off his ribs. "I brought an elephant tranquilizer. Shame I won't have to use it."

"Keep it close, just in case. I'm mad as hell," Richard said shortly, trying to take shallow breaths and not collapse back onto the bed. The painkiller the paramedics had given him in the ambulance was beginning to wear off, but it made him groggy, and he refused to request more. Someone had tried to kill him, and he wasn't going to doze off while someone else figured out who. "Where's Donner?"

"I'm here." Tall and lanky, Texas in his soft voice, the lead attorney in the law firm of Donner, Rhodes and Chritchenson strode into the room. "Jesus, you look like hell, Rick."

"Who is she, Tom? And where are my clothes?"

"We don't know yet, and right here." Light blue eyes narrowed. "But we'll find out. Count on it." Dumping a sports bag onto a chair, he yanked out a pair of jeans, a black T-shirt, and a long-sleeved cotton shirt.

Richard lifted an eyebrow. "From the Tom Donner Outdoor Living selection, I presume?"

"They wouldn't let me onto the estate to get your things. They'll fit." Scowling as Klemm finished wrapping Richard's ribs, Donner handed over a pair of brand-name athletic shoes. "What are you doing here, anyway?" he asked. "You're supposed to be in Stuttgart."

"Harry tried to talk me into staying another day. I should have listened to him." Richard rolled his shoulder, wincing again at the pull against his stitches. "I want Myerson-Schmidt on the phone."

"It's four o'clock in the morning. I'll fire 'em for you tomorrow."

"Not until I have a chance to chat with them." And not until he'd made certain that they hadn't sent a very clever—and lucky—female to test his security.

"Hell, the cops found one of the cameras batted into the treetops, mirrors blocking the gate signal, and a big hole in one patio window. Not to mention most of the pieces of a security guard and Rick Addison with his hair on fire."

"My hair was not on fire, but thanks for the imagery. And I'm not going to sit back and twiddle my fingers. I want to be there when they question her." Of course they would have to find her first. He assumed the police would, but at the same time he had the distinct feeling that it wouldn't be easy. Whoever she was, she still had him wondering about the security test, and that was after his third floor had blown up.

"Forget it, Rick. She's just someone who wanted a piece of you and messed up. She's not the first to try. And there are already five news crews by the elevator who want a few more slices."

"I think she saved my life." Stifling a groan, Richard pulled the borrowed T-shirt over his head. "And that *is* a first for someone who allegedly wanted me dead."

Tom Donner opened and closed his mouth. "Tell me what happened."

Rick told him, starting with the screeching fax machine that some idiot had programmed to call his private number every two minutes starting at 2:00 A.M., to the security call he'd overheard informing Clark that Prentiss had discovered an intruder, to the way Miss Smith had tried to stop Prentiss's advance, then threw herself on him just as the hallway exploded.

" 'Smith?' " Donner repeated.

"I would guess she was lying," Rick said with a faint smile.

"Ya think? She knew about the bomb."

Richard shook his head. "She knew something. I saw the look in her eyes when she hit me. She was terrified."

"I'd be, too, if some idiot security guard set off my explosives before I was clear."

"She could have made it past me before it went off. She didn't. She took me down. And I didn't drag myself downstairs, whatever the police think."

Of course she'd been at the estate to rob him. And, the cynical, suspicious core of him admitted that she might have been there to kill him. Something, though, had happened to change all that. And he wanted to know what, and why.

The detective he'd met at the estate leaned into the doorway. "Castillo," he said, flashing his badge as Donner started forward. "You sure her plowing into you wasn't just an accident, Mr. Addison?"

"I'm sure," Rick grunted. He didn't want to deal with the detective right now. With the explosion, this had become very personal. He wanted to be the one asking the questions, and he wanted the answers for himself. This was too much like working for someone else—and that wasn't how he ran his business, or his life.

The detective cleared his throat. "I'm more suspicious, myself. We've got out an APB, and like I said, she's bound to turn up somewhere for medical attention. I suggest you find a place to stay, and I'll set up an around-the-clock watch on you."

Richard frowned. "I don't want people following me around."

"It's procedure. You can either use the Palm Beach PD or the sheriff's department."

"No. I don't get kicked out of my own house, and I have my own estate security."

"With all respect, I'm not exactly impressed by your estate security, Mr. Addison."

"I'm not either, at the moment." Groaning aloud, he gingerly stood to pull on the faded jeans.

"Christ, Rick. I'll get a wheelchair." The tall attorney strode for the door.

"I'm walking," Richard said, clenching his jaw as he straightened. He should probably be grateful his blood wasn't pooling somewhere on the floor, but damnation, he hurt. And Miss Smith had been right there with him. "Tom, get Myerson-Schmidt on the phone now. And not some drone. Somebody who can answer some questions."

"I'm working on it." Donner came back into the room, a cell phone to his ear and a wheelchair in front of him.

Trying not to double over, Richard faced Castillo. "If—when—you find this Miss Smith, I want to know. And I want to be there."

"That's not exactly procedure, Mr. Addison."

Giving up on being stoic, Rick dropped into the wheelchair. "Fuck procedure. My taxes pay half your department's annual budget. If you're going to talk to her, I'm going to be there."

Donner glanced at him, but Richard pretended not to notice. The fiasco, and therefore the answers, belonged to him.

"I'll see what I can do."

"He what?"

Samantha flinched. "God dammit, Stoney, be careful. I need that arm."

Fat fingers surprisingly gentle, Stoney sent her shoulder an intense scowl and pinched together the long, jagged cut. "You need a hospital, honey." With his free hand he squeezed a tube of super glue along the wound.

"What I need is a heavy, blunt object so I can beat you across the head," she returned, more to cover her gasp of pain than because she was still angry. "You said Addison would be in Stuttgart for another day."

"That's what the *Wall Street Journal* thought, too. Some bank deal with Harold Meridien. Blame the *Journal* for having bad information, or blame him for lying to them. And hey, you might at least have grabbed one of the Picassos on the way out. The alarm was already triggered."

"Like you want to fence a Picasso without a buyer. And I had my hands full, thank you very much." She *had* had her hands full, with a very heavy, very unconscious Richard Addison. She'd seen a few shots of him, in the *Inquirer* during his messy divorce year before last and on one of the nightly Hollywood entertainment shows a couple of months ago, when he'd donated an obscene amount of money to some cause at some event hosted by whoever'd won the Oscar last year. Rich, divorced, and private. And annoyingly unpredictable.

"That should do it," Stoney decided, slowly releasing the hold he had on her shoulder. The glue held. "I'll bandage it, just in case."

"How's my back?" She craned her neck, trying to see.

"Good thing you were wearing Kevlar, honey. You can see the vest outline." He traced a scooped line high up between her shoulder blades. "No tank tops for a while. But I'm more worried about the gash on the back of your leg. You do much walking, and the glue won't hold."

She looked at his face. "You're worried? About me? How sweet." Placing a kiss on the end of his crooked, flat nose, she gingerly scooted off the end of his kitchen table.

"I'm serious. You must've left some blood behind. What about DNA mapping and that shit?"

She'd thought of that and had already rationalized her way out of letting it bother her. "They have to have me to match it with something," she returned, taking a slow, experimental step and feeling the glue pull at her torn skin. "And they don't have me." She glanced at his sliding-eyes cat clock above the refrigerator. "It's after five. Turn on the news, will you?"

While he shuffled in his bathrobe and slippers to the small counter television, Sam carefully shrugged into the spare pair of jeans she kept at Stoney's. This must be why mothers always told their kids to wear clean underwear, she reflected, wincing as the material slid across the bandaged gash. In case of explosions.

"You said the security guard died, Sam," Stoney grunted, flipping on the local morning news. "What're you looking for, video of the body bag?"

"I left fast," she returned, easing on a T-shirt and leaning into the refrigerator for a can of Diet Coke. "I think I avoided all the cameras on the grounds, but I'd like to know for sure."

He cocked a heavy eyebrow at her. "That all?"

"Well, I'm kind of curious about who strung that wire across the hallway, and it might be helpful to know whether Addison survived or not."

Cool as she kept her tone, Stoney would know she was worried. The explosion had shoved her into the floor and obviously rattled her brain. She'd dragged Addison downstairs almost by reflex, then realized he could probably identify her to the cops. The guard, Prentiss, was definitely dead, and if she had been the one to discover an intruder in the hallway when a bomb went off, she knew whom she would blame. This was bad. Very bad.

"Sam."

She jerked her head toward the television.

"—quiet of the night was interrupted by a fire at Solano Dorado, the Palm Beach County estate of billionaire businessman and philanthropist Richard Addison. One fatality has been reported, and the cause is under investigation and has been declared 'suspicious.' Addison was taken to the hospital for treatment of minor cuts and bruises, and has been released." The video changed to show Addison, accompanied by a tall, blond man, diving into the back of a black Mercedes limousine. Disheveled dark hair half hid the bandage that crossed his forehead, but otherwise he looked intact. And for a moment she was relieved.

"Great." Stoney sighed. "You should have left him up there."

"I don't think letting Richard Addison burn to death would have helped me any," she retorted, hiding a shiver at the thought.

"Did he get a look at you?"

Sam shrugged. "A brief one."

"They're going to be after you."

"I know. I'm good at not being found."

"This is different, honey."

She knew that, too. Someone had died. And a very rich man had nearly died. And she hadn't even managed to nab the stone she'd been after. "I was stupid. I should have noticed that someone else had already broken in and wired the place with explosives. Dammit." She took a long swallow of soda. "Who would want to blow up the stuff in that house, anyway? What's the point?"

Stoney gazed at her. "Murder?"

"But why? And why so messy?"

"Ya know, Sam," the burly black mountain in terry cloth rumbled, "if I was you, I'd be more concerned about being blamed for killing that guard than with being Mrs. Murder, She Wrote."

"Jessica Fletcher," she corrected absently, watching as the television, muted now, played some taped footage of Addison at yet another charity function with that model Julia Poole on his arm.

"And if I had a memory like yours, I'd be going on game shows, not stealing shit."

She couldn't blame the news for going overboard in their coverage of Addison; with that face and his money he had to be good for ratings. Of course a political scandal or a corporate bankruptcy would have been nice, but no, she'd had to break into his house on a slow news day. She watched him answer a question about some bit of nonsense or other. *Bored*, she thought, and a little amused at the swirl of sycophantry around him.

"I've never stolen *shit*, thank you very much, and I prefer to think of it as the involuntary relocation of objects, anyway." Taking a last swallow of soda, she dumped the can into Stoney's recycling box and grabbed up her torn and singed shirt and pants. She'd toss them in a dumpster on her way home. The vest was heavier, but at least it was salvageable, and she slung it over her good shoulder. "I'm going out for a while. I'll call you this evening."

"Where, Sam?"

She glanced over her shoulder at him and forced a smile. "Like I'd tell you."

"Just be careful, baby," he cautioned, following her to the door.

"You, too. Your buyer knew you had somebody going after the tablet last night. You might get some pressure."

He smiled, lips pulling back to reveal white teeth. "I like pressure."

So did she, usually, but not in this amount. Hard as the police might look for a missing ring or a painting or a vase, they looked harder when someone died over it. And they would look even harder when someone died in the house of a man featured last year on the cover of *Time* magazine.

She had some thinking to do. Like why someone would string explosives across a hallway in the middle of a multimillion-dollar art and antique gallery. And she wanted to know whether a particular stone tablet would be listed among the destroyed items—or if she'd be blamed for taking it, on top of everything else.

Three

Tuesday, 6:15 a.m.

Tom Donner flipped his cell phone closed. "Myerson-Schmidt confirms they didn't send anyone to test security. But they are very anxious to continue their relationship with you."

Beside him in the back seat of the Mercedes, Richard blew out his breath. Damn. He'd been hoping the elusive Miss Smith had been telling the truth. "And Prentiss? Any family?"

"Parents and an older sister, all in Dade County. Myerson-Schmidt has a counselor there with them."

"I won't intrude," he decided. "I'll have my office send them my condolences and see if there's anything else they need."

"Sir, press and police barricades," the driver said over his shoulder, slowing the stretched black SL500.

"Go through them, Ben. They're not keeping me out of my own bloody house."

"I thought you British guys were all stoic in the face of disaster."

Richard slid his gaze from the attorney as cameras and reporters rushed the car. "This *is* me being stoic. I want them gone, Tom."

"The reporters, or the cops?"

"Both."

"Yeah, well, I'll work on the press. But considering that somebody tried to kill you this morning, I'm gonna suggest you let the police do their jobs."

"Not from my front drive. I'm not going to change the way I live my life. In my line of work, if I look weak, then I *am* weak. I won't have the police barricading my house, like I'm some freakish recluse afraid to step outside. Aside from everything else, I refuse to live in an armed encampment."

"Okay. I'll do what I can. But face it, Rick—you're a valuable commodity."

They drove through the gates, which were manned by a pair of officers. Richard set aside his annoyance at having to get clearance to enter his own property, and instead kept his eyes on the house as they crossed the lush green palm grove and reached the curving drive at the front. Ruined furniture and curtains and carpets lay strewn at the edge of the cobblestones, heaped alongside more carefully placed statuettes and paintings. Already the insurance people were there, counting and examining objets d'art and wrapping the more delicate ones in felt blankets and lined crates for storage and protection—all under the watchful eyes of more police.

"A couple of broken-out windows," Donner commented, leaning across Rick to take a look, "and black roof tiles. Other than that, it doesn't look too bad from the outside."

Yet another uniformed officer pulled open the car door as they came to a stop. Richard's joints had stiffened on the drive from the hospital, and he winced as he straightened. "You should see the inside," he muttered, starting up the wide front steps. The granite blocks were still covered with tarps and equipment and groups of emergency personnel drinking coffee from his china cups.

"Sir? Mister Addison?" The officer behind them caught up at a brisk trot. "Sir, the building hasn't been cleared yet."

"It looks fairly empty to me," Richard replied, eyeing the piles of his belongings strewn across the lawn. They must have gutted the entire third-floor gallery.

"Cleared by the bomb squad, I mean. They've done the basement and the first two floors, but not the third floor or the attic."

"Then have them notify me if it looks like something's going to blow up."

"Rick," Donner cautioned, "they're on our side."

Richard frowned. He'd set up the damned estate for privacy, a place where he could escape from the cameras and reporters who always seemed to hound him. And he had to admit that without the police presence, half the tabloids would probably be jumping the walls right now. He turned around, eyeing the officer still dogging their heels. "What's your name?"

"Kennedy. James."

"You may accompany us, James Kennedy. As long as you stay out of the way."

"Sir? I'm supposed to—"

"In or out, Kennedy." Between the pain in his head and the soreness of his ribs, he wasn't in the mood to be diplomatic.

"What Mr. Addison meant to say," Tom amended, "is that he intends to cooperate fully with the police department. But he still has multiple business concerns that require his immediate attention. Your presence will ensure that we don't go anywhere or touch anything that might compromise the investigation."

"Homicide won't like it," Kennedy returned.

"We'll be careful."

"Um, well, okay then. I guess."

Danté Partino, Richard's estate acquisitions manager, fell in as they climbed the crowded stairs to the third floor. "It's a mess, Rick," he said, in Italian-accented English. "Who would do such a thing? Both of the 1190 full armor pieces, the Roman helmet, half the sixteenth-century—

"I can see for myself," Richard interrupted, stopping at the top of the stairs. "Mess" didn't begin to describe the gallery hall. "Armageddon" seemed a more apt characterization. Blackened and twisted suits of armor lay where they'd fallen, lost warriors of some obscene marble-tile-and-carpet-covered battlefield. A French Renaissance tapestry, one of the first items he'd ever collected, hung in burned tatters from the wall. What little remained was hardly recognizable. Anger curled through him. No one did this to him and got away with it.

"Jesus," Tom whispered. "Where were you standing?"

Richard took four slow steps forward, well beyond the outer edge of the chaos. "About here."

Danté cleared his throat, breaking the ensuing silence. "Rick, I want to inspect all the damaged items myself, but the insurance people act as if they own everything. They have no idea how delicate—"

"Danté, it's all right," he countered, more for his manager's sake than his own. Furious as he was, the loss of his things was only a sidebar. He wanted to know who had destroyed them. "Tom'll make certain you're consulted on everything."

"But—"

"That's how it is, Danté."

Partino nodded, fingers clenching the clipboard he carried. "Very well. But the water from the sprinklers and the hoses, it also damaged some of the paintings on the second floor. Maybe we can salv—"

"What about the tablet?" Richard interrupted. He admired Partino's passion, but it had been a damned long night.

"It's not here," Castillo said, topping the stairs behind them. "We figure that was what she was after. And you shouldn't be up here, Mr. Addison. This is a murder investi—"

"Have you photographed and fingerprinted and whatever it is you do?"

"Yeah."

"Then what kind of explosive was it?" Ignoring the hiss of Officer Kennedy, Richard stepped forward, sinking into a stiff squat close to a fire-blackened hole in the gallery wall.

Castillo sighed. "Looks like a trip wire strung across the hallway, rigged like a grenade with shape charges. You pull out the wire, and pop. Quick setup, but professional—and very effective. Perfect for covering your tracks if you're caught before you're out."

"What if she'd gotten out unseen?" Richard asked.

"Well, it'd be a hell of a way to confuse a robbery investigation."

"And a hell of a risk," Richard continued more quietly. "A couple of years for theft versus the death penalty for murder in the first degree, yes?"

"Only if she gets caught. I might risk that for the stuff you've got in here."

"I wouldn't." Richard straightened, dusting soot from his hands. "Castillo, I'll leave you to work, but please keep me apprised of the investigation. I have a few phone calls to make."

While Danté hovered over the carnage like an anxious mother hen, Tom and Richard shut themselves in the second-floor office. The huge windows overlooked the front lawn and pond, generally a tranquil enough sight, but now covered with uniforms and garbage. With a groan he couldn't stifle, Richard sank into the chair behind his severe black-and-chrome desk. It was one of the few nonantique pieces of furniture in the house, and only because the seventeenth century hadn't made allowances for computers or phones or electronics.

"What's bothering you?" Donner asked, pulling a bottle of water from the small cabinet refrigerator and sitting in one of the plush conference chairs at the far end of the room. "Other than nearly getting blown into itsy bitsy pieces."

"I told you I couldn't sleep last night."

"Because of the fax calls."

"Precisely. So I was wandering about, waiting for a decent

hour to call the New York office. The gallery would've been my next stop, intruder or not."

Tom stayed silent for a beat, taking that in. "You're firing Myerson-Schmidt."

"That's not the point. She yelled at Prentiss to stop, then hit me like a bulldozer."

"Castillo figured she was trying to save her own skin."

"No."

"Then what, Rick? Really?"

"Let's say she sneaks in, gets through all the security and grabs the tablet—even though I have a multitude of things worth more money—pauses on her way out for five minutes to rig an explosive, gets caught at it, then tries to keep anyone from getting blown up."

"Tries to keep *herself* from getting blown up."

Maybe. "But if she hadn't stopped to set up the bomb, she would have been out before anyone noticed."

Tom crossed his long legs at the ankles. "Okay, possibility number one: Robbery wasn't the objective. Like you said, she did walk right past a hell of a lot of nice stuff."

"That makes murder the objective." Richard could still see her eyes, the expression on her face as she hit him. "Then why drag me downstairs, out of range of the fire?"

The attorney shrugged. "Cold feet? Or maybe you weren't the target."

"So who was? Prentiss? I don't think so." He leaned forward, tapping his fingers on the hard black desk. "Possibility number two: She didn't plant the bomb."

"All right, then we have two intruders breaking into this fortress on the same night, one through the patio window and one by . . . some other method. One wants the tablet, and the other wants to blow something up. To blow you up."

"Except that I wasn't supposed to be here."

Donner blinked. "That's right. You were supposed to be in Stuttgart until this evening."

"The bomb would've gone off during the next regular patrol of the gallery, and I wouldn't have been here at all."

"Unless someone knows you left Germany early."

Richard scowled. "That narrows it down to just a few people, most of whom I trust implicitly. And Harry Meridien, who wanted me to stay even after I told him that I was not going to pay more than we agreed on for shares in his bloody bank."

"People talk."

"Not my people." Pushing to his feet, Richard paced the long room. "I want to talk to Miss Smith."

"So does the Palm Beach PD. And the FBI, now. You know how they hate it when influential foreign businessmen from allied countries almost get blown up."

Richard dismissed that with a wave of his hand. The maneuverings of the FBI, little as he liked them, didn't interest him at the moment. "I don't care about anyone's agenda but mine. Someone broke into *my* home, killed someone who works for me, and stole something that belongs to me. And 'guilty' or 'not guilty' doesn't begin to answer the questions I want to ask."

Donner sighed. "Yeah, okay. I'll see if I can find out how close they are to nabbing her." He shook his head. "But when we get arrested for interfering in a police investigation, I'm not representing you."

"If we get arrested, then I'm firing you for doing a sloppy job." Smiling, Rick reached for the phone. "Now leave. I have work to do."

Two flipping days. Samantha sank into the cushions of her couch and chose another channel with the TV remote. She hated sitting around under the best of circumstances, and this was far from the best of anything. Still, the media wouldn't give up the story. And while they had hold of it, she couldn't turn her attention elsewhere.

By now they'd run out of new information, and so for the last day she'd been hearing the same story with a handful of twists—the life of Richard Michael Addison, the loves of Richard Michael Addison, the philanthropy of, the businesses of, yadda yadda yadda. And then there were the facts they *did* have, and kept repeating on every news broadcast: There'd been an explosion, a guard, now identified as Don Prentiss, had been killed, and several valuable items had been destroyed. And the police were looking for a white female, height five-foot-four to five-foot-seven, weight 120 to 150 pounds, in conjunction with the investigation.

"One hundred and fifty pounds, my ass," she muttered, changing channels again. Wrong weight or not, she knew what it meant; one suspect being sought, one person they were blaming. Her.

Every instinct told her to run, so she could look at what had happened from a safer distance. The problem was, if they thought she'd tried to kill Addison, there was no safe distance. And no safe way to get there. Airports, bus stations— they'd be watching everything. Well, they could just keep watching, though it didn't make her feel any better to hear on the morning news that the police were "expecting to make an arrest at any moment." She didn't believe it, but neither was she willing to ignore the threat.

And so she sat on the couch, sipping a soda and eating microwave kettle corn, watching the tail end of the mid-morning news—and tried to figure out what had happened. As a thief, she was exceptionally gifted. Her father had said so, as had Stoney, and a few of the discreet clients she'd worked for.

She enjoyed the independence that her skills provided her. She enjoyed the challenge of her chosen profession, enjoyed the feeling that temporarily possessing some of the world's rarest objects gave her. And she enjoyed the money she received as payment, careful as she had to be about spending it. Retirement, her father had repeated endlessly while he taught her the skills of the trade. Work toward twenty years from now, not for tomorrow.

That goal was why she lived in a small, neat house outside of Pompano Beach, and it was why she worked for a pittance as a freelance art consultant for some museum or other. And that, quite simply, was why she didn't kill. People who killed in the quest for inanimate objects didn't get to retire peacefully somewhere in the Mediterranean and employ handsome houseboys.

All of which made one thing clear. If she wanted to retire, she needed to figure out who had set that bomb. She'd either been played for a fool, or she had the worst luck in history. Either way, she wanted payback. And she needed to be able to prove that she hadn't done it. Solving this mess just to satisfy her own curiosity wouldn't keep her out of prison.

The news ended with no break in the story, and she finally found something worth watching. With *Godzilla 1985* roaring and stomping Tokyo on WNBT in the background, she scooted off the couch for her computer, logged on, and checked messages. Since she wasn't interested in either penile enlargement or a free trip to Florida, she deleted them, went into a search engine, and typed in Richard Addison's name.

The preview page flooded with images, a backlog of articles on various newspaper and magazine Web sites, from *Architectural Digest* to *CEO* to *Newsweek*. "We get around, don't we, Addison?" she murmured, scrolling through the first page and calling up the second.

Most of the articles used similar pictures, as though Addison had sat for one photo shoot and left the publications to sort through the results. Despite the slightly too-long, dark, wavy hair just touching his collar, he looked like a multibillionaire, and not just because of the black Armani suit, black tie, and dark gray shirt. It was the eyes, mostly, dark gray and glinting. They said power and confidence, looking directly into the camera and announcing that this was a man to be taken seriously.

"Not bad," she commented. Okay, so maybe that was an understatement. Maybe he was gorgeous. And he'd definitely looked delicious in nothing but sweatpants, even covered in soot and blood.

Annoyed at herself for getting distracted, she clicked on the third page. Now that the references were becoming a little more obscure, she slowed. Purchases of antiques, a site dedicated to yacht enthusiasts, and an entire page of *www.divorcegladiators.com*, hosted not by Mr. Addison, but by Patricia, the ex–Mrs. Addison. *Ouch.* Samantha knew she had more pertinent things to discover about the man who'd dumped her into the middle of a murder investigation, but she clicked on the Web site anyway.

A photograph of Patricia Addison-Wallis flashed onto the screen. A petite blonde with the sculpted good looks that cost a thousand dollars per visit at a salon, the ex–Mrs. Addison answered e-mail questions and gave advice on how to avoid being taken to the cleaners in a divorce, in hopes that others would profit where she hadn't. Considering that just over two years ago Addison had caught her bare-assed with Sir Peter Wallis at his villa in Jamaica, Sam privately thought Patricia had gotten off easy. Not all cuckolded husbands would allow their ex-wives and new spouses enough funds to at least keep a nice home in London.

Her phone rang. Sam jumped, trotting into the kitchen to pick it up. "Hola."

"Samantha Jellicoe," the voice returned, male and heavily French. "So this is where you've been hiding."

Her heart thunked, then began beating again. *As if she didn't already have enough trouble.* "Etienne DeVore. I'm not hiding, and how the hell did you get my number?"

He made a derisive sound. "I know my business, cherie. And stay out of mine. It's dangerous."

A siren drifted into hearing a few blocks away, then cut off. The hairs on the back of her neck pricked, and Sam pulled aside the lace curtain to gaze out the small kitchen window at the street. Nothing, though the timing of the phone call had just become very interesting. "That was you at Addison's! You nearly killed me!"

"I did not expect you'd take a job like this one. So complicated, you know."

"Well, fucks to you, mon ami." As another thought occurred to her, she frowned. "How did you know it was me, there?"

Etienne snorted again. "Don't insult me. Anyone else would be dead. Even with you, it was too close, non? Besides, I'm trying to do you a favor."

"A fav—"

Another siren just entered her hearing, and then shut off abruptly, rather than dropping into the typical low rumbling growl as the car stopped.

"Dammit. I have to go. Etienne, if you called the cops on me, you're a dead man."

"I don't call the cops, ever. This is shit. Go, Samantha. I will take care of things."

"Yeah, right." Her mind flying with scenarios about who might have talked and why, Sam hung up the phone. She raced into her bedroom, grabbed up the backpack she always kept under her bed, and hurried back into the living room. The computer still sat there, requesting whether she would like to subscribe, for the reasonable price of $12.95 per year, to the newsletter dedicated to following the private life and business practices of Richard Addison.

She yanked the plug out of the wall, lifted the casing off the CPU, and pulled out every circuit board and wire that wasn't soldered down. Shoving them into her pack, she kicked the crap out of the rest of the unit, then took another minute to make a check of the windows around the perimeter of the house. It looked clear, and she slipped out the back door. Hopping her neighbor's fence, she hiked herself onto Mrs. Esposito's roof, wincing as the motion pulled at the wound on her thigh, and ran.

She'd left the Honda parked in the Food for Less market two blocks away, and she reached it just as a police helicopter, a news helicopter close behind it, powered overhead in the direction of her house. Her former house. Starting the car, she drove another mile and a half before she pulled into a lot crowded with hamburger and pizza and Cuban food restaurants. The pay phone worked, though she wouldn't vouch for its cleanliness. Dropping in a quarter, she dialed Stoney's number.

"Yeah?"

"Jorge?" she said in a thick accent. "Está Jorge alle?"

She heard his intake of breath. "Look, lady, I keep telling you, there's no Jorge here. No está aqui. Comprende?"

"Comprendo." Her hands shook as she hung up the phone, and she clenched them together. They'd found Stoney, or at least were keeping an eye on him. A close eye. Which meant they'd probably try to trace her call. Cursing, she hurried back to the car and headed north. How in the hell had the police found their trail so fast? She knew she hadn't left prints, and even if Addison had managed to give a good description of her, they had nothing to match it to. She believed Etienne when he said he hadn't turned her in—that wasn't his style. The cops' arrival, though, hadn't surprised him, either. Someone had talked, and they'd implicated both her and Stoney. She narrowed her eyes. No one played her for a fool. No one who didn't regret it later.

This was out of control. Rich people had things stolen from them all the time. That was why they'd invented insurance. What rich people didn't have, however, were people trying to blow up their houses, and perhaps even them. Damn Etienne. She remembered Addison's face as she'd hit him, the startled look that had replaced the mild amusement in his gray eyes. He had to know she hadn't tried to kill him. Just the opposite. She'd saved his life.

Samantha's heart jumped. He was the only witness to her involvement in any of this, as far as she knew. Etienne might have said he'd take care of things, but in her experience, that meant only things that concerned his own ass. If he followed his usual pattern, he would disappear for a few weeks and emerge counting his cut. Which was fine, except that it left her with a shitload of trouble. And so she needed Addison. She needed to convince him that she was innocent—or relatively so, anyway. Someone needed to take the blame for this fiasco, and she didn't intend for it to be her. It looked as though she was going in over the wall, after all.

Four

Thursday, 9:08 p.m.

"This is ridiculous," Richard said, hanging up the phone after his conversation with the chief of the Palm Beach Police Department. "It's been two bloody days, and still all they'll say is that they have a few leads but nothing they're free to tell me."

"Which would be true." Donner watched Richard pace from the far side of the desk.

"Except that they have a Walter 'Stoney' Barstone under surveillance." Richard glanced at the fax Donner had brought with him. "And a house they began searching this afternoon. I would say that's significant."

"It's something. But since the house is owned by one Juanita Fuentes, who apparently died in 1997, I'd guess they aren't quite sure what's going on."

"I want to go there," Richard said. "To that house." Striding to the liquor cabinet for a brandy, he rubbed at his temple. Dr. Klemm had said he probably had a mild concussion, but by now he imagined the headache was more than equal parts frustration.

"You can't. We don't officially know about it yet. And I can only push things so far, Rick, even with your name to throw around."

"I hate not knowing what's going on. And whatever anyone else thinks, she didn't act—"

"Didn't act like a killer? You said that before—but it's not your job to decide that." Clearing his throat, Donner uncrossed his long legs and stood. "I'm more concerned that the police want you to stay in Florida." He flashed a grin at Richard's frown. "I mean, I like having you here, even off-season, but keeping you in a place where things explode doesn't make me all that comfortable."

"Me, either."

"Ha. You *like* being in the middle of shit."

Richard eyed him. "True or not, I *do* like resolutions. Go do something constructive, will you?"

Tom made a truly awful bow. *Americans.*

"Yes, your majesty. I'll swing by the office and put in another call to Senator Branston. Maybe I can shake something out of her tree."

"Shake Barbara hard, or I will."

"No, you won't, because you're lying low and cooperating with the authorities in this matter. I'm the lawyer. I'm supposed to be nasty."

Donner left, closing the door behind him. Richard, though, continued to pace. He hated being handled, even by a friend like Tom. The police department's sycophantic nonsense was simply insulting. And the FBI and he went back quite a ways and had never dealt well together.

He supposed he might be considered a suspect by an exceptionally broad stretch of someone's imagination, but in reality they probably wanted him to stay in Florida because his presence would keep the media interested and convince the department to continue paying the investigators their overtime. As long as it helped somebody track down Miss Smith, he would put up with being in the public eye—for now.

He started to take another swallow of brandy, then stopped

as the skylight in the middle of the ceiling rattled and opened. With a graceful flip that looked much easier than it had to be, a woman dropped into his office. *The* woman, he noted, reflexively taking a step back.

"Thank you for getting rid of your company," she said in a low voice. "I was getting a cramp up there."

"Miss Smith."

She nodded, keeping green eyes on him as she walked to the door and locked it. "Are you sure you're Richard Addison? I thought he slept in a suit, but night before last you had on nothing but jogging sweats, and tonight"—she looked him slowly up and down—"a T-shirt and jeans, and no shoes."

The muscles across his abdomen tightened, and not—he noted with some interest—in fear. "The suit's at the cleaners." Her gloved hands were empty, as they had been the other night, and this time she didn't even carry a paint gun or a pack. Again she was in black—black shoes and black tight-fitting pants and a black T-shirt that hugged her slim curves.

She pursed her lips. "Satisfied I'm not carrying a concealed weapon?"

"I have no idea where you'd keep one, if you were," he returned, sliding his gaze along the length of her.

"Thanks for noticing."

"In fact," he continued, "you seem a bit underdressed compared to the other night. I do like the baseball cap, though. Very fashionable."

She flashed him a grin. "It keeps my long blond hair out of my face."

"Duly noted for my report to the police," he said, his mind still pondering the intriguing thought of where she might carry a concealed weapon. "Unless you're here to kill me, in which case I suppose I don't really care what color your hair might be."

"If I were here to kill you," she returned in a calm, soft voice, sending a glance beyond him at his desk, "you'd be dead."

"That confident, are you?" She wasn't armed; he could rush her, grab her, and hold her for the police. Instead, Richard took a sip of brandy.

"Mm-hm," she answered. "Who was that you sent out to shake Senator Branston's tree? Or Barbara's, rather?"

He found himself watching her mouth, the soft curve of her full lips. *Concentrate, dammit.* With a breath, Richard glanced toward the skylight again. The glass was thick, but not enough to stop a good listening device—or a bullet. So she had had the opportunity to kill him again and hadn't taken it. Interesting.

"That was my attorney. Tom Donner."

"Attorneys. My favorite people. Now why don't you move over there by the cabinet for a minute?" she suggested, walking closer. She seemed coiled, ready to move in any direction, to react to whatever he might do. Richard found it oddly . . . tantalizing. Most people played more defensively where he was involved. Miss Smith, it seemed, considered herself his match.

"This is my office, Miss Smith. Why don't you ask me nicely? Considering that you're unarmed."

The soft smile touched her mouth again, saying both that she had no doubt she could hold her own against him and that she was supremely enjoying their encounter. "Please move, Mr. Addison," she cooed.

Because he wanted to see what she meant to do next, he moved where she indicated. Stepping forward, she brushed gloved fingers through folders and papers on his desk. "I don't have any concealed weapons, either," he said after a moment, covering a flicker of annoyance when she invaded the top drawer of his desk.

"Of course you do," she said. "I just want to make sure they're not anywhere too easy to whip out." Her glance took in his faded jeans.

After a moment she backed away, giving him an all clear gesture. He returned to his desk, sinking back against the near edge. If she'd checked the cabinet behind him she would have found a .44, but she undoubtedly thought she could get out before he could get to anything he had closed away. "All right, let's say I accept that you're not here to kill me," he said. "Why *are* you here then, Miss Smith?"

For the first time she hesitated, a furrow appearing between her delicate, curved brows. "To ask for your help."

And he'd thought nothing else could surprise him this evening. "Beg pardon?"

"I think you know that I didn't try to kill you the other night. I did try to take your Trojan stone tablet, and I won't apologize for that. But thievery has a statute of limitations. Murder doesn't." She cleared her throat. "I wouldn't kill anyone."

"Then turn yourself in and tell the police."

She snorted. "No fucking way. I may have missed the tablet, but not all the statutes have run out on me."

Richard folded his arms across his chest. She hadn't taken the tablet. Curiouser and curiouser—and it didn't suit him to let her know that someone else had made off with it. "So you've stolen other things. From people other than me, I presume?"

As she glanced toward the skylight, her smooth, devil-may-care countenance shifted a little. It was an act, he realized. Fearless as she seemed to be, she would have to be desperate to drop in on him here tonight. If he hadn't been so accustomed to reading people, looking for weaknesses, he never would have seen it. She was good at what she did, obviously, but that moment of vulnerability caught his attention—and his interest.

"I saved your life," she finally said, her unaffected mask dropping into place again, "so you owe me a favor. Tell them—the police, the FBI, the news—that I didn't kill that guard, and that I didn't try to kill you. I'll deal with the rest on my own."

"I see." Richard wasn't certain whether he was more intrigued by her or annoyed that she expected him to make her error go away. "You want me to fix things so you can walk away from this, without repercussions, owing to the fact that while you've been bad elsewhere, you were unsuccessful here."

"I'm bad everywhere," she returned, with a slight smile that momentarily made him wonder how far she would go in her quest to see herself cleared of any wrongdoing. "Accuse me of attempted theft. But clear me of murder."

"No." He wanted answers, but his way. And not through some sort of compromise, intriguing though she made it sound.

She met his gaze straight on for a moment, then nodded. "I had to try. You might consider, though, that if I didn't set that bomb, someone else did. Someone who's better at getting into places than I am. And I'm good. Very good."

"I'd wager you are." He watched her for another moment, wondering what she'd be like with all of that coiled energy released. She definitely knew how to push his buttons, and he wanted to push a few of hers. "I'll admit you may have something I'm interested in acquiring," he said slowly, "but it's not your theories or your request for aid."

Returning to her position beneath the skylight, she yanked her arm down. The end of a length of rope tumbled into the room. "Oh, Mr. Addison. I never give something for nothing."

He found that he wasn't quite ready for her to leave. "Perhaps we could negotiate."

She released the rope, approaching him with a walk that looked half Catwoman and all sexy. "I already suggested that, and you turned me down. But be careful. Somebody wants you dead. And you have no idea how close somebody like me can get, without you ever knowing," she murmured, lifting her face to his.

Jesus. She practically gave off sparks. He could feel the hairs on his arms lifting. "I would know," he returned in the same low tone, taking a slow step closer, daring her to make the next move. If she did, he was going to touch her. He wanted to touch her, badly. The heat coming off her body was almost palpable.

She held where she was, her lips a breath away from his, then with another fleeting grin slid away to grab the rope again. "So you weren't surprised tonight, were you?" With a fluid coordination of arms and legs, she swarmed up through the skylight. "Watch your back, Addison. If you're not going to help me, I'm not going to help you."

"Help me?"

She vanished, then ducked her head back into the room. "I know things the cops would never have a clue how to find out. Good night, Addison." Miss Smith blew him a kiss. "Sleep tight."

Richard stepped forward to look up, but she had already disappeared. "I was surprised," he conceded, taking another swallow of brandy. "And now I need a cold shower."

Samantha gave Addison credit for one thing. He didn't sound the alarm while she slipped out of his very nice house, over the side wall, and away from his very nice grounds.

It had been a stupid idea. She'd only been in hiding for two days, and already she was taking foolish chances. Of course he had no reason to believe her, much less to want to help her—even if she had a damned good idea who had done the bombing. Not that she had any intention of ratting out Etienne to anyone—but she could damned well turn their attention away from her. Now, though, she'd given him a better look at her, informed him and thereby the police that she was still in the area, and proven that she could get through even their beefed-up security with enough ease that she could have carried an explosive with her on either occasion.

And what had she gotten out of their little encounter? Sam pursed her lips. She'd already known he was good-looking, but based on their little exchange, his temperature ran to hot and very sexy. It was fortunate that flirting had been part of her plan tonight, because she wasn't sure she could have stopped herself from doing it. It could have been pheromones or something, but in retrospect perhaps a partnership with a man she found that attractive wouldn't have been the best of ideas.

She hiked the rest of the humid mile to where she'd left her car and tossed her gear into the trunk. As she climbed behind the wheel, though, she paused again. *He hadn't sounded the alarm.* So he did believe at least part of her story. It was something, she supposed, but not nearly the level of assistance she'd wanted.

Blowing out her breath to try to rid herself of the last of the adrenaline-driven arousal he'd sparked, she started the Honda. Time for another plan. Sometime in the next day or two she would have to boost another car, and she hated doing that. Her father had once accused her of being squeamish, but he would have been more accurate to call her a snob. Any slob could boost a car. She craved the thrill of going somewhere she wasn't supposed to be, and of touching . . . time.

Ancient texts, paintings by the old Masters, vases of the Ming Dynasty, Roman coins, Trojan stone tablets—they fascinated her, and she'd been criticized for that, too, for learning everything she could about an object before she liberated it. Her father had seen them only as money, and himself as the banker, transferring funds from one account to another and taking a cut for his trouble.

Damn. Since Etienne had been less than forthcoming, she'd meant to ask Addison whether the stone tablet had gone missing or been destroyed, not that he was likely to tell her in either case. It made a difference, though; in one case the bomb had been a distraction, and in the other it had been a murder weapon. One most likely meant to kill him. Yummy, desirable Richard Addison. The only billionaire she knew who went about barefoot and wore snug-fitting jeans and had a nice ass.

Sam shook herself. "Stop it," she muttered, turning up the radio. If nothing else, her level of distraction after one conversation told her she'd done the right thing in getting out of there. So what if he gave the police her description? They'd never find her. Now she just needed to wait a few days for the official net to get tired of watching for her and develop a few weak spots. One was all she needed.

She worried about Stoney, but he'd survived working with her less-cautious father, and he could take care of himself. As for her, Milan would be nice this time of year, too crowded with tourists for anyone to notice her. What she would do later, when she wanted to return to the U.S. and couldn't because she would still be wanted for murder and attempted murder, she didn't want to think about.

Deciding she hadn't damned Etienne nearly enough, she did it a few more times. Of course he'd only been concerned with himself; she was the same way. But he'd been sloppy, and now she'd been stuck with cleaning up his mess.

For tonight, she headed back inland toward Clewiston, where her father had one of his safe houses, now hers. It was a crappy little place, but definitely nondescript. No one would think a self-respecting cat burglar would go within a mile of it.

The wounds in her shoulder and leg smarted. She needed to wipe them down again with alcohol and touch up the super glue where at least one of the cuts had begun to pull open. Tomorrow she would worry about tomorrow. And tonight she would wonder why it continued to bother her that someone might be trying to kill Richard Addison, the one witness to her involvement in any of this.

Five

"Did Danté give you the damage report?" Richard asked, sitting back against the soft leather cushions of his limousine.

Donner climbed in behind him. "Yeah, for the items he had confirmation on. He's still fighting with insurance over the values of most of the damaged stuff. The appraiser had to go throw up once."

The car rolled down the long, winding drive and through the open gates, still manned by uniformed police. "This is the third day now. How much longer are they going to be here?"

"Until they catch your bomber, would be my guess. It's a little difficult for me to complain to the police that they're protecting you too well. Which reminds me, Castillo called this morning to protest that your exiting, and I quote, 'the secured area of your home today, leaves you vulnerable to a second targeting by an assassin,' unquote."

"So I'm warned. Don't sue him if I get killed." Richard rolled his shoulders. "And I'm just going to your offices to work for a few hours." He glanced at Donner. "By the way, are you charging me for the drive to my house and then riding back with me? I told you I'd prefer to drive myself."

Tom grinned. "I'm on retainer, so I pretty much charge you for everything."

"In that case, I neglected to tell you something about last night." Donner only looked at him, so Richard drew a breath. He could keep it to himself; he actually preferred to do that. On the other hand, if something happened to him, he wanted the murder solved. "I had a visitor. She dropped in to see me after you left."

"She who? You're going to have to narrow it down a little before I can guess, Britain's Hottest Bachelor."

"I told you never to mention that to me again."

The attorney snorted. "Sorry. Who dropped in?"

"Miss Smith."

Tom opened his mouth, but no sound came out. "You— she—why the hell didn't you say anything, Rick? Dammit!" He grabbed the cell phone clipped to his belt. "This—" and he jabbed a finger in Rick's direction while he punched numbers with the other hand "—*this* is why you need private security."

"Hang up."

"No. You and your damned stiff British upper lip. She was in your house? Where? Did she threaten—"

"I'm not being stoic. And I'm not happy." Richard yanked the phone out of his attorney's hand and snapped it closed. "I paid for this phone, for your house, and to put Chris into Yale," he growled. "Don't make me regret it."

Donner's face reddened. "You—"

"Give me a little bloody credit, Tom. She's not the one who tried to kill me. And telling Castillo she came visiting won't do anyone any good."

"It won't do *her* any good, which anywhere but here would be the idea." Tom hurled the water bottle he'd snagged against the opposite seat. "Dammit! And all supposition aside, how do you know she didn't do it?"

"She told me so." Goading his attorney only seemed fair,

considering how annoyed he was. This was his problem, and he would decide how it was handled.

"Shit. Give me the phone, Addison. Fire me if you want, but you are not going to get killed on my watch."

"Very dramatic, but it's not your watch. It's mine. It's always been mine. Now just calm down and listen, or I won't bother telling you anything."

After he spat out a few more curses Tom sat back and folded his arms, his color and temper still high. "I'm listening."

"I was unconscious for at least five minutes after the bomb went off. Instead of leaving me there or finishing me off, she dragged me downstairs, risking discovery, before she got out. Last night when she dropped in through my skylight she reminded me of that fact, then recited the tale end of the conversation you and I had in my office, to prove that she could have taken me out then, as well. She confessed to having been after the tablet—unsuccessfully, by the way—and actually . . . asked for my assistance in making certain the police knew she hadn't had anything to do with the explosives."

"And you said?"

"I said no." And that, he had realized in the middle of his cold shower, had bothered him. Not because the sight of her practically gave him a hard-on, but because he'd wanted to handle this himself, and she'd tried to give him the opportunity. But it hadn't been on his bloody terms, so he'd turned her down. "After that, she warned me to be cautious and wished me good luck, since whoever had planted the bomb was at least as proficient as she was at breaking and entering, and she'd managed to get in again."

"And that's all."

"Well, in a roundabout way she offered to help me find out who planted the bomb if I would help clear her of murder charges." She'd also said a few other things, of course, but he intended to keep those to himself. He leaned down to pick up the water bottle as it rolled back to them and returned it to Donner. "In retrospect, I'm wondering if I shouldn't have taken her up on it."

Tom continued to glare at him, but the more he considered it, the more he regretted letting her slip back into the night. Beneath her cool facade she'd been worried, and for some unknown reason he found he could sympathize. And he doubted she would have offered assistance if she couldn't provide any. She didn't seem to work that way.

In a sense her world was very similar to his, though his opponents wore suits and for the most part swam through the shallows in broad daylight. If their circumstances had been reversed, he would have done exactly as she had—gone to the person with the most power to see whether he could influence the course of events. If Julia Poole or any of the other actresses and models he'd dated had found herself in this kind of trouble, she would have fluttered her eyelashes and thrown herself on his mercy, expecting him to clean things up. Not Miss Smith, however. She proposed a trade. Apparently she hated relinquishing control as much as he did.

"You really are considering it, aren't you?"

"I'm a businessman, Tom. I trust my judgment in evaluating people and situations because I've been successful at it. Yes, I really am considering it."

"And if you hypothetically did decide to team up with Miss Smith, how would you hypothetically go about contacting her?"

"So you can tell Castillo? I don't think so, my dear fellow."

"Stop acting so British."

Richard lifted an eyebrow. "As you've repeatedly pointed out over the past few days, I *am* British."

"You're my friend. If you're jumping out of the airplane, I'm right behind you—but I'm carrying the spare parachute. You keep me in the loop, and it'll stay between us. Unless it puts your life at risk."

"Life *is* a risk." Tapping his fingers on the armrest, Richard spent a few moments gazing out the window. With jolting abruptness palm trees and beach gave way to buildings and traffic lights. "So how do we get hold of someone the police can't find?"

"I don't know why the hell you feel the need to risk that thick, billion-dollar skull of yours." Still shaking his head, Donner opened the water bottle, took a swallow, and scowled at it as if he wished it were bourbon.

Ben in the driver's seat buzzed the intercom speaker. "Mr. Addison, more cameras coming up. Should I use the parking structure?"

Ahead of them on the right stood the gleaming tower that housed the law firm of Donner, Rhodes and Critchenson on its top three floors. Ranged in front of the lobby's brass-and-glass revolving doors, a dozen reporters and camera crews sprang to attention like a pride of lions scenting gazelle. Thinking fast, Richard returned the cell phone to Donner. "No, stop at the curb."

Chauffeur and attorney gave him the same look.

"Yes, I'm certain," Rick said, straightening his tie. "Tom, pretend you're on the phone, then hand it to me as soon as I stop to talk to the vultures. Make certain they've got the microphones aimed in my direction, first."

"All right. You're the boss."

Richard flashed him a grin. "Yes, I am."

Ben pulled over and sprang out of his seat, hurrying around to open the rearmost passenger door. Tom emerged first, mostly because Richard shoved him. God, he hated the press. Aside from their constant, annoying, biting-midge presence, two years ago they'd bloodied an already painful divorce and sent in hyenas to scavenge the remains. Well today they could work for him.

"Mr. Addison—Rick—can you give us an update on your injuries?"

"Was this a murder attempt or a robbery?"

"What was taken from your home?"

"Is your ex-wife considered a suspect?"

Richard took the phone Tom practically hurled at him as they waded through the cacophony of shouts. "Just a moment," he said, and lifted the phone to his ear. "Miss . . . Jones?" he began. "Yes, four o'clock is fine. I'll have Tom prepare the paperwork. Thanks for the help—I can use it. I'll see you then." He clicked the phone closed and handed it back while the shouts increased in volume around him. "I'm not at liberty to discuss precisely what was removed from my home," he continued in a louder voice, "though several antique Meissen porcelain pieces were broken in the explosion. They were personal favorites, and I do regret their loss."

He couldn't say more without alerting Castillo and the FBI, but Miss Smith seemed exceptionally bright, and he would wager that she knew precisely which art objects he owned and where he housed them. Now he'd have to wait and see whether he was correct.

"But can you confirm or deny that Patricia Addison-Wallis is—"

"Excuse me, I have a meeting," he interrupted, working to keep his jaw from clenching. Hearing the Addison and Wallis names strung together like that continued to leave him with the desire to punch someone. One of the few things the court had granted Patricia, though, was continued use of the name of which she'd availed herself for three years.

The silence of the lobby opened around him with cool, air-conditioned fingers, blissful after the humidity that had come with the sunrise and the tight, barking overlay of voice-coached news personalities. He couldn't help brushing off his sleeves and checking his collar for hidden microphones as he waited for Donner to catch up to him.

"Jesus," Tom said as he pushed past security and the rotating door. "I think I left an arm out there."

"What did you get from my blathering?" Richard asked, his voice echoing faintly as he continued toward the brass-plated elevator doors at the far end of the high-ceilinged lobby.

"I got the Jones/Smith bit, which was pretty obvious, and the four o'clock meeting. You lost me with the missing porcelain reference, though."

"Not 'missing.' Meissen. Meissen antique porcelain figures are quite the rage for some collectors. And the shop housing the largest collection in the world happens to be right here, on Worth Avenue."

"Ah. I hope your Miss Smith is smarter than I am, then."

Richard shrugged. "If not, I'll be buying a Meissen at four o'clock today for no good reason."

"This piece then, Mr. Addison?" the very helpful store clerk suggested, managing to turn, point, and show off her cleavage all at the same time. "From your description, this may be more to your liking."

Richard glanced toward the door, as he had every minute for the past twelve. They'd played his little clue on the news at least a dozen times since this morning; if Miss Smith was anywhere near a television, she would have seen it. If she'd seen it, she would understand the message he'd sent. And she would appear, as he'd requested. He drew in a breath and returned his attention to the ornate, brightly-colored pair of wall sconces, circa 1870. "Nothing wall-mounted, please. I want something for a table display."

"Of course, sir. This way, then. We've just purchased several lovely eighteenth-century pieces from an estate in Strasbourg."

With another glance toward the entrance, he followed. She was late. He wasn't used to twiddling his thumbs, and he didn't like it. When he set an appointment with someone, he expected them to arrive on time, or better yet, early. His time was valuable.

The store clerk had certainly recognized this. The "by appointment only" script on the door hadn't stopped either of them from engaging in business. It hadn't stopped her from writing her personal phone number on the back of her business card, and it wouldn't stop her from slipping the card into his bag if he should make a purchase.

Tom stayed a few steps behind, ignoring the delicate porcelains and instead concentrating his attention on the clerks and other clients. Bodyguard seemed an odd job for an attorney of Donner's reputation and prestige, but Richard had learned the value and rarity of true friendship. If dogging his heels this afternoon gave Tom some feeling of control, Richard had no problem with it—as long as the attorney didn't interfere.

"How much do these things run?" Donner asked, relaxing enough to eye a small vase.

"Mostly in the middle five figures, I believe."

"You believe? You know the price of everything, Rick."

"I told you I don't collect it."

"But—"

"That's why I chose Meissen, because Miss Smith would know I didn't have any of it in the gallery."

"You have a lot of art and antiques, Rick. How's she supposed to know that these are the one thing you don't collect?"

While the clerk eyed him hopefully, Richard pretended interest in a pastoral figurine featuring a girl with a goat. "That's not the point, and they're not the one thing I don't collect. Some people, I believe, have a great interest in G.I. Joe action figures, for example. I don't collect those, either."

"The older ones were better anyway, when they had real hair."

Rick froze, electricity shooting from the back of his scalp to his crotch. He turned his head to see the young woman perusing a pink candy tray decorated with a swan. No wonder he hadn't recognized her. This afternoon she fit Worth Avenue to perfection, in a short cotton dress of blue and yellow which showed off long, tanned legs, yellow-heeled sandals, and over her arm a white purse that didn't need the large "G" branding the flap to declare its origin.

The attentive clerk hovering just behind her only added to the aura of wealthy Palm Beach resident. For a moment he wondered whether she *was* one of the idle wealthy, stealing for thrills, but quickly dismissed the idea. Her expression was too alive, her eyes too inquisitive to allow anyone to dump her into the herd of the isolated, insulated rich.

"How do you do that?" he asked in an equally soft voice.

"The Joes? Oh, you see them at your lower-range antique shops all the time, not that I shop at those places." Still not looking at him, she moved on to the next piece.

Richard kept pace with her on the opposite side of the display table. Straight auburn hair, not a one-tone red or brown, but a dusky bronze beneath the shop lights, parted across her shoulders. And he felt it again, the electric pull between them. He wondered whether she did. "I meant your ability simply to appear, actually."

Her lips curved upward. "I know what you meant. You summoned me, so what is it?" Her gaze lifted, went past his shoulder. "And keep him away from me."

"Tom, go look at something," he instructed, feeling Donner crowding up behind him.

"I am looking at something. Miss Smith, I presume."

"Tom Donner, attorney-at-law. I don't like attorneys."

"And I don't like murderers or thieves."

"Tom, back off," Richard instructed, glancing at the expensive and delicate porcelain around them. "I asked her to meet us here."

"Yeah, and—"

"Yes, you did," she interrupted, her gaze returning to him, as if she'd evaluated Tom and dismissed him. "And why was that, again?"

"I changed my mind," he said, moving around the edge of the display to get closer to her.

For the first time, she looked surprised. "Why?"

"Do I need to explain my reasoning?"

"Yes, I think you do."

His clerk, probably sensing the drifting of his interest, approached again, and Miss Smith wandered off with her own keeper to the next display. Cursing under his breath and wishing she could be obtained as simply as a Meissen porcelain, Richard pointed at the nearest item, a cream pot on a small pedestal. "I'd like this one, if you'd box it up for me." *Want, acquire, possess.* That was how he did business.

"Of course, Mr. Addison."

"I thought the goat and the shepherdess looked better on you."

Richard pretended to ignore Miss Smith's soft commentary. "Tom, see to it."

"Like h—"

"I'm not going anywhere. And I'll tell you everything we discuss," he lied. "Give me five bloody minutes to talk to her, will you?"

"After looking at her," Donner murmured, "I can see why you're interested, but make sure you're thinking with the right body part."

"You are not my keeper." Richard stepped closer to her as she ran a finger over one of the more recent pieces. "You made a good point last night," he said in a low voice, wondering if she'd managed to stuff any of the smaller figurines into her Gucci bag. *Want, acquire, possess.* They weren't that different, and the idea made him hard. He brushed her arm with the back of his hand. "About your not being the one who tried to blow me up," he continued quietly, "and about your point of view probably being more helpful than a detective's."

She seemed to think about that for a moment. "So you'll make sure I don't get accused of murder."

"I'll do my utmost."

"And you'll make phone calls and whatever else necessary to get me out of this shit?"

"Whatever else necessary," he agreed.

"And you won't turn me in for theft."

"You didn't actually steal anything from me." He studied her face as her lips twitched. "Did you?"

"Not if you haven't noticed."

Her rather macabre sense of humor again, even if he wasn't particularly amused. They were asking a lot of one another, and since she'd attended his meeting, he supposed the next step belonged to him. "You need to trust me," he offered, "and I need to be able to trust you. When this is over, nothing additional will be missing from my home. Is that clear, Miss Smith?"

For the first time that afternoon, she looked him full in the face, her green eyes telling him just how much this visit had cost her already as she assessed both him and his words. "Samantha," she said in a near whisper. "Sam. You get my last name after I decide I can trust you."

Richard offered his hand. "Pleased to make your acquaintance, Samantha."

With a deep breath she reached out and shook his hand. Heat speared down his spine at the contact. Whatever this partnership was going to be, it wasn't simple.

Six

Friday, 4:33 p.m.

"I am not climbing into that car with you." As they stood outside the Meissen shop's front door, Samantha realized that she'd been wrong to think she'd find Addison less attractive in daylight and with witnesses.

"It's a limousine," Addison corrected, "and I'm not trying to kidnap you."

"I'd prefer to meet you back at your estate after dark." That made more sense as far as she was concerned. She'd have her own way in and out, and a little control over how deeply she became involved in this. "I know the way in."

"You're not breaking into my house again. And I can't quite see you walking past the police posted at the front gate."

"I'd like to see that," Donner countered.

She smirked at him, not having to feign irritation as they continued to argue on Worth Avenue. Strong as the instinct to get out of the open pulled at her, she wasn't about to compromise her standards. And considering that the male heat coming off of Addison was making her mouth dry, she definitely needed to keep a little distance—and perspective. Obviously she wasn't the only hunter in the mix any longer. "All my worldly possessions are about two blocks from here. I'm not leaving them behind."

Addison started to say something, then closed his mouth again. "All your possessions?" he repeated after a moment, and she sensed that she'd surprised him. Probably the idea of someone even being able to tally all their possessions, much less tote them about, stumped him.

"I'm afraid so." It wasn't quite true, since she had the storage unit rented outside of Miami, a safe house here and there, and a nice-sized bank account in Switzerland, but that wasn't any of his business. Everything she needed to exist from day to day was in the trunk of the Honda.

"We'll swing by and get it."

Sam was definitely beginning to feel more like prey than predator, and she didn't like it. This partnership had been her idea, not his. "Like hell we will," she snapped. "I drive myself to the estate, or forget it. You don't need to run my errands."

"I *want* to run your errands," Addison insisted, annoyance just clipping the edges of his warm voice.

"People don't disagree with you very often, do they?" she asked.

"No, they don't."

"Get used to it," she countered, having no intention of giving up the quarterback position. She could probably ease her way into command later, but with Addison she wanted some ground rules set.

"Why don't you just cooperate and be grateful we don't call the cops, Miss Smith?" the lawyer grunted, arms folded across his chest. Leaning back against the side of the limo, he looked like a tawny-haired mafioso with a tan and cowboy boots.

"Don't you have ambulances to chase?" she returned, glad she didn't have to work any particular charms on the lawyer. "Or do you have to be available to wipe Addison's ass?"

"I wipe my own bum, thank you very much," Addison put in mildly. "Get in the car."

"I—"

"I'm not going to keep arguing. At this moment you're free because I haven't called the authorities. We'll get your things, then we'll go back to my estate and get down to business. That's as compromising as I'm going to get, love."

For a moment she wanted to ask what kind of business he had in mind, but under the circumstances that didn't seem wise. He was right about having the advantage here. Even if he didn't call the cops, the longer they stood out on Worth Avenue in the open, the more likely she was to end up in handcuffs. "All right."

"Let's get a move on, then," the attorney said, his expression darkening as he looked past them. "Unless you want to use the six o'clock news to invite Dracula or Hannibal Lecter to dinner."

Sam glanced over her shoulder, narrowing her eyes against the glare of the afternoon sun. The sight of a herd of news cameras loping in their direction made her yelp. Not bothering to wait for someone to open the limo door for her, she did it herself and leapt inside. *No photos. Ever.* A photo meant you were labeled and remembered and recalled at convenience. "Come on," she ordered, sliding to the middle of the seat, away from the windows.

"And I thought *I* hated the press," Addison commented, sitting beside her.

Donner took the seat opposite, and the limousine rumbled with reassuring speed into the light traffic. Sam didn't let out her breath until they'd passed the last of the news vans.

"Will they follow?"

"Of course they will. I imagine we've got at least one news helicopter tailing us right now, too."

She frowned. "Then forget my car. I'll come back for it later."

"I'll send someone for it. Will that make you feel better?"

"I'll feel better if I'm the only one who knows where it is."

"You're twitchy, aren't you?" the attorney said, pulling a bottle of water from a built-in refrigerator beneath his seat. He didn't offer her one.

"Are the police after you?" she retorted.

"Nope."

"Then shut up."

Addison ignored the exchange, instead flipping a button on the door console. "Ben, take us home, please."

"Yes, sir."

Jaws clenched with a nauseating combination of nervousness and annoyance and adrenaline, Sam watched Donner tilt up the water bottle and take a long drink, condensation running down his thumb and dripping onto his tie. "Are those for everybody, or is he special?"

With what sounded like a suppressed chuckle, Addison leaned down to retrieve another ice-cold bottle and hand it to her. "He *is* special, but help yourself."

"I'm glad you're amused, Rick," Donner muttered. "This isn't what I pictured when you said you wanted her help. I was thinking more along the lines of a phone call or two— not inviting the fox back to the henhouse."

"All of Addison's chickens are safe," Sam retorted. "Does he really need to be here?" She turned to Addison, who was watching her with that amused, sexy expression on his face.

"For now, he does."

"Great." She'd meant to sound more annoyed, but no man had any right to look that good three days after a bomb had nearly blown him to pieces. Her uncertainty about this whole deal grew, and she tried to drown the butterflies in her stomach with a swallow of water. *Uncertainty, or lust, Sam?* With the heated vibes ricocheting between them, she had a good idea which it was.

"What changed your mind about me?" she pursued.

"Curiosity." He sat back, as at ease and relaxed in his expensive blue suit as he'd looked the night before in jeans and bare feet. "So, Samantha, do you have any idea who might have taken the stone tablet and planted that bomb?"

Sam froze with the bottle halfway to her lips. "The tablet's gone?"

He nodded. "Disappointed?"

She deserved that, she supposed, and let the comment pass. "It makes a difference." Scowling at the attorney's cynical expression, she drank more water and silently cursed Etienne a few more times. And whoever'd hired him. *That,* she needed to find out. "A difference about the intent of the crime. Not a difference to me. Speaking of which, Addison, do you have any idea how you're going to help me?"

"I have an idea or two. But I do expect your help in return. I won't give you something for nothing. That's not the way I do business."

"Me, neither."

Actually, getting something for nothing was precisely how she preferred to do business. But this was anything but business as usual. Everything she'd learned in her life screamed that she couldn't trust him, couldn't trust anyone. Her freedom and her life were her responsibility. Yes, she had a damned good idea who'd taken the tablet and more than likely planted the bomb. Etienne wasn't going to confess, and she wasn't going to turn him in. Throwing Etienne's boss to the wolves suited her just fine, but she needed time to find the bastard before the police found her. Hence she'd answered Addison's televised invitation, and now she was riding in his limousine.

Addison nodded, sending a warning glance at the attorney. "We'll all make an effort to cooperate here."

"I'll do my part, but I reserve the right for griping and future 'I told you so's,'" Donner said, settling back with his water.

"That's helpful," Sam noted.

"I wouldn't have to be saying it if you hadn't broken in, Miss Manners."

"But you'd still have a theft and an explosion, Harvard. And no one to help you figure it out."

"Yale. And you—"

"Enough, children," Addison broke in. "Don't make me stop the car."

Smirking at the lawyer, Sam sat back. Her father must be spinning in his grave right now. His daughter was riding in a limousine with an attorney and one of the wealthiest men in the world. She knew exactly what Martin Jellicoe would do with the opportunity—steal Richard Addison blind, deaf, and dumb. That thinking, however, was why her father had spent the last five years of his life in prison. She'd learned the lessons of restraint and patience, even if he hadn't. As she glanced again at Addison, she decided that the restraint lessons would come in especially handy.

She gazed out the window past the attorney to watch the palm trees and coastline fly past, and wondered what she'd gotten herself into. Every mile took her farther from her gear and her car, farther from the safety net of the city and its crowds. For God's sake, she didn't even have a change of clothes with her. But she could play this game; she *would* play it, because she didn't have any other choice.

They approached the front gates, a uniformed cop standing in front of either post. Sam couldn't help sinking lower in the seat as they slowed. No, she wouldn't have liked doing this on her own, but then, she wouldn't have driven up to the front door. The limo driver rolled down his window, held a brief exchange with one of the officers, and the gates opened.

"See, you're safely inside, as I promised. No need to go over walls, dig tunnels, or anything."

Samantha turned around to watch the gates close again. "You have lousy security."

"We have two cops at the front gate," Donner said.

Facing forward again, she scowled at the attorney. "And they didn't even check the trunk or the passengers in the limo. If the idea is keeping Addison safe, you might want to suggest they log everybody's identification and check that no one's holding anyone hostage before they open the gates. I know you gave them a description of me, because I heard it on the news. And yet here I sit."

Richard kept his gaze out the window. Samantha had a point. The deference with which the Palm Beach police treated him was expected, given his status in the close-knit, elite community, but he would be a fool to rely on it for anything more than keeping the press away from his front door. They certainly hadn't kept his visitor out last night—or just now. "Worried about me?" he asked.

"You're my way out of this," she returned, the tease coming into her voice again.

"Then try to be honest with me."

"I'll do my best."

"Thank you."

Tom looked skeptical, but Richard suspected she was telling the truth. Even so, he intended to keep his perspective. She might give off more heat than the Florida sun, but she was playing a game, just as he was. The only difference was that she wanted to get away free, and he wanted . . . her. "I do occasionally conduct business on the estate," he said. "I also entertain. Guests are to be expected. And you have to admit, you're not precisely dressed like a thief at the moment." He took the occasion to run his gaze down her long legs.

If she noticed the scrutiny, she didn't say anything about it. "I could have been naked or draped with ammunition bandoleers, Addison, and they wouldn't have blinked."

"Point taken. And since all I have is your first name, you may as well call me Rick."

"I'll decide what I might as well do," she returned, though her tone softened a little. "But thanks for the offer, Addison."

So she *would* put up some boundaries. That was interesting—and even more intriguing.

Ben drove up the long drive and stopped, coming around to open the door for them. Samantha jumped out first, obviously relieved to have escaped the limousine intact. Richard watched as she did a turn on the front steps. She'd probably never seen the estate in daylight.

"I'll give you a tour later, if you'd like."

"You're not her damned host, Rick," Tom whispered, as they followed her to the front door. "You're a target. And you may think she's cute, but I don't trust her. She's been here twice already. Uninvited."

"And now she's invited. Back off, Tom. I'll meet you in my office in a few minutes. Get William Benton on the phone for me."

"Benton? You—"

"Tom."

"Yes, sahib." Donner strode through the foyer and up the stairs, sending a last glare at Samantha. She didn't seem to notice, because she was busy running her fingers over the vase on the front table.

"Why would you keep a fifteen-hundred-year-old vase so close to the front door? Don't you get hurricanes here, or do your gates keep those out, too?"

"It's—"

Frowning, she leaned closer to study the pattern, tapping the rim with the tip of a fingernail. "Oh. You own fakes?"

"I thought it was pretty," he said, grinning and impressed. It had taken Danté nearly an hour to figure it out. "And it was a replica, for a fund-raiser. How much do you know about art?"

"I can recite the best seller list, but I prefer antiques. What kind of staff do you have here?"

"Don't thieves know that sort of thing before they break in?"

"*You* weren't supposed to be here. Your staff while you're not in Florida is six during the day and two at night, plus hired security, and a room where your art acquisitions manager stays sometimes when you keep him here working late. I don't know who shows up when you're in residence."

"A dozen or so full-time staff," he supplied, "though I haven't called most of them back yet. The police thought I

should keep personnel to a minimum, and I don't want to endanger anyone."

"Makes sense. Do you have a butler?"

"Yes."

"Is his name Jeeves?"

Rick gave an appreciative smile. He was rapidly discover-
ing that the charm he'd seen in her was part of her character.
She'd obviously figured out how to use it to her advantage,
but he couldn't help enjoying it. At the same time, he
wouldn't forget how good she was at this. "Sykes. He is
British, though, if that makes you feel better."

"So they travel the world with you, going from house to
house?"

As she spoke, she wandered out of the foyer and into the
downstairs sitting room. Several antique pieces of furniture
housed various figurines and china plates, and Richard followed her to lean against the doorframe. She seemed a little
more at ease with Tom absent; given her occupation, he could
see why she wouldn't like lawyers. Again she ran her fingers
along the fine-grained wood of the seventeenth-century writing desk, as though she had to touch it to judge its value.

The sensuality of her hands kept distracting him. But this
wasn't a bloody date; it was a murder investigation. He drew
a slow breath, watching the fluid grace of her movements.
Damn, she was mesmerizing.

"Do they?"

Richard blinked. "Beg pardon?"

"The servants, Addison. Do they follow you around?"

He cleared his throat. "Some of them do. Most, like Sykes,
I keep on salary at a particular house year-round. He stays in
Devon at my estate. There's a lot to maintain whether I'm
there or not, and some of them have families and don't want
to move around. Why?"

"Call me suspicious."

"Of *my* staff?"

"Don't tell me the police didn't ask you any of this," she

said, glancing over her shoulder at him before moving on to the china cabinet.

"They did. None of my staff anywhere matched your description, however, and they remain focused on finding you."

She sighed. "That figures. For my edification, then, how many of your staff knew you were coming back to Florida early?"

"Just the flight crew, my driver Ben, and the housekeeper Reinaldo. I was staying at a hotel in Stuttgart, so I didn't have to inform anyone there where I was going. But it wasn't one of my staff."

"How about their family members?"

"No."

"Well, it wasn't me. What about personal . . . friends in Germany?"

"You mean do I have a fraulein in Stuttgart?"

He thought a blush crept up her cheeks, but with her face in profile he couldn't be certain. It surprised him. She seemed so worldly and capable, yet she could blush.

"Sure. Do you?"

"Not on this trip. I was there on business."

"Hm."

"Hm what?"

"I'm thinking. Give me a moment." Sam wandered past him into the hallway again and back toward the front door.

"What are you thinking?"

She shot him another look, a half smile still on her face. "What are *you* thinking, Addison? You'd never have invited me in here if you really thought I'd set that explosive, so who are your suspects? What are their motives? Any other signs of breaking and entering? I mean, I said I'd help, but you have to do some of the work."

The antique grandfather clock in the main hall chimed six times. "I don't keep an enemies list." He smiled briefly, noting that she still refused to use his first name. He wondered how many other roadblocks she might attempt to set up and how much he would be able to find out about her. He had her first name, which was more than he'd known last night, but given the reluctance with which she'd handed that out, this wasn't going to be easy. Thankfully, he liked a challenge. "And no, the police didn't find any other doors or windows forced open," he continued. "We did assume that it was you who used the mirrors at the front gate and cut open my patio window. Would you care for dinner?"

Her expression drew tighter. "I'm not staying."

"You're safer here than anywhere else, especially until we can find a way to convince Detective Castillo of your innocence."

"I'm safe here unless someone tries to blow you up again, you mean. You're charming, but I prefer to keep breathing." Taking a last step forward, she curled her fingers around the handle and pulled open the door.

"I will sound the alarm if you try to leave," he said quietly. She wasn't getting away. Not yet.

One hand still on the door, she stopped. "I thought we had an agreement."

"We do, love. You will help me, and I will help you. I thought I'd grill some steaks, since you and Tom are here."

"Does Harvard sleep at the foot of your bed, too?"

"He's my friend, and he thinks I'm being foolish. I therefore expect him to annoy me to a certain degree. Don't worry; he'll leave soon."

Her shoulders heaving with the breath she took, Samantha faced him again. "Steak sounds delightful. But then I'm afraid I must depart for my chateau."

"Your chateau in Pompano Beach? I'd avoid going there, if I were you."

"Pompano Beach. That's near here, isn't it?" she asked, not batting an eye. "Is that where you think I live?"

"Someone thinks so. Now come along, and I'll show you to a room. I have a few minutes of business with Tom, then we'll start dinner."

"You can't keep me prisoner here," she said as she brushed past him, heading deeper into the house.

"I'm merely making certain we're both in a position to up-hold our ends of the bargain." He closed the distance between them. "You are a self-confessed thief, Samantha. Don't expect me to forget that."

"I don't. But I'm not going to forget anything, either. Where's my cell?"

It wasn't worth arguing about what she chose to call her accommodations. But he could change his mind about which room he would give over to her. Richard led the way upstairs to the second floor. "You'll find some clothes in the closet and appropriate toilette items in the bath."

"Your ex-wife's?"

His jaw closed over a retort. "I frequently entertain visitors on short notice," he said instead. "I've found it prudent to keep a few extra items about to make certain they're comfortable here."

"Not defensive at all about that failed marriage thing, are you?"

He was beginning to get the feeling that she didn't miss anything. Well, he was fairly observant, himself. She followed him down the hall to the suite at the far end. Unable to help a small smirk, he pushed open the door. "Here you are."

As Sam brushed past him, he leaned in to smell her auburn hair. Raspberries. Very nice. And surprisingly hot.

Halfway into the room, Samantha stopped, and he watched as she took in her surroundings. Off to her right the gleam of tile and mirrors would give hints of a huge bathroom, while open double doors on the left revealed an over-size bed draped in cool green and gray. A small balcony stood outside the wood and glass doors straight ahead, with a set of curving red stone steps leading down from it to the grotto pool. In the central sitting room, green overstuffed furniture in the English Georgian style invited her to sit in front of the fireplace or watch the plasma television set into the wall above it.

"This would be the green room?" she asked after a lengthy silence.

He grinned. "Actually yes, it would be. Do you like it?"

She nodded, a genuine smile on her lips. "It's nice."

"Why don't you find something to wear suitable for a barbecue, and I'll be back for you in a few minutes," he said, pleased that the room pleased her.

"Are you going to lock the door?"

"Would that stop you?"

Her lips twitched. "No."

"Then I won't bother."

"I'll change, then, if you take that off." She tweaked his tie. "It makes me nervous."

"I doubt anything makes you nervous," he returned, the quick touch of her fingers against his chest stirring him farther down. Yes, he'd bloody well figure her out. And soon. "Don't go anywhere."

"And don't take anything. I know."

He tossed the room's key onto the coffee table, figuring she would feel more secure with it in her possession. The master key remained in his pocket. With a slight smile he headed down to the opposite end of the hall toward his office.

This was certainly more interesting than purchasing a failing cable television station, as he'd been scheduled to do this week. *Damn*. He would have to push back some meetings—if he had been the bomb's target, he didn't want to put anyone else in danger. And he wanted to concentrate on Samantha—and their agreement.

Seven

Friday, 6:18 p.m.

Samantha had observed enough powerful, ego-driven businessmen to know that this was all something of a game for Richard Addison—especially where it involved her. She could play to that, if she needed to. But all she really cared about at the moment was getting the police focused away from her, and away from Stoney, so they could escape Florida for a while and so she could avoid being hunted down for murder.

Stoney. She desperately wanted to call him, to find out if the police were doing more than tapping his phone. Whether they'd had assistance or not, they'd found him within two days. But Walter Barstone had worked on the shady side of legal, as he put it, for thirty years. He hadn't done that, and made quite the living at it, by being careless. Which meant that somebody was talking.

Lips pursed, she looked at the phone sitting on the bed stand. It would certainly confuse matters if they traced a call to Stoney back to Addison's estate. As her illustrious host had said, though, at the moment she was safe. She wouldn't risk it. Not yet, anyway.

She found the walk-in closet in the huge bedroom and dug in. Wearing a dress and heels was something she did with regularity, usually when she had the opportunity to case a house or other establishment. Nice things were usually kept in nice places, and she needed to blend. Skirts and pumps hampered her movements, though, when she was actually working. And even if she wasn't stealing anything tangible tonight, she was definitely working.

Apparently most of the guests who stayed in the green room came without their own bathing suits, but toward the back of the closet she found some sweats and T-shirts and even a few glittering evening gowns and a tuxedo. He expected her to relax, and so she would look relaxed. Half-closing the closet door, she pulled off her dress. Folding it carefully, she slid it into her purse, then yanked on a plain blue T-shirt and a pair of yellow shorts just long enough to cover the bandage high up on the back of her thigh.

A couple of boxes of athletic shoes in varying sizes lined the floor, but she opted for flip-flops. They fit her relaxation theme for the evening, and from the way Addison had been looking at her legs, the more of them she left exposed, the better. Tonight the name of the game was distraction. Besides, being ogled by a guy that good-looking was doing nice things for her ego—and several of her body parts.

Taking a moment to more closely admire the suite's tasteful furniture and artworks, she wandered to the glass doors leading to the balcony. The grotto pool below glinted in the lingering sunlight, with the near side shaded by overhanging palms and birds-of-paradise. On the left, closest to the west wing of the house, stood a large brick barbecue grill surrounded by an artistic grouping of wrought-iron patio tables and chairs.

So she was going to eat steak grilled by a billionaire. Weird—and not even close to what she would have expected. She stayed out of prison by figuring people out quickly, and

Addison frustrated her. Rich men didn't do manual labor. She wondered whether his staff knew that he liked to barbecue. Probably. The police probably didn't, because who would suspect that a man who could afford to buy a country would like to stand out by his pool and flip his own steaks? Not her, until today.

Frowning, Sam pushed open the double doors and strolled out to the balcony. The evening breeze coming in from the ocean felt cool and comfortable against her bare legs, and she took a deep breath. The tension knotted into her shoulders didn't ease, but she was growing used to the sensation.

Her flip-flops smacking against the bottoms of her heels, she went down the red stone steps to the pool deck. She was being an idiot, taking unnecessary risks. But with this alliance, Addison had gone from being the only witness against her to being the only man who could help clear her, and until that happened she didn't want him dead. Etienne had nearly killed him once, and she couldn't afford to assume that he or someone else wouldn't try it again.

The barbecue was Spanish-style brick and stone, with a stainless-steel grill across the top and a steamer hood to one side of the main unit. The gas was off, as it should have been, and she knelt to reach under the unit and feel along the pipe. She wasn't quite sure what to expect; the bomb in the gallery had been clever but hastily rigged, and easy to see if you knew where to look. She knew next to nothing about explosives except for the opening-a-safe or popping-a-dead bolt variety, but she did know a great deal about subterfuge and misdirection.

The pipe jointed smoothly up in the direction of the coal box, and she stood again. With a grunt of effort she lifted off the grill and dug her hands into the dusty coal, shifting chunks aside to run her fingers along the igniter.

"Put your hands where I can see them, and do it slowly."

Shit. Sam closed her eyes for a moment, then slowly withdrew her blackened hands from the barbecue. She should have known better than to trust anyone. Ten miles from her car and her gear, she couldn't do much more than kick off her flip-flops and make a run for it—and hope that whoever was behind her had poor aim.

"Turn around."

Her hands still well away from her sides, Sam turned. *Cop*, she thought instantly. Plainclothes, detective, probably homicide. And no doubt he had her description written on that little notepad in his jacket pocket.

"Are you carrying a weapon?"

She shook her head, forcing her brain into action. "I work here," she offered, keeping her voice low and calm. "Nobody checked the barbecue, and Mr. Addison wants to grill tonight."

"Didn't you use the same story the other night?"

Sam frowned, her heart pounding. "What are you talking about? Have we met?"

"Move away from there and lie face down on the deck, fingers interlocked behind your head."

Sighing, she pasted a mildly annoyed look on her face. "I'll get coal in my hair."

"I'm not gonna say it again."

As she knelt on the stone deck, she spied Addison coming down the balcony stairs. For his sake, it was a good thing the cop had a gun. Nobody played her. She couldn't believe he'd done it so easily, fooled her so quickly. She obviously hadn't been thinking with her head. The handcuffs the detective pulled from his belt with his free hand sent a shudder of panic through her. She'd never been caught before.

"Detective Castillo," Addison said, stopping at the foot of the steps, "it's all right."

"It is now," Castillo grunted. "Stay away from here, Mr. Addison. I'm calling in the bomb squad to check your barbecue."

So Addison hadn't been the one to turn her in. "That's what *I* was doing, you idiot," Sam snapped, immediately returning to her act. "Will you please tell him, Mr. Addison?"

"She works for me. You suggested I get private security, and I hardly have much faith left in Myerson-Schmidt. I had Donner hire her for me."

"When?"

"This afternoon."

The detective slid his gaze sideways, eyeing Addison. "*She's* your security. Dressed like that."

"Well, yes."

"You don't mind if I do a little check on her, do you?"

"I gave all my references to Mr. Addison," she put in, deciding to lay it on as thickly as possible. "Are you cleared to be here, Detective?"

"This is my investigation. And I would like to see those references for myself."

"Of course, Detective Castillo," Addison broke in. "In fact, I insist on it—though I'm completely satisfied with her credentials. You might want to call William Benton, at—"

"Bill Benton the spook?"

"Ex-CIA. We play golf together. He recommended her."

For the first time, Castillo looked uncertain. With another dour look at her, he holstered his gun. "Fine. I'll need her name."

Shit. Better the devil you kind of know than somebody you didn't know at all, she decided, sending another glance at Addison. He'd come through for her—this time. "Samantha," she answered, her mind racing. Being connected to Martin Jellicoe might hurt, or it might help, since she evidently hung out with ex-CIA. "Sam Jellicoe. I actually specialize in security for valuables, but I'm branching out."

The detective gazed at her sharply, his hand straying back to his weapon. "Jellicoe?"

She drew a breath. Man, she hated guns. "I'm his kid. Making up for Daddy's bad ways, you might say."

"I didn't know he had a kid."

"I'm the white sheep of the family. Nobody talks about me."

The two of them looked at one another for a long moment, each assessing and distrustful, until Addison stepped between them. "Anything else, Detective?"

Rubbing a finger along his moustache, Castillo shook his head. "No. But if you've got a record, Miss Jellicoe, I'll be back. And I'll be keeping an eye on you, regardless."

"Good. I'm looking to expand my fan club," she returned, watching the detective as he spent another few minutes in low-voiced conversation with Addison and left the patio, heading for the main drive. Not until he was out of sight did she return her gaze to Addison. "You were supposed to clear me, not make me into two people."

He shrugged. "It'll give us some time. Who's your father, Samantha Jellicoe?"

"None of your damned business, Rick Addison," she bit back, rattled. Jesus. In five minutes the entire Palm Beach PD would know who and where she was. And ten minutes after that, Interpol would have her name and location.

"Now, now, what about trust?"

"I'll talk about him when you talk about your ex-wife. Deal?"

Addison's gaze hardened. "That's not—"

"Never mind that," another voice growled from behind her. As she whipped around, startled, Donner grabbed her by the elbow. "What the hell were you doing down here?"

"Let me go," she snapped.

"Tom—"

"If you want to lie to the cops that's one thing, Rick. But she was down here, alone, up to her elbows in the barbecue. I saw her. We both did. And I want to know what the hell she was up to."

Sam took a steadying breath. Good questions, but she was not in the mood. Not with the lawyer. "I'm going to ask you once more to let me go," she muttered, stilling under his hard grip.

"And I'm going to ask you once more, what the hell were—"

Pushing toward him, Sam sank down and swept her left leg into the back of his knees. As soon as he was off-balance she yanked backward and heaved up. The attorney went over her shoulder and into the pool, headfirst.

"Karate?" Addison asked calmly, folding his arms and ignoring the roar of splashing and curses coming from the pool. His gray eyes danced with amusement.

She'd noticed it before, but the Brit was one seriously good-looking man. "I'm just mean," she returned, and headed up the steps. "I'm going to wash my hands. And your barbecue's fine, as far as I can tell. I didn't think anyone would have checked it."

He'd bought her some freedom with the stupid private security story, but he hadn't cleared her. On the other hand, unless Addison wanted to look like a complete idiot and possibly find himself charged with interfering in a police investigation, he had tied his own hands as well.

Sam elbowed open the bathroom door and stuck her filthy hands into the green marble sink. Now they were both neck deep in crap, and she was staying for grilled steak. A deal, after all, was still a deal.

When she came back down to the pool, the deck was deserted. A dripping-wet trail ran from the shallow end to the other set of steps, which led, she remembered from the blueprints, to a hallway lined with other bedroom suites, ones not as large or as elegant as hers. Yep, Addison liked her. With a small smile she dragged one of the wrought-iron chairs around, so her back wouldn't be to Donner's refuge, and took a seat.

The humidity always eased in the evenings as the breeze picked up, and she took a deep breath of air scented with jasmine and sea. Over her shoulder amid the scattered planting of birds-of-paradise and low begonias, a frog began chirping. Nice.

A young, Cuban-looking man walked around the side of the house toward her. "Would you care for something to drink?" he asked in a light accent.

"Iced tea?"

"Straight or fruity?"

"Raspberry, Reinaldo," Addison's voice came as he

emerged from one of the ground-floor doors opening onto the pool deck. "For both of us. And a Coors for Tom."

The strain was gone from her face, but he wouldn't precisely call her relaxed. To the casual observer she probably looked completely at ease, but as a fellow game player he could see the veriest bit of an edge to her. He wondered if she ever completely relaxed.

"Harvard's still here?"

"Tom doesn't discourage easily. He's changing." And making another phone call to Bill Benton, improving on the details of Samantha's story now that she had a last name. It was costing him Dolphin season tickets and a nice suite at the stadium, but he never had much time—or inclination—to attend the games, anyway. English football—now that was a sport.

"I'm not apologizing to him."

He hefted the tray he carried onto the barbecue. "He shouldn't have grabbed you. How do you like your steak?"

"Medium."

While he started the barbecue, Reinaldo came back with their drinks. Richard couldn't help a grin as Samantha took the Coors and moved it to the table farthest from where she sat. He also noticed that his iced tea was allowed to stay where it was, next to hers. Taking advantage of that fact, he made sure the coals were lit and took the seat beside her.

"Will Castillo find that you have a record?" he asked, sipping his raspberry tea.

She eyed him, obviously weighing whether or not the answer was any of his business. "No. Nothing definite, anyway. I work for museums and galleries. Legitimately."

"Good. That'll make things a little easier."

"What things?"

"Clearing your name and figuring out what happened here. What did you think I meant?"

She kicked her bare toes against the table leg. "I'd like to see your security room."

Studying her over the rim of his glass, he wondered

whether Donner was right, and he was thinking with the wrong body part. Showing a thief his security system, giving her access to the video and sensor controls, was insane. But he needed to keep her there unless he wanted to sit back and let Castillo do the work. "Very well. If you'll show me exactly how you got in here the first time—and the second time."

"I'm not starting a breaking-and-entering school, Addison."

"But the second time you didn't leave any signs of entry. Our bomber may have entered the same way." He frowned. "Why didn't you go in that way the first time?"

She shrugged, as if the answer was so obvious she couldn't quite believe he'd asked the question. "Target location. Cutting through the patio window the other night was faster, and I was dodging security guards."

"Why did you pick Tuesday morning?"

Her gaze touched his, amused. "You weren't here, and you'd announced that you were sending the tablet to the British Museum."

"How did you know I wasn't here?"

Now the slight smile touched her mouth. "You told the *Wall Street Journal* you'd be in Stuttgart until Thursday."

"What's so funny?" he asked, wondering what she would say if she knew he'd canceled a dinner with a senator and her husband to barbecue at his poolside for her.

"My guy said you can't trust somebody who lies to the *Journal*."

"Your guy?" he repeated softly, curling the question at the edge.

"My broker. My fence. The person who sells the things I steal."

"Oh. I thought you might have had a partner," he said.

"No. I work alone, these days."

He was actually a little more relieved than he should have been at the confirmation of her solo career. "I don't suppose you'd suspect 'your guy' in any of this?"

"I'd suspect Tom Donner first."

He shook his head. "Tom's not a thief."

"No, he's a lawyer. That's worse. And you trust him, which is stupid."

Richard narrowed his eyes. "We're talking about *your* friend—not mine. Does this 'guy' have a name?"

"I would imagine so," she said casually, taking another sip of iced tea, "but I'm trusting you with *my* freedom, not his."

He couldn't shake the feeling that she knew something specific about all this—and not any of that thief's intuition nonsense. "If it bears on this investigation—"

"If it does, Sherlock, then I'll think about it. But it doesn't. I . . . Great."

He didn't have to turn around to know that Donner had returned poolside. "Tom, how—"

"I'll just be over here," the attorney interrupted, picking up his beer as he sat at the far table.

His look at Samantha was less than friendly, but Richard wasn't overly concerned. Donner knew he'd stepped too far, and while tossing him into the pool might have been extreme, so were the circumstances. "I was just going to ask how you wanted your steak."

"Are you doing that mushroom-and-onion thing?"

"Hans is in the kitchen sautéeing as we speak."

"Medium well, then."

"So you barbecue a lot?" Samantha asked, dividing her attention as she kept an eye on Donner. She hadn't been kidding; Sam Jellicoe didn't like lawyers. She did, however, seem to like him, and he found that perversely pleasing.

"When I'm here," he answered. "Tom and his family are good sports about being my culinary victims."

"I doubt they mind."

Halfway over to check on the coals, Richard glanced back at her. "What do you mean?"

"Come on. He's practically attached to your butt as it is. You think he's going to object to being asked over to the Florida version of Buckingham Palace for dinner?"

"Was that a compliment?"

"Not from where I'm sitting, attached to your butt," Donner grunted.

"Solano Dorado is nice," she offered.

"Thank you."

Green eyes met his, then slid away again. "You're welcome. But then you already know that I lie all the time."

Donner took another swallow of beer. "This is all very cute, but I'd still like to know who tried to blow Rick to hell, if y'all don't mind. Since it wasn't you, Jellicoe."

Richard was beginning to wish Tom hadn't stayed for dinner. Besides the fact that he would prefer being alone with Samantha, he wanted her to relax a little, or he'd never get more than a glimpse of the information he wanted. "After we eat, Tom. For now, ask Miss Jellicoe what she thinks of Meissen porcelains, why don't you?"

"I'd rather ask what she thinks of Trojan stone tablets." Donner clanked his bottle on the ornate iron table. "But you didn't try to snatch it for yourself, did you? Who were you going to sell it to—or do you steal things, then look for a buyer?"

"I work on contract," she answered, surprising both men. "My guy gets a request for an item, sometimes a location, we agree on a price and the timing if necessary, and I do some research, then go in and get it."

Sliding the steaks onto the grill and smothering them with mesquite sauce, Richard thought about what she'd said. "The tablet was only here for a fortnight, but it wasn't a secret." He pursed his lips, considering just how personal he could make his questioning before she managed another change of subject. "Without betraying any confidences, did your guy indicate whether this buyer asked for my piece specifically?"

"Trojan stone tablets aren't exactly off-the-shelf items," she returned, giving him a slightly superior look, as though she would have expected him to know something like that. He did, actually, but this was her turn for show-and-tell. "There are only three in existence, if I recall," she continued, fiddling with her glass. "But yes, they would have wanted yours specifically."

"Why?"

She stayed silent for a moment. "I don't know. Convenience, I would guess. The other two are in private collections in Hamburg and somewhere in Istanbul. And maybe price."

Tom snorted. "You mean his stone tablet was cheaper than the others?"

Her soft lips twitched. At least Richard imagined they would be soft. "Maybe," she returned. "Or the buyer could be U.S.-based. Getting contraband items from one country to another can be expensive—and tricky. Especially now."

"Hm," Richard mused, flipping the steaks, "it was going to London in a few days. You may have a point."

"But we're not after my buyer," Samantha pointed out. "We're after someone who uses explosives in enclosed spaces, and whoever might have hired him." Rising, she strolled over to the barbecue, watching as Richard fiddled with the steaks. "That smells good."

So did she. "It's my best recipe."

"I really would like to see the gallery again. It might give me some ideas."

"About other items you can liberate?" Donner suggested, without heat.

Samantha leaned back against the barbecue and smiled sweetly. "How'd you like to visit the bottom of the pool again?"

"Children," Richard cautioned, taking the plate of sautéed onions and mushrooms from Reinaldo as the housekeeper appeared from the kitchen. "Behave yourselves."

"I gave my word that nothing would end up missing from the premises, Donner. I keep my word."

"I thought you lied all the time."

Her eyes cooled, but her smile became more coy. "Only about some things. You know, Addison, I could find you a parrot to do the same work as Donner, and it'd only cost you a cage and some birdseed."

"Yeah," Donner countered, "but the bird would crap all over his paperwork."

Richard flipped a steak. "I'm declaring a truce," he said, sensing, even if Donner didn't, that the lawyer stood a fair chance of ending up back in the pool. "Anybody who doesn't wish to abide by it can get the hell off my property." He held Samantha's gaze. "We'll go see the gallery after Tom leaves."

"Great. Are you giving her a key, too?"

Richard ignored his friend's grumbling. Besides, this guest didn't need a key. "Have a seat, Samantha," he said quietly, smiling. "I make great steak."

Eight

Friday, 8:03 p.m.

Addison was right about one thing. He knew how to grill the hell out of a steak.

As dusk settled around them the pool lights kicked on, followed by trails of lights edging the flower beds and into the palm trees around the pool deck. Reinaldo emerged from the house with table candles, which he set out with practiced precision.

"This is starting to look like a date," Samantha murmured, glancing at Addison. "Unless it's for Harvard."

"It's not for me," Donner said from his table across the pool deck. With a stretch, he rose. "Speaking of which, I'm outta here."

"B' bye."

He scowled at her, then put an arm across Addison's shoulder as they headed toward the house. "I'll have some of the insurance paperwork ready tomorrow. You want me to bring it here, I assume?"

"Yes."

As they rounded the corner of the house, Sam sat back to take another deep breath of flower-scented air. At this moment she had to think she'd made the right decision in coming to see the billionaire. Otherwise, she would have been holed up in that dingy old house in Clewiston, scouring the television for news and hoping she wouldn't have to run until airport security got tired of looking so hard for her.

"Ready to see the gallery?" Addison asked as he reappeared. He'd worn jeans to barbecue, with a green T-shirt hanging loose to his hips and an open gray shirt over it. He'd thrown on flip-flops as well, and the light breeze ruffled his hair with gentle fingers. She wouldn't mind running her fingers through that wavy black mass herself.

Sam swallowed. "The security room first."

He was still wary about her having access to that; Sam could see it in his face, and that was why she'd pushed for it. They were doing the trust test, and he could just sweat a little, too.

Addison motioned her toward the front drive. "Around this way, then."

He led them back into the house through the repaired patio door. "Impressive," she said, looking at it. "Do you keep spare patio windows around, or do you own the repair company?"

"Neither. I'm just charming."

That, he was. "What happened to the other glass?" she asked.

"The police have it," he answered. "Dusting for prints, I would imagine."

"They won't find any of mine."

"I should hope not. If there's anything you can think of that might tie you to the other night, you'd best tell me about it now."

"Not a thing comes to mind," she said. "I told you that I'm good at what I do."

"I don't doubt it. I'm just trying to catch any problems." Addison headed into the bowels of the house beyond the kitchen. A set of stairs led into a basement area, with an electrical room, pool pump and water heater room, then the security room.

"Mister Addison." A man wearing the tan uniform of a Myerson-Schmidt guard stood upright so hastily that his chair rolled backward. Sam stopped it deftly with the sole of one flip-flop and slid it back to him.

"Louie. We're just sightseeing." Addison's gesture gave her the run of the room.

Twenty monitors dominated the room, stacked in fours with a master computer in the middle and another two units to one side for playback purposes. "Is there usually just one guy in here?" she asked.

"Unless there's a big party," Louie said, resuming his seat, "one is all it takes."

"How come we surprised you when we walked in?" she pursued. "Didn't you see us coming?"

The guard cleared his throat. "I've been monitoring the outer perimeter cameras," he returned, his expression becoming defensive. "With all due respect, ma'am, you wouldn't have gotten indoors at all if Mr. Addison hadn't been with you."

She had several responses to that, none of which he would like, but she nodded. "Okay. The cops have the tapes from the other night, I suppose?"

"Yes," Addison answered. "Anything else?"

"The gallery."

They crossed back to the front of the house and started up the main stairs. The Picasso still hung on the landing, apparently having escaped all fire, smoke, and water damage. That had been a several-million-dollar piece of good luck for Addison.

"Does this sort of thing happen to you often?" she asked.

He slowed. "I've had death threats before, but this is the first time anyone's gotten this close to actually killing me."

"Nice line of work."

"Look who's talking." Addison shrugged. "The fact that somebody invaded my home to do it makes me *very* angry."

"But what if the bomb wasn't supposed to kill you?"

"It was meant to kill someone under my roof, which means under my protection."

"Your protection?" she repeated with a faint smile. "You sound like a feudal lord."

Addison nodded. "Something like that. Be careful up here. There's still debris lying about, and the floor's got some weak spots."

Yellow police tape stretched the width of the hallway right at the top of the stairs, but he pulled it loose as though it was nothing more significant than a spider's web. The way Addison stood there, the way he eyed the destruction of the gallery with a deep, cold anger, made it clear just how personally he took what had happened.

"Wasn't there more armor?" she commented, stepping past him.

"My estate manager sent some of the more salvageable pieces out to an armorer, to see what he could do with them."

"They were beautiful." For the first time Samantha reached the door that had secured the stone tablet, to find it hanging off twisted hinges and blackened with soot.

Richard stood back and watched her. He'd been over the floor himself already, but it fascinated him that she looked at it differently, that she saw things he would never have conceived of. *She* fascinated him.

"This is your secure room, right? Double-bolted, with infrared crossing the floor?"

Keeping in mind that he would ask how she knew all that later, he nodded. "Yes. With video on the far wall, facing the door."

"And nothing showed up on tape, I presume."

"Nothing so far, according to Detective Castillo."

"If you're so concerned with people invading your privacy, you maybe should consider putting more cameras inside the house," she suggested.

"That would protect my things, not my privacy." Walking closer so he could keep her in sight, he saw her squatting in front of the broken door, running her finger along the secondary lock. "What do you see?"

She straightened, brushing her hands off on her borrowed shorts, leaving black soot smudges across the yellow. "I was going to pick the secondary lock and cut the main," she said after a moment. "Whoever did this thought the same thing. You can see the nicks the tools made."

"A professional."

"Yes." She shrugged, moving into the room. "And . . . sometimes thieves do carry guns, even grenades, in case they get cornered or caught."

"You don't."

Samantha flashed a smile. "I don't get caught. I'm just trying to figure out what this was—a robbery or an assassination attempt."

"And you can determine that by looking at tool marks?"

Slowly she nodded. "There were no signs of forced entry but mine anywhere on the estate, you said, but this is pretty obvious."

"And?"

"And so he didn't have to be careful here, because he knew he was going to blow up any evidence."

She walked the edge of the room back to the video camera, but Richard stayed where he was. No signs of forced entry, but an obviously cut lock here in the middle of the house. Nothing on the video according to the police, though he'd had copies of the tape made and would go over it himself.

The number of people with access to the estate in his absence was almost endless; gardeners, security, housekeeping staff, pool maintenance, estate management, plus a select number of friends who were welcome to use the house whenever they chose. Though keys to the secured areas were harder to come by, they did exist—but not for the thief, apparently.

Finally she stopped at the fallen pedestal that had cradled the tablet. "This fell with a lot of force. The tablet would have broken."

"You're leaning toward the bomb being planted to cover the theft, aren't you?"

Samantha glanced up at him. "Maybe. At the least, someone knew the value of what was in this room and didn't want it ruined in the process of whatever the hell he was doing."

That was the third time she'd referred to the thief as a "he." Normally he wouldn't have found the masculinization odd—except that she was a thief, herself, and *definitely* female. "Does an assassin make an effort to preserve antiquities?" he pursued.

"I don't know—I'm not an assassin." With a quick grin she moved back into the gallery. "On the other hand, he didn't give a damn about anything sitting out here, or the rest of the stuff in the house if your fire sprinklers hadn't worked." Samantha frowned, then cleared her expression as she glanced at him again. "How much is a good suit of sixteenth-century armor worth these days?"

"Half a million, give or take."

"Ouch."

"How did you know? About the bomb, I mean."

She moved back to the large hole blown in the gallery wall, crouching to look at it more closely. "I didn't. I mean I almost stepped into the wire, but then saw it at the last second. It pissed me off, actually."

"Why?" Richard studied her expression, trying to ignore the abrupt tightness across his chest at the thought of her stepping into the middle of that bomb. She'd broken into his house, violated his sanctuary. But now he apparently worried about her.

"You had fairly top-line security everywhere, ineffective as most of it is, then a damned wire across the hall. It was just stupid. Guards, guests, would trip on it all the time and set off the alarm, or get hurt. And then I noticed that it wasn't quite parallel to the floor, and that . . . bothered me."

He crouched beside her. "Asymmetry bothered you. In the middle of a robbery."

"It bothered me that everything else in this house is tasteful and meticulous and well thought out. It didn't fit, and it obviously hadn't been approved by you. It wouldn't have been there for one thing, and for another, it wouldn't have been crooked. I wasn't completely sure, though, until I saw Prentiss marching toward me and not even glancing down."

And he'd thought himself reasonably observant. "I would have walked right into it," he muttered. In the dark, distracted and annoyed by the idiotic fax call, thinking about two meetings, a contract, and next week's scheduled trip to Beijing, he wouldn't have seen it until he tripped over the wire. And then he would have been dead. "Thank you," he said quietly.

A smile dimpled her cheeks. "Yes, well, look what it got me."

He was definitely beginning to think he'd come out ahead in this little partnership so far. Richard stood, and because he wanted to touch her, he offered his hand to help her to her feet. She gripped his fingers and stood, gazing at him from beneath her long eyelashes.

Jesus. Richard knew he was being played, that she'd probably gazed at other men in the same teasing way, knowing that they'd give her whatever she wanted. He still couldn't help reacting to it. To her. Slowly he smiled back at her. As long as he knew what was going on, he might as well enjoy it. "Do you have any theories, then?" he asked, letting her go after a moment and backing up again to give her room while she continued toward the far end of the gallery.

"Just this one side wired," she noted, "which would say to me that whoever did it left in this direction. Unless he didn't."

"That's not very helpful."

"I know. It's just . . ."

"Just what?" he prompted.

"I'm not used to looking at a robbery from this side. I mean I know what *I* would do in a given circumstance, but this definitely isn't me."

"Aside from the bomb, what else makes it different to you? I'm not looking for trouble, Samantha. I'm trying to figure this out, too."

She blew out her breath. "Right. Well, I like to get in and out fast. I look at blueprints, photographs, or whatever, find the quickest, easiest way to get what I want, and go with it. Leaving evidence of a break-in really doesn't concern me, as long as none of it points specifically in my direction."

"Once an object's gone missing, it's obviously been stolen," he commented, and saw her nod. "It makes sense."

"But this guy didn't want anybody to know he'd been here. So, from what I see, there's only one conclusion." Slowly she paced back toward him again, stepping over a crushed, decapitated knight as she did so. "He knew the layout really well, and he came in both to steal the tablet and to blow up your gallery."

"So he didn't mind killing."

"Or he intended to kill. But not you. You weren't supposed to be here."

"Nor were you."

"All right, let's go from there," she returned, fine eyebrows furrowed in concentration. "Who was here on—"

"Let's go there from downstairs," he interrupted. "Do you like raspberry sorbet?"

"Boy, you're smooth," she said, giving him an appraising look. "You do remember that I was trying to steal from you."

"Yes, but do you like raspberry sorbet?" he repeated, allowing himself a smile at her expression. She was too damned sexy for his peace of mind, but at least he seemed to get under her skin a little, as well. Where he wanted was under her clothes.

"Sure."

As they reached the dining room, he let her move ahead of him. Lowering his gaze to admire her backside, he abruptly noticed blood running down her left thigh. "Samantha, you're hurt," he exclaimed, taking her shoulder to pull her to a stop.

"No, I'm not."

"Your leg is bleeding."

She shrugged free of his grasp. "Looking at my legs, were you?" she asked coolly, glancing at Reinaldo and Joseph, the other dining room attendant. "Don't worry about it. It's just a cut. Do you have any super glue?"

"Super what?"

"Never mind. There's some in my purse upstairs." She turned around to exit.

Richard blocked her escape. "I'll send Joseph for it." Before she could protest, he waved a hand at the young Latino, who nodded and bolted out the door. "Sit—no, bend over. I'll take a look."

"I don't think so, your lordship. Not before dessert. And don't make such a fuss. I'm fine. My guy patched it. I just pulled it open, squatting up there."

"Get me a clean cloth," he barked, and Reinaldo reappeared a moment later with a hand towel. Gauging the antagonistic look in her green eyes, he pointed Reinaldo back toward the door. With a half grin, the housekeeper vacated the dining room, closing the door behind them.

"What do you think you're—"

"Take off your shorts."

She tried to face him, but he pushed her forward over the table. "This isn't very romantic. Aren't you even going to offer me a glass of wine first?" she said over her shoulder.

"You got this saving my life," he growled, holding her down with a hand against her spine. "Why did you say you weren't hurt?"

"It's not a big deal."

"Yes, it is. Now stop fooling around and take off your damned shorts. This isn't a seduction. I want to make certain you're all right." Just then Joseph reappeared, her purse clutched in his hands. "Put it down and get out," Richard ordered.

Samantha held still for a moment until the door closed again, then, with a not-quite-easy sigh, she unbuttoned the yellow shorts and slid them down.

Noting both her cute pink underwear and her smooth, warm skin, he knelt behind her. Trying to curb his rather ungentlemanly and impractical urge to slide his hands up the insides of her thighs, he took her purse and dug into it. He'd actually been imagining having Samantha bent over a table like this since she'd dropped through his skylight, but not under these circumstances. "Super glue?" he asked, holding a tube of something in front of her.

With a tight nod, she snatched the purse from him. "This is personal property."

"Yes, but whose?"

She snorted. "Fuck you."

"I deserve that, I suppose," he returned. "Do you really want me to do this? I can call a physician. He'll be very discreet. I promise."

"No. Just pinch the sides together, run glue over it, and hold it there for a minute. And don't get any on your fingers, or we'll be stuck together."

"Ah. And we wouldn't want that."

He thought he heard her attempt a chuckle, which he considered a good sign. "No, I really don't want your hand stuck to my ass. Especially with Donner already attached to yours."

It was a very nice ass, actually, trim and muscular and well suited to her long legs. He gingerly peeled off the tape and the bandage high on the back of her thigh, drawing in a sharp breath at the sight of the wound. "This isn't just a cut," he muttered, carefully cleaning the blood from her leg. "You need the emergency room."

She was silent, and after a moment he noticed how tightly her fists were clenched across the table. God, it must hurt. Wiping at the wound again, he gingerly pushed the two edges together and glued.

To her credit, she did no more than gasp, but it had to be killing her. "Almost there," he murmured. "Then we'll have some wine and sorbet."

"Addison?"

"All right, finished," he said, blowing gently to make sure the glue had set and carefully moving his fingers, stroking his palm down her leg as he did so. Nobody had that much self-control. The glue held. "How's—"

He didn't finish speaking because she fainted dead away, collapsing bonelessly into his arms.

Nine

Samantha awoke to the sound of men muttering. Peeling open one eye, she took in dark draperies inches from her face. "Green," she mumbled into a soft pillow, trying to remember where the hell she was.

Footsteps approached from somewhere beyond the curtains. "Good morning," a deep voice rich in faded Brit said, and she remembered.

"Oh, shit," she breathed, pushing up onto her hands and knees.

"Samantha, it's all right. You fainted."

As she shifted, the rest of the room came into view beyond the bed hangings. Addison alone would have been bad enough, but he had someone else with him: A thin, bald man with Drew Carey glasses and a goatee. "Who the hell are you?"

"He's my physician," Addison said. "Dr. Klemm."

She rose onto her knees, silk sheets sliding from her shoulders to her calves. He'd put her in damned silk pajamas, too. Pink ones, yet. Rescuing her hardly called for him to put her in appropriate nighttime wear. A British gentleman who apparently liked his women in dainty pink. Stifling a half-amused grumble, she squirmed through the heavy luxury to sit on the edge of the bed. "I told you, no doctors."

"And I told you he would be discreet. You have nothing to worry about, love."

She had several very good reasons to contradict that statement, but as she opened her mouth to do so she realized that her thigh actually did feel better. Her shoulder did, as well, and she experimentally rotated her arm. When she felt reasonably sure that she was grateful, she looked up at her host.

He was casual again today, once more in jeans and a black T-shirt with an open white shirt over it, and brand-name athletic shoes on his feet. "You don't look like a billionaire," she commented, pretending it didn't bother her that she'd been completely vulnerable for eight hours. Dammit. Passing out had not been part of the plan, and she needed to pull herself together.

"No? What do I look like, then?"

"A soccer player, or a professional skier or something," she returned grudgingly, admitting to herself that it was true. "One of those guys who pose for jock calendars."

Addison grinned, the expression lighting his gray eyes. "I'm hell on skis."

The doctor cleared his throat. "Ahem. Well, if anyone cares, your leg took fifteen stitches, young lady, and your shoulder took seven. Super glue is very clever, but I wouldn't recommend it on a regular basis. Rick said I'd probably never see you again unless you were unconscious, so I put in the dissolving kind of stitches. Don't pick at them."

Hm. Discreet and competent. It couldn't hurt to know a doctor like that—one who made house calls, yet. Sam smiled at him. "I don't know why Mr. Addison thinks I'm so hostile," she said, ignoring the sound Addison made. "From the way my cuts feel, I think I owe you lunch, Dr. Klemm. With dessert."

"Apple fritters?"

Her grin deepened. "My favorite. And I know a place that makes the best in the county."

"Then you're on, Miss Jellicoe."

Addison stirred, stepping between them. "Any other medical instructions, George?"

"Not really. I'd avoid the pool and baths for a week to ten days, but quick showers are fine." The doctor gazed at her for another moment, his expression mildly amused. "I took the liberty of changing the Band-Aids on your back and slopping on some antiseptic. There's some more ointment on the table." He indicated a white tube of something on the nightstand.

"Thanks. I'll call you for lunch."

"I'll be waiting."

Addison gestured toward the main part of the suite. "I'll see you out, George." As they left, he glanced over his shoulder at her. "Stay there. I'll be back in a few minutes."

She waited on the bed until the hall door closed. Her borrowed shirt and shorts were nowhere in sight, but her pink bra lay on the chair beside the bed. *Great.* So he'd seen her naked. She wondered whether he approved her size *B*'s. Most of the models who claimed to date him were considerably more top-heavy. At least he'd left her panties on.

Trying to convince herself that she didn't care what he thought didn't work any better than pretending she didn't enjoy the attention he paid her. Sam stood and burrowed back into the massive closet, which seemed to have given birth to even more clothes overnight. More jeans and T-shirts and blouses and shorts, most of them mysteriously in her size. Somebody had a personal shopper. Selecting a blue-and-white short-sleeved blouse and some jeans, she retrieved her bra and headed into the main sitting room.

Well, he might have seen her tits while she was passed out, but he wasn't going to see them this morning. Teasing and flirting was one thing; giving him the grand prize would mean losing her best leverage—and considering the way he made her skin tingle, it would also mean losing her perspective. She locked the main door and headed for the mammoth bathroom, closing and locking that door as well, just for good measure.

The shower felt heavenly, and only stung her cuts a little. She found deodorant, a toothbrush, and toothpaste waiting for her in the medicine cabinet, and by the time she had dried and combed out her hair she felt almost like her usual self. If not for the small matter of an arrest warrant hanging over her head and a very handsome British guy playing hell with her libido, she would have called this a good morning.

She half thought Addison would be sitting in the room waiting for her when she emerged, lock or no lock, but he was nowhere in sight. Then someone knocked on her balcony window, and she nearly popped her stitches. "Jesus," she muttered, stalking forward to push the curtains aside.

"Hungry?" Addison asked from the far side of the glass door, grinning at her disgruntled expression.

She unlatched the door and opened it. "Don't you ever work?" she asked, noting the table, two chairs, two place settings, and two stacks of pancakes and glasses of orange juice with what looked like a heaping bowl of fresh strawberries in the middle. Reinaldo stood down on the pool deck, obviously awaiting further orders.

"Coffee, I assume?"

"Diet Coke, if you've got it."

He lifted an eyebrow but didn't say anything. Instead, Addison waved at the housekeeper. "A Diet Coke, and tea for me." He pulled the chair out for her. "Have a seat."

"Any word from Harvard or Castillo this morning?" she asked, reaching for a strawberry and biting it in half.

"It's only seven-thirty," he returned. "Give them a little time. Are you feeling better?"

"Yes." She grimaced. "I'm not usually like that. I said I would help figure this out, and I will. I guess I was just more tired than—"

"Samantha," he interrupted, his expression serious, "considering the circumstances under which you received those wounds, you don't have to make excuses for anything."

The backs of her thighs tingled at the look in his eyes. Heat. She'd been with men before, but she couldn't recall one that gave off that masculine heat, the electricity, the way Rick Addison did. Maybe he thought size *B*'s were a nice change. "All right."

"So eat your pancakes."

Reinaldo came with the tea and Coke, and Sam occupied herself with popping the tab and pouring it into the very nice glass he'd supplied, complete with palm-tree-shaped ice cubes. She'd acknowledged yesterday that she wanted to trust Addison, when a long time ago she'd learned she couldn't trust anyone but herself.

"You don't have to sound so magnanimous," she commented around a mouthful of pancake and maple syrup. "You undressed me."

"Yes, but I didn't look."

"Liar."

Addison laughed. The sound was low and genuine, and it made her chuckle in return. Their eyes met, and her laughter faltered a little. Who would have thought—Samantha Jellicoe enjoying the company of someone like Richard Addison. No, not someone *like* him. Him. Over and above the role-playing and the unexpected lust, she was beginning to enjoy *his* company—and that was trouble.

"All right, I looked a little. But it was necessary." He sipped his orange juice. "I can't believe you did those acrobatics in my office and threw Tom into the pool while you were injured like that."

Relieved at the change of subject, she shrugged. "I would bet you've been playing hurt."

"Yes, but I went to the hospital."

"I saw, on the news." She reached up and flicked his black hair out of the way, revealing a small butterfly bandage across his left temple.

Addison caught her wrist. "You watched me on the news?" he asked, his lingering smile warming her in some nice places inside. *Keep your distance, Sam.*

"I . . . wanted to know how much trouble I was in."

"Have you ever been in this much trouble before?"

He still held her arm, his fingers gentle on the pulse running along her wrist. A light breeze rustled through the bordering palms, stroking along her skin and sending a strand of hair across her left eye. "No. Not that I recall."

Richard wanted to kiss her. He wanted to lean across the table and touch his mouth to hers, to taste the syrup and strawberries on her lips. If she'd been any other woman in the world, he would have done it. This one, though, required care and caution, and so with surprising reluctance he released her, bending only enough to brush the wisp of hair from her eyes. "We'll get you out of it."

The cell phone on his belt rang. When he flipped it open, Tom Donner began barking at him before he could even finish saying hello. "Jesus," he grumbled, grimacing at Samantha, "will you stop shouting?"

Tom lowered his voice, but it didn't make his news any more palatable. Halfway through the diatribe Richard cut him off. "Just bring the insurance papers and get over here," he growled, slapping the phone shut.

"Bad news?" Samantha asked. She'd been watching him during the entire conversation, her absurd Diet Coke in her hands.

With a deep breath he pushed away from the table. "Do you know Etienne DeVore?"

Samantha frowned, her fingers tightening on the glass. "Why?"

"You do." Coming around the table, he gripped her arm again and pulled her to her feet. The warning came into her eyes, but he ignored it, yanking her back into her borrowed suite. Abruptly he wasn't thinking of kissing her as much as he was worried about keeping this maddening woman alive. "How well do you know him?" he demanded.

"Not well," she snapped, pulling free. "Why?"

"He . . ." Richard counted to five, pacing to the door and back. "The police found him this morning."

Her fine brow furrowed. "Etienne? You've got to be kidding. Spider-Man couldn't catch DeVore. As for the Palm Beach Po—"

"He's dead, Samantha."

Her face went gray. Richard strode back to catch her, but she waved him off, instead sitting on one of the overstuffed Georgian chairs. "Oh. Oh."

He took the seat beside her. "You *were* close. I'm sorry." However tough she obviously was, he had no business telling her the news with the finesse of a sledgehammer. At the same time, he wanted to know just how well she'd been acquainted with someone the Paris police referred to as "le chat nuit." Of course she was a creature of the night, herself—which was why it could well have been her body being dragged out of the Atlantic and identified by Interpol agents.

"How—" She stopped. "Where?"

"North of Boca Raton. They found him washed up on the beach." He took a breath, abruptly wishing he hadn't been the one to give her the news. "Donner said they didn't have an autopsy report yet, but he'd been shot."

Samantha balled her hands into fists and pressed them against her eyes. "Shot," she repeated dully. "Etienne said he always figured he'd die old and rich and surrounded by half-naked women on some island he was going to buy." Abruptly she stood, walking to the patio door and back again. "We never expect we'll get shot, or blown up, or even caught, you know. If you think you're going to fail, you don't do it. But Jesus. I liked Etienne. He was a pain in the ass, but he was so . . . alive."

"I'm sorry," he repeated, sensing as he had on a few previous occasions that this was the real Samantha—and that above and beyond the lust, he liked her.

"It's not your fault. Etienne chose to live the way he did, the same as I do. He—" She blanched again. "I need to make a phone call. Shit." Spinning toward the hall door, then returning to him again, she actually knelt at his feet. "I need a phone they can't trace," she said, her face pale and very, very worried. "I can't—"

Richard pushed to his feet, grabbing her hand to touch her, even if she didn't want him to comfort her. Even if he wasn't certain how to go about comforting her. "Follow me."

Her hand gripped his with surprising strength, but he pretended not to notice as they strode down the hall to his office. He locked the door behind them and directed her toward the desk.

"You could get in trouble for this," she said, sitting behind the chrome and steel as he indicated.

"I'll manage. Line three. It's direct."

She picked up the handset, then paused, looking at him. Richard waited for her to ask him to leave; he wasn't going to volunteer to go. Whatever she decided, though, she didn't say. Instead she pushed seven numbers in quick succession. A local call, though he couldn't make out more than two or three of the numbers she dialed.

"Stoney?" she asked, and her shoulders visibly relaxed. "No, it's all right. Shut up. What are biscuits without honey when you golf?" While Richard scowled, she smiled a little into the phone. "How's your pillow? Good. Good. Bye."

"What the hell was that?"

She hung up the phone, closing her eyes. "He's okay. I should have realized, but with Etienne, I wanted to be sure."

"Samantha, no secrets."

Green eyes opened again, studying his face. "I don't know about that," she murmured. With a deep breath she stood. "But I need your help again."

"That's fine—if you explain to me about the biscuits and pillows. Otherwise, forget it." He'd heard the name Stoney before, from Donner's fax. Walter Barstone, the man the police had under surveillance. Her "guy," no doubt.

"It's code. Once we settled in around here, we came up with an area-specific code. We do that for wherever we are."

"And?" he prompted.

For the first time since his phone had gone off at the breakfast table, brief humor touched her face. "You hate not knowing things, don't you?"

He wasn't the only one, but this wasn't the time to be sidetracked. "Explain, please."

"Biscuits without honey are buttered. That means Butterfly World."

"The aviary off Highway 95."

"You know your tourist attractions," she complimented. "When you golf you say—"

"Fore," he interrupted, understanding beginning to dawn. "Four o'clock. We're to meet him today, I presume?"

She shook her head. "There's no 'we' in 'me,' Brit. Forget it. Just get me into town, and I'll take it from there."

"No. I'm not letting you out of my sight."

"You stand out too much," she complained. "Everybody notices you, so they'll notice me, and they'll notice my guy."

"Stoney," he corrected, lifting an eyebrow when she glared at him. "You said his name. Besides, I happen to know the police have surveillance on a Walter Barstone. I'm very useful."

"You're too conspicuous."

The idea of going with her, especially now that she was protesting it, continued to grow in appeal. She was going after information, and he was going to be there when she got it. Otherwise, he'd never be able to stay even with her on this, much less half a step ahead. And unless he was mistaken, DeVore's name hadn't surprised her. "I can blend."

"Right. At Butterfly World."

"Yes. And if you want off this estate, you'll have to give me your word that you and I will be going together."

Samantha ran a hand across her face. "Addison, I understand that this is . . . different, and exciting for you. Thieves, secret codes, police investigations. But two people are dead. You're too valuable a commodity to risk on stupid stuff like this."

Obviously she didn't know much about his life. "This involves me," he said in a low voice, "as much as it involves you. Aside from that, if someone follows your Stoney and they see you, both of you will be arrested. Like it or not, I am your passport, my dear."

"Do you always get your way?" She stalked back to the office door.

"Yes."

As she opened it, she glared over her shoulder at him. "Fine. Seeing you will probably make Stoney crap his pants, anyway."

"Oh, that's nice," Richard returned. At least she had recovered her sense of humor. "Let's fetch my tea and your breakfast soda and go for a walk."

"A walk."

"Around the grounds. The police couldn't find any sign of entry but yours, but I'd like you to take a look, anyway."

"Okay."

"Besides, I promised you a tour." And he wanted her to understand that he wasn't going to betray his word or her trust. Not unless she changed the rules, first.

"I thought Harvard was on his way."

Damn. He'd forgotten. "I'm sure he'll find us."

She sighed, a little color returning to her cheeks. "I'm sure you're right."

He actually had Reinaldo fetch her a fresh Diet Coke, chilled in the can. It was a luxury generally only found at home or in your better convenience stores. She told him as much, but he only grinned at her. For a rich man, he had quite the sense of humor. And today it helped, to have a reminder that life wasn't all tense nighttime excursions and friends turning up dead when you least expected it.

She reflected that yesterday she'd considered playing the dumb bimbette, lulling him into thinking she'd managed to break into his estate by sheer luck alone. Today she could admit that she felt relieved at not having to play that game with him. The problem was that he seemed to like, to appreciate, this version of her and what she brought to the table. She wasn't used to . . . being herself. And she didn't like the way she was enjoying their conversations, and forgetting she was there to help herself and not him. It left her feeling off-balance. And in her line of work, off-balance meant arrested—or dead.

"What about here?" he asked, gesturing at a section of high, curving stone wall along the north side of the estate.

"It's possible," she returned, leaving the cobbled path to move in closer to the wall. "You have a good eye for sneakiness."

"I'll take that as a compliment."

Addison followed her into the foliage; he had, all four times she'd headed off the path. Sam wasn't certain whether it was because he enjoyed shoving through cobwebs or because he was afraid to let her out of his sight in case she bolted. From what she was learning of Richard Addison, it was probably a combination of the two.

"Stop," she ordered, as the wall surveillance camera swung in their direction.

He moved past her. "We're allowed to be seen," he said, deep amusement in his voice. "I'm the owner, remember?"

Crap. "Right. Old habit." Sam watched the camera make its slow, half-circle rotation. Positioned every forty yards or so along the wall, they had an asynchronous pattern, which made sense. Halfway between the wall and the house, a half circle of light posts stood, each one fitted with a motion detector. "Did you consult with Myerson-Schmidt," she asked, "or was this stuff already here when you bought the place?"

"Both. The cameras were here, but my people commissioned the motion sensors. Why?"

"You have blind spots. It's really crappy security, Addison. Especially with no cameras indoors. Even with the guards roaming around at night."

"If it's so . . . crappy, as you put it, why did you bother with the gate sensors and the hole-cutting?"

She shot him a smile, sliding between a huge fern and the back wall. "There's no fun in entering if you're not breaking, too." Sam glanced down and stopped.

"So basically you made a mess because you could."

"Something like that," she said absently, squatting to finger a crushed begonia leaf.

"Did you find something?" His voice had sharpened, and in less than a heartbeat he was crouching beside her.

"I'm not sure. Somebody squashed this, but it might have been the cops during their search. There're footprints everywhere around here." She straightened, backing away from the wall and looking upward.

"A blind spot," he supplied.

"Yes, and a pretty clear run from here along the creek bed to the house. Only one, maybe two sensors to duck. Hm."

"What?"

Something caught her eye about halfway up the wall, and she couldn't help her quick grin. *Gotcha.* "Boost me up, will you?"

Obligingly he cupped his hands at the base of the wall. She stepped into the stirrup, and he boosted her skyward. At eye level, the print was easy to see.

"You already knew it was DeVore who came in with the explosives, didn't you?" he asked from below.

Damn. Either she was slipping, or he could read minds. "Once you get to a certain level of expertise and object value, only so many people could have done it," she hedged.

"And DeVore is one of those people."

"Yes."

"Are you?"

She ignored that, running her fingers along the slight curve of the shoe print. Etienne was careful, but in the middle of the night it wasn't always possible to wipe all the mud off your shoes before you scaled a wall. But the fact that he'd been so careful on the way out meant something. No one was supposed to know he'd been there at all. Why? His style was similar to hers, so why had he cared this time?

"What did you find?" he asked.

Samantha shook herself. *Concentrate, idiot. You could still get blamed for all of this.* "The front part of a shoe print," she said, pointing. "He was climbing the wall, digging his toes in for purchase. He had mud on his shoes. Most of it's caked off the wall, but you can still see the smudge. On the way out your adrenaline's up, and it's hard to be as careful."

"That's good to know."

"All right. Down, please."

She clasped his shoulder as he let her down, and she found herself a scant breath from his face as he straightened. He had to be several inches over six feet, because straight on, her eyes were level with his collarbone.

"You knew who did this," he repeated. "Why didn't you say anything?"

Sam shrugged. "Honor among thieves, maybe. And personally I'm more interested in who hired Etienne, and whether it was for the tablet or to kill you. He . . . called me and told me to stay out of this."

"But you're here anyway."

"I'm stubborn that way. Besides, his warning came a little late. And I want to figure this out."

"As do I." He nodded, but he wasn't looking at the wall. He was looking at her. Moving forward slowly, as though he was worried she would bolt, Addison lifted her chin in his long, elegant fingers and leaned down to touch his lips to hers.

Before she could decide whether she wanted to push him away or throw her arms around his neck and roll naked in the begonias with him, the soft warmth of his mouth left hers. He straightened, gazing at her with a slight smile on that very capable mouth.

Keep your cool, Sam. She needed him more than he needed her. Who *wanted* whom more, however, remained a question. "Cheeky, Addison. What was that for?"

"Admiration, Samantha," he murmured, running his thumb gently along her lower lip.

"Oh." And because she'd enjoyed it, and because he

looked so smug and in control, she leaned up and kissed him back. She felt his surprise, then the heat as his mouth molded to hers. And then *she* pulled back.

"I admire you too, Addison," she said, then walked away from him, with little of her usual grace and composure.

Ten

Tom Donner and four phone messages were waiting in his
office when Richard returned inside. He brought Samantha
along with him, mostly because he didn't want her flitting off
to Butterfly World without him. He'd be a fool to doubt for a
second that she could disappear from the estate anytime she
felt like it.

"Reinaldo said you'd gone for a walk," Donner commented, his long legs stretched out as he lounged in one of
the conference table chairs.

"I wanted to take a look at my outside security, which is
apparently crap." Richard slid a glance at Samantha, who'd
strolled to the window and was looking out at the pond. She'd
scarcely said a word since they'd kissed, so apparently neither of them intended to apologize or make an excuse. Another few moments of their mutual admiration, though, and
he would have needed a cold shower again.

"It's state-of-the-art crap," Tom said, his gaze also on the
estate's houseguest. "Castillo wants to come by and show
you some photos of Etienne DeVore, to see if you or anybody

at the estate recognizes him. Apparently this guy's got outstanding arrest warrants on him for cat burglary or suspicion thereof in eight countries."

"Did they say when it happened?" Samantha asked in a quiet voice, not moving.

Donner's feet hit the floor. "You knew him, then. Great. It's a regular thieves' convention here. Do we put out drinks and hors d'oeuvres, or do y'all prefer to break in and help yourselves?"

"Stop it, Tom," Richard said, his attention on Samantha as he wondered how many countries might have warrants out in regard to her nocturnal activities. "They were friends."

"Great," the attorney repeated. "No, I don't know when it happened. I imagine Castillo'll have more info after the autopsy."

"Etienne called me on Thursday, after the break-in. He warned me off this job and seemed kind of pissed that I'd shown up. If whoever he was working with heard him, then . . ." She drew a breath, straightening her shoulders and facing them. "Then they may have killed him for talking. If not, then I don't know. It could have been random, I suppose."

"But you don't think so." Richard offered her another soda from the office fridge, but she shook her head.

"He wouldn't have been an easy target for a stranger."

"Did he have a guy?"

She shot him a brief smile. "Nobody specific. He liked to work directly with a client."

"Are you completely sure he was the one who took the tablet and set the explosives?" Tom asked.

Her eyes lost focus, as though she was thinking of something far away, and Samantha half smiled again. It was a sad, lonely expression, and Richard gripped the back of a chair to keep from approaching her.

"Even if he hadn't called me and practically admitted to it, I already told Addison you can count the thieves of Etienne's caliber on one hand," she said. "I'd still like to see the surveillance videos for the north side of the grounds."

"We'll do that before we go," Richard said.

"And where are *we* going?" Donner queried.

Samantha snorted. "Like we'd tell you."

"We're going sightseeing," Richard interrupted, dropping into a chair. "What else did you bring for me?"

"The initial insurance estimates for the destroyed items. Danté's bringing up the official valuables list in a few minutes so I can compare market values against what the insurance guys are likely to offer. I also have some updated viewership statistics for the WNBT buyout. Connor sent them over after you canceled your meeting. I think he's getting nervous that you'll back out."

"It didn't occur to him that I might have a few personal matters to attend to, what with my house blowing up and all?"

Donner grinned. "Apparently not."

"His loss, then, if he lets the delay drive down his price."

Samantha sighed, pushing away from the window. "This is all very fascinating, but I don't think you need me for it."

"Where are you going, then?" Richard asked, prepared to tie her to a chair if she didn't answer.

She shrugged. "I promised not to take anything from here," she said, pulling open the door, "but you do have neighbors, don't you?"

Richard lurched to his feet. "Samantha! My house is *not* going to become your new base of operations. You will *not* steal from my neighbors."

The look she gave him was at least as annoyed as it was amused. "I was joking. I do have some self-control. I'll be out by your pond, or something." Halfway out the door, she paused. "But watch who you're ordering around, Addison. Our agreement was for your estate. As for the rest of the world, I'll do as I damned well please. A steak and some Diet Cokes doesn't mean you own me."

When she was gone, the door closed behind her, Richard took his seat again. "Dammit."

"She's a thief, Rick. You've found a use for her now, which is fine, I suppose, but—"

"But what, Tom?" Richard retorted, his temper flaring before he could yank it back under control. "I can't 'save' her? You think she's a charity project or something?"

"You're a philanthropist. Maybe you can't help it."

With a forced smile, Richard pulled over one of the stacks of papers Donner had brought for his review. "Samantha's not the only one with self-control. But I'll do as I please, as well."

"Uh-huh. Don't rattle your saber at me; I just work for you."

"I know, I know. On the phone you said you'd found out something about her father."

The problem wasn't Donner, and it wasn't even Samantha Jellicoe. As they became better acquainted, Richard wanted to make excuses for what she did: She had had a poor childhood; she gave her profits to the poor; someone had blackmailed her into a life of crime. At the same time, he sensed that none of that was true. She was a thief because she enjoyed being a thief. And she was bloody good at it.

Whatever her father had done—and from Castillo's reaction to the name he assumed the senior Jellicoe had been a thief of some notoriety—she was a bright young woman. If she'd wanted to find a different career for herself, she could have and would have done so.

"Okay. I called in some favors at the DA's office, and we found a Martin Jellicoe, who served five years of a thirty-year prison sentence in a maximum security prison." Tom pulled over some more papers and flipped through them. "I assume it was maximum security because he broke out of everywhere else. Three times."

"What did he do?"

"Stole things. Lots of things. From just about everywhere, apparently. And there's pretty much a consensus that he got away with a lot more than they found him guilty of. Florence and Rome were putting together an extradition request in 2002, which they've since dropped."

"Why?"

"Because he died in prison that year. Heart attack, from

the autopsy report." Donner glanced up at him. "Remember the whole *Mona Lisa* theft fiasco a couple of years ago?"

"That was him? Jesus." A frightening thought jolted cold through him. "It was *him*, wasn't it? Not her?"

"It was one of the jobs they convicted him of. Besides, how old is your Miss Jellicoe? Twenty-four, twenty-five? I doubt she could have pulled it off at sixteen, Rick. They suspected a partner in some of his jobs, but he never fingered anybody. If it was her, though, she's way more than some pickpocket."

"I realize that."

"Rick, I'm serious. They stole things from some very wealthy and very powerful people. And most of it's never been seen again. Crown jewels, original Monets, the captain's logbook from the *Mayflower*."

Richard sat back, turning his gaze to the window. She was out there, sitting on a bench facing the pond and tossing what looked like bread crumbs to the fish who resided there and the ducks who were visiting. He'd told her that he admired her, and he did; not for her career, but for the spirit she displayed and her obvious skill.

"So, all I'm going to say is that when this is over and you've cleared her of breaking in here, she's not going to become a schoolteacher."

"Drop it, Tom."

"The next time she takes something, it'll be because you lied to the cops and let her—"

"*Drop it.* Now." He took a deep, slow breath. "One thing at a time."

"Well, here's one more thing for you, then." Donner shoved the style and events section of the *Palm Beach Post* in his direction. "Page three."

He already knew what page three meant. It was the society page, featuring photos of the richest and most famous who happened to be in Palm Beach, and who or what they were doing. Directly after his divorce every tabloid in the world had seemed to feature him every day with a different woman, whether he actually knew her or whether they happened simply to be crossing the street at the same time. Once Donner had gotten through with a dozen lawsuits they'd become a little more cautious, but in the ensuing year and a half, he'd become a little less so. Divorce hadn't made him a monk, for Christ's sake.

The photo was quite good, considering the distance the photographer had been from the limousine. Donner leaned against the car while he stood with a slight smile on his face, talking with "mystery woman," who thankfully had her back half-turned to the camera. "Don't tell her about this."

"I'm not telling her anything. That's your department."

With a last look he closed the paper and shoved it back at Tom. "All right. Show me the insurance report."

They had moved from estimated loss compensation to going over the expense of repairing the damage to the walls and floor of the gallery when Danté knocked at the door. "Rick, Tom," he said, half-bowing as he took a seat at the table. "I did a new invent—"

"Was anything missing other than the stone tablet?" Richard interrupted. If more items had vanished, his partnership with Samantha was going to have to alter. He'd begun to trust her—or at least her opinion on the theft. If she'd lied . . .

"Just the tablet taken. The damage to some of the other pieces, though, is horrific. I—"

"Wait a minute."

Rising, Richard went to the window. Nothing else was missing. Thank God. His relief didn't make any sense; as Tom had said, she'd done a lot of damage elsewhere. But he *was* relieved.

She'd never been arrested for anything—he knew that. At the same time, he was perfectly aware that she'd done at least some of what Tom had claimed. She was too good, too practiced, for him to fool himself into thinking for a moment that this was the first job she'd attempted. And he hadn't become successful by ignoring reality.

He unlatched one of the windows and pushed it open. "Samantha!"

She started, looking over her shoulder at him.

"Will you join us for a moment?"

With a quick nod she rose and disappeared back along the path toward the house. Whatever they knew or thought they knew about her, it could wait. He'd made a deal, and he would honor it. As he'd told Donner, one thing at a time. He would worry later about what to do with her when this was finished.

People had every right to protect their property, and to attempt to stop anyone who tried to invade their domain. Etienne had been cocky and more than a little greedy, but he'd understood the rules and the danger as well as she did. To hear that he'd been found floating in the ocean, full of gunshot wounds—that wasn't a death in the line of even a thief's duty. That was just murder. And that wasn't part of anyone's game. *Game*. This one had stopped being amusing at the moment of the big boom.

"Did you find out anything more about Eti—" she began as she pushed open the office door. A third man had joined them, and she stopped her sentence abruptly. "You must be Danté."

Richard had stood as she entered the room, his English manners showing. "Samantha, this is my art acquisitions manager, Danté Partino. Danté, my new security consultant, Samantha Jellicoe."

God, she wished he would stop handing everybody her name like that. It jolted her every time she heard it on his lips. "Hi," she settled for, taking the seat beside Addison when he motioned her to the table. "What's going on?"

"Danté's been compiling a list of my damaged and destroyed artworks. I just wanted you to hear it."

"Trying to make me feel guilty?" she murmured.

"No. You didn't blow anything up. I want your opinion."

She didn't quite see why, since her concern was only for the bomb and for whoever had wanted the tablet—and now, for whoever had killed the man who had taken the tablet. Even so, she nodded.

"Security consultant?" Partino repeated, eyeing her much as Donner had when they'd first met. "With Myerson-Schmidt?"

"No, she's independent," Addison replied, giving her a look of veiled amusement. "Miss Jellicoe specializes in security for valuables. Go ahead."

Partino read through the list, item after item, each one followed by its original, then estimated current market value, the amount of damage, and if it was repairable, how much that would cost. He knew his stuff. And Sam couldn't help remembering that her host had at least three other residences, and that as far as she knew, all of them were choked with antiques and works of art. For her, it would have been Christmas, the Fourth of July, and Thanksgiving, all rolled into one.

She had trouble concentrating on the lengthy soliloquy, though, with Addison sitting so close beside her that she could feel the warmth of his body seeping into hers. Sam wondered what he would do if she simply grabbed his face and planted another kiss on his unsmiling, sensuous mouth.

Yeah, right. This was his game, but the stakes were much higher for her. *Ignore the attraction*, she ordered herself. She was in too much shit for anything else. If Etienne could be shot and killed, it could happen to her, too. She shifted, leaning closer to look at the paper he was holding. It could happen to him.

"Anything catch your attention?" he murmured, looking sideways at her.

Sam blinked. "No. It's all sellable, but no one thing more than any other—except for the stone tablet, which somebody really wanted, obviously."

"Miss Jellicoe," Partino returned, "not to doubt your expertise, but I assure you that a preeminent collector would recognize the value of every item in this collection."

"Tell that to the guy who only stole one thing and didn't care about blowing up everything else."

Partino twitched. "I do not recommend poor-quality art-works for purchase. Everything here is of the highest quality."

"You tick off everybody, don't you?" Donner asked her, with a low chuckle.

That was enough of that. "Well, here's Harvard, a guy who wouldn't know a Rembrandt from a Degas," she shot back. "Let's take a look at him."

Donner narrowed his eyes. "Whatever you're implying, I don't appr—"

"I was invited to this show," she snapped, standing. "Play with yourselves for the encore."

Half-expecting Addison to call her back, she slipped out the door and back down the hallway to her bedroom suite. Somebody, probably Reinaldo, had put a bowl of fresh fruit on the coffee table, and she snatched up an apple, tossing and catching it while she tracked down the remote for the theater-sized television and turned it on.

A moment of searching found WNBT, the station Addison was after. Godzilla again trampled Tokyo, this time in the company of Monster X and Rodan. It figured.

Twenty minutes later the doorknob behind her rattled and turned. Though she was certain who it was, habit and a strong sense of self-preservation made her glance up over her shoulder. "When you buy a television station, do you change the format?"

Addison closed and locked the door, then dropped into the chair beside her and set two cans of soda on the coffee table. "Not always. Why?"

"First of all, don't you use coasters?" she asked, leaning forward and slipping two Victorian flower-patterned coasters beneath the drinks. "This is a Georgian table, you know. Two hundred and fifty years old."

"Two hundred and thirty-one years old," he corrected.

"Secondly, this is the only station around here that shows the classics." She gestured at the huge screen with the re-mains of her apple. "This is Godzilla Week, for example."

"I see." Helping himself to a peach, he bit into it. Juice ran down his chin, and he wiped at it with his thumb, absently licking the sweet liquid off. "Godzilla being one of the classics, of course."

Oh, yum. "Most of 'em. A few of the ones from the late seventies turned Godzilla into an environmental avenger, which is just silly. After all, he's a by-product of nuclear testing. He's supposed to be bad."

"Why do you steal things?" he asked abruptly, his gaze still on the rampaging monsters.

He seemed genuinely curious, but the more he knew about her, the more dangerous he was. "Why did you marry your ex?" she countered.

Addison shifted in his chair. "Sooner or later you're going to trust me enough to tell me," he said without heat.

"Sooner or later you'll do what you promised, and I'll be out of here," she returned, tossing the apple core into the wastebasket by the door. *Two points.*

"Do you want to leave?"

"Now?"

"Yes, right now. Today. This minute. Do you want to go?"

No. "What I want to do," she said slowly, finding it difficult for the first time to meet that deep gray gaze of his, "is to go to Butterfly World."

He pushed to his feet, reaching over and taking her hand to pull her up beside him. "Fine. Let's go now, and we'll have time to sightsee a little."

"You're weird." She couldn't help grinning at his chuckle.

"I'm mysterious," he corrected. "You should appreciate me more."

If she appreciated him any more than she was beginning to, they'd be naked on her borrowed bed right now, and screw the consequences.

Eleven

Saturday, 1:18 p.m.

"We are not taking your limousine." Samantha folded her arms across her chest.

Trying not to smile, Richard stood on the front steps beside her and decided not to ask why she had such a prejudice against his limousine. "I didn't say we were, love."

"You told Ben to bring the car around."

A yellow Mercedes-Benz SLK rounded the house and cruised to a halt in front of them. "Yes, but I didn't say which car."

"Doesn't James Bond drive a BMW or something?" she asked, heading for the passenger side as Ben exited the driver's seat. "Banana yellow. Very inconspicuous."

"I'm not James Bond. Shut up and get in."

She liked the car; he could see it in her tease of a smile as she sat. Samantha ran her hand across the dash, which was another good sign. She seemed to learn by tactile sensation. It would be interesting to see if that continued into the bedroom. He shifted, abruptly uncomfortable. *Cold shower. Think cold shower.*

Finally, she buckled in and grinned at him. "Can we put the banana's top down?"

Obligingly he pushed a button on the dash. The trunk lid popped open, and the roof lifted and swung backward into the trunk with one fluid motion. "Better?"

"Cool," was all she said, as they rolled down the drive.

The police still stood at the outside gate, but they were beginning to look more bored than hopeful of catching a bomber. Of course they'd already found the bomber washed up on the beach, whether they'd realized it or not. He glanced at Samantha, leaning one arm on the window frame, her chin tucked along it.

"The police identified DeVore and consider him a suspect," he said, "but since I described a woman inside my house, they haven't given up looking."

"They probably figure he had a partner. Tracking him won't lead them any closer to me, but I'm definitely not in the clear." She shot him a look. "Yet."

"Has he ever used explosives before?"

"I don't know all the jobs he's pulled, but I wouldn't be surprised. He wouldn't have called to warn me away if we'd just been competing for a simple grab." She shrugged. "He's done hits before, but he always said it wasn't as much of a challenge. People move around and make themselves vulnerable. Objects stay put, and you have to go to them."

"Were you and DeVore ever . . . partners?"

She sat back and punched on the stereo. "Oh, that figures," she scowled, as Mozart drifted into the car. "Partners. I assume you mean in bed as well as in crime. In crime, no."

Gripping the steering wheel, his stomach clenching in a jealousy that was as unexpected as it was ridiculous, Richard nodded. "Then I'm sorry again."

"Quit apologizing. It wasn't your fault. People drop in and out of my life all the time. I'm used to it."

"Cynical, aren't we?"

"I try to stick to what I'm good at. Besides, you shouldn't be complaining. You're 'in' at the moment."

For how long? he wondered. "It was a comment. Not a complaint."

Samantha flashed her quicksilver grin. "Good. Anyway, I'm just hoping Stoney will know who Etienne was contracted with. If not, we'll be stuck at about the same place the police are." Auburn hair whipped across her face, and she pulled a rubber band from her Gucci bag to pull the wavy mass back into a pert tail.

"I thought we were trying to blend," he commented. "So why the expensive handbag?"

"It's all I had with me. Besides, it'll help me look like a tourist. I hope you brought a corny baseball cap or something."

"Sorry, I didn't dig into the corny section of my wardrobe this morning."

She studied his profile for a moment, while he pretended to keep his attention on the highway. Thank God the traffic was light.

"Just keep your sunglasses on. You're not wearing a suit, so that should help. We'll get you a Gilligan hat or something."

"No, we won't."

Samantha was silent for a moment, though she eyed the stereo with such keen disappointment that it was almost comical. "You told watchdog Donner where we were going, didn't you?"

"I trust him, Samantha. And—"

"I don't. Never trust somebody who knows how much you're worth."

"Everybody knows how much I'm worth."

"Yeah, but everybody doesn't have the kind of access he does." She drummed her fingers on the window frame. "Your death's gotta have a huge profit built into it for him."

Richard frowned, already putting the notion out of his head. Tom Donner was his closest friend. The idea was ridiculous. And he was careful about whom he let into his life, these days—with one glaring exception. "I trust him," he repeated. "Drop it."

"Okay. If it makes you feel any better, if I were you, I wouldn't have gone anywhere with me unless I told somebody I trust, either. I just wouldn't have picked Donner."

The compliment, double-edged as it was, pleased him. "You can change the CD if you want," he said, "but—"

She leapt at the stereo. Mozart cut off, to be replaced by Beethoven, then Haydn. Sitting back, she folded her arms. "Are there only dead people in your CD changer?"

"You like antiques. I thought you'd appreciate classical music."

"I do—but not in a James Bond car with the top down."

"I am not bloody Ja—"

With a quick flick she switched off the CD and started punching radio stations until something with heavy drums and electric guitars and vaguely in-tune screeching lit up the equalizer. She hit the volume and sat back again while he laughed.

"What the devil is that?"

"Who cares? It's got a beat."

Leaning her chin along her arm again, Sam squinted against the warm breeze whipping into the car. She loved Florida. Europe owned the prize for picturesque villages tucked into old pine-and-oak forests, but the dichotomy here fascinated her. They flew past long expanses of marshy grass, broken by tiny houses set back from the highway on dirt roads with rusted-out cars decorating the front lawns. More scattered groves of two-hundred-year-old elms and hanging willows spread along creek banks, their giant hurricane-bowed forms dwarfed by needles of glass and steel in the business areas.

And Palm Beach, even without the allure of the country's wealthiest residents cramped into a few square miles of paradise, fascinated her even more. Insulated beauty and antiquity and modern corruption—the perfect place for a high-class cat burglar. She slid a glance at Addison again. In her line of work she wasn't supposed to like surprises. Surprise again.

On the other hand, surprise did have its drawbacks. Sam angled her head a little more to see the reflection of the side view mirror. "Change lanes," she said.

"What for?"

Reminding herself that Addison was a businessman and not a thief, she kept her relaxed pose. "Because I want to see if the car behind us changes lanes, too."

He kept his gaze on the road. "That beige sedan?"

"You noticed?" she asked, surprised enough that she straightened.

Addison nodded. "It's been behind us since before we got on the highway, but this *is* a main thoroughfare, love."

"Okay, so you're observant, but you need to practice paranoia. Change lanes. Head toward the exit."

"Does this happen to you often?"

She flashed a grin. "Only in the past week or so. Usually the idea is that nobody knows who I am."

"Too late for that." He slid his gaze to the rearview mirror. Half a minute later, the sedan changed lanes to match them.

"It could still be a coincidence," he muttered, but kept his attention on the mirror as he moved to the outside lane. The sedan followed. "Or not."

"See, paranoia can save your life. Floor it."

"Don't you want to know who it is?"

"Jesus. Curiosity killed the cat, Addison, and I'm a cat."

"I'm a wolf," he returned, and slammed his foot on the brake.

High-tech antilock braking system or not, the SLK's tires smoked as they jolted to a halt. Traffic was fairly light, but Sam couldn't help a gasp as a big rig veered around them, the driver giving them the one-fingered salute and yanking on the air horn. "Christ."

The sedan didn't have antilock brakes. Brakes squealing, it fishtailed wildly, missing them by only a few inches as it skidded onto the mud beyond the narrow service lane. The driver yanked it back under control before it rolled into the swamp grass. The guy knew how to drive, and that answered a few questions right there. It ground to a halt a dozen yards past them along the side of the road.

"Voilà," Addison said, accelerating again and pulling over in front of the sedan.

"Right, unless they're armed."

Addison shifted, removing his seat belt and in the same motion pulling what looked like a Glock .30 from the glove box. "I like to be prepared."

"No guns," she grated, undoing her own seat belt and vaulting out of the car. "Besides, you'd only get arrested." The sedan's passenger door creaked open. "Good afternoon, Detective Castillo," she called, approaching as he emerged. *Be friendly*, she told herself.

"What the hell was that all about?" the detective growled.

"That was my fault," Sam returned, feeling Addison coming up behind her. "I noticed we were being followed, and I suggested that Mr. Addison pull over." She mustered a pained grin. "I'm afraid he panicked."

"Like hell I did," Addison broke in. "Why are you tailing me?"

"They're not tailing you; they're tailing me," Sam countered. "But I told you, Detective, I'm a good girl. I'm afraid to say, though, that you might have tipped off anybody who *was* tailing Mr. Addison." She gestured at the sedan, not having to conceal her contempt. "Nobody rents '91 Buicks to tourists, and no self-respecting cat burglar or assassin would drive an old beige car. You drive better than reporters, so you had to be cops."

"Ah. Then why'd you try to kill us like that?"

Addison pushed past her. "She didn't. I panicked, remember? Is there something you wanted, Detective?"

"No. Nothing in particular. But just remember, Mr. Addison, if you get killed, then I get fired. You shouldn't be out here."

"I'll be careful." Addison slipped his hand around her upper arm. "Shall we, Samantha? We'll be late."

"Sure. And don't worry, Castillo. It's my job to keep him

safe." She shot him a grin. "However much a pain in the ass *that* is."

The cop's moustache twitched. "I almost believe you, Jellicoe."

"I'll have to work a little harder, then."

They slipped back into the SLK, and Addison put it in gear. "Do you think they'll give up?" he asked, his attention on the rearview mirror again.

"Probably. But just in case somebody else had the same idea as Castillo, how fast can this thing go?"

Richard eased back out onto the highway, turned up her hellish rock station, and floored the accelerator. "Let's find out."

Castillo watched the bright yellow car as it headed south and went into the road version of hyperdrive. "Shit."

As he returned to the passenger's seat, Officer James Kennedy beside him started the Buick. "Do we keep following 'em?"

"Nope."

"I could call Highway Patrol and have 'em pulled over for speeding."

"Nope."

"Then what do we do?"

"Head back to the station and pull up the insurance claims for Addison's stuff. Just because he's rich doesn't mean I'm not allowed to conduct this damned investigation."

"You think he's in on it?"

The detective looked at the eager face of his driver. "I think *she* is, and I think he's with her of his own free will. There's more to this than a theft and a bomb. But thinking doesn't get me dick, and sitting here is wasting my time."

Kennedy turned under the highway for the northbound on-ramp. "Ha. I told his attorney he should've hired me for his security. He's gotta be hiding something, hiring that bimbo instead."

Castillo freed a stick of gum from his pocket and opened

the wrapper. "Considering who we pulled out of the water this morning, that bimbo may now be the best cat burglar in the world. Show some respect."

As the police turned north on Highway 95, a black BMW with dark-tinted windows left the gas station on the opposite side of the road and headed south at high speed.

The Butterfly World parking lot was fairly crowded for a Thursday afternoon, but as far as Sam was concerned, that was a good thing. Being inconspicuous with Addison beside her was a difficult enough prospect without a deserted tourist attraction to add into the mix. "Over there's fine," she said, pointing.

Addison pulled them into the spot. "Is everywhere a potential trap?" he asked, unlatching his seat belt and sliding from the car. "I presume that's why we're three feet from the exit and a quarter mile from the entrance."

"Today everywhere is a potential trap," she answered, slinging her purse over her shoulder and closing the banana car's door behind her. "We're just lucky that was the cops back there."

"But you knew that before we stopped, didn't you?"

His tone accused her of something underhanded, but she refused to let it get to her. She shrugged. "Like I said, whoever belonged to an old beige car wasn't one of your friends—or enemies, and the people I know have more self-respect. Which left cops, or press. And I'm glad it wasn't the press."

A smile touched his sensuous mouth. "I do believe, my dear, that you're even more camera shy than I am."

Sam nodded. "Hence the blending."

"Blending. Right." He held his hand out, and she hesitated. "Happy tourists, remember?" he teased, flexing his fingers to beckon her closer. "Maybe we're newlyweds on our honeymoon."

"You're putting way too much thought into this, Addison,"

she said, taking his hand and pretending that her own imagination wasn't on overdrive.

His warm fingers curled around hers. "Rick."

Sam nodded, not ready to say it yet. "Let's go. They stop letting people in at four o'clock, and kick everybody out at five."

"So no one gets in after we do."

"That's the idea."

He seemed to be catching on to her little tricks and idiosyncrasies with alarming speed, but she'd already noticed that he wasn't a slouch by any stretch of the imagination. She and Stoney would have to change all their passwords and signals, but they'd done that before, when her father had been arrested. It was a pain in the ass, but necessary to their continued safety.

As they reached the ticket booth, she couldn't help looking over her shoulder, but no beige Buick drove into the parking lot. Addison had broken the land speed record on the way down, so she didn't think anyone short of NASA could have kept up. Not looking, though, would have driven her crazy.

"Two adults, please," Addison was saying to the young lady in the ticket booth.

"You've only got an hour left before closing," she said in a soft Southern accent.

"That's fine."

"That'll be $29.90."

Before Sam could protest, he pulled bills out of his tight jeans pocket, accepting the tickets and the change with a smile. He took her hand again, guiding her to the gates. "You notice I paid cash," he murmured, leaning close, "because someone might be able to trace a credit card purchase."

Goose bumps rose on her arms. "You learn fast, Addison," she said, hoping Stoney wasn't watching. She shivered as his mouth brushed her ear. Muscles contracted, and she forced herself to draw a slow breath. *Stop it*, she ordered herself, as they passed into Butterfly World.

Double doors secured the aviary, preventing the butterflies

from escaping. They went through the first set, and were trapped in between when Addison pulled her closer. "Say my name," he ordered in a low voice.

"Come on, Stoney'll be waiting."

"Say it."

"Go to—"

"Say it, Samantha."

"You have to be in control of everything, don't you?" She forced a chuckle. "Man, it must drive you crazy that you can't make me do something I don't w—"

He lowered his mouth to hers, sweeping his free hand around her waist and drawing her against his flat, muscled abdomen. Heat swept down her spine as his lips molded to hers. This wasn't a tentative kiss, as the first one in his garden had been. This kiss told her exactly what he wanted, and how much he wanted it. And the best and worst of it was, she wanted it, too.

The warm humidity of the aviary hung in the dim foyer, still and dark and close. He pressed her back against the inside door, mouth hard and demanding against hers, shifting and moving and drawing her in.

"Easy, Tarzan," she managed, gulping a breath of the hot, moist air. "Someone will see—"

"Say my name," he repeated, teeth finding her lower lip.

Christ. "Rick," she muttered thickly, her mind sinking into a damp, Addison-filled haze as he pressed her harder against the door. "Happ—"

Her bottom nudged the door handle, and the inner door flew open, propelled by their weight against it. Still attached at the mouth, the two of them stumbled into the aviary.

Several of the other late-arriving tourists turned to look at them curiously, and she gave a careless laugh, taking his hand and swinging it playfully. "We're newlyweds," she said to no one in particular. None of it was easy when she didn't have any breath left in her body, and when she was practically having an orgasm just from his kiss, but it seemed to work.

She'd gone only three feet when he tugged her back against him. "Stay close, Samantha."

"Hm. Was that kiss out of admiration, too, Addison?" she whispered back.

"No, that was lust. What's with the humming and arm-swinging?"

"We're blending. And you started it. I just suggested a hat, but then you had to swallow me whole."

"You were snacking, too. Was it an act, then? Should I be grateful you didn't throw me into a pool?" he continued in a soft voice.

"If I'd wanted to drop you, I would have," she whispered back, pulling him forward. "Come on, honey."

"Was it an act, Jellicoe?" he repeated.

"Maybe." *Men.* "Don't get your testosterone up, Addison. This is going to be difficult enough to pull off with you tagging along. I don't need another complication right now."

He moved in closer to her again, his gaze dark and heated. "You've already got one."

Shit. "Will you knock it off? Jesus. What brought this on, anyway? You were civilized in the car."

"It's been building all day," he said with a little more humor, "but I was driving, then. Now I'm not."

Several of the female tourists were gazing at Addison over their husbands' shoulders or through the rain forest ferns. She wasn't certain whether it was because they recognized him or because he was looking particularly handsome in a predatory, carnivorous kind of way, but she had to admit to a brief sense of satisfaction. He wanted Samantha R. Jellicoe. *Eat your hearts out, girls.*

"Look at the butterflies," she instructed. "That's why we're here."

His hand in hers tightened, then relaxed. "Any sign of your guy?"

"Not yet. He's probably in the gardens behind the main aviary." A bright blue butterfly the size of a postcard fluttered in and lit on Addison's dark hair. "Don't move. You have a friend."

"Great."

Sam chuckled. "I wish I had a camera. What does butterfly poop look like?"

Carefully he shook his head, and the butterfly flitted off into the warm faux jungle. The classical music playing softly in the background seemed both appropriate and amusing—everybody was a critic. Beneath the high, domed ceiling hundreds of butterflies of every color and size darted among the trees and flowers, while a fine, warm mist jetted out from hidden fixtures in the walls and the tropical growth.

"This is pretty," Addison said, echoing her thoughts.

"Maybe we should have come earlier."

"Maybe we'll have to come back and do the tourist thing for real."

"Mm. Like a date?" she murmured.

"I could rent it after hours. We'd have it all to ourselves."

She couldn't help imagining herself spread-eagled among the ferns, Addison on top of her and butterflies flitting over their heads. "Show a little restraint, will you?"

His smile made her wet. "I'm showing a great deal of restraint." Trying not to hurry, they made their way along the dome's meandering path toward the far doors. "Are you going to tell me what Stoney looks like?"

Through the clear netting of the dome Samantha caught sight of him sitting on a bench in the rose garden. The relief that ran through her was so strong it made her shake. Attached to her hand, Addison slowed and looked down at her.

"What is it?"

"Stoney's a cross between Hulk Hogan," she said, pulling her hand free and moving forward again, "and Diana Ross, with a nose that's been broken about a hundred times and a little silver cross around his neck."

She pushed through the two sets of doors and turned onto the left path, by the sign that read ENGLISH ROSE GARDEN. As

Addison drew even with her again, she slowed. The precautions they'd taken to set up the meeting would be for nothing if she stampeded now.

Stoney saw her and stood, then caught sight of Addison at her elbow. Immediately he turned around and started strolling in the opposite direction. They had an "all clear" code word, but she hesitated before she said it aloud. Nothing was clear, and having Addison here wasn't doing either of them any good. But she had given her word that she and the rich guy were partners, and if she left without talking to Stoney, she was going to implode. "How about those Dolphins?" she said in a carrying voice, facing Addison.

"What?"

"Shut up and play along," she said under her breath. "Think they'll make it to the Super Bowl this time?"

"Ah, well, now that Dan Quayle—"

"Marino."

"—Marino's retired, I don't know."

"You're a Dolphins fan, are you?" a deep, musical voice said from over her shoulder.

She jabbed a finger at Addison. "Oh, he's a transplant, but I'm working on it. This is Richard Addison."

"Walter." Stoney stuck out his hand, looking friendly despite the slap of his words. "You've gone insane, Sam. The three of us can't be seen together."

After Addison shook Stoney's hand, Sam followed suit, clutching her fence's thick, agile fingers for a moment longer than she needed to. "Did you hear about Etienne?"

"I heard. And until you called me, I thought you'd be the next corpse to wash up on the beach." The emotion was buried deep in his voice, but she knew him well enough to hear it.

"He called me right before the cops showed up at my house, and basically told me I was in some deep shit. Do you know who he was working for?" Mushy sentiment could wait for later.

Stoney glanced at Addison. "I need a little bit of an explanation first, honey."

"Samantha and I have an agreement," Addison put in. "She helps me figure out who tried to blow up my house and why, and I clear her of any breaking and entering—and murder—charges."

"She saved your life, you know."

"I know. That's why I'm here."

"I told her hanging around to drag you down the stairs couldn't have been a good idea, and she'd probably get into more trouble for being nice; but Sam can't even stand to squash a spider."

"Stoney, shut up," she said brusquely. Great. Her deepest secrets exposed. "I'm guessing that Etienne's client or the broker is the one who killed him. Do you have any idea who he was working for?"

"Right. Okay. Somebody European. Etienne flew in from overseas. If he was working through a broker I'll find out, but I don't think he was. He hated sharing the finder's fee."

Addison made a disgusted sound at Stoney's choice of wording, but she barely spared him a glance. "And now for the Final Jeopardy question, Stoney. Who hired *us*?"

"You don't know?" Addison whispered, clasping her elbow.

Taking a half step backward, Stoney cleared his throat. "I got the call through O'Hannon. As soon as this shit happened I phoned him, but he hung up on me. Now he's not answering."

Sam glowered at her broker. *Dammit.* "You took a third-hand job? Why didn't you say so?"

"Because the money was great, and because you wouldn't have taken it if I told you. I've known Sean O'Hannon for fifteen years."

"You're right. I would never have worked for O'Hannon. Jesus. He's scum, Stoney. Find out who he was brokering for."

The mountain nodded. "How do I get hold of you?"

"Call me on my cell phone," Addison said, writing the number on the back of his entrance ticket. "It's not registered."

"That okay with you, Sam?"

"It's not okay, but it's the safest way to do it. We need to figure this out, Stoney. The sooner the better."

Stoney looked at her for a moment. "Can I talk to you in private, Sam?"

"No secrets," Addison shot, his jaw clenching.

"Let go," she snapped, shrugging free of his grip on her elbow. "I'll be right back."

"Samantha—"

"Wait here." Favoring him with a slow smile, she leaned closer. "Rick," she purred.

She and Stoney strolled a few yards down the path, walking among the fragrant roses. Addison sat on the vacated bench and looked mad enough to chew bricks, but he deserved at least a point or two for staying put.

"What the hell's wrong with you, Sam?" Stoney grunted, as soon as they were out of earshot.

She didn't have time to play dumb. "I assume you're talking about the rich guy. It's . . . necessary, at the moment."

He tilted his head at her. "Necessary to what? Your safety? Hon, two men are dead, both connected with that stone tablet and that house—and that guy."

"I know."

With a frown, Stoney took her hand again. "I don't get it, but I trust you."

She squeezed his fingers. "Well, that's nice to hear."

"This was bad from the start, and that's my fault, but you know that sticking with him is asking for trouble."

"What do you know?" she returned. "Really?"

"Something went to hell. O'Hannon was terrified when I called him, and I can't think of a damned reason why Etienne would use something as sloppy as explosives without a reason."

"This whole thing bothers me. Keep some feelers out. That stone tablet went missing from the estate, so unless Etienne stashed it, somebody's got it. If you hear of anybody offering or buying, let me know. You hear anything, let me know."

"And you're going to stay with the rich guy until you solve his little mystery?"

"I don't know."

"Yeah, well I see the way he's looking at you, Sam. It's not *your* best interest he's thinking of. He's a guy who gets what he wants, damn the consequences."

She wasn't entirely certain about that, but then she was daydreaming of having sex with Addison. "I'll watch out for myself, Stoney. I always do. Just do what you can."

"All right. Shit."

He turned away, but she caught his arm. "And be careful, okay?" she whispered. "You're the only family I've got."

Stoney flashed a quick, concerned grin. "Boy, do I feel sorry for you."

She watched him out of sight, then returned to Addison. "Shall we finish the tour of the garden?"

"I don't like secrets, Samantha." His face was set, and he made no move to rise from the bench.

"You have a life other than this," she returned hotly. "Well, so do I. I've known Stoney my entire life. He's worried about me, all right?" Blowing a strand of hair out of her face, she offered her hand.

Slowly Richard reached up and grasped her fingers. "To my surprise," he said, standing, "I find that I worry about you, too."

Twelve

Saturday, 6:15 p.m.

Patience might have been a virtue, but it wasn't something Richard had a lot of experience with, or fondness for. He wanted answers. Samantha had given up on the car stereo, and Haydn echoed softly from the speakers as they headed north. She hadn't objected when he put the car's top up, which Richard attributed to her state of distraction rather than her tiring of the tourist charade.

Her fingers drummed against the door handle. "If I start telling you everything I think you need to know," she said into the relative silence, "it's not just my freedom and safety that'll be in your hands, Rick."

Rick. She'd let him in, a little. "You're here to help me solve this."

"Well, really I'm here so you'll help me—but I'm trying to keep my end of the bargain."

"So what do you want, my word that nothing you say will go beyond me? I can't do that, Samantha. In the first place, I don't like the idea that everything I've earned and collected is up for grabs. In the sec—"

"No," she interrupted, sitting straighter. "I'm not in this car with you because of a theft. I'm here because of a bomb." Her lips twisted as she weighed her next words. "I'll make you a deal. Use whatever information you want that has to do with Etienne DeVore. Anything else I tell you or that you might figure out, use it to protect your own things, but you can't tell the police about it."

"No deals."

"Then stop the car and let me out."

"No."

She hit the button to unroll the window. "Fine. I'll jump."

"Don't be ridiculous." He rolled her window up again and locked the control.

Glaring at him, she unfastened her seat belt and reached back to unlock her door. "I can't make you a better deal. If you don't like it, then we part company. Now."

The idea of killing someone to gain an object offended her; he had sensed that almost from their first meeting. He supposed that would have to be guarantee enough for now. The fact that he wanted sex with her figured into the decision as well, of course, as did the way he had a difficult time believing her flirtations were purely mercenary—any more than his were.

"Fasten your bloody seat belt."

"Is that a yes?"

"Yes. Subject to further discussion."

Samantha nodded, buckling in again. "This is complicated."

She had no idea. "I like complicated. Now, shall we stop at Rooney's Pub for dinner, or shall I phone Hans and have him throw something Italian together for us?"

"You do that a lot," she commented.

"Do what?"

"Give choices so a person feels like they're making the decisions, but the whole thing's really under your control."

Richard smiled. "Irish, or Italian?"

"Isn't Rooney's a little off the path for James 'Diamonds up the Wazoo' Bond?"

"I'm not James Bond, ouch, and quit stalling."

"Irish, then."

And that made sense, too. A public place, where the personal discussions couldn't get too personal. Best start before they reached the pub, then. "Speaking of Irish, tell me about this O'Hannon who hired Walter Bradstone to hire you."

"He's scum."

"So you said. What else? And be blunt, if you can."

She shot him her quicksilver grin. "Smart ass. He's based in London. Never leaves, in fact, because he's afraid to fly, afraid of water, and afraid of small spaces." Samantha shifted, curling one leg underneath her so she half faced him. "I don't like working with him because he's always squeezing or undercutting his procurer."

"How so?"

"He'll tell you he has a buyer for an item at fifty or a hundred thousand below market, but it's an easy job, yadda yadda yadda. So you take it, then find out his buyer's willing to go fifty or a hundred above market."

"Which would go straight to him, with no percentage to his procurer."

"Yes."

Keeping his gaze on the darkening highway, Richard gripped the wheel a little harder. "If he had an especially good deal going, but there was likely to be a lot of publicity from it, would he set somebody up to take the blame—especially somebody he didn't work with a lot, or somebody who maybe spoke her mind and told him he was scum?"

When she didn't answer, he looked over at her. Her mouth set into a grim line, she stared at him, green eyes going hazel in the dusk. "You think that bomb wasn't for you."

"Would he do that, Samantha?" he pressed.

"Jesus." She ran her hand through her hair, yanking out the rubber band so that soft, disheveled waves of auburn fell to her shoulders. "He might. That would explain some things. Dammit. God fucking dammit!"

Cursing under his own breath, Richard pulled the SLK to the side of the highway before she could start punching things. With the car still rolling she jumped out, striding forward and back with hands stiff and fisted at her sides. He joined her outside but leaned his backside against the car and let her fume.

The idea that she might have been the target had occurred to him the evening she had jumped through his skylight. He had had no motive then, only a feeling about it. Since then he'd discovered a warning from a now-dead thief of exceptional skill, a job arranged through someone Samantha didn't trust, and a missing stone tablet—but not much else. And the police had even less.

"Why would he set you up?" he asked.

"Money. He doesn't respond to much else, and he doesn't care about anything else."

He watched her pace past him and back again. "Tell me what you think of this scenario," he said, glancing at his watch. It would be dark soon, and if she was a target, he didn't want her exposed on the side of the road like this. "O'Hannon sent DeVore in to steal the tablet, and sent you in as a convenient scapegoat. Whoops, you were killed by your own bomb, which you set as a distraction to help you get off the estate. And then because he's scum, O'Hannon kills De-Vore so he doesn't have to split the profits."

"It might work, except for two things. One, O'Hannon's a coward, and I'm not sure he would have the guts to kill any . . ."

She trailed off as a black BMW approached along the highway, changing into the closer, outside lane and slowing as it drew even with them. Richard took a step toward the passenger door and the Glock he'd shoved back into the glove box after Samantha's protest. In the middle of the other traffic the car didn't stop, though, and accelerated as it passed them. Great. Good Samaritans, cops, and assassins, beware.

Samantha kept her gaze on the BMW, too. "And two, if I'd been killed, the police would expect that I would have had the tablet on me. The tablet's missing, so somebody else would have to be involved. And if that person was Etienne, who took the tablet from him? O'Hannon wouldn't be here himself. He would have had to hire someone, and all this would definitely be cutting into his profits."

"Maybe O'Hannon was hoping we'd all figure the stone had been destroyed in the explosion, along with you."

"Maybe. I just can't figure why he'd want Etienne dead, if he even hired him in the first place. Guys who kill their procurers don't last long in this business." As she reasoned it out, she calmed down, her hands slowly relaxing and her striding slowing to pacing. "I need to think it through," she muttered, coming to a stop in front of him.

"Let's think over a plate of shepherd's pie," he said, pulling the passenger door open for her. "Come on."

Close as they were to Palm Beach, traffic on the highway was fairly heavy. No one else slowed to take a look at them, though, and they merged back onto the road without any trouble. Richard was more concerned over Samantha Jellicoe than the traffic. Unsavory as he considered her line of work, if someone was trying to kill her because of it—or for any reason—he intended to do something to prevent it. He wasn't even certain when he'd made that decision, or when *he'd* become *her* bodyguard—just that he had.

Fifteen minutes later he pulled onto Clematis Street and turned into the parking lot at Rooney's. The pub looked crowded, as it generally was, with the sound of Irish music drifting out over the street. Despite the lack of privacy he liked it; pieces of authentic-feeling Britain weren't that easy to find in Florida.

"Ah, Mr. Addison," the hostess greeted him with a broad smile. "Two tonight?"

"Thank you, Annie. In the back, if you can."

"Of course we can."

He motioned Samantha to follow Annie toward the rear of

the pub. When he was in town they always held a table in reserve away from the crowded bar, solely in deference to his
preference for quiet and privacy. Samantha took the seat facing the front door, which didn't surprise him, and he shifted
his own chair around the side of the table so they were at
right angles, and he could see the billiards room entry over
her shoulder. James Bond or not, he was beginning to feel
like a bloody secret agent.

He ordered a pint of Guinness for each of them, then
scooted closer to Samantha as the waitress left. "This is unusual for you, I take it?" he murmured. "The bomb, not the
pub."

"I just can't believe Etienne would . . ." She swallowed.
"But I don't think he knew I'd be there. Otherwise, he
wouldn't have been so pissed off when he called."

"I can't believe O'Hannon would be willing simply to use
your death as a convenience."

"That's still supposition. I would guess there's more going
on than convenience."

"Then tell me what it might be."

Samantha paused in her study of the room to look at him.
A slight smile touched her lips. "You sound angry."

"I am angry." He took the hand she rested on the table and
curled his fingers around her palm.

She jumped a little, but didn't pull her hand away. "This
changes everything, you know," she said. "If you're not in
danger, you have no reason to help me out." Samantha took a
breath. "In fact, it would be stupid of you to stay involved
with this."

"I'm still missing a Trojan stone tablet," he said in a low
voice. "And once you slept under my roof, you fell under my
protection, too."

"Being the feudal lord again, are you? The Earl of Palm
Beach?"

His lips curved. "Like you said, no one deserves to die
over an object. And I'm going to make bloody certain it
doesn't happen to you."

"That's pretty arrogant, your lordship." Even so, her fingers tightened around his. "And I appreciate it."

"You saved my life, Samantha. Turnabout is fair play."

A waitress came up with two pints, and Sam occupied herself taking a long drink. Nothing like this had ever happened to her before. When the police had arrested her father in the middle of an "easy" grab of a miniature Grecian frieze, she'd been devastated. A thousand scenarios, a thousand different plans to break him out or escape the country or commit another crime to make it look like her father was innocent, nothing had even come close to fruition. Even making stupid, useless plans had felt better than blind panic at the idea that she was alone.

Eventually she'd gotten used to the idea of not being able to see him, of not being able to attend the trial, and of not being able to visit him in prison. When he'd died just over two years ago, she'd been relieved. After that she didn't have to plan every move with a thought toward what she would do if he suddenly appeared on her doorstep, and she didn't have to feel guilty about being free while he was locked in a small room for the rest of his life.

Every job she did had a certain risk built into it. But no one had gone out of their way to try to kill her before, and certainly no one had tried to use her as a convenient scapegoat corpse. Rick's scenario was a stretch, but it made a degree of sense that nothing else had so far.

Addison ordered two shepherd's pies while she downed her pint and requested another. Even after a night's sleep and stitches she felt battered and bruised, inside and out. Learning from Stoney about O'Hannon's involvement made a few more puzzle pieces fit, and angry as Addison's theory left her, she'd go with it for the moment, too. She needed to sound some of her own theories out, and she wanted to do it with the man sitting beside her and sipping his own pint with much more reserve than she showed.

"You said DeVore wouldn't have a problem with killing someone," he said, nodding at the couple who strolled past, both of them staring at him with undisguised curiosity, "but you didn't think he would hurt *you*."

"I don't. Assuming that he either didn't know who he was after or that someone lied to him about it makes this much more complicated, though. If it wasn't meant for me, then I would want to know if someone's put a hit out on you. That makes more sense, anyway."

"And why is that?"

Their pies arrived, and she inhaled the scent of hot vegetables, potatoes, and veal. Once they were alone again, she cut through the mashed potato crust and steam rose from the bowl. "I'm not worth the trouble, frankly," she said.

"Allow me to disagree." His jaw was still clenched; his eyes had been fairly glinting with suppressed anger and tension most of the way back from Butterfly World.

"Disagree all you want, but it's true. Money-wise, it doesn't make sense. Not even for the tablet. Ten percent is a good share of a grab, and I can't imagine Etienne committing a theft and a murder for 150,000 dollars."

"So O'Hannon or someone paid him more than that."

"Why? There has to be a profit in it for everyone involved." She scowled. "I'm not even sure Etienne would do any job for change like that. I only took it because I was bored. My cut—unless they didn't pay because I was dead—would be ten percent, plus something to whoever capped Etienne. There has to be more money in it somewhere, if it involved killing."

"Unless this is personal."

"Against me?"

He shrugged. "Done anything especially nefarious, lately?"

"Not that I recall. How about you?"

"Not that I'm aware of. Are—were—you still on good terms with DeVore?"

"We were okay. I hadn't even seen him in almost a year." Sam concentrated on her shepherd's pie, savoring the tender, lightly spiced flavor and washing it down with the Guinness.

No wonder Addison liked to eat here. "I've actually been . . . quiet, lately."

Gray eyes snapped up to hers. "How so?"

Jesus, he never let anything go by without comment. "Crikey," she said in an exaggeration of his soft British accent, trying to cover an uncomfortable surge of self-consciousness. She was so unused to talking about herself. "It's nothing. The Norton Museum received an endowment last fall, and all kinds of works have been coming in. I've been helping with the cleaning and cataloging."

"Your legitimate job," he said softly, a slow smile touching his mouth again.

"Drop it, Brit."

"Fine. Eat your pie. And save room for a slice of Ultimate Chocolate Cake, Yank."

Bright light flashed in her eyes, and she jumped, instinctively throwing an arm in front of Rick. He moved nearly as fast, grabbing her and keeping her in her chair.

"Easy," he whispered, his gaze on a man standing a few feet away, a camera in his hands. "The press."

"Shit."

"Happy?" he said in a louder voice. "You've got your photo, so please leave my friend and me to finish our meal in peace."

The photographer grinned, a leer that made her want to kick in his teeth. "Does your 'friend' have a name, Mr. Addison?"

Rick's grip on her shoulder tightened. "If we don't tell him, they'll make a very large deal out of it," he murmured in her ear, making the motion look like a caress.

The camera flashed again. "No. Please," she returned. "I hate . . ."

"Samantha Jellicoe has a legitimate reason to be seen with me," he said in a surprisingly gentle voice. "Trust me a little."

Every nerve screamed for her to run and hide, and at the same time she knew he was right. She blew out a shaky breath. "Sam Jellicoe," she grated with what she hoped was a professional-looking smile.

"That's 'o' 'e,'" Addison added helpfully.

"And your relationship?"

"I'm his artworks security cons—"

"We're dating," Addison said over her explanation.

"*You sh*—"

"And I am consulting with her regarding security," he continued smoothly. "Anything else?"

"Address would be nice."

"If you're trying to goad me into threatening you, you're very nearly there. I'll need your business card. Now."

Jovial Richard Addison was gone, replaced by the hard-assed businessman she'd heard about and read about online. Sam wasn't the least bit surprised when the reporter lowered his camera and dug into a pocket for his card, which he handed over without further comment.

"Thank you, Mr. . . . Madeiro," Addison continued. "I'll expect the *Post* to report this information in an accurate and respectful manner. Good evening."

"Good . . . evening."

As soon as the reporter's back was turned, Sam jammed Addison in the ribs with her elbow. With a grunt he doubled over. "Don't ever do that again," she hissed, shoving her chair back and standing.

Twisting, he grabbed her arm and yanked her back hard into her seat. "Leave the damned introductions to me," he growled back, refusing to release his grip even when she pushed at him again.

"What's your damage?"

"I wanted to keep your involvement in our little investigation quiet," he retorted, bracing his free arm against his rib cage. "Whoever paid DeVore to set that explosive might not know any more than the thief who escaped was female. I date on occasion, Sam, and I don't use personal security. Now you stand out as both security and an art expert."

She snapped her jaw closed. *Fuck.* Addison let her go, and she sat where she was, trying to get her breathing back to normal and searching for words she very seldom—never—used. "I'm sorry," she said. "I screwed up."

"It happens," he grunted back. "We'll have to be more careful with you now. That's all."

"I didn't pound you that hard." Sam reached over and touched his rib cage. "Are you all right?"

"I acquired some bruised ribs the other night when a very nice young lady tackled me and saved my life."

"Oh, God. I'm really sorry, Rick. I just—"

"You didn't like that I said something personal about you. I get it. The whole kissing-newlywed-hand-holding thing was just for show."

The fact that he was wrong didn't make her feel the least bit better. It wasn't like her to react so violently to a little subterfuge; hell, she lived by subterfuge. "Stoney was right," she muttered, downing the rest of her drink. "I am going insane."

He made her sit with him through dessert, and considering that it was chocolate and heavenly, she didn't object overly much. As they returned to the car, though, she put a hand on his arm. If someone was out to kill her, she didn't want her equipment sitting around being useless ten miles from where she was staying. "Okay," she ventured, "since this partnership thing seems to be going all right so far, can I take you up on your offer to move my car into Harvard's parking garage?"

"Certainly." If he was surprised, he kept it to himself, facing half away from her as he keyed the remote to unlock the Mercedes. "Where to?"

She gave him the directions, and fifteen minutes later they pulled up beside her nondescript blue Honda. "Okay, you want to lead me to the garage?" she asked, climbing out of the SLK.

Under the streetlights he studied her face for a moment. "You're not bolting anywhere?"

She shook her head, wishing she had the guts either to grab him or flee into the night. "You're still my safest bet."

With a slight scowl Rick waited while she started the Honda and eased back into the street. Under any other occasion the caution with which he drove, making sure they were never separated at a light or even by another car, would have been amusing, but she was still too busy mulling over whether anyone might want her dead to be anything but appreciative.

The night attendant waved Addison through without blinking, and whatever Rick said to him, it got her into the parking garage without so much as a word. She picked a spot close to the exit but out of sight of the street, parked, and got out. "Is there room for my gear in your trunk?" she asked, leaning into the SLK's window.

"That depends. Do you tote ladders and grappling hooks?"

"I keep those in my purse."

"I wouldn't be surprised."

He pushed a button and opened the trunk while she went around to the back of the Honda and did the same. Nothing had been disturbed, thank God, and she hefted her knapsack into Rick's car as he emerged, following it with a duffel bag and a hard-sided case where she kept the most delicate equipment. Shoving his trunk closed, she leaned back on it. "Thanks."

"You're welcome. But I do have a question," Addison said, as she climbed back into the SLK beside him and headed back to his estate.

Feeling a little more relaxed now that she and her things had been reunited, Sam sank into the leather seat. "Shoot."

"Do you ever steal from the museum where you're working?"

So much for small talk. "Would you have divorced your wife if you hadn't caught her with Sir What's-His-Name?"

"Peter Emerson Wallis," he said in a stiffer voice. "In England we'd call this conversation tit for tat. Is that what we're playing?"

"Yes," she decided, gauging his dislike for discussing his ex. "You answer my question, and I'll answer yours."

"That's a deal. And the answer is yes, probably."

That was unexpected. "Why?"

"First you answer my question, love."

Sam drew a breath. The issue of how much he needed to

know and how much she wanted to tell him was becoming more complicated with every second. "No, I don't steal from the museum where I'm working. Your turn."

He shrugged. "I imagine it would have taken a little longer than three years, but . . . she didn't like my lifestyle."

"Women throwing themselves at you and mentally undressing you every time you stepped out of doors?"

"That, and my being occupied with business most of the time." He turned onto the main highway. "Your turn. Why don't you steal from your museum?"

"I don't steal from *any* museum." She frowned into the darkness, seeing the faint reflection of her face in the window. "It's just stupid. The things there are . . . where they should be. No one person gets to hold history."

"That's not stupid. It's interesting."

Her father had thought it was stupid. It was his persistence in hitting museums and galleries, though, that had finally gotten him caught, then convicted. Angering one collector was different than angering a country when you made off with a national treasure.

She shook herself out of her reverie. "Were you friends with Sir Peter Wallis? Before, I mean?"

"Yes. We went to Cambridge together. We even roomed together for a year."

"Good friends."

"For a time. He was extremely competitive, though, and it got a bit tiresome. Cars, business deals, women."

"He won, then."

Addison glanced at her. "Because he took Patricia from me, you mean? I suppose so. He . . . fooled me with his claims of friendship. And that actually made me more angry than his theft of my wife."

"You don't get fooled often."

"No, I don't."

"If you were so mad, though, why did you let them keep one of your houses in London?"

"You know a lot about me, don't you?"

She favored him with a short smile. "You're all over the Internet."

"Smashing. I let them keep the house in London because it shortened the divorce proceedings, and because it seemed . . . fair, not that I was overjoyed to do it. I knew she hadn't been happy in our marriage, and I didn't do much to amend that situation." He shrugged. "Maybe it was so I could have the final word."

Just when Samantha was congratulating herself on getting a handful of answers out of him for the price of just one question, he slowed and turned into his drive between the two bored policemen. This time they barely glanced at the two of them before opening the gate.

"They're getting complacent," she commented, stretching as they crossed through the palm grove and stopped in front of the house. "Your crappy security just lost about half its effectiveness."

They climbed out of the car, and Rick caught her arm as they reached the front door. "You owe me an answer," he murmured, turning her to face him.

She managed a smirk. "I thought I got that one by you. All right, what's the question?"

Addison gazed at her for a moment. Reaching out, he brushed a strand of hair from her face, then leaned in and kissed her. Soft and warm and lingering, it sent heat down to her toes and everywhere in between. His tongue glided along her teeth, and without even thinking she opened her mouth to him. She went wet. Just when she thought she would melt into him, he backed off an inch or two.

"What's your answer, Samantha?" he whispered against her mouth.

Thirteen

Saturday, 9:21 p.m.

Mouths locked in an embrace, Rick gave way as Sam towed him up the front steps. As she dug into his pants pocket for the front door key, her fingers brushed his straining cock through the denim, making him jump. *Jesus.* With a grin she pulled his face down again, kissing him hot and open-mouthed while she fumbled the key into the lock and turned the doorknob.

They stumbled into the foyer. Rick closed the door and pressed Samantha back against the heavy English oak, cupping her face as he kissed her. Their tongues teased and met in a swirl of heat and mutual lust—need—that had him near to reeling. God, when she made a decision, she didn't hold back.

He wanted her right there on the marble floor, on the couch in the nearest sitting room, on the staircase. Only the knowledge that several security guards wandered the estate at all hours kept him from sprawling onto the floor with her. As he ran his hands down her spine, pulling her against his hips, he dimly recalled that he hadn't felt this way in a long time. Sex was fun; it wasn't an all-consuming need for possession. Until tonight. Until Samantha Jellicoe.

"Rick," she moaned, yanking the open shirt down his arms, throwing it over the fake Ming vase, then pulling the black T-shirt from his jeans.

"Upstairs," he said, using every ounce of hard-won willpower to push away from her again. Before she could argue he grabbed her hand and towed her toward the stairs.

If she'd said no, he wasn't sure what he would have done. He'd been hard and aching for her since they'd climbed into the car that morning. Separating the woman from the job had been driving him insane. It made no sense that he could want her and disapprove of what she did, all at the same time. That was why he kept looking for loopholes. She liked working in museums, and she didn't steal from them. There was no reason she couldn't give up one part of her life and continue with another when she so obviously enjoyed it.

At the top of the stairs the need to taste her again overwhelmed him. Stopping at the landing, he pulled her against him, savoring her mouth, the soft warm skin of her throat. Holding her against the wall with the weight of his body, he reached between them and undid her jeans, slipping his hand in under her panties to cup her. She was wet for him already.

"Naughty," Samantha breathed.

She moaned, pressing herself harder against him as he slipped a finger up inside her. Everything she'd learned in her life, from her own experience and from listening to the stories of others in her profession, told her that what she was doing was a very bad idea. Clients or victims—you couldn't trust either one of them. Nothing she'd done since the night of the explosion, though, made any sense at all.

A shadow moved at the far end of the hall, and she tensed. Fun was good, but not in front of witnesses. "Rick," she muttered unevenly, tearing her mouth from his and shoving at him, "stop."

He seemed to sense that she meant it, because he withdrew his hand from her jeans, turning as one of the security guards emerged from a connecting hallway and came toward them. From his carefully bland expression the guard had seen precisely where his employer's hands had been, but with a nod he kept walking toward the west wing.

"Shit," Addison said, his breathing harsh. "Come on."

"This isn't a good idea," she protested with her last remaining breath of sanity. She did not belong in his bed, however much she was coming to enjoy his company and his attention—and his very naughty hands. He made her lose her concentration. She couldn't be soft; her life, and perhaps his, depended on it.

"It is a very good idea," he returned, kissing her again, hot and aggressive. "I want to be inside you, Samantha."

"This is a business deal," she protested, even as she allowed him to draw her forward again, toward the east wing of the house, where she'd never been.

"No, it's not." He turned, gazing hard at her. "Scared?" he asked, his tone taunting her to admit to it.

Sam met his mouth with hers again. "Never."

When he pulled her through a door, shutting and locking it behind them, she knew instinctively that they'd entered his private domain. Dimly lit by a lamp in the corner, a massive sitting room of royal blue and oak sprawled before them. She would wager that no security guards or anything resembling a camera were allowed in here—ever.

"Nice, Your Dukeness," she muttered, then couldn't breathe as he slid his hands up under her shirt to cup her breasts.

"Very nice," he agreed, closing his teeth gently over her earlobe.

The hell with restraint. She could back off again later. Sam pulled his shirt off over his head, noting the wrapping around his ribs and the bandage high on his shoulder. They'd both been marked by what had happened, and if this gorgeous, sexy man wanted her, she was not going to argue. Tomorrow could wait until tomorrow. Tonight she was going to get lucky.

Her T-shirt hit the floor next, and as he wrapped his arms

around her to unfasten her bra, she indulged in another melting, faintly chocolate-tasting kiss. His thumbs grazed her nipples, and she moaned again.

"I meant to tell you before," he said, holding her back a little so he could run his fingers in slow circles around her breasts, pinching and rolling her nipples between his thumb and forefinger so that they hardened, "you have lovely tits."

"Thank y—"

Rick bent down and took her left breast into his mouth, sucking and caressing with his tongue. Sam arched against him, tangling her hands into his dark, wavy hair. "Oh, God," she muttered, her knees turning to Jell-O.

They sank to the floor just inside the doorway, carpeted like the rest of the sitting room entry in dark, thick indigo. Rick laid her down so he could peel her out of her borrowed jeans. "I didn't compliment you on your great ass, either," he said, bending down to run his tongue with maddening slowness from between her breasts to the band of her panties. "It just didn't seem appropriate when I was applying the super glue."

"You're a true gentleman," she managed, lifting her hips so he could slip her underwear off.

With a grin he tossed the skimpy things somewhere over his shoulder. "No, I'm not," he returned, pulling her knees farther apart to continue the downward trail of his tongue. He dipped his head lower, to her dark patch of hair, driving her into a near frenzy with his mouth and his knowing fingers. He slipped a finger inside her again, and she bucked.

Good God. Well, she wasn't going to be the only one to lose control. "Get up here," she gasped, pulling him upright so she could reach the fastening of his straining jeans. Sitting up so she could unzip him, she did it slowly, smiling a little breathlessly as his hands covered hers to hurry her along. Samantha tugged him closer by a belt loop, fastening her mouth to one hard male nipple and suckling. He moaned, tangling one hand into her hair while he finished unzipping his pants with the other.

Wondering for a fleeting moment if it was his money alone that kept all those swimsuit calendar babes satisfied, she yanked his trousers to his knees. Nope, it wasn't just the money. "Nice cock," she whispered, gently closing her fingers around his hard, erect penis and caressing its length while he threw his head back.

"Thanks. You're seeing it at its best."

He was glorious, lean and muscled and more professional athlete than billionaire. Rick pushed her flat onto her back again. A hot haze closed around her mind as he lowered himself down on her, taking her mouth again in a deep, consuming kiss. Fingers in his hair, she drew him down the length of her body again, until he stopped for another taste between her legs. God, the Internet didn't mention how good he was in bed—or on the floor. She arched her back as his tongue darted inside her. "Oh, my God," she moaned.

"Samantha," he murmured, rising up again to run his tongue in leisurely circles down her shoulders and suckle her breast again.

She kneaded her fingers into the taut muscles of his back. *Let go*, she told herself. Control, decisions, she could worry about later. *Just enjoy. Just be.* Pressure built inside her as his slow, expert hands moved down the length of her, breasts to toes, and back up again led by his mouth, until she couldn't even breathe in more than gasps. "Rick—Richard—I want you inside me. Now."

"I—Fuck." He raised up, shifted off of her.

"What? What, dammit?" She felt suddenly cold. And very, *very* annoyed. Someone was going to get the crap beat out of him.

"Don't move. I'll be right back."

She watched as he strode, fully aroused and magnificent, into the bathroom and then emerged a moment later. "Ah, body armor," she breathed, reaching up to wrap her arms around his shoulders and pull him back down on her again. He had her brain so clouded with lust that she wouldn't even have thought about protection, and that wasn't like her at all.

Neither, though, was falling into bed—onto the floor—with someone like Rick Addison.

"Ready or not," he murmured, nudging her knees apart again.

"Ready. Definitely ready." With agonizing slowness he eased inside her. Sam's head fell back, and she closed her eyes as he filled her, the hot, tight slide of his body inside hers so exquisite she couldn't breathe.

"No, Samantha. Look at me," he groaned, burying himself completely.

She clasped herself against him, forcing her eyes open to meet his dark gray gaze. He felt huge, rock hard, as he began to pump his hips, and she arched to meet him. Fire. He felt like fire, and she burned. Heat seared through her. Sam slid her arms around his shoulders, locked her ankles around his hips as he moved. Digging her hands into his back, his buttocks, she met every thrust, filling and tightening until, with a mewling cry, she shattered.

He slowed his pace but kept moving, in, out, in, out. "Mm, you feel good," he murmured.

Sam couldn't speak, couldn't do anything but gasp for air and float into the white haze covering her mind. She went on and on, his slow rhythm pushing her further than she'd ever gone before.

"Christ," she finally mumbled, forcing her eyes to focus. "Do that again."

Rick chuckled, leaning in for another deep kiss. "I'm not stopping now."

Increasing his pace, he reached back to draw her legs farther up around his waist. She complied, the movement bringing him in deeper and harder. As she felt tension building in both of them, Sam flexed the muscles across her abdomen, tightening around him. Hell, she didn't work out for nothing.

He groaned, planting his hands on either side of her shoulders and thrusting deep and hard and fast. With a surprising punch she came again, drawing him over with her.

He came with a deep, satisfied groan, settling his weight

down on her and resting his head on the floor beside her neck. Samantha kept her arms around him, finally closing her eyes. Listening to his harsh breathing in her ear, and feeling their hearts pounding together, she realized what it was that made her want him so much. In Richard Addison's arms, she felt safe.

A few moments later, he lifted his head, dark hair hanging across one eye, to look down at her. "The bedroom's over there. Shall we?"

She chuckled breathlessly, kissing him again, running her fingers down the straight, sweaty line of his spine. "How much body armor do you have?"

"Not nearly enough, plainly," he returned, standing and drawing her up into his arms to carry her naked to his dark blue bedroom.

Richard opened his eyes slowly, careful not to move. A week ago, the last thing he would have expected would be to wake up in bed with someone like Samantha Jellicoe beside him. Now she lay tucked against his side, one hand curled over his chest and her breath soft and even in his ear. Auburn hair tumbled across her face and tickled his shoulder. His arm beneath her was completely numb, but he didn't care. Good God, what a night. He'd been right in his observations that she learned by tactile experience; he didn't think there was an inch of his body that she hadn't explored with her hands or her mouth.

Both before and after Patricia there had been women: Models and actresses, mostly, because they hadn't minded the loss of privacy that being seen with him usually entailed, or the lack of time he had to spend with them between trysts. With Samantha, both were going to be a problem. Her need for privacy was as much a part of her as her hands. And then there was the fact that she thought as soon as they'd figured out what was going on here, she was going to leave, to go on with her life as it had been. She was wrong about that.

Her eyes opened, immediately alert, immediately remembering where she was and why. "Mm. Good morning," she said with a coy smile, giving a cat-like stretch.

"Good morning."

He rescued his arm, flexing his fingers to get the blood circulating. He put his surviving arm behind his head to watch her, the play of her muscles beneath her skin as she sat up, the satisfaction in her face and the lift of her pert breasts as she stretched her arms over her head. Despite the fact that he was going to have to go through the bother of buying another damned box of condoms, he went hard again.

She angled her eyes over to the blanket just below his waist. "Yikes. I thought you Brits were calm and dull."

"Shall we go for the seventh inning stretch?" he murmured, sitting up beside her and cupping a hand over her left breast, feeling the nipple grow hard against his pressing palm. "That's American, isn't it?"

"Jesus, seven?" she said, arching her back at his touch. "I thought it was just one continuous orgasm."

"For you, maybe. Safety forces me to keep count."

Samantha laughed, turning to throw her arms around his neck and kiss him on the mouth, ears, throat, chest, everywhere her mouth could reach. Last night she'd been open and very responsive, but this was the first time he'd heard her really laugh. Grinning back, he lifted her onto his lap, careful not to pull at the stitches in her thigh as he eased her legs around his waist and impaled his length slowly into her.

By the time they were finished it was considerably later, he'd missed another meeting on the WNBT sale, and they were both starving. "I'll ring down to have Reinaldo bring up some breakfast," he said, reaching over to grab the phone off the nightstand.

She lay on her stomach where he'd left her after the last at bat. "No. I need a shower. And clothes. And clean underwear."

"I'll send for some."

Samantha turned her face toward him. "You are not buying underwear for me," she stated. "I have some in my bag, in the car."

"I'll have that brought up, then," he returned, vaguely annoyed. "Unless you're trying to escape."

She smirked at him, rolling on her side to gaze at him full on. "I'm currently naked in your bed, your lordship. But we still have a deal that isn't about sex."

"We'll still have a deal if I send out for food and clothes."

"Hey, rich guy," she retorted, twisting to sit up and slide her legs off the side of the bed, "quit trying to show off. I'm not impressed by your ability to purchase pink panties. Go find me a robe or something."

"Hanging off the back of the door in the bathroom. Get it yourself, thief."

With a quick grin and a peck on the cheek, she scooted off the bed and scampered naked out of his bedroom. Richard sat up again to watch her go. He still couldn't figure her out. She was so damned tough, yet so delicate at the same time. Samantha Jellicoe fascinated him, and a night spent inside her, on top of her, beneath her, and beside her hadn't lessened the sensation one damned bit.

He wanted a shower, himself, and joining her in the bathroom seemed a bloody good idea. With a groan he stood. In thirty-three years of life he hadn't had too many nights like that one. Hell, he couldn't think of any, offhand. With a grin, he made his way through the wreck of last night's clothes in the sitting room. She emerged from the bathroom just as he reached it.

"I'm going down to the car," she said, tying a white silk robe around her waist.

Richard reached around the door and pulled free another one, shrugging it on. "I'll go with you."

"I'm not going to run away," she said, softening the complaint by tugging his blue robe closed and knotting the tie around his waist.

He waited for her to add "yet," but even when she didn't, the word still seemed to hang between them. Making himself smile, Richard pulled her up against him and kissed her. "And I want to make sure I get some breakfast."

"Fine."

Running a hand through his hair so he wouldn't frighten the help, he followed her downstairs. She headed for the front door, and he tucked an arm around her waist. "It'll be in the garage," he said, redirecting her toward the back of the house.

As he expected, she tolerated his arm around her for a few moments, then shrugged free. He didn't think it was the public display of affection that bothered her; instead, except for last night, she seemed to have a need for space around her, literal and figurative. Well, he'd just have to work at getting her to realize that holding hands didn't mean she was vulnerable or trapped or weak. Not where he was concerned. For this morning, falling into step behind her and watching her swaying backside beneath the soft silk robe sufficed.

He didn't question that she knew where the garage was; she'd mentioned studying blueprints of the house. Her reaction when they stepped through the door beside the kitchen didn't surprise him, either.

"Holy crap!" she exclaimed, her voice echoing beneath the high ceiling. "This is not a garage; this is a . . . stadium."

"I like cars," he said by way of explanation, taking her hand to lead her around the herd of new and antique vehicles to the yellow SLK. "Have you ever had sex in the backseat of a Rolls Royce?" He slid his hand into her robe pocket, caressing her thigh through the thin material.

She smirked at him. "No, not that I recall."

"We'll have to remedy that. How about a Bentley?"

"Knock it off. You're gonna kill me."

He didn't even care that he probably looked smug and self-satisfied as he popped the SLK's boot open. "We may as well bring it all upstairs," he said, reaching in for one of her bags.

She hauled out her knapsack. "You don't mind having this stuff in your house?"

"I have *you* in my house," he replied, then stopped the rest of what he was going to say as he looked down.

His knuckles scraped against something hard and flat lying half out of the duffel bag. Brow furrowing, he pulled the sack open to free the cloth-wrapped parcel and jam it back inside.

"Hey, that's private prop . . ." She trailed off as the easy expression on his face locked down. Her throat tightening, Sam followed his gaze. "Oh, my God."

Fourteen

Sunday, 10:36 a.m.

"Good morning, Mr. Addison. Hope you don't mind me just barging in, but your security said you were in here." Detective Castillo strolled in through the wide double doors at the front of the garage.

With a curse, Richard stuffed the Trojan stone tablet back into the duffel and whipped around. *Jesus Christ in a hand-bag.* Beside him, Samantha had gone white, her hands gripping her knapsack so hard he could see the tendons across her knuckles. Only his years as a very disciplined, very successful businessman kept his face and eyes calm. "Detective Castillo. I thought we were going to meet at Donner's office later this morning."

"Yeah, but I thought you'd be more comfortable here. Besides, I've seen the way you drive when you're annoyed, and I didn't want to put the general citizenry at risk." Keen dark eyes took in the pair of robes, two sets of bare feet, and the way Addison's and Jellicoe's shoulders brushed.

Keeping a cool, slightly annoyed smile on his face, Richard nodded. He knew Castillo had seen them touching, and he knew that from now on Samantha's actions would reflect on him—and vice versa. And considering what lay in her duffel bag, they were both in a shitload of trouble.

"Actually, Detective, I think we'd be even more comfortable in the kitchen," he said. "If that's all right with you."

"Does that offer come with coffee?"

"It does." None of Samantha's things looked outwardly like thieves' gear, but Castillo already had doubts about her story. And surprisingly, Richard's first thought was to protect her—even with the damned tablet in her duffel bag. *Bloody hell.* He wanted to put a fist through something, but instead finished hefting the duffel and the hard-sided case out of the trunk. "Would you mind giving us a few minutes to dress?"

The detective shrugged. "Sure. Need some help carrying those?"

"No, I think we've got it." Samantha had recovered the power of speech, sounding now as calm and cool as she always did. As cool as a professional thief and liar. "I'm just moving some of my . . . personal things in," she continued.

"Yeah. I read in the paper this morning that the two of you are dating." Castillo took a step backward as Richard slung the duffel over his shoulder. "You might have mentioned that yesterday. And if you don't mind my asking, Miss Jellicoe," the detective continued, falling into step behind them, "where are you moving your personal things from? I mean, I looked you up in the computer, but it shows no place of residence. Not even a driver's license."

Splendid. Her car was probably stolen, too. Richard wasn't certain whether he was more furious with her or with himself for being duped. And now he was concealing evidence—and a felon, apparently—from the police, all because he couldn't rid himself of an obsession with a female who had already admitted that she lied all the time.

"I've been staying with a friend," she answered, giving a small grimace. "No offense, but with my father's reputation,

I tend to get harassed by the cops when I settle in somewhere. It's easier not to. Settle in, I mean."

"Someone—you—should write a book about your dad."

Samantha snorted. "Nobody'd believe it. Besides, he made sure I stayed on the sidelines."

The detective grinned in turn. "Even so, I bet you have a few stories."

"Buy me a beer sometime, and I'll tell you what I know."

"That's a deal."

She *did* charm everyone in sight. "I'll have Hans get you some coffee, Detective," Richard put in. "Can you wait fifteen minutes for us?"

"Make it twenty," Castillo agreed, allowing himself to be guided into the kitchen, where Richard dispatched instructions for coffee and breakfast.

As soon as the door closed behind him, Richard whirled on Samantha. "What in hell is—"

She stepped in and kissed him. It wasn't passion; her lips were tight and trembled a little, but it shut him up. "Not here," she whispered. "Security."

Shit. "My room," he snapped, hefting the duffel again and striding away. He knew she would follow; he had the damned stone tablet with him.

Richard slammed the door as she slipped in behind him. "Why did you lie to me?" he roared, slinging the bag onto the couch.

Samantha flinched at the venom in his tone. "I didn't."

"God dammit. I should turn you over to Castillo right bloody now!" He ran a hand through his hair, looking as though he'd prefer taking more violent action than shouting. This man, the one with the hard, icy eyes, was the one who owned a good portion of the world—and obviously Sam had just landed on his bad side. Six feet plus of angry Brit scowled at her as he paced like a wolf looking for a vulnerable place to bite.

Time to remind him that she had teeth, too. "I don't know

what's going on," she snapped, refusing to back down. "I didn't fucking put it there."

"I am not a stupid man, Samantha," he snarled.

"I am *not* lying. Somebody—"

"What, somebody else put it there? Whatever the hell game you're playing, it's over. Now."

"Why don't you check with Donner? He seems to live in your pocket. I doubt there's anybody with more access to you and this est—"

"Don't change the fucking subject! This is *your* duffel!"

"I didn't do this, Rick," she whispered, unable to keep her voice steady. She'd spent her life dancing at the edges of a vortex. When her father had been arrested she'd felt it sucking at her, trying to pull her into the depths, but she'd managed to keep her footing. Now, for the first time, she'd slipped and fallen in. She couldn't think of any act, any lie, not even any truth, that would pull her out. "I didn't do it. And that is the truth."

"You came here for it."

"Of course I did. I never lied about that. But I didn't take it. If I had, I wouldn't have come back for your help. And I damned well wouldn't have brought it with me. I don't know what's going on, but I don't like being played for a fool, either."

"Then how did it get here?" he demanded, pulling the tablet free.

"I don't . . ." She stopped. As long as she was denying his accusations, staying on the defensive, she couldn't think. "Let me see it," she said in a calmer voice.

He glared at her, his shoulders heaving with the deep breath he took. "Like hell. Put on some clothes. I'm calling Tom before Castillo figures out what's going on." He jabbed a finger at her, then clamped his jaw shut, curling his hand into a fist. "Dammit, Samantha. What do you think you're pulling?"

She shook her head, willing him to believe her. "Nothing. Prentiss died while somebody—Etienne—stole that tablet.

And then Etienne died, I presume at the hands of whoever he was working for. It doesn't make any sense that it would be in my duffel. Not when two people are already dead because of it. Somebody wanted it enough to kill for it. Twice."

For the first time since they'd entered the bedroom suite he dropped his eyes from hers to look at the old, chipped stone in his hand. "No, it doesn't make sense," he finally said. "None of it makes any sense."

"It does to someone." Sensing the lessening of his anger, she ventured a step closer. "Someone who just gave up over a million dollars to frame me for murder. Let me see it, Rick."

His gaze went from her to the phone on the end table. She knew what he had to be thinking, trying to decide: If he went to Castillo downstairs, probably both of them would be arrested. If he called Donner, he'd probably get out of it, but she wouldn't. After the longest half minute of her life, he held the tablet out to her.

Sam let out the breath she'd been holding. "Thank you," she said, before she took the tablet from him.

"Why?" he grunted.

"For not . . ." An unexpected tear ran down her face, and she wiped it away, surprised and worried. She never cried. Never. "For giving me another chance to figure this out," she amended.

Richard felt as though he'd just stepped into a chasm with his eyes closed, going on blind faith that he'd find a bridge beneath his feet. But her hand shook when he placed the stone in it. This was the first time he'd seen her truly unnerved.

"It's beautiful," she murmured, running her fingers over the rough surface, carved with runes and symbols by some scribe dead more than three thousand years.

She held it with such reverence. That, more than anything she said, convinced him that she'd never touched it before. But then he *wanted* to be convinced of her innocence. Even more, he didn't want to feel that gut-wrenching . . . disappointment again, as he'd felt when he'd opened the door to see Patricia and Peter rolling around in his bed three years ago, and as he'd felt when he'd opened her duffel bag in the garage a few minutes ago. And so he kept his eyes and every ounce of his attention on her as she paced the room, the tablet in her hands, and her fingers delicately tracing the etchings.

"What are you thinking?" he asked.

"Somebody went to a lot of trouble to make me look guilty," she said slowly. "No one knew where my car was. Not even Stoney, or Harvard."

Dismissing her paranoia about Tom, he dropped onto the couch beside the duffel bag. "Could they have done it before you put the bags in your car?"

Samantha shook her head. "The duffel was under my bed. After I left Stoney's I stayed home for two days until the cops showed up."

"You realize you're not helping yourself," Richard noted, somewhat bolstered by the notion. If she'd been guilty, she would have thought of an excuse already. She liked answers, as he did, and she was deft at providing them.

"Why did you open the duffel in the garage?" she asked.

Richard lifted an eyebrow. "Are you going to accuse *me*, now?"

She made a frustrated sound. "Paranoid much? What made you open the duffel bag?" she repeated, resuming her pacing.

"Actually, the bundle was partially sticking out, and I opened the bag to stuff it back . . . in." He scowled. "You wouldn't have just thrown it in like that. You would have been careful, and reverent, like the way you're holding it now."

"Well, someone wants you to think I did steal this, after they tried to keep me from it before," she said, returning to the couch and sitting beside him.

"That means you were the target. Not me. And not my staff."

Her expression faltered a little. "Boy, somebody really doesn't like me."

"Or somebody really wants you out of the way. But why?

Why hire you, then try to kill you, then plant evidence on you when that didn't work?"

"And why give up the tablet?"

"Finding it on you would probably keep the police from looking any farther afield."

She nodded. "I'd buy it if I were Castillo," she agreed, hefting the tablet in her hand. "But . . . Argh. Something is just wrong."

"What?"

"I'm—or the mystery woman we're pretending I'm not is—still the only other suspect, right? I'm already in trouble for this, with or without the tablet."

Rick glanced at the wall clock. "Which reminds me, Castillo's going to be wondering where I am."

Taking the cloth back from him, she carefully placed it and the tablet on the coffee table. "Do you have any information on the tablet?"

"I have a copy of the insurance portfolio and photos in my office. Why?"

"May I get them while you change?"

"The door's locked."

Standing, she gave him a quick smile, though her eyes still looked as worried as he'd ever seen them. "That's not a problem."

He rose as she went to the door. "Samantha, I—"

She turned back, walking up to him. "Don't say anything to get yourself into trouble, Rick. It seems like every time you take a step to help me, you risk getting into a hell of a lot of shit." Drawing a deep breath, she tucked her fingers around the front of his robe. "But if—if you have to say something to Castillo, could you yell or something? So I'll have a head start."

Whatever was going on, he wasn't saying anything to Castillo. Not yet. And the reason was very simple: He wasn't ready to let her get away from him. Richard brushed a strand of auburn hair behind her ear. "If I turn you over to Castillo, it'll be because I've satisfied myself that you did this. And in that case, I won't be warning you first."

"Fair enough."

He kissed her, releasing her reluctantly as she slipped back into the hallway. They'd passed the point where he could distance himself from her; hell, he'd been the one to announce to the paper that they were dating. And he realized, even if she didn't, that this was not a simple partnership. He'd been screwed in business partnerships before, and he hadn't been nearly as furious as he'd been this morning.

The way things were going, if she was lying to him, neither of them was getting out of this alive.

As far as Sam was concerned, while the trail grew more complicated, part of it also became very simple. She hadn't mentioned her new theory to Rick, and she wouldn't until she was certain. Every instinct she possessed, though, screamed that whoever had initiated the tablet's unexpected return had easy access to the estate—too easy to be an outsider. It didn't explain the damn bomb, but she wasn't turning her back on anything—or anyone.

Sam opened the door to Rick's office with a paper clip, making it look as though she had a key for the benefit of any patrolling security and her own peace of mind. Even with permission it was more difficult than she expected to saunter in as though she had every right to be there and go through his desk drawer—which was weird, because usually she did it without permission. Addison was obviously getting to her.

The tablet photos and detailed ownership history were in a file marked with a number she assumed to be part of the reference system for his large art and antique collection. The idea of staying there and looking through them made it feel too much like thievery after she'd given her word to be good, so she took the file and left the office for the relative safety of Rick's private suite.

Safety. She hadn't realized how foreign the concept had become to her until last night. It seemed like . . . never since she'd last felt completely relaxed and at ease, and safe. And safety was a powerful aphrodisiac—almost as powerful as the lure of Richard Addison, himself.

"Danger, Will Robinson, danger, danger," she muttered, putting the folder down beside the tablet and digging deeper into her duffel for clean clothes.

This situation was becoming extremely dangerous, and not just because people were dying and cops were walking around the estate at will. Her first thought this morning when she'd seen Rick's face and followed his gaze down to the tablet in his hand hadn't been for her safety. It had been that he wouldn't believe she hadn't done it. She was *supposed* to worry about herself before anyone or anything else. That was rule number one. Take care of yourself.

Ignoring rule number one for the second time that morning, she went to Rick's bathroom to take a shower instead of resuming her study of the tablet. She needed to think things through, and the shower was great for that. At the same time, neither did she want to touch the tablet again without Rick in the room. She evidently needed his protection even more now, but above that, she wanted him to trust her, which was absurd under the circumstances—hell, she would have been ready to arrest herself a half hour ago.

When she emerged from the bathroom she had a vague list of suspects, but she needed Rick to confirm who had access to the estate, and who had been there both the night of the robbery and either last night or this morning. And she wanted to look at today's paper, just to confirm what Castillo had said, that her face had appeared on the page along with her name. *Good God.* As if she didn't have enough to worry about.

So she wouldn't be tempted by the tablet, she went out to Rick's private veranda and sat in the shade of an umbrella to let her hair dry. She could go back to the room he'd loaned her, but then whoever'd been able to dump the tablet in her duffel would have no trouble at all getting into Rick's suite and taking it back.

"Why are you smiling?"

She nearly jumped out of her skin as Rick stepped onto the veranda from the pool deck stairs. "Jesus Christ!" she gasped, putting a hand over her heart.

"Sorry," he said, brief amusement touching his eyes. "I thought you had nerves of steel."

"That's Superman or something."

"Ah. And you're Catwoman."

"Cool. Where's the cop, Batman?"

"I just walked Castillo out to his car."

"What did he want?"

"Showed me some photos of DeVore, wanted to know if I recognized him. He wanted to ask you the same questions, but I mentioned some words like harassment and attorney, and he agreed to put it off."

"So is Etienne officially a suspect now?"

"Yes. He flew into Miami three days before the robbery, and they found copper wire in his hotel room, the same stuff that wired the bomb to the walls."

Even with the evidence and his own sort-of confession, she still couldn't believe the witty, self-centered Frenchman had tried to kill her. "What about the woman you saw?"

"Apparently I might have been hallucinating."

"Apparently."

"All they need is the tablet, and I think they'd be satisfied with the whole thing." He sat opposite her. "And why were you smiling?"

"Oh. I just thought it was funny that I tried to steal the tablet, and now I'm sitting out here protecting it."

His gaze sharpened. "Protecting it? What did you find out?"

"I just didn't want to look at it without you here," she returned, noting that today he looked more like a billionaire than a jock, with tan slacks and a white shirt open at the neck and the cuffs rolled up. Loafers with no socks completed the image, though she had the feeling he used clothes like she used personalities. "I have a couple of theories, though."

As for her, she needed to decide if her image was going to

be rich guy's date or his security consultant. The way he had looked her up and down in this morning's shorts and tank top, overlaid with a shirt to hide the shrapnel scrapes on her back, the date attire worked better on him. But she needed to find her own balance.

"Tell me."

"My duffel bag. Aside from the wanting me to look guilty thing, the only time somebody could have gotten to it was between when we left your car out front and when we went into the garage this morning."

"Somebody got onto the property again. I figured that. We'll go through the video in a few minutes."

"I'm not so sure he hasn't been here all along," she said slowly, watching his expression.

"Explain."

He didn't scoff, only demanded to know her reasoning. It was something of a relief, she realized. "Etienne didn't come back and plant the tablet. Someone else did."

A muscle in his jaw jumped. "You think it's one of my staff. But you'd never even met them until two days ago. Why frame you?"

"I don't know. But the only people who were here for both events are you and me—and maybe somebody who works here."

His eyes narrowed, and he stood to look over the veranda at the spread of his estate. "For a few hours I thought I could get away with just suspecting DeVore. But you're right. The bloody tablet never left the estate. Shit."

"I'd like to look at it and the file more closely. Maybe we'll find there's a history we're missing, or . . . I don't know. Or we can sit on our asses and wait for the cops to settle for blaming me."

"I don't like sitting on my ass. Especially when you're being targeted." Rick pulled open the veranda door and ushered her back into his suite. They sat on the couch, and she flipped open the file.

"Were you selling the tablet to the British Museum, or donating it?" she asked, spreading the photos out around the tablet and concentrating on the detailed trail the tablet had taken since its unearthing. Several century-long blank spaces didn't even bother with suppositions about the stone's whereabouts between its more public appearances.

"I'm donating it. Does that make a difference?"

"I don't know. This is all so . . . strange." She flipped another page. "Yeesh. According to this, your tablet's one of the things that persuaded Calvert and Schliemann about the location of Troy. This is why they dug in Hisarlik in 1868."

Rick smiled. "I know that."

"I didn't. I had a short timetable. Not enough time to do as much research as I'd like." Scowling, she turned from gazing at the tablet to pick up one of the photos. "I'd never use it to frame somebody, not when I wasn't even a suspect. It's way too cool for that. Too . . ." She trailed off, staring. Something in the photo caught her eye, and she shifted it closer to the tablet. "I'll be damned."

"That's not right," Rick said a moment later, leaning against her shoulder to look. He gestured at the photo, then at one of the symbols on the tablet. "On the photo the engravings here are faded almost to nothing. On the tablet you can see both of them."

"The carvings are all deeper than they look in the photos," she said half to herself, picking up another picture to make certain the shallow look of the original carvings wasn't just a trick of the light or the camera. "Wow. I don't believe it. This is a—"

"It's a fake," he cut in, picking the tablet up and turning it over in his hands.

The ramifications left her distinctly light-headed. "You have a good eye for detail," she said slowly, her mind retracing everything they'd learned so far about the robbery.

"You're not surprised, are you, Samantha?" he asked, his thigh brushing hers.

"Like I said, I'd be more surprised at somebody pitching the original at me for no good reason. But the question is, is this a good enough counterfeit to work as a donation to the British Museum?"

He glanced at her. "For a while, probably. With only three in the world they were gobsmacked to be getting it. And before the robbery, they—and I—wouldn't have had any reason to suspect anything. After display, though, they'd do some studies. That's why I was donating it." Richard straightened. "You're not suggesting I tell the police that I temporarily misplaced the tablet, then go ahead with donating the fake."

With a quick grin, she shook her head. *As if he would.* "No. But I'm wondering if someone had that in mind. The real one isn't here, but that might explain why the fake is."

"So framing you was just convenient? 'Oops, I forgot to make the switch?' That puts the reason for the bomb back into question again."

"Yep. And how about this?" she countered, shuffling the photos again. "Why make a good-quality fake if you're just going to blow it up?"

"You don't," he said slowly. "My estate gets recompensed the same amount whether the thing is stolen or lost or destroyed."

Rick stood. She thought he meant to pace, as she did when she was trying to decipher a particularly complicated knot, but instead he went to the phone and dialed. She made herself sit still, trusting him not to do something that would endanger them—or her freedom.

"Kate? Hi, it's Rick. Is Tom in?"

Sam rolled her eyes. Even if she didn't half suspect him, she had to admit that she liked antagonizing Donner. Besides being fun, it might piss him off enough to get him to make a mistake.

"Tom. Who the devil does my payroll? No, not mine personally. The payroll for the estate. I need to know who's been here over the past . . . three weeks, say."

Sitting forward, Samantha slid the photos back into their file. "You might also check outside services who have the same person here on a regular basis."

"Right. Tom, no, you don't need to bring it by in person. Just fax it to me. But I need it today, so you'll have to go into the office. And I also want a list of outside services personnel who are regularly assigned here." He paused again, listening, his stance going from alert to aggressive. "None of your bloody business."

"He's talking about me, right?"

"Hush." He turned his back on her, striding to the veranda door with phone in hand. "All right, all right, yes—something new's come up. Be here at ten tomorrow morning with a trial attorney—Macon, maybe—somebody who takes client-attorney privilege seriously."

As he punched the phone off, he walked back to the couch. "Don't argue," he said, before she could open her mouth. "I believe in being prepared for any contingency. If Castillo or somebody gets hold of this"—and he gestured at the tablet—"you are going to be in serious trouble. Fake or not, I don't want you caught with it."

"That was probably the thinking of whoever dumped it on me. Do you want me to hide it somewhere?"

"I'll take care of it."

"Rick, with all due respect, you're a smart guy, but you don't have some of my talents. I know how to hide things. I'm in this shit deeper than you are, and I'd just as soon you not end up in jail because I asked you for help."

"Bit late for that, my dear," he said, brushing hair back over her shoulder. "As we say in Britain, in for a penny, in for a pound."

God, just the touch of his hand on her hair made her all shivery. On impulse she leaned over and kissed him. Rick wrapped an arm around her shoulder, pulling her in closer and deepening the embrace of their mouths. As before when he began touching her like that, her mind shut down. It was so tempting, just to sink into him, to let everything go away. Everything but pleasure and heat and Richard Addison. It would work for a while, until someone decided to drop the gun that had killed Etienne into her purse or something.

She pulled back, but he pursued her, sliding her down onto her back with her head resting against the duffel bag. A warm hand slid up under her shirt, cupping her breast.

"Rick, stop," she protested, in a choked-off moan of pleasure.

"I want you," he murmured, ducking his face into her neck.

"Good God." Shuddering, she shoved at him. "We fucked all night. Stop distracting me," she muttered, pulling back through his arms.

"I think that's a compliment."

"I want to see the videos for last night and this morning, Rick."

"Later."

"Whoever this is, he's been a step ahead of us all the way," she said, putting a hand over his sensuous mouth when he would have argued with her. "I want to at least pull even. Ahead would be nice, too, don't you think?"

With a curse, he blew out his breath and sat up again. "All right. We'll look at the video." He looked over at the tablet. "And where do you recommend we put this? Under the bed?"

"I don't think so."

After she wrapped it back in its protective cloth, she dumped out her knapsack, folded a shirt around the bundle, and slid it in. "There. That'll do until we get it out of your room and somewhere safer."

Rick, though, was toeing through her knapsack refuse. He bent and picked up a broken computer board. "And this is?"

"Part of my home computer. I heard the police coming, and I didn't want them accessing the system."

He gazed at her, his expression part lustful and part worried. "We are seriously going to consider another line of work for you when this is over with," he murmured.

At the moment, it almost sounded like a good idea.

Fifteen

Sunday, 11:54 a.m.

Ronald Clark had been moved to the day shift after the break-in, and he was seated in his chair before the bank of video monitors and computers when Richard led Samantha into the security room.

"Mister Addison," the guard said, standing. The Adam's apple bobbed above his tie, and his thinning blond hair was slicked back in a distinctly unflattering style. A cop wannabe, she decided immediately, who probably couldn't figure out why he kept failing the psych profile part of the entrance exam.

"Clark. Miss Jellicoe and I would like to review the tapes for the garage, starting at about nine last night and up through ten this morning."

"And for the front drive at the same time," Samantha added.

Clark sat again. "Um, okay. I'll put 'em up on those screens over there. It'll take me a minute."

"What time did you start your shift this morning, Clark?"

Samantha pursued, brushing a hand against Richard's arm as she passed him.

She intoxicated him just by being in the room. And she'd accused *him* of being too distracting. Since she'd dropped into his office to ask for his help, she'd become his obsession. To date he'd canceled three meetings, four conference calls, and a flight to Miami. The cost of his neglect could potentially come to millions, but a few one way or the other didn't matter all that much. It seemed more important that when Samantha was around his heart raced, his pulse heated, and life became more . . . alive. The glimpses of the clever, funny woman beneath the cool, professional facade fascinated him.

"I came in at six," Clark answered, looking from his employer to Samantha. "Louie Mourson had the night shift. Why?"

"No reason," Richard answered, following Samantha to the monitors in the corner.

The look she aimed at him said otherwise, but he wasn't about to accuse people who worked for him without a damned good reason. She gripped his shoulder, going up on her toes to reach his ear. "He was here both times," she whispered. "Don't be so quick to dismiss coincidence."

"I dismissed it where you're concerned," he returned in the same soft voice.

Samantha grimaced. "Yeah, well, you were here both times, too."

The monitor flickered to life. They were looking at a video of the garage taken from the southeast corner, giving the camera a view of both the wide front doors and the smaller door leading to the house. Unlike the outdoor cameras this one was fixed, rather than rotating back and forth.

Samantha nodded her approval. "That's good placement," she said, "except you don't have a redundant camera. If someone figures out how to get past this one, they're in."

"Not everybody is an expert at electronics and burglary," he muttered, keeping his voice low so Clark couldn't overhear.

"Anybody who could get this far into the estate without being detected would be an expert," she shot back at him huffily.

"Could you get in and out of there without anyone knowing?"

"Oh, they'd know I'd been there, but not until after I stole that hot blue Bentley Continental GT and left again."

So she liked the Bentley. Next time they went somewhere together, he'd let her drive. Of course she apparently didn't have a driver's license, but that seemed the least of their worries. "Can we speed up the tape from here?" he asked over his shoulder.

"Yep. Just use the keyboard there under the desk. It's all set, Mr. Addison."

From the meter in the corner of the screen, it was three minutes after nine o'clock, and the Mercedes hadn't yet been returned to the garage. Samantha pulled out the keyboard and tapped a key, and the tape glided into high speed. After about forty-five minutes, the car zoomed into view, taking its place among the others.

Samantha backed the tape up again to watch the entry at regular speed. Ben Hinnock drove the SLK into its spot, got out, wiped a smudge off the windshield, and left through the wide doors, which closed behind him. At eleven the pre-programmed lights dimmed, leaving the garage in heavy shadows.

"That's stupid," she muttered, keying the tape into high speed again. "Like the cars need dark so they can sleep or something."

"How can you see anything with the tape going that fast?"

"Just watch the trunk. That's all we need to see, unless you want to sit here for thirteen hours."

"Okay. But what do you suggest we do if we find something, Samantha?"

"If we find something, then we show it to Castillo, say we looked in my bag because of it, and 'wow, look what we found.'"

He lifted an eyebrow. "You're frightening."

She kept her eyes on the screen, but her lips twitched in a fleeting smile. "You scare the hell out of me, too."

Richard leaned his hip against the table, settling in for a long, nonblinking surveillance. "We should have had breakfast first. Or at least coffee."

"Soda. Coffee's for amateurs."

"Did I mention that you're very stra—"

"Whoa." Moving fast, Samantha froze the tape. "Did you see that?"

Richard stiffened. "What? Nothing moved."

"No, not that. The time." She backed the tape up, then sent it forward again at normal speed. At seven-fifteen the tape bumped and jumped to seven-nineteen. Nothing else in the picture changed. "Four minutes."

"That's what happened with the secure room's video the night of the robbery." He looked at her. "How easy is that to do?"

Samantha shrugged. "If you know the system, it's fairly simple. If you're sure it's not our friend Clark," she whispered, gesturing, "then it was done somewhere between here and there, and done so that it didn't set off any alarms."

"Wouldn't Clark see that the screen was blank?"

"The camera picture might have looked normal, and it just wasn't recording. Or the image might just freeze, or something." She swiveled in her chair. "Clark, what time do you take your morning break?"

The guard ran a hand across his balding pate. "I've been going up to the kitchen for coffee at about seven-fifteen, but just for five minutes or so. Then I usually don't take another break until nine-thirty."

"You're pretty consistent, then?"

"Well, yeah. Hans said he'd shoot me if I tried to make my own coffee in there, and he doesn't have the first pot ready until after seven, most mornings."

"Hans is very protective about the reputation of his coffee," Richard supplied with a slight smile. "He won an award for it, once."

"Too bad I don't drink it, then."

She pushed the tape into fast-forward again, but nothing moved until after ten o'clock, when the two of them strolled into the garage, hand in hand and wearing their dressing robes. Richard watched as they flirted in fast motion, noting with a deep rush of satisfaction the way she gazed at him when he wasn't looking. Castillo came into the picture as they were both bent over the boot, and thankfully nothing of the tablet showed in the video.

Sam stopped the playback. "Just in case, we should look at the front drive video, too," she said. "Maybe whoever it was walked by on their way in or out."

"Except that you don't think whoever it was has been going in and out," he reminded her. "They've been here all along."

"It's looking more and more like somebody who knows the household routine and has a good working knowledge of the security system."

"The part I still don't get is the bomb," Richard said, taking her hand as she rose. Perhaps it was sappy, but he felt the need to touch her every few minutes, to make certain she was still there, and to show whoever might be watching, himself included, that she belonged to him—whether she realized it yet or not.

"May I please have some breakfast? Or it's brunch now, I guess," she asked in an exaggerated pleading voice as they returned to the hallway. "I'll think better when I'm not starving."

"On my veranda," he agreed.

"On *my* veranda," she countered. "I can see the front drive from there."

He couldn't blame her for being paranoid. If she hadn't been good at what she did, she'd be dead. "I'll put in an order with Hans and check my office to see if Donner's sent me that fax yet."

She nodded and would have headed up the stairs, except that he took her wrist and turned her back to face him. "What?" she asked.

"I can't seem to get enough of you," he muttered, and touched his mouth to hers again.

"You're not so bad yourself, for a rich-guy Brit," she replied a little breathlessly. "Mind if I stop off in your room for my stuff?"

Her stuff—which would include the fake tablet. "Samantha. You—"

"I don't want that thing found in your private rooms, regardless," she said in a tone that surprised him with its seriousness. "I won't do anything with it until you get there."

Richard knew better than to fight a battle he couldn't possibly win. "All right. I'll see you in a few minutes."

She smiled a little at him. "I'm not going anywhere. Partners, remember?"

He remembered. He just hoped she did.

Rick had missed the main difficulty in all this mess, Samantha mused as she strolled toward his private rooms. Him. She made her lifestyle an excuse for not dating much, though she had to admit that most men she ran across seemed rather . . . dull. When their most exciting activity was Pilates, they really couldn't compete with her evenings. Rick Addison could compete, and in spades. And he intoxicated her. She'd known him for less than a week, and already she felt like an addict. How would she make herself leave at the end of this?

"Miss Jellicoe."

With a start, Samantha turned around. The prissy Italian acquisitions manager, his curling black hair styled to perfection, strode up to her. "Partino?"

"Si. I just wanted to welcome you to the company."

She frowned. "Beg pardon?"

"I saw the newspaper this morning. Rick has hired you for art security."

"Oh, that. Yes, just until we get this mess figured out."

"I made some calls. You work for the Norton. You are an expert in art and antiquities."

He almost made it sound like an accusation, so she smiled. *Charm time.* "I'm not trying to take your job or anything. I'm here for security, and that's it. And just temporarily."

Partino smiled brightly back at her, though she couldn't help noticing that the expression didn't touch his dark eyes. "Of course. That's just as well, anyway."

"And why is that?"

His smile deepened. "You are not the first employee to try sleeping with the boss, Miss Jellicoe. None of them still work here."

She narrowed her eyes. "I think that's more my business than yours."

He nodded. "Yes. You understand, we must all look out for our best interests."

"Oh, I understand that."

"Good day, then." With a bow, he turned on his heel.

She shrugged off the slightly slimy feeling the odd little man left behind. He probably wasn't feeling quite his best, anyway. An acquisitions manager who allowed art objects to get stolen couldn't feel very secure about his own continued employment.

At the same time, as far as she knew it was the first time anything had gone missing from the property—a pretty good track record, considering the quality of the stuff Rick collected. And Partino had worked for Rick for a good ten years. What happened to the little Italian wasn't any of her business, though if she'd been the one to take the tablet, she supposed it would be her fault if he were fired. Too weird.

Her room and Rick's were in opposite wings of the house, and she was out of breath by the time she'd hauled her knapsack, duffel, and kit down what felt like a mile of hallways and galleries. Yeesh. She was going to have to hit the gym—though if she and Rick continued exercising as they had last night, that would probably take care of her daily workout.

She smiled as she shouldered open her suite door and dragged the duffel inside. If they continued as they had last night, she'd be dead in a week. What a way to go, though.

The knapsack would have to stay packed until Rick came in, since she remained determined not to touch the tablet outside of his presence. She had more clean underwear and clothes in the duffel, though, and nice as the things were that Rick provided, she felt more . . . independent in her own clothes.

Hefting the heavy duffel again, she dragged it to the bedroom. In the entryway something pressed against her thigh, and she instinctively backed away an inch.

It was too late. With a faint pop the safety pin at the end of a wire pulled out of the grenade taped to the inside bedroom wall. Gasping, she slammed her hand around, just catching the lever against the grenade as it started to spring away.

The movement overbalanced her, but she managed to keep her fingertips pressed against the lever as she stumbled against the doorjamb and fell to the floor. "Oh, my God," she rasped, not daring even to breathe. On the far side of the door another grenade wobbled, the pin hanging on by a fraction. Her leg, tangled in the wire, jerked, and the pin slipped another millimeter. "*Rick!*"

Richard whistled as he strolled toward Samantha's private rooms. A bowl of sugared strawberries in his hand, he couldn't believe he would be in such a good mood with a thief and a murderer potentially loose on his estate. But neither situation could quell the thought that last night he'd had what was probably the best sex of his life. And come hell or high water, he was going to have more within the hour.

"*Rick!*"

The fear in the scream froze his blood. Dropping the strawberries, he sprinted to Samantha's room. The door was half-open, and he charged in. "Samantha?"

"Here!"

He saw her legs across the bedroom doorway, one of

them at an odd angle. "What happened?" he barked, lunging forward.

"*Stop!* It's a grenade!"

Stopping at the doorway, he leaned into the room. She lay on the floor, half on her back, one hand pressed against a grenade secured with duct tape to the wall at about thigh level. On the other side, another grenade teetered, still with the safety pin in—but only because the wire hadn't pulled it completely free. Her left leg was tangled in the wire.

"Jesus. Don't move." Grasping the doorframe, he leaned over her toward the second grenade.

"Don't! Get out of here! Just call somebody!"

"Right," he answered, concentrating on keeping his hand steady as he touched the end of the pin. "In a minute." Shoving with his index finger, he pushed the pin back into place. Holding it there, he stepped over her. With his free hand he untangled the wire from her leg. The first grenade's pin dangled at the far end of it.

"I'm going to call for help, then we'll put the other pin back in," he said, trying to keep his voice steady. If she hadn't been so quick with her hands . . . Good God.

"Just leave the pin," she countered. "I'm okay. Call from the sitting room, then get out."

Carefully shifting the wire to lessen the pull on the intact grenade, he stood, making his way to the nightstand. "I'm not going anywhere. If you want to fight about it, come over here."

"Shit. Don't be stupid."

"Quiet. I'm on the phone." He called Clark.

"Yes, sir?"

"Clark, call the police. Inform them that there's a grenade in the green suite, and that my girlfriend is holding it together with her hand."

"A gr . . . Right away, Mr. Addison. Do—"

He hung up. "How're you doing, Samantha?" he asked, coming to squat beside her.

"Better than you, you idiot. Tell the rest of your people to get out. And I'm not your damned girlfriend."

He'd made her angry, which at least brought some color back to her face. She was still alarmingly pale, but the stark terror had faded a little from her eyes. "It says you are in the newspaper."

"Yes, well, I'd like to take a look at that."

"Later. Let me get the pin."

"No. It's safer this way. It's a pretty crude set-up, but I don't want to risk us igniting the fuse by stuffing the pin back in. Or by pulling the thing off the wall, if that's what you're thinking."

Sweat beaded her forehead, but she still managed to sound like a complete professional. "By God, you're amazing," he murmured, rising to call Clark again and tell him to evacuate the building, but to allow no one out of the gates. As soon as he finished, he returned to her side.

"You're subscribing to the killer-in-residence theory, then?" she asked, shifting a little.

Her arm must be aching by now, Richard thought. He moved behind her so she could brace her back against his side and take a little of the strain off her shoulder and arm. What he wanted to do was grab the grenade himself, but heroic though it might have been, it would also have been abysmally stupid. At the moment, she had this under control. "I subscribed to it before, but now I want to make certain we don't let them slip out and manufacture an alibi. I am going to kill whoever tried to do this to you, Samantha."

Ten minutes later the bomb squad entered the room. From their expressions, this wasn't the kind of scenario they were used to encountering. Even so, they dragged in a bomb-safe container along with their heavy padding and face and eye protectors. They outfitted Samantha as well as they could with one of her arms plastered to the wall, then went to work on securing the grenade.

His refusal to leave probably annoyed the hell out of them, but he didn't much care. He wasn't leaving until she did.

Finally, with yet another piece of duct tape, they secured the lever to the grenade and dragged Samantha backward. "All right, all civilians out of the house," the lieutenant ordered.

"Like I wanted to stay," Samantha commented, letting Richard pull her to her feet.

She was shaking, and he put an arm around her waist to help her from the room. Down two flights of stairs and out on the front steps, she pulled free.

"All right. I'm sitting now," she said, plunking herself down on the white granite steps.

Richard sat beside her, putting an arm back around her because he couldn't not do it. "You're certain you're all right?" he asked quietly, kissing her hair.

"I didn't even see it. It was so stupid," she burst out.

"What happened?"

She blew out her breath, rolling her shoulders and obviously trying to calm herself down. "I carried my stuff in, then dragged the duffel bag to the bedroom so I could put some of my clothes away. My leg hit something, and I moved back, but I heard the pin pull." Samantha shrugged. "I slammed my hand around and caught the lever before it popped, then I realized there was another grenade on the other side of the door. That one not going off was just dumb luck."

"Luck, and very quick reflexes."

"It should never have happened. I know better than to let my guard down." To his surprise, a tear ran down her cheek.

Richard held her tighter. "Don't say that. Someone tried to outsmart you for the second time, and it didn't work."

Samantha shrugged out from under his grip, then slammed her fist against her knee. "I have never been so damned scared in my life."

"This is over," he said. It was too late to save her, but he couldn't help his instinct to want to protect her. While her fear had subsided, she was obviously still angry as hell. As for him, his heart was still pounding. "We are leaving."

"No. The answers are here." She shook her head, gazing at

him. "And I *really* want to find them now. It seems our theory was right; it's me somebody wants dead."

Castillo's car rolled up the drive and stopped. Samantha stiffened beneath Rick's arm, but he refused to let her go. "You have to trust me," he murmured. "I won't let anything happen to you."

"It's not you I'm worried about trusting, Rick. And don't forget, that tablet is still in my knapsack, in my room, surrounded by twenty cops."

"You've had a busy morning, haven't you?" Castillo said, climbing the shallow steps until he drew even with them. "Everybody okay?"

"Nobody blew up," Samantha said, reaching for her usual sardonic humor.

"That's a plus." The detective continued up the stairs. "Stay here, Mr. Addison, Miss Jellicoe. I'll go take a look."

Richard was glad to see him go. He needed a few minutes to decide how much information he needed to relay and how many lies he would have to spin to do it and still be able to protect Samantha—from the police, from whoever had tried to kill her again, and even from herself.

Sixteen

Sunday, 1:30 p.m.

"I should call Tom," Rick said, though he didn't move.

Samantha wiped at unaccustomed tears. It was the adrenaline; she was still shaking with leftover energy. She was used to the punch, but being nearly blown up was nothing like the thrill of a well-executed burglary.

"How much are you going to tell Castillo?" she asked, grateful that Richard pretended not to notice her stupid crying.

"Enough so we can figure out who's been setting bombs in my house." With a grim look he reached for his belt and pulled free his cell phone.

"He's going to say it was me, you know."

"That's why I'm calling Tom. Even if Castillo decides to arrest you, we'll have you out on bail in an hour."

Another rush, this time of fear, hit her, and she lurched to her feet. "No. I am not—"

"Samantha, calm down. I won't let—"

She backed away another step, easily evading his grasp. "It's not up to you. I am not going to jail just so you can put on your shining armor and rescue me. No."

Rick got to his feet. "Wouldn't you rather be cleared than have Castillo and the police watching you every second of your life?"

He had no idea what it was like to live her life. "I'm used to hiding, and I can't be cleared," she hissed, her trembling starting all over again. She was not going to be hysterical. She didn't get hysterical. Not even when people tried to kill her and other people she was beginning to trust then suggested it would be a good thing if she went to jail. "If I go in, I'll never get out."

"Calm down." He kept his voice quiet and even, probably anticipating that she might run. She wanted to run. Hell, she'd already scoped out an exit. "All right. Don't worry. You're not going anywhere. Just sit down, and let me call Donner."

"I'll calm down," she returned, "somewhere else."

"Someone just tried to kill you," he said more sharply. "You're not leaving my sight."

"Then follow me," she shot back, turning on her heel. "I'm going for a walk."

She heard his low growl, then his feet on the drive. He was following her. Feeling a little easier despite herself, she headed toward the pond.

Castillo looked out the veranda window. The room Miss Jellicoe used had been cleared, with no further devices found. She should have been killed; from what the bomb squad said, she had either set up the event, or had the fastest reflexes they'd ever seen. Considering the study he'd been making over the past few days of what was known about her father's career and about some other thefts attributed to him but not proven, his hunch tended toward the fast reflexes.

Out on the front drive she and Addison were arguing about something, and he imagined that it had to do with how much they were going to tell him. If this crap had happened anywhere but at Solano Dorado, he would have had them both taken down to the department for questioning. But after twenty years of working in the middle of the Palm Beach elite, he knew the chain of command by heart—especially when high-powered movers and shakers like Richard Addison were involved: Addison knew the governor, who knew the commissioner, who knew the captain, who knew the chief of detectives, who knew Castillo.

At the same time, he was willing to bet his badge that Jellicoe had been the woman Addison had seen the night of the burglary, the one he also credited with saving his life. Obviously, though, she hadn't been the only cat in the house. He had a body in the morgue, but Etienne DeVore wasn't doing any talking other than to say that he'd been shot twice and dumped into the ocean to drift away.

The chief had made it clear that he wanted DeVore connected to the explosion and subsequent death of young Prentiss. That would be the end of the homicide investigation and the end of his involvement with Richard Addison and company. It was a shame, then, that he hated puzzles with missing pieces. Something much larger than a stolen tablet was going on, and he badly wanted to figure out what it was.

The head of the bomb squad gave him the technical details of the almost death of Samantha Jellicoe, and armed with that information, he decided to go for a walk by Addison's pond.

"Harvard's on his way, I presume?" Samantha sat on the cool grass at the edge of the pond, her attention ostensibly on the small green frog perched on the rock beside her.

Richard strolled back and forth along the path a few feet away, too restless, too concerned that whoever had wired the grenades remained on the grounds to relax. She'd accused him of wanting to be her knight in shining armor, and she'd hit the target spot on the bull's-eye. "Yes. He's bringing my list of employees with him."

"Good. I bet he was pissed."

Keeping in mind that "pissed" meant drunk in England and angry in America, Richard nodded at her back. "Quite."

"He thinks I'm bad luck."

"He thinks you're dangerous. Of course, it doesn't help that you intentionally antagonize him."

"But it helps me feel better, which is what's important."

"You might at least call him 'Yale.' He did graduate top of his class there." Finally deciding that the number of police currently on and around the premises would probably keep anyone from lobbing more explosives at Samantha, and mostly because he wanted to be closer to her, he sat down beside her. The frog looked at him and jumped into the pond.

"You scared him." Samantha leaned a little in his direction. "Why am I dangerous?"

He had the feeling the epithet flattered her. "According to Tom, it's because you have too many secrets and a sad excuse for a lifestyle, and you thereby put my life in jeopardy."

"And according to Richard Addison?"

"Ah. According to him, he doesn't quite know what to make of you, but concedes that you are extremely distracting, and that you tempt him to do things he probably would never have considered before making your acquaintance."

"Like lying to the police?"

"Something like that." Actually he'd committed that particular sin before, but not about something as serious as murder. As Castillo approached along the path, though, he pushed that memory out of the way. "Detective."

"Frank's good enough." Castillo sat on the rock vacated by the frog. "The room's clear," he said, "and they're working the rest of the house. I've got a couple of my guys questioning the staff, but nothing's popped so far. That was smart, keeping everybody bottled up on the grounds." He leaned forward, peering into the pond. "You got fish in there?"

"Koi," Richard answered. "This time of day they pretty much hide beneath the rocks and lily pads."

"Kind of like whoever set those grenades out," Frank commented, reaching into his pocket. "Do koi like sunflower seeds?"

"It'll probably kill them, but what the hell. It might draw them out."

Castillo tossed a few seeds into the water. "What we have here," he said in a mild, conversational tone, "is a kind of stalemate. Oh, there they are. Wow." He dumped another handful of seeds into the pond, watching as the large, bright-colored fish swarmed up to the food.

"A stalemate?" Richard prompted, noting that Samantha had edged as far from the detective as she could without actually getting up. She might play friendly with Castillo, but she obviously wasn't going to do any talking today.

"Yeah. I have all these puzzle pieces, but no picture to go by. For instance, I would have bet that DeVore, that guy I asked you about this morning, was the one who broke in here and stole the tablet and set the explosives. But he's dead, so he didn't plant the grenades this morning, and he doesn't match the description you gave that night of the female you claim saved your life."

Risking a glance at Samantha's set, unyielding expression, Richard took a breath. "What if I was mistaken about that female, Frank, and she was here by my invitation?"

"Well, that would definitely help point the finger at De-Vore, except for the grenades this morning."

"It wasn't the same guy," Samantha said brusquely, plucking at the grass and keeping her gaze on the pond.

"The bomb squad tends to agree," Castillo said in the same mild voice, continuing to flick seeds into the water. "Their theory is the first one was done by a pro, and the second by an amateur, trying to copy the style of the first one."

Samantha actually nodded. "Shape charges are a lot harder to come by than grenades. And the pins should've been pulled already, with the wire triggering the levers to spring off. No chance of anyone stopping the explosion. Even that, though, gives the victim four or five seconds to get out of the way."

Richard closed his eyes for a moment. It amazed him, that she could so calmly discuss the flaws of a bomb set-up that had nearly killed her half an hour ago. He opened his eyes again, looking at her rather than Castillo. "What if I were to tell you, Frank, that a fake version of the tablet appeared this morning, with at least one of the video cameras deactivated in just the same way they were the night of the robbery?"

"What?" Castillo started to his feet, then changed his mind and settled back down again with visible effort. "I'd want to see the tape anyway." He cleared his throat. "I would also need to narrow down the time during which the grenades could have been set. What time did you leave your room this morning, Miss Jellicoe?"

"She spent the night elsewhere," Richard answered, so she wouldn't have to. "In fact, I suppose the grenades could have been put there anytime over the last twenty-four hours."

"I don't think so," Samantha said quietly.

"Why not?" both men asked at the same time.

She took a breath, so clearly reluctant to speak it was almost amusing. "I was in the newspaper this morning—as a security and art expert." She glanced at Richard. "That was my fault."

"Done is done," he said, reaching over to cover her hand with his, then pulling back from the caress before she could. He knew how to fish; the difficulty with Samantha was that she was far more sleek and deadly tiger shark than timid minnow. He wanted her, but neither did he wish to lose an arm—or any other appendage—in the process.

"I don't . . . like accusing people without any proof," she said in an even more reluctant tone, "so I'm just telling you this for purposes of information. Danté Partino made a big deal about welcoming me to the company this morning, and about making sure I knew that he knew about my museum background."

"What? That's ridic—"

"Did he threaten you?" Castillo interrupted, shifting again to face her.

She grimaced. "Look, I'm not going to—"

"Samantha," Richard cut in sharply, "did he threaten you?"

"No." Her frown deepened. "He suggested that I wouldn't

last long. And—shit—he also said he knew where I'd spent the night."

"God dammit." Richard lurched to his feet.

"Just a minute, Mr. Addison," Castillo said, rising to put himself between Richard and the house. "Are you absolutely sure that's what Partino said to you, Miss Jellicoe?"

Probably not liking the idea of two men towering over her, Samantha climbed to her feet, as well. "May as well call me Sam." She sighed. "And yes, I'm sure. My memory's pretty close to photographic."

Castillo dug into his pocket again, this time for a radio. "Mendez, find Danté Partino for me. Be nice, but stay close to him."

"Affirmative," a female voice said through the speaker.

A photographic memory. That explained why she'd suspected so quickly that the tablet was a fake. She'd seen photos of the original somewhere. In a way, it also explained why she was so tactile; she literally memorized everything she touched. Including him.

"You can't arrest him because of what I said," Samantha protested, backing away a step.

"No, but I can ask him some questions based on what you said," Castillo returned, his expression unexpectedly understanding.

Apparently Samantha Jellicoe had another admirer. Of course it benefited her to have a cop on her side, though that might have been the idea. But at the same time, the tough, capable lady reluctantly handing out evidence to put the blame on someone else, felt like the real Jellicoe.

"I want to be there," Richard said. This was still his party.

"Yeah, I figured that. First I want to look at the video you were talking about."

"Of course you do," Sam muttered, her expression growing glummer by the moment.

Richard couldn't help grinning. "Don't worry," he murmured in her ear. "Cooperation in the face of adversity builds character."

"Bite me."

"Later, my dear."

She moved closer. "As long as I choose the place," she breathed as they returned to the house.

Jesus, she was going to make him insane. "That's a deal."

"When Castillo sees the tape you're going to have to explain that we found the tablet in my personal bags and didn't tell him about it," she continued a beat later.

Well, that was nearly as effective as a cold shower. "I made you a promise," he returned in the same low voice. "I keep my word."

Samantha didn't say anything, but her hand slid against his. Wordlessly he twined his fingers with hers. Bloody hell, this was getting complicated. And now one of his own employees had just become a suspect in an attempted murder. The oddest thing was, he had an easier time accepting Partino's guilt than he had ever had believing that Samantha might be involved in a murder.

His cell phone rang. "Addison," he said, as he flipped it open.

"Rick, tell the cops to let me through the goddamned gates," Donner's voice spat at him.

Richard lowered the phone. "Frank, please let Tom Donner through the gates."

Castillo scowled. "We were having a nice conversation here. You sure you want your attorney to ruin it?"

"I totally agree," Samantha said with the glimmer of a smile.

Wonderful. Now the thief and the cop had a mutual admiration society. "I think it's for the best, yes," he insisted. "Besides, he's got some information with him that we might be able to use."

"Okay." Frank lifted his radio again and gave the order.

Raising the phone to his ear, Richard listened for a second while in the background Tom continued to argue with the police stationed at the front gate. "Tom? Give it a second. They'll let you in."

"Bummer," Samantha muttered.

He tugged her closer with the hand still wrapped around hers. "Be nice to him," he said quietly. "We might need him soon."

Seventeen

Sunday, 2:15 p.m.

Frank Castillo kept his mouth shut as he watched the garage tape, up to and including the images of Rick and Sam digging in the trunk of the SLK, then talking to the detective. Samantha swallowed, staying close by the door and waiting for the inevitable accusations and attempted arrest. One thing was for sure—if they meant to take her to jail, she was going to make them work for it.

Donner didn't utter anything articulate either, but the noises he made said clearly enough that he understood the significance of the bathrobes and hand holding. Shit. He'd probably like to see her rotting in jail for life. Of course if he'd orchestrated this whole thing, he wanted her dead, not just in prison. Hm. Did boy scouts know about hand grenades?

"Okay," the detective finally said, sitting back. "He had four minutes to stash the tablet. He could have done the grenades any time after that—unless it was more than one guy."

"I don't think so," Sam said reluctantly, wishing she had

enough of her father's uncaring attitude about everyone else that she could keep her mouth shut.

"Why not?" Rick asked.

"The plan would seem to be making sure I looked guilty, then dead," she returned.

"Danté Partino's been with you for ten years," Donner said, though his own face was grim. "Are you sure about this?"

"*I'm* sure enough to ask him to come down to the station for some questions," Castillo said, rising.

"I still want to be there when you talk to him," Richard said, as they left the security room.

Sam grabbed Addison's arm as the other two men headed back upstairs. She could hear Castillo warning Clark not to discuss with anyone what he'd overheard. "I saw the cops carrying off a broken bowl of something from the hallway outside my room. What was it?"

"Sugared strawberries."

"My favorite." Running her hands up his chest, she stretched onto her toes and kissed him. In a second his arms were around her, pulling her closer against his tall, lean body. Adrenaline tingled and surged through her again, this time welcome and electric, and accompanied by a hefty helping of arousal. "Thank you," she murmured against his mouth.

Rick nudged her backward, pressing her between himself and the wall. With lips and tongue he kissed the base of her jawbone below her ear, and she moaned. His hands slipped under her tank top and up along her spine as he caught her mouth again.

"Rick, are you coming?" Donner called down the stairs.

"Just about," he murmured, lowering his arms with obvious reluctance. "Yes," he said in a louder voice.

"Are you sure you want to go to the police station?" Samantha asked, nibbling at his chin. "I'm feeling very grateful right now."

He groaned as she tangled her fingers through his dark hair. "I have an idea," he suggested in a whisper. "We'll take the limo, and we can fool around in the back seat."

It tempted her, despite the destination. "I am not going to the police station."

"Yes, you are," he murmured, kissing her again, teasing at her with his tongue. "If we're right about Danté, at least he and DeVore are involved. I'm not sure whether two's the lucky number, or if it's a whole damned conspiracy. And until I do know, you're not getting out of my sight."

She pushed him away. "No, Rick. I'm serious."

He backed off a little, studying her face with his cool gray eyes. After a long moment he nodded. "Okay. We'll do it here, then."

She couldn't help her snort of derision. "That's awfully cocky of you, don't you think?"

Rick gave her a quick smile. "Yep."

She followed him back upstairs and into the kitchen. Castillo stood by the big double oven and barked orders into his radio. Donner was on his phone, as well, but when Rick raised a hand they both stopped talking. It must feel good to be the boss.

"Gentlemen, I'd like to do this here," he said. "In my office."

"If we do it here," Castillo said, lowering the radio, "I can't advise him of his rights. He won't have an attorney present, and nothing he says will be admissible in court. And no, Donner doesn't qualify, because he works for you."

"You said you weren't going to arrest him on my say-so, anyway," Samantha put in gruffly.

All three men looked at her. She squared her shoulders. *Let them look.* No one was going to jail because of something she'd said. If she acquired a reputation for being a rat, no one in her circle would ever trust her again.

Castillo pursed his lips. "Friendly questions only, then. But just to make it clear, Mr. Addison, I don't work for you. I'm here to solve two murders and an attempted murder. Whatever it takes."

"Rick. And I appreciate that," Rick returned. "Do we know where Danté is?"

"With the rest of your staff, evacuated to the tennis courts."

Donner pushed to his feet. "I'll get him."

"No. *I'll* get him," the detective said. "Your office, Rick. But this is my investigation. If you step out of line, I'll take you in for obstruction. You're already pushing it with me."

"Agreed." Rick watched him out the door, then turned to Donner. "Where's that list of employees?"

The attorney dug it out of his jacket pocket. "You're insane, Rick. You do know that, don't you?"

The look Rick gave him was startlingly dark, even to Samantha's jaded eyes. "You didn't see how close Samantha came to being killed an hour ago," he snapped. "In *my* bloody house. So help me or get out, Tom. I'm not joking."

Donner glared back at him. After a moment he blew out his breath and seemed to deflate. Wordlessly, he handed the sheet of paper to Rick, then led the way out the door. "There are six people, not including you and Jellicoe, who were here both the night of the burglary and this morning."

"Is Danté one of them?"

"Yes."

As they headed out of the kitchen, Samantha spied a copy of the morning paper on the counter. With a questioning grin to Hans the cook to secure his permission she snatched it up, shuffling through it as they walked to Rick's office. It took her a moment to find the society section.

"Page three," Donner said, glancing over his shoulder at her.

From his expression, he thought she must be flattered and thrilled to have her photo in the paper, especially with Addison as her companion. Yeah, that was her, publicity seeker extraordinaire. Harvard would never believe that she would have been happier facing another pair of grenades than seeing her face and her name in a newspaper.

"It's a nice picture," Rick said, slowing to draw even with her.

The paper had opted to use the first photo the reporter had snapped, probably because she'd looked like a deer in the headlights for the second one. So she and Rick sat in casual conversation, an easy, relaxed smile on his face as he gazed at her. Her expression was one of fond annoyance, while his hand covering hers spoke of trust and affection.

"Weird," she muttered, uncomfortable. She skipped her eyes down to the caption, which named her as Sam Jellicoe, the date of billionaire Richard Addison, and an art and security expert.

"What's weird?"

"It's like . . . evidence," she fumbled, closing the paper again.

He took it from her. "Evidence. Of what? That you like me? That I like you? Is that so bad, Samantha?"

"It's a frozen moment," she muttered. "It doesn't say that two minutes later I bashed you in the ribs, or that—"

"—or that an hour later I was fucking you," he whispered, his lips brushing her ear. "Which I intend to do again. And again."

She shivered. "Grenades are safer than you."

Rick chuckled. "I'll take that as a compliment."

"As the voice of reason in this happy little band," Donner said, waiting at the office door for Rick to produce the key, "I'd just like to know how seriously we're taking the idea that Partino killed the security guard, the guy in the ocean, and tried to kill Jellicoe. Danté. Our Danté. The little guy with the hair gel."

"I'm voting for the third one only," Sam said. "The others don't make sense coming from Partino. Not yet, anyway."

"The bomb squad said they think the bombs were set by two different people," Rick seconded.

"Okay, then what the hell's the motive?" the attorney asked, sending a look at Sam.

"That's what we're going to find out. Have a seat, Samantha." Rick took the chair beside her, while Donner sat at the head of the conference table. "From the conversation he had with Samantha, my guess would be worry over her presence."

"I know how he feels. You are being a little friendly with his job competition."

"Which I would hope doesn't give him free rein to blow her up," Rick said sharply.

"If."

"Yes, 'if.' But that's not what I mean. He made a point of saying he knew you were an expert, didn't he, Sam?"

She nodded. "Yes."

Richard had positioned himself so he could see the door, and as soon as Danté Partino entered the room in the company of Frank Castillo, he knew. The excitable Italian was quiet but couldn't seem to keep still, tugging on his right ear and cracking his knuckles until Richard was half-surprised his fingers didn't fall off.

In business dealings this was the moment Richard always looked forward to, the moment when his opposition had realized they had no chance against him and that he was about to drop the hammer. Today he had to clench a fist against his thigh to keep from hurling himself across the table and beating the bloody hell out of his art acquisitions manager.

"Rick, Tom, everyone is well, yes? The police made me evacuate my office." Partino's eyes edged toward Samantha, then away again without making contact.

Dead man, Richard said to himself. Danté Partino was a dead man. "Yes, we're all fine," he returned smoothly, offering his calm, professional smile.

"Mr. Partino," Castillo said, taking another seat at the large mahogany table, "I'd like to ask you a couple of questions just to clarify some points in the burglary investigation."

"Of course. Anything I can do to help."

"The tablet. You said its value was approximately one and a half million dollars."

"That's right."

"What did you base that on?"

Richard shifted impatiently. This wasn't about the damned tablet; it was about who'd tried to kill Samantha. She didn't seem to mind the turn of the conversation, though. In fact, she snagged a few blank sheets of paper from Donner and was making pencil drawings of koi. She was actually pretty good. He wondered if she'd had formal training or if it was natural ability. Natural ability, probably. Sam Jellicoe, Renaissance woman.

"Um, value is always based on comparisons with other, similar objects and what they have been selling for."

"But I thought only three of these existed in the entire world. Have any been sold lately?"

"No. But Rick's original purchase price in January was a little over a million dollars, and the Greek-and-Roman-collectibles market has been quite strong over the last few months. I keep up with all the auctions and public sales. It is part of my job."

"What about the other destroyed pieces?"

"The same rule applies. The value of the armor is generally much easier to judge, since there is more of it on the market. A few of the pieces, unfortunately, were very rare, and their insurance value is accordingly placed much higher. I'm sure Tom could give you that information—the claims are settled through his office."

Samantha continued to sketch, seemingly paying no attention to the conversation going on around her. Considering that they'd held it here for her benefit, Richard began to feel a little annoyed. "What are you doing?" he muttered.

"Seeing into the future."

Danté glanced at the page upon which she was sketching. Unless Richard was mistaken, the estate manager's ruddy complexion paled a little. He looked down, himself—and stifled the abrupt urge to smile. She'd moved on from fish, and was drawing a very nice scaffold and hangman's noose. He didn't know if she had an innate sense of how to play "good cop/bad cop," or if she was angry as well and simply choosing her own method of showing it.

"What's the procedure with the damaged but repairable items?" Castillo the good cop pursued, jotting down notes on his pocket pad.

Samantha began sketching the hanging victim, who had dark, gel-slicked hair and wore the exact suit Danté currently had on.

"They are assessed by both the insurance company and a reputable art expert. If repairs will not harm the value of the object and can be made without compromising its authenticity, then they are authorized. If not, the insurance pays a compensatory amount based on the reduced value of the item."

"So the owner really loses no money whether an item is stolen or destroyed."

Partino nodded eagerly. "Precisely. In fact, if an item is known to be weakening on the market, destroying it immediately might be to the monetary benefit of the owner."

"Your point being?" Richard asked sharply.

"I am only answering the detective's questions, Rick. I have a responsibility to tell the truth." He sat forward. "And that is why I must tell you that your female friend here is an art thief."

Samantha's hand stilled, and she slowly looked up to meet Danté's gaze with glittering eyes. "Beg pardon?"

"Yes. Her father died in prison as a known art thief. In fact, I wouldn't be surprised if she has the tablet, and tried to kill me with the first bomb so that I couldn't discover who she was. She can't be trusted."

"And the second bomb?" Richard asked, clenching his fist so hard his fingers were going numb.

"To make herself look innocent, undoubtedly. Have you searched her belongings, Detective Castillo?"

"They might believe you, Partino, if you hadn't hired a chimpanzee to make the fake for you," Samantha retorted, rising and flinging the pencil and paper in the estate manager's face before either Rick or Castillo could make a move to stop her. "No wonder you tried to kill me before I could take a good look at it, but you'd have to blow up everybody over the age of seven if you wanted to keep that shit a secret."

"You know nothing," Danté returned, standing opposite her and slamming a fist against the table. "I know you tried to kill me, and nothing you say will change that. The police will find out the truth."

"They already have," she shot back. "You just placed yourself close to the first bomb, and nobody said I was close to the second one—except for you. So it's too bad you don't have the original tablet, because you could probably use the money from it to buy your way out of a murder conviction, you stupid fuck."

"Bitch!" he yowled, lurching across the table at her.

Donner and Castillo grabbed him by either shoulder and shoved him back into his chair. At the same time Richard shot to his feet and pushed in front of Samantha. "Enough!" he bellowed.

"What did you use for a mold?" Samantha taunted from over his shoulder, "Play-Doh? Or did you have somebody do it freehand with a sledgehammer?"

"I'm not saying anything! I want a lawyer!"

"You'd better get one," Castillo said grimly. "Danté Partino, you're under arrest for attempted murder and theft and whatever the hell else I can think of on the way to the station."

"No! I didn't do anything! It was her! I didn't take anything! She has the forgery!"

Richard stormed around the table and grabbed Partino by his tie. "What forgery?" he growled.

Partino's face went white. With an audible gulp he clamped his mouth shut. "I want a lawyer," was all he said, and he kept repeating it while Castillo called in a uniformed officer with a pair of handcuffs.

When the acquisitions manager—former acquisitions manager—had been escorted from the room, Castillo faced Richard again. "I'll need the fake," he said.

"I'll get it for you."

"I'm going with you. Evidence contamination and all that."

They left the room, though Richard paused long enough to send warning looks at both Samantha and Donner before he exited. Tempers were already high, and he didn't want to come back to find one or both of them bloodied.

"Partino's right about Jellicoe, you know," the detective said conversationally.

For a moment Richard kept silent. "And you have proof?" he finally asked.

"No. If I did, she'd be in handcuffs right along with Partino."

"Then she's innocent until proven otherwise," Richard returned. "That is still the creed you Yanks go by, isn't it?"

"Yeah. You're not surprised by the accusation, though." Castillo glanced sideways at him. "I figured you wouldn't be."

"As far as I'm concerned, she's done nothing wrong. Her father was the convict. Not Samantha."

Castillo sighed. "She's a pretty toy, Mr. Addison, but if I were you, I'd keep one hand on my wallet. She's as slick as they come. Hell, I've been catching crooks for twenty years, and I'd still be tempted to give her a head start."

"You're not me."

"That's right. And if I do uncover something, she's going to jail."

"You won't uncover anything." He wasn't quite as certain as he sounded, but neither did he doubt Samantha's creativity or cleverness. Castillo wouldn't find anything—not here, anyway.

In Samantha's room, still littered with members of the bomb squad investigative unit, he lifted the knapsack from the couch and pulled the faux artifact free of its protective cloth. "Here you are."

"And you found this in your trunk, with her bags."

"Yes."

"This morning."

"Yes."

"Tell me again why you didn't let me know that when I was in the garage with you?"

Richard gave his charming smile. "It took us a little by surprise."

Nodding, Castillo took the wrap and put it back over the fake tablet. "Okay. I'll have my expert verify that it's not genuine. My take is that Partino saw that nice photo of you and Sam in the paper this morning and decided he needed to protect himself and his job. He planted the tablet so everybody would stop looking for the real one, then he planted the grenades to keep anybody from figuring out the tablet he'd placed in her bags was a phony."

"I'd agree with that."

"Yeah. Proving it'll be a little tougher. And I still need to know why he had a fake, where he got the grenades, and where the original is."

All three questions troubled Richard, as well. Why steal a tablet and keep the fake hidden when he could have used it to disguise the robbery? Or if, as Samantha thought, her friend Etienne DeVore had taken the tablet, why did Partino have a fake? And why the first set of explosives?

Dammit, everywhere he turned he found more questions than answers. And whether Danté was under arrest or not, he couldn't shake the feeling that this wasn't over. He left Castillo at the front door and went back upstairs to his office. "Where's Samantha?" he asked as soon as he stepped into the room.

Donner sat alone at the conference table, flipping through the newspaper. "She said she was starving and went to get something to eat."

"Right." He'd forgotten that neither of them had eaten since dessert at Rooney's last night. "Want a sandwich, then?"

"No." Another page turned.

With a tired grimace, Richard sat at the table. "So what do you think of all this?"

"You don't want to know, Rick."

"Mm-hm. I'm going to tell you to speak now or forever hold your peace, Tom."

"Okay." The attorney flicked the newspaper closed. "One, you're sleeping with a known thief. Two, if that tablet you found had been the original, you'd be under arrest right now for insurance fraud. Three, you let Danté go to jail without so much as blinking. Four, I don't think you commit two—

three, almost—murders over a stone tablet. So fifth and last, what do you commit multiple murders for?"

"Danté had something to do with this."

"Enough to let him get thrown in jail? Hell, you've only know Danté for ten years, so why not toss him away at the urging of someone you've known for under a week and whom you caught breaking into your estate twice?"

Had it really been less than a week? Decisiveness had never been a problem for him, but Christ. "If Danté had nothing to do with this, I'll have your firm defend him. Honestly though, Tom, who do you think's more likely to be lying?"

Donner glared at him, then stood to pull a bottle of water out of the fridge. "Crap. Between you and me, I think if Jellicoe had done it, she wouldn't be here. And she wouldn't be trying to pin it on someone else."

"Wow. I bet that hurt." Despite the joke, Richard felt somewhat grateful. What Donner would say if he knew how strongly Sam seemed to suspect the attorney, he didn't want to speculate.

"You have no idea." Taking a swig of water, the attorney headed for the door. "I'm going to go down and see that Danté has proper representation. It'll make us look better in the long run, anyway. Someone has to keep you popular with the media and the local community."

Richard joined him as they walked down the hallway. "I choose not to comment on that. But if he did as I suspect, he'd best stay in jail for his own protection."

At the front door, Donner stopped again. "Okay, one more question."

"Yes?"

"You and Jellicoe. Serious?"

"I don't know." Part of him didn't want to think about it. She was there, and he enjoyed having her around. As Tom had pointed out, they'd known one another for less than a week. It would take more than a week to figure this out—to figure her out.

"That ain't good," Donner returned with an exaggerated

drawl. "Why don't the two of you come over for dinner tonight?"

Richard grinned before he could stop himself. "Are you kidding me?"

"No. I mentioned her to Kate—not any of the particulars, don't worry about that—and she suggested you come over for dinner. Some chicken parmesan thing, probably. About seven?"

"Sure. Why not?"

Eighteen

Sunday, 3:21 p.m.

Samantha watched as Hans trimmed the crust off a fine-looking cucumber sandwich. "You are an artist," she stated, resting both elbows on the counter.

The tall Swede glanced at her. "It is only a sandwich, miss."

"Sam. And yes, it is, but I always do things in such a hurry." Frequently, in fact, she forgot to eat until her stomach reminded her. That was one of the oddest and most compelling things about being in Rick's company; she could take time and watch him grill steak or wait while his world-renowned chef made her a sandwich, and then take the time to enjoy it. "There's a . . . peace about cooking, isn't there?"

Hans smiled. "I think you may be an artist, as well." He handed over the china plate and pulled a chilled can of Diet Coke from the beverage refrigerator. "Most of Mr. Addison's guests don't know where the kitchen is, much less notice the way their crust is cut."

"Their loss. It's all in the details, Hans."

Armed with lunch, she headed upstairs. It would serve

Donner right if she returned to the office and ate in front of him, but she needed to think and so headed for the library. It was one floor up and half a wing away from Rick's office, but according to Hans, it was also one of the most interesting walks in the house.

She didn't know whether Rick personally acquired the pieces for his collection or whether he assigned the job to underlings like Partino, but the mix was both eclectic and fascinating. She could only imagine what treasures his other houses contained. A shame she'd never see them, since the only way to do that would be to commit a robbery, and she wouldn't attempt to steal from him again.

A wall mosaic of Roman floor tiles, red and blue and yellow, meandered all along part of one hallway. Carefully she ran a free finger along the delicate ceramics, awestruck at the idea that citizens of Rome had walked on them four thousand years ago. A display of Roman coins behind a protective glass shelf came next, followed by a stand of Roman spears and helmets.

She wondered how significant it was that so much of what Rick collected had belonged to warriors: knights, centurions, Samurai, Conquistadors. He was something of a warrior in the business world, she supposed, and judging by the quality and quantity of his possessions and conquests, he was the twenty-first century's equivalent of Alexander the Great—or Genghis Khan.

Sam stopped in the library doorway. "Holy crap," she muttered.

One entire wall consisted of floor-to-ceiling windows. The other three were lined with books, with more freestanding shelves spaced at intervals across the room. He even had a college-sized research table on one side, and of course classical marble busts of Greek deities at the ends of the shelves. If she'd been in a thieving mood, the stuff here would have had her in raptures. Even doing a straight stint, goose bumps rose along her bare arms.

Putting her lunch on the table, she went to browse. The

contents of the shelves were even more impressive than the busts. First editions of everything from Twain to Stoker, and even a first folio of Shakespeare's *The Tempest* stood behind a glass-enclosed shelf.

In a few minutes she'd figured out the system and found a book on Greek antiquities. The trail of the three Trojan tablets had been fairly legitimate—at least over the past three hundred years or so, and because of their rarity they'd also been photographed on numerous occasions by several historical researchers. They were some of the very few writings widely believed to originate in Troy, though even that remained a subject of argument and speculation. At any rate, they were ridiculously old and precious.

With one currently missing, the remaining two in Hamburg and Istanbul became more valuable than ever. It was probably time someone figured out precisely where they were—and whether anyone had tried to steal them, lately.

"I don't know what you said to my chef," Rick's voice came from the doorway, "but he's now creating a dessert of some kind in your honor."

She grinned. "Just so it's not Jellicoe Jell-O or something."

"How charming were you?"

"I just asked for a sandwich," she said, licking mayonnaise off her finger and turning a page, "and complimented him on his culinary skills. I'd heard somewhere that his coffee won an award."

"Well, whatever you did, Hans was practically giddy when I was in there a moment ago," the cultured British accent continued, low and musical.

She shrugged. "All I asked for was peanut butter and jelly, but he thought jam would better suit my sophisticated palate, and I ended up with a cucumber sandwich on rye." And some very nice chocolates, which she'd already eaten.

"Perhaps he was looking for a polite way to say that you can't tell your jellies from your jams," Rick said with a chuckle.

"Yes, but who can, these days? Oh, and by the way, you'll

be stocking peppermint ice cream from now on. Hans put in an order once he found out it was my favorite."

"Have you ever met anyone you couldn't charm?" he murmured.

"There's Donner." She glanced at him over her shoulder, smiling at his somber expression. "I'm just charming, Batman. Can't help it."

"So you are. And amazingly hot, as well." He strolled up behind her and slid his hands along her shoulders.

"Careful of my stitches," she muttered, trying to concentrate. Finally, she found the page she'd been looking for. Sam set aside the sandwich, wiped her fingers on her napkin, and tugged the book closer.

His grip on her tightened for a moment, then relaxed again. "What are you doing?"

"Trying to figure out the location of the other tablets."

"And why is that?"

She glanced up over her shoulder at him. The bland, cool look on his face didn't surprise her in the least. He was angry.

"Oh, I don't know," she drawled. "I missed yours, but there are still two other tablets out there."

"Don't you dare," he said in a low, hard voice.

"You know," she returned, shrugging out from under his hands, "I think you should set aside a little of that income of yours to buy yourself a sense of humor."

For a moment he was silent. "You need to realize that despite our . . . intimacy, I really don't know you all that well."

"In that case, *you* need to realize that ordering me to do something is very likely to piss me off and make me do the opposite just to aggravate you."

He pulled out the chair beside her and sat. "Point taken. So why are you really after the location of the other tablets?"

"You learn fast, anyway," she grumbled. "I need to know where they are so I can do a little research and find out if anyone's tried to steal them recently."

"I can call my office in London and probably find out who owns the pieces," he offered.

She looked sideways at him, a blush creeping up her cheeks. "Okay, this is a stupid question, but what sort of business do you do?"

Rick laughed. "You don't know?"

Sam shrugged, her color deepening. "I didn't have time to read most of the Internet articles. You buy things and sell them, but I figured there had to be more to it than that."

"Ah. As the saying goes, I have my finger in several pies, but yes, mostly I purchase properties, improve or renovate them, and sell them again. On occasion I'll acquire an entire business for the same purpose."

"So what are you going to do with WNBT?"

He smiled. "Well, the Godzilla programming seems fairly popular. Maybe we'll go with all monsters, all the time."

"Cool."

"Actually, the station's been running at a loss for the past four years. My idea is to bring in a few of my people and see what we can do to fix that little problem."

"You have people," she repeated. She knew that, of course, but she couldn't help being curious to learn more about him. The whole time she'd been there, he'd been so focused on her that it seemed almost odd to remember that he had a job—a very successful business empire—that needed his attention.

"Tom's one of my people. I have others."

"How many?"

"It varies. Somewhere around six or seven hundred at the moment, I would imagine. That includes architects, contractors, carpenters, accountants, computer programmers, attorneys, my secretary, butlers, and whoever else I need for whichever projects we're working on."

"Cool," she repeated. His statement, though, brought another question to mind. "And why am I here?"

"We have a partnership," he returned. "One that you proposed."

So she had. But the rest of this, she'd never anticipated. And she would never have planned anything more than conning him into assisting her, then bolting, because being with him was very bad for business. Bad for business—and for her peace of mind. "And why are we sleeping together, then?"

"Because we want to. To be perfectly honest, Samantha, you fascinate me. I find getting you out of my thoughts to be an impossibility."

She cleared her throat. "That can't be good."

He sat closer, feathering her hair behind her ear with gentle, clever fingers. "Why not? Do you want to be somewhere else right now?"

Yeah—naked in his bed again with his warm, hard body inside hers. "Well, this place is pretty nice."

A muscle in his jaw twitched, and before she could talk herself out of it, she leaned in to kiss him.

He kissed her back, teasing and pulling, molding his mouth to hers while heat arrowed down her spine. Sam tangled her fingers into his hair, moaning softly as his mouth made promises she hoped his body would keep.

"You taste like a garden," he murmured, lifting her onto his lap.

Beneath her thighs she could feel him already, hard and ready. "It's the cucumbers."

"No, it's you," he corrected with a low chuckle, running a hand up under her shirt to cup her breast.

Sam gasped as his fingers crept beneath her bra to glide across her nipple. Jesus. They'd spent the night doing this, and had only been out of bed for five or six hours, and already she craved his touch, his caress, his heat again. When his tongue and lips found the base of her jaw she went boneless, sinking into his embrace.

He pulled off the loose shirt and the tank top she wore under it, tossing them onto the floor behind them. Her bra followed a moment later, and both his hands went to work, fingers rubbing and gently tugging.

"I hope to hell you have body armor with you," she moaned, pulling his shirt from his trousers and undoing the buttons.

"I actually put some in my wallet this morning," he returned, laughter in his voice. "I haven't done that since college."

"Smart boy."

His cell phone rang. "Shit."

There was no question about whether he would answer it or not. Sam merely turned her attention to kissing his throat as he pulled the phone free and flipped it open.

"Addison."

She felt the muscles tense across his chest, and lifted her head. His face had gone still, all of his attention focused on the other end of the phone. For a long moment he said nothing. Then his gaze met hers.

"She should hear it from you," he said, and handed the phone to her. "Walter," he said, his voice low and hard.

Her heart jumped as she lifted the receiver to her ear. "Stoney?"

"Hey, darlin'. I tried O'Hannon's phone again this morning, and a cop answered it. He wouldn't give me any details, and I had to hang up before they traced my call, but Sean O'Hannon's dead."

Sam took a breath. She didn't like Sean O'Hannon—never had, and never would. But he had worked in her realm and was one of her kind. And he'd been involved, somehow, with the Trojan tablet. "Do you have any idea how it happened?"

"The cop—bobby, whatever they call 'em there—said an explosion. That's all I know." He was silent for a moment. "Sam, I'm gonna disappear for a few days. I'm thinking you should do the same."

Rick slid his arms around her, not in passion now, but in comfort. She leaned her head against his shoulder. "Be careful," she said. "You call me at this number as soon as you can and let me know you made it."

"That number?" he repeated, the tone of his voice changing a little. "So you're staying with the rich guy?"

"If I don't, I'll steal his cell phone," she answered, though that was only for Stoney's benefit. She wasn't going anywhere.

"Fair enough. Keep your head down, baby."

"You, too."

The phone clicked dead, and she handed it back to Rick. He put it on the worktable, keeping his arms around her and slowly rocking back and forth. Why was it, she wondered, when in reality it couldn't possibly make the least bit of difference, that she felt so safe in his arms? She drew another slow, deep breath, trying to collect her thoughts, and her emotions. God, she'd been so hot for him a moment ago.

"We should tell Castillo," she suggested, and felt his approving nod against her cheek. "But only that I knew O'Hannon, and that he had expressed an interest in Trojan tablets and now he's dead. Not that Stoney had anything to do with anything."

"Stoney who?" he agreed, his low voice reverberating against her shoulder.

"I, um, should get dressed," she said, becoming very conscious that she was naked from the waist up.

"I suppose so. For now." Holding her a little away from him, he kissed her again, long and slow and deep. "You're certain you're all right?"

"Yeah. My little band of bad guys seems to be shrinking at an alarming rate, but hey, it's all part of the excitement of the job, right?"

"Right." He hugged her again, then helped her off his lap and back to her feet so she could gather up her bra and shirts. "Why don't you see if you can narrow down the location of the other two tablets a little, and I'll get on the phone with Castillo. It's"—and he looked at his watch—a Rolex, of course—"eight at night in London, so I'll give Sarah a call at home."

Sam paused. "Sarah?"

"My secretary." A small, wicked grin touched his sensuous mouth. "She's very loyal, and sensitive to all my needs."

"I bet."

What did she care? She'd only known him a few days, and in a few days more they would go their separate ways, and she'd never set eyes on him again, except as the subject of a special on *E!* or something. As Partino had intimated, she hadn't been his first, and she certainly wouldn't be his last.

He caught her arm as she pulled on her loose shirt over the tank. "I'm a rather single-minded individual, Samantha. And I've already told you, you have my attention."

"I'm not jealous, Addison." She took her seat again. "You're fun. Now move it. I'm busy." Ha. That would show him. He hadn't been her first, either.

"Fun," he said slowly, not moving from his stance behind her. "I'm fun."

"Yes. Go away and buy an island or something."

Before she could finish her smirk he yanked her chair, tilting it back on two legs. She flailed, trying to keep her balance, while he leaned over to look down at her upturned face. "Telling me what to do is a good way to convince me to do the opposite, just to spite you," he murmured, and covered her mouth with his in an upside-down kiss that curled her toes.

"Point taken," she managed, grabbing on to the edge of the table to pull herself upright again.

"Not yet, but you'll take it soon," he whispered, and strolled out of the room, whistling.

"Shit," she muttered, shivering, and went back to the book.

As he finished his conversation with Frank Castillo and hung up his office phone, Richard realized that he hadn't informed Samantha they would be dining out that evening. Well, it would undoubtedly cause an argument, and considering the day she'd had so far, he'd give her a bit more time to recover herself.

Castillo had been highly interested in the demise of Sean O'Hannon, though if anything it made more trouble for the police where Danté Partino was concerned. With a death in England, Partino had likely had a very limited role in this mess, if any at all.

He sat there, gazing out over his garden and pond. When he'd flown in from Stuttgart last week, he'd intended to buy a television station, spend a day or two relaxing with Tom Donner and his family, arrange for Danté to ship the tablet to the British Museum, and with a handful of business detours follow it back so he could stay a few weeks at his main house in Devon.

Instead he'd nearly been blown up, had the tablet stolen, missed the deadline on WNBT, gotten Tom thrown into his pool, and met Samantha Jellicoe.

Of course there were additional highlights: dead thieves, mysterious tails, Sam nearly getting killed in the room he'd given her, fake tablets, a man he'd known and trusted for ten years arrested, and some really fine sex.

Samantha had called him "fun." While he had no personal objection to the term, he knew what she meant by it, and that was what he didn't like. "Fun" meant something you did for an afternoon or while you had nothing better to do.

That should have been perfectly agreeable to him—but it wasn't. In the American vernacular, it pissed him off. He still wanted her in his bed, in his arms. And if he wasn't finished with her, she wasn't allowed to be finished with him.

Whichever body part he was thinking with, though, he was well aware that there was more to this than the vertical and horizontal maneuverings of the two of them. O'Hannon's death meant that for certain someone else was involved. As far as he could tell, the number of people who had something to do with the tablet for one reason or other was at least six: Samantha, Stoney, DeVore, Partino, O'Hannon, and whoever had killed O'Hannon.

"Why?" he muttered to himself. Yes, it was rare and valuable, but so were a great many other things. Why this one, why here, why now?

Someone knocked at his door. "Come in," he called, then remembered that he'd locked it for his phone call to Castillo. He started to rise, but the door swung open before he could get to his feet.

"Okay," Samantha said, pocketing something that looked like a paper clip, "tablet number one is in the possession of

Gustav Harving in Hamburg. Number two belongs to the Arutani family in Istanbul, but apparently there are several prominent families by that name."

"Good enough for a start. I'll call Sarah. We should actually be able to do this through completely legitimate connections."

She gave a brief smile. "That'll be a nice change, won't it?"

He had a few other things he needed to go over with his secretary, but he preferred to discuss them without Samantha being present. "Do you have plans for this afternoon?" he asked.

"Yeah," she answered, her voice rich with sarcasm. "*Godzilla vs. Mechagodzilla*. How about you?"

With a chuckle, he rose. "Might I join you? You can explain the finer points of giant monster warfare to me."

"Sure." She shrugged, studying his expression. "You want me to leave you alone now, right? Just sit around and not do anything?"

"And stay out of trouble," he added. "I need to make a few more phone calls. I won't be long."

"I'll be in my room, then."

She turned on her heel, but he caught up to her, sliding a hand down her arm. "I thought we might go out for dinner again tonight," he said, wondering how she would react to what he was about to tell her. Damn, she kept him on his toes.

"Okay. Won't Hans be hurt, though? He does worship me, and I was hoping for an ice sculpture carved in my likeness."

"It'd melt in a second flat. And Hans will survive." Richard kissed her cheek. "I'll call Kate and confirm."

She stiffened. "Kate? Kate who?"

"Kate Donner. Tom's wife. They've invited us over for dinner."

Her expression folded into a comical mix of horror and disbelief. "You're kidding me, right?"

"Nope. We're to be there at seven."

Sam backed toward the door. "No way. Forget it. I am not doing the domestic."

"It's just one evening," he cajoled, advancing as she retreated, in their own private version of the double-dare tango. "The Donners are just about my only venture into the domestic, as you call it. I happen to enjoy it."

"I'll tell you what," she returned, running a hand down his chest. "We stay here, and you can have your way with me."

Richard grinned. "I intend to do that anyway, when we return." He kissed her again, this time on her warm and soft mouth. "You like new experiences," he said. "This'll be one for you."

With a grimace she unlocked his door and pulled it open again. "Fine. But only because I owe you, Brit."

"Thanks, Yank."

Nineteen

Sunday, 5:48 p.m.

Samantha could hear the soft whir of her father spinning in his grave. By no stretch of the imagination would Martin Jellicoe have been able to picture his daughter preparing for a date with Richard Addison—at an attorney's house, of all things. He wouldn't see any profit in it, and even worse, he would happily point out that the venture had the high likelihood of a negative outcome for her.

She had her own reservations, but they were more along the lines of just how deeply she was becoming involved with this man. Sex was one thing; and supremely pleasurable as it had been, it had also put Rick firmly on her side. She'd be an idiot not to make good use of that and not to be flattered by it. But dating him was a whole different matter. It wasn't just her looking after her own best interests; it was becoming entangled, meeting his friends, passing herself off as what—his girlfriend? His lover?

Her heart beginning to pound, Sam dug into her closet of borrowed clothes. "What the hell am I supposed to wear?"

From the sitting room she could hear Rick laughing at her.

"Wear whatever you want. But Godzilla's attacking the mechanical one. I thought you said Godzilla was always bad."

Picking a sundress, she walked to the bedroom door. "No, I said he was best when he was bad. How does this look?" She held up the short red and yellow dress.

He craned his neck to look over the back of the couch. "It's nice. But—"

She scowled. "But what?"

"The scratches and cuts on your back will show."

Crap. With the antiseptic Dr. Klemm had given her, the cuts had stopped hurting, and she kept forgetting about them. "What are you going to wear?"

"What I've got on."

"But you look nice."

"Thank you. I'll spill something on my shirt, if you like."

He was teasing her again, as he had been from the moment he realized that the idea of dining with Tom and Kate Donner unsettled her. She'd agreed to go, though, partly because he'd intimated that she was a coward if she refused, but mostly because after he'd charged to her rescue with the grenades that morning, she'd felt like she owed him something.

"Found anything?" Rick asked, leaning into the closet.

"Go back and tell me what's happening," she said. "I'll show you what I find."

"Something in green would be nice. In honor of Godzilla."

"Get back to the couch, fella."

He raised his hands in mock surrender. "All right, all right."

Despite herself she was chuckling, which in itself was frightening. She couldn't be that connected to him yet, that seeing him happy made her happy.

This new life was so strange—and so tempting. She shook herself, pulling another summery dress off its hanger and shutting the closet door so she could try it on without him commenting on it. She needed to stop being distracted by the soft pleasures of this life. In her line of work, softness equaled imprisonment—or death. Work. She was working, trying to figure out what was going on.

And while she might still have a halfhearted question or two about Donner's involvement, she had none regarding Danté Partino's. When the cops had carted off the estate manager, they'd also taken boxes of paperwork from his office. For such a prissy man, he'd kept a cluttered work area, but she hadn't commented on that. Rather, she intended to visit it later tonight to see what might be left. If that failed, finding out where Partino lived should be simple enough. Since Rick had taken the tracking down of the other two tablets out of her hands, she needed to do something. Sitting on her ass drove her crazy, and she wasn't about to forget that someone seemed to want her dead. As opposed to Addison, who just wanted her.

"Okay, how's this?" she asked, putting a firm clamp on her nerves. She would fit in tonight, because that was what she did. If not for Addison's irritating ability to decipher exactly what she was thinking and feeling, she would count this evening as an easy job. Okay, fairly easy.

"You did pick green," he said, standing again.

"It has short sleeves and a high back," she explained patiently. "If you think I look like the monster who ate Tokyo, though, I'll go change again."

"You don't look like Godzilla," he returned, the warm smile lighting his lean, handsome face. "You look great."

Sam blew out her breath. "Good. Now for hair and makeup."

"You don't need any."

"Good answer, but I'm not asking for flattery. I want to look . . . nice. Like for normal people. I assume Mrs. Donner is normal, anyway. I know Harvard isn't."

"You got on Tom's bad side, since he thinks people occasionally try to take advantage of me. He really is fairly normal—though my experience in that area is rather limited."

"Mine, too." The big battle between the Godzillas was

heating up, so she took the seat beside Rick on the couch. Makeup could wait until Tokyo was saved. "May I make a guess?" she asked after a moment, slanting him a look.

He was still gazing at her. "Of course."

"No one takes advantage of you, do they? Ever."

"Nope."

"But your friend Peter Wallis did."

His jaw clenched. "There's one exception to every rule, I suppose."

"Just one?" she returned.

"You're talking about Danté, I presume?"

She'd meant Donner, but nodded anyway. "You trusted him."

"I did, but it's not the same. I've known him for a while, but he's not in the same category as Peter. And because of Peter, I choose my friends carefully these days, Sam. I've been disappointed once. It won't happen again."

She met his gaze again. "So which category am I in?"

Gray eyes touched hers. "You're a whole new category, I'm afraid." He ran a hand slowly up her thigh. "A very interesting one."

Heat began at the point of contact and slid up her leg. "Okay, another question."

"You're making me miss the movie, Yank."

She ignored the protest; he obviously had no true appreciation of campy monster movies. "You've been sitting on this couch with me for half an hour, and you're being a perfect gentleman."

"Ah. You mean why aren't we naked and making passionate love to one another?"

Oh, boy. "Yes, something like that."

"Because we have to be somewhere in an hour, and I don't want to rush right now."

"You did this afternoon."

"That was before we heard about O'Hannon. Now I find myself . . . concerned over your continued safety, and I intend to take my time with you later tonight and savor every inch of your very attractive body."

She shivered. God, he made her feel so . . . weak. "It won't last, you know," she said, trying to put some mental distance between them.

A frown furrowed his fine brow. "What won't last?"

"This." She gestured between them. "You and me. Face it, we're novelties to each other. But this is almost figured out. Once we know who has possession of the tablet, the story's over. I have no reason to stay, and you certainly have better things to do than screw me."

He stood, anger in the precise, spare movement. "Nice. I'm going to get a beer. Meet me downstairs at half past six."

"Fine."

Halfway to her door he stopped and turned around, stalking back up to her and placing his hands on her knees so their faces were inches apart. "A lot of people have thought they had me figured out," he said in a low voice, eyes glinting, "and a lot of people have regretted making that assumption."

"Rick, it's just a fact. I'm not—"

"You've given me what I assume to be your opinion on several occasions now. I would appreciate if you would wait until I offer my own before you chisel it in stone on my behalf."

With that he was gone, the door closing gently behind him in spite of—and probably because of—the fact that she would prefer he slam it. Dammit. Nobody was this difficult to figure out. She was good at assessing people's character in a few seconds. Her life frequently depended on her skills in that department. Addison seemed genuinely worried about her and genuinely insulted that she didn't consider this a possible long-term relationship.

Solve this and get out. That was the solution. She was here on her own terms, and for her own reasons. When she left it would be because *she* wanted to, not because he decided it was time for her to shove off. As she returned her attention to the humongous television, Mechagodzilla went down for the count. Ha. At least some things in the world went the way they were supposed to.

She put on her makeup and did her hair about five times before she was satisfied that it looked presentable, then deliberately waited until twenty minutes to seven before she appeared downstairs. Richard Addison could dictate all he wanted, and she could just as easily remind him that she was an independent contractor.

While she anticipated him being angry and pacing in the foyer, waiting for her, she actually had to go and find him out on the pool deck and nursing what smelled like gin. "Ready?" she asked, unable to keep the snippiness from her tone.

He stood. "Is it time?"

She would have given him the raspberry, but then he would know that he'd annoyed her. Instead Sam nodded, leading the way out to the front drive.

The blue Bentley sat—no, crouched ready to leap forward—in front of the steps. Despite herself, a low thrill ran up her spine. She was going to ride in a goddamned Bentley.

"Here," he said, and tossed her the keys.

Sam started to comment that she didn't have a valid driver's license, but luckily talked herself out of that stupidity almost before the thought could form. "Oh, Mama," she sang, sliding behind the wheel as Ben held the door for her.

"How much is this thing worth?" she asked, turning over the engine and gunning the motor for the hell of it.

"A lot. Try not to kill us."

Unable to hide her wide grin, Sam punched the car into gear and smashed her foot down on the accelerator. They flew down the drive and barely missed clipping the gate on both sides as the surprised cops leapt out of the way.

"Which way?"

"Turn right at the intersection. I'll give you directions from there." He'd buckled on his seat belt, but other than that didn't seem concerned about any damage she might do.

Once they'd left estate row and crossed the bridge to reach

the wealthy, more uniform residential neighborhoods of
Palm Beach she slowed to a more conservative pace. In this
part of town kids on bikes and roller blades and razors cluttered the sidewalks, and she certainly didn't want to damage
any of them. They all looked so . . . oblivious to the idea that
bad people existed in the world. She couldn't remember ever
being that naive. A horrifying thought struck her.

"They don't have kids, do they?"

"Turn right," he said, adjusting the airflow from the vent
on his side of the car.

"Oh, good God. You didn't tell me there'd be kids."

"You were one once," he said, amusement deepening his
voice. "I'm certain you'll cope."

"I was never a kid. How old are they?"

"Chris is nineteen, but he's not home. The semester's
started at Yale."

"Yale. That's far away. So far, so good. Now give me the
bad news."

He chuckled. "Mike's fourteen, and Olivia is nine."

Sam groaned. "This is a damned ambush."

"No, it's not. They're great kids. And Kate's a good cook.
The third house on the left."

The houses here were austere, with large yards and gates
for privacy. The Donners' was ungated, but had a nice white
picket fence running along the street side just for appearance's sake. Holy cow, a white picket fence.

Richard kept his attention on Samantha as they turned up
the short drive. He'd cheated by not giving her all the details,
but she'd made him mad, so fair was fair.

From her reaction this really was her first trip to suburbia—
or at least her first trip to a nice, normal family's home for dinner in suburbia. The house of hers the police had ransacked
was in the middle of a run-down housing tract, but somehow
he doubted that she socialized much with her neighbors.
From the official report, none of them had known her as anything but that nice, quiet niece of Juanita Fuentes.

She put the Bentley into park but didn't turn off the engine.

Instead, she sat there looking as though she'd like nothing better than for a hurricane to hit and sweep them into the ocean.

"Come on. Take a deep breath, and let's go in."

Giving him the evil eye, she shut off the car and opened the door. Then she froze again. "Shit. We weren't supposed to bring them a present or something, were we?"

Richard wondered if Jane had had this much trouble with Tarzan's first polite family dinner. It would be fun, guiding her into civilization. "I took care of it. Pop the boot."

"Trunk, Addison. If I can't say jelly, you can't say boot."

He wasn't going to argue with her at the moment, but dug for a pair of small, wrapped gifts. "Shall I carry them, or do you want to?" he asked, closing the boot—trunk—with one elbow.

"I'll drop 'em." She scowled, falling into step beside him as they walked up the cobbled path to the double front doors. "No, give me one. It'll give me something to do with my hands."

Judging which of the two presents was the less breakable, he handed it over to her, then jabbed the bell with a forefinger. He'd also declined to tell her that she looked more than great; with her wavy hair loose around her shoulders and her lips tinted a faint bronze, she was stunning. She'd done something with her eyes, as well; the green of the dress deepened their color to emerald, with impossibly long, black lashes.

"Okay, they're not home," she said after about five seconds. Let's go."

"Coward."

That got her attention, as he'd thought it would. Her back went ramrod straight, and her lips thinned as she clenched her jaw. "I faced a damned grenade today," she growled. "Two of them."

The door swung open. "Then this should be easy," he murmured, and stepped forward to greet Tom.

He'd always liked the Donners' house. It felt . . . warm,

and intimate and inviting, in a way a twenty-acre estate never could. This was a home where people lived, not a showplace where one entertained heads of state and held charity balls and stayed for a month or two out of the entire year.

"Kate's still in the kitchen," Tom said, closing the door behind them. He tried to cover it, but Richard saw the appraising look he gave Samantha. She'd be in for more in a moment, but warning her would only have made her bolt.

Or maybe it wouldn't. Samantha shook Tom's hand, giving him a warm grin and showing no sign that she considered him some sort of archnemesis. "This is nice."

"Thanks. We tore the old house on the lot down about six years ago and had this one built. We're still tweaking, but that's part of the fun," Donner replied, with the pride of a man who'd personally supervised the placement of every bit of wood and plaster. "Would you care for a drink? We've set out some lanterns on the patio."

"A beer for me," Richard said, his attention on Samantha.

"A beer would be great," she agreed.

So no Diet Coke now, apparently. She took in the living room area with what looked like genuine interest. Even when she was nervous she came across as smooth and at ease. It had to be a survival instinct—but she'd let him see her nervousness. Did it mean that she trusted him a little? Or did she just want him to think that?

Feet thundered down the stairs to their left. "Uncle Rick!"

He turned as Olivia thudded into his chest, wrapping her arms around his waist. Grinning, he returned the embrace, smacking a kiss on her upturned mouth. "How are you, my butterfly? You look grand. And you've grown at least six inches, haven't you?"

"Only three," the nine-year-old replied, grinning up at him. With her cropped blond hair and light blue eyes, she'd be a boy killer in a few years, and she knew it. "What did you bring me?"

"First, say hello to my friend. Sam, this is Olivia. Olivia, Samantha."

Olivia offered her hand, and Sam shook it. "Pleased to meet you, Olivia." She glanced at Rick. "Now stop torturing her, and hand over the present."

He brought the gift around to the girl's eye level and handed it over. "Now you said Japanese and red, so if it's not the one you wanted, it's your own fault."

"Oh, I know it'll be the right one," she said, her eyes dancing as she tore off the ribbon and lifted the lid off the box. With great care she reached her fingers into the package to pull out the small porcelain doll clad in traditional Japanese kimono of bright red with white orchids. She squealed. "This is the exact one I saw in the book!" she exclaimed, wrapping a free arm around him again. "Her name's Oko. She's so pretty. Thank you, Uncle Rick."

"You're welcome."

Tom was grinning, too. "Go show your mom, Liv."

"Mom! Look what Uncle Rick found for me!" she yelled, and stampeded toward the back of the house.

"She collects porcelain dolls from around the world," Donner explained, glancing at Samantha before turning his gaze back to Rick. "And you paid way too much for that, I'll bet."

He shrugged. "She appreciates them."

"Yes, she does." Samantha smiled a little. "She called you 'uncle.' "

"I've known her since she was born," he returned, still wondering what was going on in that agile mind of hers.

"Rick, you've outdone yourself," a warm female voice came from the doorway, and he looked up, smiling.

"Kate," he said, going forward to kiss the petite blonde on one cheek.

"How did you know we were looking for that exact doll?" she asked, reaching up to wipe lipstick from his jaw. "We haven't been able to find it anywhere. And believe me, we looked."

"Actually, Olivia faxed me a picture of it in London, and asked me to keep my eyes open for it. You know me. I can't resist a challenge."

"Uh-huh." Her blue eyes slid from him to Samantha, still holding the other present and looking far more comfortable than he would have thought possible for her. Thank God he'd come to the point where he knew it was a facade. "You must be Sam. I hear you threw Tom into the pool. Good for you. He can be a real pain in the neck."

"Well, thank you so much," Donner grumbled.

"Hi," Samantha said, with a return smile that for a moment looked almost shy. "You have a great house. I love all the exposed pine."

"That was Tom's idea. Once I convinced him that I didn't want a little house on the prairie, and he toned it down a little, I think it came out nicely."

Samantha's smile widened. "Hm. I thought he'd be more the *Bonanza* type."

Kate laughed. "You should have seen the original plans. Antlers on the walls and everything. It was hideous." She put a hand around Samantha's arm. "Do you cook?"

"Sandwiches and popcorn," Samantha answered, her expression even more disarming. "Not even close to what you can do, from what I've heard."

"Ah, I love pressure." Kate smiled again. "I need some olives sliced, but I didn't want you to think I was insulting you with menial labor."

With a sound halfway between a snort and a laugh, Samantha grinned again. "I'm great with slicing." She handed the other present back to Richard and headed for the kitchen with Kate and Olivia.

"Where's Mike?" Rick asked Tom, hefting the remaining gift.

"Baseball practice. He'll be back in another twenty minutes or so." Donner led the way to the wet bar at the back of the parlor. "What the hell's with Jellicoe?"

"What do you mean?"

"Come on, Rick, she was pricklier than a cactus with me at your house, and now she's Miss Congeniality?"

Richard took a breath. He could wish he'd been the only

one to realize that, but then Donner was supposed to be observant. "She's adapting."

" 'Adapting.' "

Since he'd brought a thief into the Donner house, he supposed he owed them an explanation. "It's what she does," he said in a low voice. "She fits in. She's a survivor, and that's how she does it."

Tom pulled two bottles of Miller beer out from under the bar. "So which of her adaptations is the one you've been screwing?"

"All of them." Charm or deceit—they were so close, but he'd seen her worry and her fear and her passion. That was the real Samantha. It had to be. "Change the subject," he suggested, putting the box on the bar top.

"Okay. I saw you let her drive the Bentley. Interesting."

"Why so?"

The attorney handed him one of the bottles. "You don't let me drive the Bentley."

"I'm not trying to impress you."

"But you're trying to impress *her*? I thought it was the other way around."

"I can't keep it straight any longer." Richard leaned his elbows on the bar. "How much does Kate know about her?"

"Only what you told the paper; that she's an art and security consultant, and you're dating her. Oh, and I added that she's helping with the tablet theft and dumped me into the pool."

"Okay. Thanks."

"I will tell her the rest, you know."

"I know. But at least she'll have the chance to make up her own mind about Samantha first."

"Or she'll think whatever Jellicoe wants her to think."

"Stop it, Tom. It's not like that. She's just trying to get out of this alive."

Tom's eyes were searching and somber. "You're serious about her, aren't you?"

"I seem to be." He wasn't in the mood to discuss it in depth yet, however, so he straightened. "I did let her drive the Bentley, after all."

"Which is my poin—"

"Anything new with Danté?"

"Fine. I was still down at the station when you called about that O'Hannon guy. They told Partino, but considering that it fairly well cleared him of the DeVore killing, he didn't look all that happy."

"No? How did he look?"

Tom glanced around, looking for wandering children. "Like he was about to shit his pants. I did find him a lawyer."

"Who?"

"Steve Tannberg."

Rick nodded, approving. "I'm glad you went outside your firm."

"Yeah. Didn't want to risk a conflict of interest down the line. I did get kinda pissed when Tannberg came out of interrogation without him. From what Steve said, though, Danté prefers to stay in jail. He says it's to protest his unfair treatment by his former friends, but—"

"But you think he's scared he'll end up in pieces once he's back out on the street."

"Something like that."

"He's still not talking, though?"

Donner grimaced. "I'm not supposed to know this, but I think he actually wants to confess about the tablet. If he does, though, he'll be owning up to tampering with the video."

Richard nodded. "Which helps put him in Samantha's room for the grenades."

"I was thinking more along the lines that it would mean he had something to do with the original theft and Prentiss's death, but that works, too."

"Sorry." Richard took a long swallow of beer. "I can't seem to stop thinking about her."

"Well, after seeing the way she looks tonight, I can't entirely blame you for that. Wow."

"I know."

"Dad?" Olivia wandered into the parlor. "Mom says you're busted for not bringing her a grasshopper and Sam a beer."

"Crud. I'm on my way."

Instead of leaving, though, Olivia continued her approach. "Are you dating Sam?" she asked, taking Richard's hand in her small one.

"Yes, I am."

"Why?"

"Because she's smart, and I like her."

"She knew that my new doll was made by hand in 1922, and that they used a real lady's hair to make her hair. And she split some of the olives with me when Mom wasn't looking. We put them on our fingers."

"Yes, she's pretty cool," Richard agreed.

Olivia laughed. " 'Cool.' You're so old."

Tom only laughed as Olivia ran off again. "You *are* old," he said, when Richard lifted an eyebrow at him.

"I'm younger than you are."

"Yeah, by four big old years." He handed over another bottle of Miller and lifted the glass he'd made up for his wife. "Come on, before I get busted again."

They headed into the kitchen—and Richard stopped. Kate had put one of her I'M A CHEF, RELAX aprons on Samantha, who stood at the counter with a knife in one hand and a stalk of celery in the other. The muscles across his abdomen tightened in pure lust. Who would have thought that Sam looking domestic would give him a hard-on?

She smiled as she saw him. "Look, I've been promoted to celery."

Laughing, Kate turned off a burner and slid a boiling pot of pasta over to one side to cool. "By the end of the evening I'll have her mixing ingredients."

Samantha chuckled in obvious good humor. "Look out Wolfgang Puck."

Unable to resist any longer, Richard strolled over to put the beer on the counter next to her, then tilted his head around to kiss her lightly on the mouth. "You are so boss," he murmured.

Samantha grinned, popping an olive into his mouth. "Groovy."

Twenty

Sunday, 7:50 p.m.

Samantha couldn't remember ever being in a house that felt so calm. If someone had described it to her, in her limited experience she would have thought it deathly boring. Surprisingly, though, the Donners' house was far from that. Cozy, perhaps, and comfortable, but not dull. It pleased her, even when she realized that she was beginning to hope Donner was a boy scout and that her reservations about him were more because of his career than because of him personally.

"Sam, will you carry the salad out to the table?" Kate asked, pulling a stack of plates down from a sunny yellow cupboard.

"Sure."

Olivia led the way with a tray of salad dressings, and together they marched out to the covered patio. Donner had lit lanterns at the perimeter of the wood and lath, probably to keep the bugs away. Around the border of the large garden, lights had been set into the ground, shining upward into the flowers and lush green foliage.

The Donners had obviously put a great deal of time and

effort into their house, and it showed. "Have you always lived in Florida?" she asked Olivia, as the girl carefully arranged bowls of salad dressing around the tossed salad in the center.

"Yes. We had a smaller house closer to my dad's office when I was little, but he built this one for us because we were getting too big to squeeze into the old one."

Sam smiled. She couldn't imagine living her entire life within ten or twenty miles of where she'd been born. She didn't even know where she'd been born.

Kate appeared, carrying two plates laden with chicken and pasta. "There're more on the counter," she said, setting them on the table.

Rick and Donner helped tote out the drinks and parmesan cheese, and they all went out to the patio together. They'd set a place for the middle boy, Mike, but Kate left his plate in the microwave.

At the doorway Samantha hung back, touching Kate's arm. She needed to know for sure about Donner one way or the other before she could let herself relax. "Where's the bathroom?" she asked.

Kate gestured toward the hall at the far end of the living room. "Second door on the left, just past Tom's office."

"Don't wait; I'll be right out." With a smile she headed back into the house.

Dinner, she'd already decided, would give her the best opportunity to do a little searching. Afterward, there would be Donners all over the house, and if Rick and the lawyer went off to get some work done, she'd be completely closed out of anywhere interesting. She found the bathroom and closed the door so it would look as though she was inside. That done, she slipped into Donner's office.

He probably had a corner office or something at his law firm, but she would wager that if he was up to anything underhanded, he would keep the evidence away from work. His desk was neat, with only a phone, a computer, and some framed photos marring the expensive mahogany surface. Sitting in the chair, she pulled open the top drawer. Pens, a few sticky notepads, paper clips, and three jacks—that was it.

Sam fingered the jacks. Kid's toys, probably Olivia's. She lifted her eyes to the desk photos. One of the whole family filled the largest frame, on the Yale campus from the background building. The oldest Donner offspring, Chris, had obviously received the best genes from both parents—tall, blond, and confident-looking, his father probably thought he'd make a great lawyer. The other photos were of the younger boy, Mike, playing baseball, and one of Olivia dressed in what must have been a Halloween fairy princess costume. And there was one of Donner and Rick, both grinning, each holding some kind of deep sea fish they'd obviously caught. Rick's was bigger.

Early in her career she'd learned to trust her instincts, learned that she could look at a room and tell the character of the person who inhabited it. Here she had an entire house, designed and built by Tom Donner and family. Blowing out her breath, she slowly pushed the drawer closed again and sat back.

"Satisfied?" Rick's quiet voice came from the doorway.

She jumped. *Shit.* "I was . . ."

He pushed upright, walking into the room. "You were what?"

Sam stood as well, returning the chair to its former position. "I was looking for proof that he had something to do with the tablet or the murders."

"Why?"

She could have made up a story, but she'd begun to realize something; she liked being straight with Rick Addison. "Because you refused to suspect him, and I wanted to be sure you weren't being played."

"And? Did you find anything?"

Sam grimaced. "Much as I hate to admit it, Donner's okay."

He stopped beside the desk and reached out to take her

hand. Unsure of his mood, she hesitated, then gripped his fingers. If he blabbed to Donner about this, she'd probably be asked to leave the house. And surprisingly, she wanted to stay a little while longer. Rick drew her up against him, tilting her chin up with his free hand.

"I told you," he murmured, "I choose my friends carefully. Which means that you are the only person who's allowed to play me."

"I'm not—"

His mouth covered hers, hot and hard and breathless. Then, before she could do more than close her eyes and wonder how long it would be before the Donners came in looking for them and found them sprawled naked on the lawyer's desk, he broke the embrace. Rick looked at her, fixing her smudged lipstick with his thumb. "Just remember," he said, shifting his grip on her hand to pull her toward the door, "that I know what you're doing, and that I have a finite amount of patience for games."

He'd never lost control, she realized. He'd done exactly what he meant to, heat her up to boiling and make her lose her composure, while he stayed perfectly cool. *Dammit.* They returned to the patio, and Kate smiled as Sam took the seat beside Rick.

"Salad?"

"Yes, please."

Samantha mentally shook herself. So Rick was a game player himself. She already knew that. Now she needed to be calm and enjoy the evening, because the Donners were genuine, normal people, and she wasn't likely to have this kind of opportunity very often.

"Which bits did you cook?" Rick asked.

"I only chopped," she said, "and sampled a little. It's great."

"It smells great," he agreed, taking the salad bowl from Kate and handing it to her.

Drawing another breath, she managed to transfer a mound of salad into her salad bowl with a fair amount of aplomb.

She'd shared meals with her father and with Stoney, but they'd been mostly take-out pizza or pasta. Fresh, home-prepared food with fresh salad and steamed vegetables was a rarity.

"I'm home!" a young voice called from the interior of the house.

Kate stood, going to the patio door. "Your dinner's in the microwave."

A towheaded boy emerged a moment later, his plate balanced in one hand and a can of soda in the other. As he caught sight of Rick, his serious face brightened. "I thought that was your car out front," he said, grinning and taking the seat on Rick's other side.

"I left a gift for you on the bar," Rick said, putting an arm around Mike's shoulders and giving him a playful squeeze.

"After you eat," Kate said, before the boy could rise. "And say hello to Sam. She's a friend of Rick's."

"Hi," he said, his ears flushing red.

She smiled back at him. "Hello."

"I didn't mean to be late," he continued with a look at his father, digging into his chicken and pasta. "The coach made us run extra laps because Craig and Todd started throwing water balloons."

"Just Craig and Todd?" Donner repeated.

Mike grinned. "Mostly. They're the ones who got caught, anyway." Seeming to think he needed a diversion from that statement, he turned to Rick again. "Is it true you almost got blown up?"

Rick shrugged. "It wasn't that exciting."

"We saw you on the news," Olivia chimed in. "You looked really mad."

With a chuckle, Rick reached for the ranch dressing. "I *was* really mad. I had to wear one of your dad's shirts."

Olivia giggled. "We tried to make color tags for all his clothes so he'd match, but he didn't like it."

With a sigh, Donner took a swallow of beer. "I have no secrets anymore."

Kate reached over to pat his arm. "That's all right, Tom. We don't mind that you can't dress yourself."

Sam could barely remember to eat. The byplay among the members of the Donner family fascinated her. Nobody tried to outdo anyone else, no one said anything more cutting than a humorous tease, and nobody talked about how dull and ignorant and ready for fleecing the rest of the world was in comparison to themselves. She was glad she'd satisfied herself already about Donner's innocence, because after this she wouldn't have wanted to find anything incriminating.

"Sam, what do you do?" Mike asked, passing a basket of cheese bread.

"I'm . . . freelancing at the Norton Museum right now," she answered smoothly, wishing she'd realized somebody in this nice, open, honest household was bound to ask her that question. "They got a big donation, so I'm helping them buy things and clean them up."

"Did you and Uncle Rick meet because somebody stole one of his antiques?" Olivia asked.

"Yes, we did," Rick put in smoothly.

Beginning to feel a little panicked, Sam took a quick look around the patio. *Keep it together, Jellicoe. You're doing fine—just act normal. Whatever that is.* "Kate," she said, a little too abruptly, "isn't that a Phalaenopsis?"

Donner's wife smiled. "Yes, it is. Wow. I'm impressed."

Sam felt her cheeks heat. "I like flowers. I'd love to have a garden, but I . . . just have never had the time. Yours is magnificent."

"What's a Phalaenopsis?" Rick asked, craning his neck to look.

Kate gestured at the pot set in front of one of the patio uprights. "The purple flower there. They're also called moth orchids. I couldn't believe when it started blooming last month. It never has before."

"I have a nice garden, too," Rick protested, grinning. "Several of them, in fact."

"Yes, but you employ like seventy gardeners, Addison."

She glanced between Kate and Donner. "I would bet ten dollars that Kate does all the flowers herself, and Tom does the water fountain and the tree trimming. You have a gardener, but he only does the lawn."

Tom was looking at Rick. "You told her that, right?"

With a laugh, Rick dug into the back pocket of his slacks for his wallet. "I didn't say a word about it. Samantha is extremely observant."

He flipped a ten-dollar bill onto the table, but Sam shook her head and pushed it back to him. "Two fives, if you please."

"Crikey," he said, exaggerating his accent while the kids laughed. Two fives appeared, and he pocketed the ten and the wallet again.

Sam picked up the money and handed one of the bills to Olivia, and the other to Mike. "I should have bet you more," she mused, chuckling at him.

"Definitely," Olivia chimed in.

Rick shook his head. "I'm not betting against you anymore."

"Thank you, Sam. Can I get my present now?" Mike asked, around his last mouthful of vegetables.

"Yes, you *may*. And turn on the coffee maker."

The fourteen-year-old bolted from the table, while Sam hid a grimace. *Coffee.* She'd known the evening had gone too smoothly. Blech. But okay, she could drink coffee with the normals one time.

Mike returned a moment later, and ripped into the package with none of the delicate care his younger sister had exhibited. "Oh, yes!" he shouted, flinging the paper over his shoulder.

"Michael!" his mother said sharply, but she was grinning. "Look! He found one!"

Donner frowned. "Um, forgive me for being ignorant, but don't you have one of those gold guys already?"

"Dad," Mike said, with an exaggerated roll of his green eyes, "it's not a 'gold guy.' It's C-3PO."

"Yeah. The *Star Wars* robot. I know that. But don't you already have one?"

"I have the 1997 version, made by Hasbro. This is the 1978 model, from General Mills Fun Group." Mike held up the black box, which was dotted with starlight and a photo of C-3PO. "Look. His waist is thicker, and his legs aren't articulated, and his eyes are the same gold as his skin—not yellow like in the newer version. And it's in the original box."

"So it's better."

"It's the original, so it's rarer. You have to be careful, because some guys buy the new ones and repaint the eyes gold, then seal the joints on the legs and feet so he looks like the older one. You can tell when you look at his feet, though. The markings are completely different. But some guys want him so bad that they're easy to fool. There're pretty good fakes all over the place."

They continued chatting about the merits of the 1978 C-3PO, but Sam only half listened. Something that Mike had said tickled at the back of her mind. Something that hadn't occurred to her before. Something about why someone with a prestigious, steady job like Danté Partino would risk jail—or worse.

"Samantha," Rick murmured, leaning close to her ear, "what is it?"

"Hm? Oh, nothing. Just thinking."

"About what?" he pressed.

"I'll tell you later."

"Promise?" he whispered, sliding a hand along her bare arm.

"Promise."

"How do you know about moth orchids?"

She shrugged, shivering as his fingers twined with hers. "I like reading gardening books."

"I want to kiss you right now," he whispered.

Maybe he wasn't totally in control, after all. Good. "You already did kiss me," Sam smirked, pulling her hand free and glad she hadn't tried to explain that gardens fascinated her, mostly because of the permanence they represented. You couldn't move around a lot and still have a garden. "So try to resist me," she chastised. "There are children present, you goof."

" 'Goof,' " he repeated, a slow smile touching his eyes. "I don't think I've ever been called that before."

Kate cleared her throat. "Shall we adjourn to the sitting room for coffee?" She gazed at Rick. "Or tea, in your case. How about you, Sam? Coffee, tea, hot chocolate, soda?"

"Soda, please," Sam answered, grateful. "I'll help you clear the table."

"Not necessary. That's what children are for."

"Mom," Olivia giggled again. "We're not slaves."

"Yes, you are. Clear, slaves. Clear."

As they left the patio for the sitting room, Rick waited for Kate to take him aside and interrogate him. He knew Tom had only given her the bare bones of Samantha's story. But knowing Kate, she'd probably figured out a great deal more about his date than she'd been told.

Thank God he'd gone looking for Samantha when she'd vanished off to the bathroom. And thank God he'd taken a moment to observe, instead of barging in and yelling at her for violating his friends' privacy. Seeing the way she'd looked at Tom's photos had abruptly made him wonder what her life had been like before he'd come across her in his gallery.

Mike and Olivia seemed to like her, mostly because she didn't talk to them like they were children. She didn't seem to know much about being a kid, herself—not the way the two youngest Donners did. He wondered what kind of child-hood she'd had, but without knowing anything much, he already assumed she hadn't had a mother who baked cookies on a regular basis. Hm. He hadn't either.

Something during dinner had caught her attention. He hadn't a clue what it might have been, but she would tell him. Everything about her fascinated him, and the way her mind worked most of all.

She sat in her short green dress between Kate and Olivia, who had brought in a few more of her miniature dolls to show off. He enjoyed finding items to add to what the children already enjoyed collecting, especially when he could procure something for them that they wouldn't be able to obtain or afford on their own. His childhood hadn't been precisely normal, either—perhaps that was why he enjoyed collecting items from other peoples' lives. Rick gazed at Samantha. *Do we seek what we know, or what we lack?*

Kate stood. "Who wants an ice cream sundae?" she asked.

Olivia's hand shot up, followed by Tom's, and then Mike, his own, and lastly, Samantha's. Obviously she was holding back to see what the correct procedure for dessert might be. Still adapting, though he'd begun to have the feeling that somewhere this evening, the acting had stopped.

"Rick, give me a hand," Kate ordered, heading for the kitchen.

Ah, here it came. Taking a breath and offering Samantha a supportive smile, he climbed to his feet and followed. "Yes, ma'am," he said, entering the kitchen.

"Grab the bowls out of the cupboard, will you?" she asked.

He pulled six of them down and laid them out on the counter. Kate began scooping mounds of ice cream into them, while he went into the refrigerator for chocolate syrup and cherries. It was a simple routine, and one he'd probably performed at least fifty times.

"Rick, how much do you know about Samantha?"

"Enough for the moment," he answered. "Why?"

"I don't like the thought that you'd let anyone . . . dangerous into this house, with my children."

"She can take care of herself," he returned, leaning back against the counter, "and I think someone may be trying to hurt her. But as for her being dangerous to you, never."

"You're certain about that?"

"Yes, I am."

Kate started pouring on syrup, then set the container down again. "I like her," she said slowly. "But she's not just an art consultant, and we both know it."

"And?"

"And so why is she with you?"

"I told you, I like her. And she saved my life, the night of the robbery. We're working together." He lifted an eyebrow, challenging her to contradict his statement.

"I can see that," she said quietly, and shooed him out the door.

Olivia had fallen asleep across her father's shoulder by the time they stood to leave. To Samantha's credit, she shook Tom's hand again, and even accepted a hug from Kate on the drive. Richard couldn't disguise his surprise, though, when she handed him the keys to the Bentley.

"You didn't like driving it?"

"I loved driving it. But if you're behind the wheel, you have to keep your hands to yourself, and I can think."

He slid into the driver's side of the car. "Does this thinking concern whatever was bothering you during dinner?"

"Yep."

"The thing you promised to tell me about?"

"Yep." She glanced at him as she belted in. "You're really not angry about the B and E?"

It took him a second to figure out that "B and E" meant breaking and entering. Someone needed to publish a *Thieves' Jargon to Kings' English* dictionary. "I'm really not angry."

Her shoulders relaxed a little, as though she'd expected a fight. "Good."

"So how much thinking do you have to do?"

"Just drive."

Chuckling, Rick turned the car down the drive and out to the street. Samantha was right about one thing; if she'd been driving, he wouldn't have been able to keep his hands off her. He'd been vaguely uncomfortable all night, and now that they were alone again, the ache in his groin became much more keen.

She sat in silence for several minutes, staring blankly out the window. Unused to seeing her pensive, Richard turned the radio onto some rock station or other.

Finally, she took a breath. "Okay. This is what I was thinking. Would somebody like Danté Partino risk his freedom, his reputation, and his career over the sale of a million-and-a-half-dollar artifact?"

"He did, obviously."

"I'm not so sure about that."

Richard nearly missed stopping at a red light. "Beg pardon? You don't think he planted the fake or the grenades? Why—"

"No, I think he did. But he's a snob. He likes the prestige of his job. I don't think he would take a risk like that for one item. And I don't think you kill people over one item—not unless it's the Hope diamond or something. He had a fake—and what else would he have it for, except to slip in place of the real one? Why should we assume—"

Making a hard right, he turned them into a deserted strip mall parking lot. He understood what she was saying, and the idea both angered and shocked him. "You think he's done this before," he snapped. "Without my knowing about it."

"Does he do any work at your other properties, or just this one?"

Richard slammed a fist on the dashboard. "He does some acquiring for elsewhere, but he lives in Florida. He likes the weather here."

"How much time do you generally spend in Florida every year?"

"A month or two during the Season, a few weeks over the rest of the year."

"Maybe he likes that about the estate, too."

"You're taking some huge leaps, Samantha. I mean, I can see that maybe he got carried away and a little greedy, and wanted to put something over on me with the tablet. But you're saying he's done it before to me, and repeatedly."

"I'm surmising, Rick. I don't know for sure. I'm just saying it makes sense. I need to look at some of your other artworks."

It did make sense, and that infuriated him. "Shit. Bloody hell."

"You told me to tell you what I was thinking," she protested. "Jesus. Forget I said anything. If you're going to get mad, I'll just keep it to myself next time."

"No, you won't," he answered. "I'm not mad at you. I'm mad at myself for not even considering the possibility before now."

"I'm probably wrong. It could be a fanatic tablet collector, or even somebody who's just crazy, and he's got Partino scared to death."

"We'll take a look in the morning."

"In the morn—"

"Yes, in the morning. No skulking about by moonlight—and I want to be certain before your suspicions go any farther than us."

On impulse, he tugged on her arm, pulling her close so he could kiss her. She opened her mouth to him, slipping her tongue between his teeth to match his own exploration.

His cock, already at half-staff since they'd left the Donners', strained at his trousers. "Jesus," he rasped, reaching out to turn off the key and slam the car into park.

She came over onto him, wrapping her agile hands into his hair and sinking into his chest. "You taste like chocolate," she murmured against his mouth, yanking his seat belt off and sliding a hand down to cup his straining crotch. "Mmm."

Feeling less articulate, Richard shoved a hand down the front of her dress to fondle her right breast, feeling her nipple bud under his rapt attentions. She pushed harder against his hand, and his head banged the driver's window. "Damn."

"Back seat," she moaned, pushing his hand out from under her dress before she executed a skilled twist over the front seat and pulled him over on top of her.

Richard didn't pause to admire her acrobatic skill as he balanced between her legs, sliding his hands up her thighs to her waist, pushing her dress up as he caressed her. He wanted to devour her, to bury himself in her, to keep her prisoner with him so she could never escape. Her urgent hands undid his slacks and yanked them and his boxers down to his thighs, while he took the easy way out and simply ripped off her lacy white panties.

"And I thought you were so in control," she panted, grinning as she wrapped fingers around him and stroked.

He slipped a finger inside her, half-thrusting against her hand. "Jesus. With everything but you."

"You wrecked my damned underwear."

"I'll buy you more."

"I don't want you to buy me underwear. I want you inside me. Now."

"Body arm—"

"Now," she repeated in an impatient moan, lifting her hips.

He didn't need another invitation. Richard plunged into her, burying his cock to the hilt. She gasped, arching her back and wrapping her ankles around his hips as he thrust, hard and fast, over and over, into her tight heat.

God, she made him insane. Like this, when every nerve in his body seemed attuned to her, to the fast beat of her heart and her harsh breathing and her moans and the warm slickness of her body inside and out, he could admit one thing— the fact that she was a thief and a liar and a game player excited him. "Mine," he growled, lowering his face to her neck as he felt himself building to crescendo. "Say you're mine."

"You're mine," she repeated with a triumphant groan, digging fingers into his ass and biting his shoulder as she came, pulsing and bucking around him. Even as he realized she was right, he followed her into breathless, mindless oblivion.

Twenty-one

Monday, 12:46 a.m.

By the time they pulled up to the gates of the estate, even the cops on duty looked half-asleep. If not for O'Hannon's murder they would have been gone by now, but Castillo was obviously protective of the community's wealthy elite. With barely a cursory glance at them one of the cops keyed the gates open, and Rick drove up the winding drive.

Halfway back Sam had realized that her underwear was hanging off the rearview mirror, and with a sigh that he seemed to find very amusing she'd yanked it free and stuffed it into her purse. Okay, so it was funny, and so she felt so relaxed she could barely keep her eyes open as they stopped at the front door.

"Should I carry you in?" he asked, giving her a smug grin as he pushed his door open.

"I'd say 'bite me,' but then we'd never make it inside." Stifling a yawn, she got out of the car. With a self-conscious tug at the short dress covering her bare bottom, she led the way to the door.

Rick unlocked it. "You're not wearing any underwear," he

sang in a low voice, bending down to kiss her neck as she passed him.

Her knees went rubbery. "Cut it out," she snarled, batting at him. "Security, remember?"

"Our photo was in the paper, darling. I don't think it's a secret that we're dating."

"That's not dating. That's . . . bedroom stuff you just did with your mouth."

He grinned. "No, it's not. You should see my bedroom stuff."

She glanced up the stairway, looking for wires or anything else that shouldn't be there. With Etienne dead and Partino arrested, they were probably safe—but someone had killed O'Hannon, too. "I saw your bedroom stuff in the car," she said, unable to resist a sly grin. "Not bad."

His "bedroom stuff" had kept them out until past midnight, and from the look in his eyes, he wasn't finished, yet. She'd thought him distracting before, but that had been an understatement. And it wasn't just the sex, exceptional as that was. There was something intoxicating about a man who walked into a room like he owned it—and knowing that he probably did. For someone in her profession, the members of which spent their time blending in, adapting to whatever situation arose, his blatant confidence was mesmerizing.

She started up the stairs, only to have him grab her elbow. "I'll go first."

Sam scowled at him. "Be serious. You do the rescuing, your lordship, and I'll do the scouting."

He didn't like it; she could see that. Rick Addison possessed a great deal of common sense and intelligence, however, and after a moment she thought was more for effect than because of actual disagreement, he nodded and gestured her to proceed.

They passed the Picasso on the landing, and she tried to sneak a look at it. In the dimness she couldn't begin to see whether it was authentic or not, though, so she supposed Rick had been right to suggest they wait for morning.

In truth, the idea of going straight to bed appealed to her immensely. After last night and the adrenaline rush of this morning, then the fun in the back of the Bentley, she felt tired to her bones, but the idea of having Rick in bed with her again filled her with . . . satisfaction, even more than it filled her with lust. Too bad she'd decided to go down and check Partino's office tonight. She could probably have waited for daylight, but she'd already ignored just about every instinct she had. It was past time for a thieves' refresher course.

"I'm going to check your room and mine, just to be safe," she said over her shoulder, keeping to the side of the hallway where the moonlight shone brighter.

"Let security check my room in the morning," he countered. "We're going to your room, and you're not my bodyguard."

"I don't want you walking into a bomb, Rick. I trust me more than I trust them. I'll check your room."

"You're worried about me," he announced.

"You grill a good steak," she said. Great. She'd realized that this . . . partnership of theirs seemed to be evolving into a complex tangle of her emotions and his, but now even he could see it.

He drew her around to face him, kissing her deep and slow. "Thanks. We'll both go check tomorrow," he suggested. "You've got to be more tired than I am, and I can barely keep my eyes open. No sense in stumbling about without a good reason—especially when whoever killed O'Hannon is still somewhere around."

"Okay, okay." She pulled out of his arms and continued down the hallway. "But I didn't think people like you ever got tired."

"Only when we're around people like you."

The hallway and her suite were both clear, and she pulled off her dress and yanked on a clean T-shirt and underwear while Rick was in the bathroom. Sam decided to lie down on the bed for a minute while she waited for her turn.

When she woke up Rick lay on his stomach beside her on

the bed, one arm draped across her shoulder, his long lashes shuttered and his breathing slow and even. She felt thick, as if she'd slept too heavily, and she stayed there for a moment, trying to make herself wake up.

He looked so beautiful lying there, and she knew, as she'd sensed from the moment she'd caught that one quick, startled look at him the night of the robbery and then the longer one when she'd hauled him downstairs, that she could never let anything bad happen to him. More than anything she wanted to snuggle closer into his arms and go back to sleep, but if she meant to carry through with her part of this odd partnership, she needed to get back to work.

Carefully, she slid out from under his arm and in the same motion stood, easing her weight off the bed. She shrugged into some shorts and headed barefoot into the main part of the suite. The security guards roaming the hallways concerned her; she had no reason to hide from them, but this was practice, and she wasn't going to just allow herself to be seen.

Partino's office was on the ground floor at the opposite end of the hallway from the security room and accessible from both the front utility stairs and the ones at the rear, which also accessed the estate's private gym. She went down the back way, the quiet and dark like old familiar friends. It did feel good to be using her skills again, though the keen rush wasn't there; if anyone saw her, they would just nod and let her pass.

Even so, she felt a definite sense of triumph when she slipped into Partino's office unnoticed. The police had confiscated his computer and desk files, which would likely hold information about any recent transactions. Recent activity, though, didn't necessarily interest her.

She unfastened one side of the police tape that crossed the front of Danté's two large file cabinets. Pulling a small length of copper wire from her pocket, in a second she had the first drawer open. The files were in a numerical order which she assumed to be some sort of cataloging in order of acquisition. Sam went back to the desk, but if a master list existed, it was at the police station.

"Okay, we'll do this the hard way," she muttered, returning to the file cabinet.

The first file contained a photograph of the medieval tapestry that had been hanging in the gallery the night she'd broken in. Neat writing detailed when the purchase had been made alongside the initials RMA, so she assumed that Rick had made the purchase himself. Price paid, which property housed the item, and its precise display location also filled little squares on the form.

In addition, Partino kept an up-to-date list of current market values for comparable items, dating back ten years. Man, the guy was anal. Anal, but accurate.

She glanced through the files in order, though she only pulled out a few for closer examination. Some items were as small as a single Roman coin, while others were as large as a fourteen-meter fresco by Lorenzetti, painted in the mid-fourteenth century.

She kept slowing down to look at the photographs, wishing she had more time to study them and to see the works in person. Rick had acquired the majority of them himself, despite his stated reliance on Partino. His eye was remarkable.

By the third drawer she realized she hadn't seen the file for the Picasso from the stairway. With three more drawers to go through, she couldn't be sure it was missing—yet. The stone tablet file was back in Rick's office, but something didn't seem right.

The door handle rattled, and out of pure instinct Samantha dove into the shadows behind the desk. Rick leaned into the room, glanced around, and started to close it again. Then he stopped, his gaze focusing on the open file cabinet. "Shit," he cursed. "Not again."

Frowning, Sam rose out of the shadows to his right. "Sorry," she muttered.

He gave a visible start. "Jesus Christ. You scared the bloody hell out of me. What are you doing down here?"

Rick hadn't bothered to put on a shirt, but stood there in his slacks and bare feet, hair disheveled and eyes sleepy, much as he looked the first night they'd met. He'd even gotten annoyed with the wrap around his ribs and torn it off this morning. "How did you know I'd be here?" she countered.

"You weren't there when I woke up." He yawned, running a hand through his hair and giving it an even more riotous look. "I followed my nose. Scary how well I'm getting to know you, isn't it?"

"Yes," she answered slowly. It *was* scary, and unsettling—and arousing.

"So, explain."

She flipped on the overhead light, making him blink and give her an annoyed look. "Okay. I'm not quite sure, but I thought I might find something interesting in here."

"Something the police missed?"

"Something they weren't looking for, maybe."

A slight smile touched his sensuous mouth. "All right, Inspector Morse, what did you find?"

"Morse? You're so *BBC America*. Why not Sherlock, or the American favorite, Columbo?"

"It's three o'clock in the morning. You're lucky I didn't trip over a landmine, darling." He slipped his arms around her, pulling her against his chest. "Talk."

Taking a deep breath, she nuzzled her cheek against his warm shoulder. "You're not going to like it," she murmured.

"I figured that. Try me."

"I think some of the files are missing."

"Samantha, I've collected antiques for better than sixteen years. That's a thousand files of past and current acquisitions. And even if a file is missing, it doesn't mean—"

"Do you have a master list somewhere, or do I need to go through the rest of these?" Her hunches were wrong on occasion, but they were right often enough that she had no intention of ignoring them.

"Stubborn, aren't you?" he muttered, freeing his arm from around her and opening the top left-hand drawer of Danté's desk. "Anything to convince you to come back to bed, then."

She followed his gaze. "If that's where the list is supposed to be, it's not there. I already looked."

"The police must have it, then. I'll get a copy tomorrow."

"Rick, there's something wrong here." Grumbling, she returned to the file cabinet. "Partino's got a room at the estate, doesn't he?"

"Down in the servants' quarters. He almost never uses it—it's just for nights he works late or wants to stay the weekend."

"It's the nights he works late that interest me, Brit."

He blew out his breath. "This way, then."

"You don't have to come. It's three o'clock in the morning."

"Yes, I do. It's three o'clock in the morning."

The files weren't in the small room Partino used for his rare overnight stays at the estate. As she looked through the near-empty chest of drawers it was difficult to miss the difference between the lavish suite Rick had loaned her and the tiny room with its twin bed and half bath that the estate manager had for his use.

"I would suppose the next step is to do an item-by-item check to see which of the files is gone."

"*If* any of them are gone," Rick amended, yawning again. When she didn't answer he gazed at her for a long moment, his face shadowed in the dark room. "All right. How certain are you that we have a problem here?"

Sam grimaced. "I'd bet your Bentley that something's not right with this—and that if we could figure out which files are missing, we'd know what the problem is."

"Let's go check the files, then."

God, that would take hours. And while it would confirm what she already believed, it wouldn't answer one large question—where the other files were, if they weren't at the estate. "I have a better idea."

"If it involves what's under your shirt, I'm all for it," he said, taking her hand in his as they returned to Partino's office.

He liked to hold her hand. She'd noticed that right away,

and while it made her feel . . . confined, it also gave her a rush every time he went out of his way to touch her.

"Let's say I'm already sure that the files aren't anywhere here at Solano Dorado," she said.

"Okay, I'll accept that."

"So, let's also say I suggest that I go to Partino's house and take a look there."

Rick came to a stop so abruptly that she stumbled at the pull on her arm. "Beg pardon?"

"The cops will have been there, but they're only looking for something to link him to explosives and to the tablet. Those files are important—Partino's so anal that he wouldn't have pulled them out of order in the file cabinet otherwise. And he couldn't have destroyed them without giving himself a heart attack."

"Samantha, you're suggesting breaking and entering. B and E. Whatever the devil you call it."

"And your point is?"

Rick glared at her in the moonlit hallway. Waking up to find her gone from the bed had sent him into an odd almost-panic, even though logic told him she would stay until she'd figured out what was going on. At the same time he'd been dismayed to realize that he was beginning to draw the investigation out. How many "wait until tomorrows" would she accept? Still, this seemed insane. "No, Samantha. We'll talk to Castillo about it tomorrow."

She returned his gaze for a heartbeat, then nodded. "Bed, then."

As she started past him, he yanked her hand, turning her back around. "How stupid do you think I am? No, Samantha."

Samantha put her hands on his shoulders and gazed up at him, her green eyes luminous in the moonlight. "Look at it this way, Rick. I owe you one. So unless you have a dungeon with a really good lock on it, I'll see you in the morning."

"I will not—"

"If you don't want me to come back, I won't," she interrupted. "But I *am* going to figure out what's going on. I *know* that Partino tried to kill me. He had a reason, and if what I'm starting to think is true, it wasn't jealousy."

"Sam—"

"You keep saying what's happened is personal. Well, it is. To me. And now that I have a clue, I'm going to follow it. I've never had much faith in cops."

Turning on her heel, she strode down the hall toward her suite. Her tools were there, and she was right about his odds of stopping her.

"I'm going with you," he muttered blackly, following her.

And so half an hour later Rick turned off the SLK's lights and drove the last half block in darkness. "I feel like a felon," he murmured, parking around the corner.

"You'll be one, if you go in there with me and get caught." Samantha pulled on a pair of black gloves and yanked a dark baseball cap down over her hair. "Why don't you just wait out here and be the wheel man? You'd probably get probation for that."

Christ. She was comfortable enough with what they were about to do to crack jokes. "I go where you go." He outfitted himself with his own pair of leather gloves and a ski cap.

"Nice. Remind me to get you a baseball cap, though. It hides your baby grays better." She slipped out of the car, closing the door gently behind her. "Don't lock it," she cautioned. "Noise, lights, takes too long to get back in, all kinds of bad stuff."

"I don't intend to make a career out of this." He closed his door, pocketing the keys. "But thank you for the lesson in criminal behavior."

He could name a few of his own business ventures that hadn't been entirely aboveboard, but he also used what he acquired to help the less fortunate, to fund causes he found worthy—and he figured that kept him on the plus side of good. Samantha was quite simply a thief, with any number of motives and plans she kept concealed from him. Yes, she had her own morality; she didn't steal from museums, didn't like guns, and she frowned on people killing or dying for an object. But she was still a thief. A damned good one.

She spent a moment looking up and down the street, then strolled up the sidewalk. At Danté's front walkway she turned in, going right up to the front door with Richard trailing behind her. Considering that it was nearly four o'clock in the morning, he felt amazingly alert. He'd never tell Samantha, but he could almost see why she did this on a regular basis. Knowing that they could be caught at any moment, that they absolutely were not supposed to be there, made this moonlit stroll more exciting than any bank deal or leveraged buyout.

Samantha knocked on the door, and his heart nearly went through his chest.

"What are you—"

"Shh. I'm not going to break in if his elderly mother is here to support him in his time of need, or some other shit," she whispered back.

"Right, right."

They stood there for what felt like an hour, and then she put both hands on the doorknob. In the dark he couldn't quite see what she did, but a second later the door opened. "Come on."

"How did you know there wouldn't be an alarm?" he asked.

"There is one," she said as she went in. "He put a sticker in the front window. If it's standard, we have thirty seconds to turn it off, or the whole neighborhood wakes up. Coming?"

On the wall at the far end of the entry she went straight to a small, glowing box. This time she produced what looked like a small battery with wires and clips. She popped the front of the unit off, and a few seconds later it beeped.

"Cool. Fourteen seconds to spare," she muttered.

"Now what?"

"Have you been in here before?"

"No."

"Then we look for an office." She started forward, then slowed to glance over her shoulder at him. "Out of curiosity, why haven't you been here before? Even if you and Partino weren't good friends, he has worked for you for ten years."

"Do you really want to have this conversation now?"

"Did he ever invite you over and you refused, or has he never asked?"

She wasn't just chatting, he realized; she was still looking for clues, hints, to answer her questions about Danté. "I don't recall that he's ever asked."

"So you really weren't friends at all, then."

"He came to my wedding."

"I bet the Queen came to your wedding," she shot back with her quicksilver grin, and slipped through a doorway.

"Her Majesty is very polite, that way," Richard returned, amused despite himself.

"Here we go," she said, and he followed her into a large, neat office. She was already at the tall filing cabinet and gestured him to the desk. "Let me know if it's locked."

He could bloody well open a desk on his own. The top drawer was secured, and as he jiggled it he heard the file cabinet door slide open. She was good. He'd realized it before, of course, but seeing her in action was supremely impressive. He rattled the drawer again, lifting and pulling, and with a low crack of splitting wood, it came open.

"Subtle," she said over her shoulder.

"Hey, it worked."

Richard reached in to flip the latch and unlock the rest of the drawers, and began his search. Personal receipts, movie rental stubs, tax information—everything had its own, alphabetized file. Even the pens were segregated by color.

"Look for weird deposit receipts, anything that doesn't fit with what you pay him."

"We're looking for art files, Samantha. Nothing else. Let the police do the rest of the investigating."

"Are you being noble, or are you afraid you'll find something?"

"If he did what you think he did, I am not going to jeopardize the trial that will send him to prison for a very long time." Rick had to slow when he came across a neat file of

Catherine Zeta Jones photos. Interesting, though he made a point of not lusting after married women, himself. Not everyone subscribed to that doctrine. "That was my philosophy with Patricia and Peter—give them enough rope to hang themselves."

"Remind me not to get on your bad side," she returned, closing a drawer and diving into the second one. "So which of them pissed you off more?"

"Shouldn't you be concentrating on something else right now?"

She gave a faint snicker. "Did I mention that B and E gets me really hot?"

Christ. "Peter did."

"But Patricia was your wife."

"She was unhappy, and she told Peter. Instead of telling me, he decided that fucking her would be the way to go. My friends don't shake my hand while they're screwing my wife."

"But you dumped her, too."

Rick drew a breath. "My wife doesn't sleep with other men."

Her responding surprised silence didn't surprise him; even three years after he'd walked in on them, he still remembered the sounds, the smells, the abject astonishment that he'd been fooled so easily. She'd asked, though.

"Ah. Bingo," Samantha murmured a moment later.

He pushed the desk drawer closed. "What did you find?"

"Your files. Files with the same numbering system as the ones at the estate, anyway." She pulled a handful free, setting them on the desk, then a second stack and a third. "About thirty or so, I'd say."

"Let's take a look."

"We could," she returned, "but it's almost daylight." Pursing her lips, she looked from him to the files. "Correct me if I'm wrong, but aren't these actually your property?"

"Yes. But what happens if he ends up on trial for something we find in these files, which he knows to be in his house?"

That stopped her for a minute. She'd probably never taken anything with an eye toward its later legal use, before. "How about if we find something, we tell Castillo our suspicions and ask him to get a search warrant? I can always slip the files back in here, if I need to."

Richard shook his head. "Let's get them to the estate and take a look first. We can decide how important they are later."

That earned him a smile. "I kind of like having a partner," she said. "With a little practice, you might make a good thief."

"Horniness factor aside, no thanks." Gathering up the stack of files, he gestured her to lead the way out. "Let's go."

She disengaged her wires from the alarm and scooted out the door, closing and locking it while she counted quietly to herself. "Clear," she said as she finished.

They slipped back down the street and into the car. As he started the engine, Samantha leaned over, grabbed his chin, and kissed him hard on the mouth. He kissed her back, wishing both that they'd taken a car with a backseat, and that they weren't parked thirty yards from a broken-into house.

"Does it always go that smoothly?" he asked, trying to return his mind to the drive home and away from the keen discomfort in his crotch.

"No. You're good luck." With another deep kiss she sat back to slip off her gloves and hat. "And thanks."

He pulled into the street, turning on the headlights once they'd rounded the corner. "Thanks for what?"

"For trusting me enough to go through with that. I know you didn't like it."

He hadn't liked the theft, but the thrill of it hadn't been so bad. Telling her that, though, seemed distinctly unwise. "We'll see whether it was worth it or not."

Less than an hour later they sat on the floor in Danté's office, stacks of manila folders around them, and went through the captured files. They looked practically identical to the ones left at the estate, and Samantha frowned. "This sucks. I know there's something here."

"We need to look at the art that goes with the files," Rick said, grabbing one of them and flipping through it again.

She started over, looking first at one of the estate files, then at one Partino had absconded with. Everything looked in shape, until she flipped to the page of comparable market values. In the recovered file Danté had been diligent to the day for the entire three years of the item's presence at the estate—until seven months ago, when the notations stopped.

Frowning, Sam opened the previous file and looked at it once more. As with all of the others she'd checked so far, it had been updated through last month. Okay, that was interesting. Setting the file aside, she went on to the next one.

It showed the same termination of market value figures, but eleven months ago rather than seven. The comparable value had continued to climb steadily until then, so it didn't look as though he'd written the painting off as a loss and simply forgotten it.

"Rick? Take a look at this."

She showed him the figures on both sets of files, watching his expression grow darker and harder as she went. "You were right," he finally muttered.

"Maybe. We still have to see the artworks before any of this means anything. And we'll have to go through every file that's still here to make sure it's not some accounting glitch."

"Let's get to it, then."

Richard's weariness had buried itself into a hard, heated anger. Samantha kept repeating that she could be wrong, but he'd already learned to trust her instincts.

"How many is that?" he asked, stretching his back.

"I don't know. About eight hundred." Samantha tossed another file into the "normal" stack. "Out of a thousand, thirty files out of date isn't that many. Maybe he moved them for some reason, and just forgot them. I mean, updating a thousand files once a month is pretty labor intensive."

"I don't understand why you're defending him. He tried to kill you. Besides, the only files with missing figures are the ones he had at his house. And he didn't stop making the entries all at once. He didn't forget anything."

She grimaced, retying her hair yet again into the ponytail that only seemed to hold for five minutes before it collapsed. "I . . . It's . . . It's like a code of honor. I break the law on a regular basis, Rick. I don't know what the hell I'm doing, ratting out somebody just like me."

Rick leaned forward, cupping her cheek in his hand. "You're not just like him, Samantha. In fact, you're not like anyone I've ever known."

"Don't get mushy," she muttered, pulling back so she could stand. "I'm going for a soda. Do you want tea, or coffee?"

With a groan he rolled onto his haunches and used the desk to climb upright. "I'll go with you." Bending down, he collected the "questionable" files. "And these are coming along, too."

"Nobody knows they're here," she said, opening the door for him. "I don't think they're going anywhere this morning."

He caught her hand in his free one. "Nothing else is getting away from me," he said, wondering if she understood exactly what he was saying.

"We still need to check the actual items that go with these," she returned, jabbing a knuckle into the stack of files. "You may need to call someone in."

"No. I'm calling *you* in. If we're wrong and it gets out, it could ruin the value of my entire collection. If we're right, I still want to be the one deciding how much the police need to know and figuring out who the bloody hell else is involved."

He understood what she'd said about her "code," though it bothered him a little. To this point she'd been fairly forthcoming with her theories, but she seemed to need to prove them to herself before she mentioned anything to him. And even talking to him was different than talking to the police. Richard could only imagine her reaction if she was asked to testify at Partino's trial or something. She'd run, and he'd never see her again. He hefted the files. All the more reason to be absolutely certain where they stood before they brought anyone else into this little mess.

When he strolled into the kitchen with Samantha, he couldn't help grinning at the adoring look on Hans's face. "Hans, a cup of coffee and a Diet Coke, please."

"Of course. But I have found a new café mocha you might like, Miss Sam. Much less coffee aftertaste. Would you care to try it?"

"I trust you, Hans," she replied, smiling at the chef.

"Splendid. And might I suggest omelets for breakfast?"

"Sounds good. Rick?"

He nodded, wondering just when he'd lost control of his household. "That's fine."

The morning had come in overcast and humid, so he guided her to the library rather than the patio. That would give them more space to spread out the files, anyway. He wondered how much time it would have taken him to notice that they were missing, if he'd even thought to look. And as for what they represented, it would never have occurred to him.

According to Samantha, he didn't think like a criminal. In her eyes, no one made up a fake tablet and expected to get it past the British Museum on their first venture into crime. If she was right, Partino had started small, and some time ago, working up to where he felt comfortable stashing the tablet on someone else and assuming both that it would pass muster and that his chosen dupe would take the blame.

"I could use a nap," she said, sliding into a chair.

"And I really want a shower," he returned, dumping the files at the head of the research table. "Now, in fact. It's been a long day and a half. You'll stay here?"

"Not if you're going to your room. I haven't checked it, yet." With what might have been a sigh, she stood again. "I should do that anyway, before anyone else stumbles into something."

"Samantha, I told you—"

"I heard you," she interrupted, picking up the files as she headed out the door. "It doesn't mean I have to obey."

Grumbling, he caught up to her and took the folders out of her arms. He couldn't stop her, but he could at least be there in case something went wrong. His suite, however, was clear of any explosives and murderers, and all but one thief.

"Okay. I'll be in the library eating your omelet," she said with a faint grin, reclaiming the files and turning on her heel.

"Samantha."

She faced him again. "Yep?"

"You really looked nice last night at Tom and Kate's."

Her lashes dipped. "Thank you."

God, she was lovely. "But don't tell Hans you've been slicing olives; you'll ruin your image with him."

"Don't worry. I don't want any more of your employees thinking I'm after their jobs."

As Richard stepped into the shower, he realized that what Samantha had proposed made the whole issue of Partino's involvement more problematic. The only evidence they had linking Partino from the grenades to the fake tablet to the original theft was the jump in the video surveillance tapes. If nothing came of the missing market comparisons in those files, they would have only speculation, unless Castillo had come up with something.

He would call the detective after breakfast. Because whether Samantha realized it or not, if Danté was eliminated as a suspect, she became the most likely culprit once more. He didn't believe it, and Castillo didn't seem to, either, but with his high profile, someone would be found guilty of the crime.

Richard dunked his head under the water. Damn. Somewhere this all made sense. Somewhere a trail existed, leading from the theft all the way to whoever now possessed his bloody tablet. And the sooner they discovered that path, the better for Samantha—and the worse for her reasons to stay around.

Twenty-two

Monday, 8:03 a.m.

They decided to start with the Picasso, both because it was convenient, and because Sam hadn't been able to get it out of her thoughts since she'd set eyes on it. She didn't even particularly like Picasso; something seemed vaguely not right about a person who took women apart like that, whatever his supposed statement.

"I can't do it on the wall," she complained, standing with her nose almost touching it. "Can we take it down?"

"I'll call Clark and have him deactivate the alarm," Rick said, straightening from the banister, where he'd been leaning behind her.

He went down the half flight of stairs and into the study, where she could hear him briefly on the phone. "Okay," he said, emerging to give her the thumbs-up.

"This is so much like cheating," she grumbled, lifting the bottom of the painting away from the wall and unhooking the pair of wires that connected it to the alarm system. She did the same with the top two, then lifted the thing off its fastenings.

"Too easy?" Rick asked, taking it from her. "We may as well do this in the library. The light's better there, anyway."

Rick had decided he was perfectly satisfied to abide by her assessment of the artworks. She wouldn't have felt comfortable admitting it, but the level of trust he showed both in her and her abilities surprised and pleased her. At the same time, it felt very strange. What he'd asked her to do was completely legitimate and completely enjoyable.

She'd parlayed her skill into jobs at museums, but that had mostly been to pass the time between robberies. Until now, she'd simply thought thievery was all she knew how to do, and the only thing she truly enjoyed. Her father had taught her how to pick pockets in Rio when she'd been five. Both her days and evenings had been filled with school as she grew up; whatever she could scramble together of mathematics and history and language during the day, and breaking and entering at night.

"Rick?" she asked, following him into the library.

"Yes?"

"Did you always want to do this?"

He looked at her as he set the painting down on the work table. "Check to see if my four-and-a-half-million-dollar Picasso is a forgery? No."

"No, I mean what you do. Buying companies and property and selling them again."

"Not specifically. I majored in business in college," he said, sitting opposite her. "Everything just seemed to . . . fall into place. I enjoy it, thankfully."

"If you didn't, you wouldn't be doing it nearly as well as you do." Sam snapped on the table light and redirected it over the painting.

"A compliment—which I won't return," he said with a slight smile, meeting her gaze, "except to say that you are a remarkable woman."

"Thanks." They'd opened the file with its photographs, but Samantha didn't think she needed them. "It's too neat," she said after a moment, ducking down to rest her chin on the table so she could look across the surface of the paint. "Nothing overlaps."

"Like somebody knew what they were painting before they started," Rick supplied, pulling out a photo and examining it before switching his attention back to the canvas.

"It's faster; you don't have to let a layer dry before you brush on the next one. People don't realize that sometimes artists change their minds in midcreation." She straightened, glancing at him. "Is this the same frame you purchased it in?"

"I'm sure it is," he said, checking the photo again for comparison.

"Let's turn it over for a second," she said, "but don't let the surface touch the table, just in case we're wrong. Reinaldo's a little too liberal with the furniture polish."

Sure enough, two little indentations marked the top inside corner of the frame. To her it screamed that someone had used a tool to carefully lever the original painting out of its frame and replace it with this one. She pointed the markings out to him, and he began to swear.

Laying the painting carefully faceup again, she took the photo from Rick just to make sure that she was right about this. It was a fairly good fake—probably worth a few dollars itself, and enough to fool anyone who had no reason to suspect that it was anything but the original.

"Selling a fake is harder than just replacing something in the middle of ownership," she said, half to herself. "When you're buying, you're naturally suspicious, and for a painting worth this much, it's expected that you'll have it examined by someone who knows what they're doing. Forgeries and fakes do get by sometimes; some of them are actually better than the artist's real work. But after the painting's passed inspection and it's been hanging on the wall for a while, who's going to notice if one day it looks a tiny bit brighter or neater or sloppier?"

"Are you trying to make me feel better?" he asked in a low voice, his gray eyes flat with anger.

"I'm just saying it's a smart way of doing business."

"It's not business," he snapped. "It's damned bloody thievery."

He had every right to be angry. If every folder here on the table meant a forgery now sat in place of an original, he'd been taken for millions. For someone of his arrogance and ego, that had to smart.

"You should still have an expert look at this," she said quietly. "I came in thinking it was fake. I'm looking for things to justify that."

Richard slammed to his feet, making her jump. "I'm calling Tom. He'll know somebody we can use."

"Actually, I was thinking of my boss at the museum, Dr. Irving Troust. He's got the training, and a good instinct for this kind of thing."

"I've met him," Rick said, pacing to the wall of windows and back. "Where does he think you've been this last week, anyway?"

"Visiting a cousin in California."

"Hm. What if he's been reading the paper?"

Sam flushed. Shit. If he'd been reading the paper, he would have seen a photo of her having dinner with one of the world's premiere citizens. "Crap," she said aloud.

"Well, at least you have something you can fall back on if you get fired from the museum. That whole criminal underworld thing, right?"

"Hey. Don't be mad at me, rich guy. I wasn't trying to fool you with anything."

He glared at her for a moment. "No, you were trying to steal from me."

"And I've been trying to make that up to you."

"I have this feeling," he snapped, dragging fingers through his dark hair, "that every time someone I know says he was robbed, I'm going to think of you."

"That's *your* problem, isn't it?"

"How do you do it? Just walk in and take something?"

Samantha frowned. "It's what I do. Back off. Be mad at Danté, not me. I didn't betray you."

"Not yet."

She pushed to her feet. "So that's what this is about? I promised I wouldn't steal anything from you."

"I'd prefer a promise that you won't take anything from anyone."

Sam stared at him for a moment, her insides clenching. "Fuck this. You don't *ever* get to tell me what to do. I am what I am. Deal with it."

He was pacing, pausing only to snap retorts back at her. "And if I choose not to?"

Shaking her head, she turned on her heel. "Then deal with this." She strode for the door.

"Where the hell do you think you're going?" he bellowed, pushing aside a chair and charging after her.

She slammed the door as he hit it, and wedged one of the Roman spears between the handle and the doorframe. "I'm calling a cab! And if you open the door, you'll break one of your stupid B.C. spears!"

"Sam!"

Taking the stairs in two jumps over the banister, she ran to her room and dialed information, then had them put her call through to a cab company. Addison could pay the additional fee involved for the automatic connection. That done, she stuffed her things into her knapsack, grabbed her duffel bag, her case, and her purse.

"Shit, you have a lot of crap, Sam," she growled, kicking open the veranda door and dragging her things down the steps to the pool deck.

She'd known it would happen, eventually. Damn, damn, damn. Richard Addison thought he could control everything—including her. If she'd stayed any longer, he'd have her in a straitjacket. No one got to use her talents, then criticize her for having them. As if he didn't get off on what she did. Hell, if she hadn't been a thief, he probably wouldn't have looked twice at her. Hypocrite. Stupid hypocrite. "Hypocrite!" she yelled back at the house.

He hit her from the side. Before she could do more than shove her duffel backward, they both went into the pool.

The cold water sent a jolt of shock through her. She barely had a breath of air, and her first thought was to get to the surface. As she broke through, gasping, her second thought was to kill Rick Addison.

"You fuck!" she yelled, taking a punch at him.

He dodged it, dragging her arms around behind her. "Stop it, Samantha!"

"Let me go!"

Rick dunked her. She surfaced again, coughing. Oh, that was enough of that. Sam took a deep breath and went under on her own. Arching her back, she pulled him forward, off-balance, then pushed up underneath him. He went over and down again, headfirst. Her arms came free, and she kicked to the edge of the pool.

She snagged her knapsack with one foot, but her heavy, hard-sided case had slid into the deep end. Shit. Maybe she could drag it out with the pool net. However furious she was, she was not leaving without her stuff.

"Samantha, get back into this pool," Rick growled, grabbing her foot as she hopped up to the edge.

"How many teeth do you want to lose?" she asked, bracing her hands on the hard flagstone.

"Back in the pool," he repeated, making a quick tug.

She slid back in, fisting her hand to let him have it in the jaw. Before she could connect, he swept her up against him and kissed her.

His warm mouth on her cool lips was startlingly arousing, and she lingered against him for a moment before shoving away. "I am not kissing you," she snapped, backing toward the edge again. "I am mad, and I am leaving."

"I'm sorry."

Sam scowled. "You tackled me into the pool!"

"It stopped you, didn't it?" He backed away a little, treading water. "I thought we needed to cool off a little."

"Jerk."

"Yes, ma'am." He shook dark hair out of his eyes. "You were right. I don't like what you do, but what you do is why we met. I'm sorry."

She took a deep breath. "I am a thief, Rick. I was raised to be one, and honestly, I enjoy the challenge of it. Pretending I have a 'real' job somewhere else isn't going to change what I do. This"—and she gestured with her dripping hand between the two of them—"is ridiculous."

Rick stroked back to her. "Are you enjoying being here?" he asked, gripping the edge of the pool beside her head. His eyes, lashes thick with water, were serious. "Other than the bits with the explosives, of course."

"Of course I like it here. You have a beautiful home."

"And do you enjoy being with me?" His voice was softer, now. A cool hand cupped her cheek, and she leaned into it without thinking.

"You're okay," she hedged.

"You're okay, as well," he returned. "Stay. We'll figure out the rest later."

"Rick—"

He shook his head. "You can't leave before we figure out this theft mess, anyway. Not solving it will drive you mad, and you know it."

Rick leaned in again, stopping with his mouth an inch from hers. She could feel the pull between them. His hands on her body, his weight on her, the deep satisfaction in his eyes when he came inside her—she craved him. And that scared her.

What he'd said had been right. She couldn't be a thief and be with him. She didn't know how to stop being one, and she wasn't ready to give up the other. The walls were closing in around her. Sam closed her eyes. Shit. She could put off deciding anything for today—for a week. That was fair. She could do that.

"Samantha?"

Slowly, feeling his breath on her skin, she closed the distance between them and kissed him.

Nibbling on her lower lip, Rick drew her into his arms. "I'll take that as a 'yes,' " he murmured, kissing her again.

When he slipped a hand down the back of her shorts, though, she snapped open her eyes again. "Cameras."

He scowled. "Shit. I hate security."

"So do I," she murmured, deciding it was fair to push him a little.

"Cease and desist," he returned, his frown deepening. "I apologized."

"You also threw my case into the deep end," Samantha accused.

"I'll get it." Rick turned and kicked off, diving down to retrieve the heavy case. For a moment she wondered whether he'd be able to lift it with him or not, but he managed to make it to the surface along the back wall. "Jesus, this is heavy," he gasped.

Clambering out of the pool, Sam padded over to help him pull the case, then himself, out of the water. "Serves you right," she said without heat, "for throwing me in the pool. Dr. Klemm said no swimming for ten days."

"Oh, so him you listen to," Rick said, hefting up her duffel and soaking-wet knapsack and carrying them back up to her room himself.

"I like him." The case felt twice as heavy as it had before when she drew the handle over her shoulder. "Man, now I have to dry all this stuff off. I hope you didn't ruin any of it."

Richard wondered if she expected him to say that he would replace anything the water had wrecked. He would— as long as the items were personal ones, and not saws or knives or whatever it was she used to break into homes.

That had been close. The Roman spear had suffered for it, but thankfully they were fairly common. He probably should have let her leave; she'd pointed him in the direction he needed to go with the investigation, and, strictly speaking, he didn't need her active assistance to turn the information over to the police. Except that he didn't want to turn everything over to Castillo yet—not until he had enough evidence to provide answers, at least for himself. For that, he needed Samantha Jellicoe.

Aside from that, he didn't want her to leave. For the last day or so, he'd sensed that she was being herself—Sam Jellicoe, imaginative, quick, humorous, surprisingly intelligent, and definitely mercurial in her moods and thoughts—and that he was in way over his head. He was used to being in control, of knowing where people stood. She made him insane—and he enjoyed the sensation as much as he hated it. "I'll tell you what," he said. "You explain to me what they are, and I'll help you dry them off."

"And everything in my knapsack," she insisted, stepping into the trail of drips he'd left going up the stairs.

"You're rather wet, yourself," he pointed out, lust tugging at him again.

"Yes, I seem to be," she murmured, giving him a sly smile.

He went hard. "I'm going to ruin another pair of your panties," he whispered as they reached her room.

"Call Dr. Troust first," she said, putting her hands on his damp shirt to keep him away. "I don't want these accusations resting on me."

"Fine. I suppose you have the number?"

She gave it to him, and he called while she ducked into the bathroom. Dr. Troust was both surprised and flattered by the call and agreed to stop by first thing in the morning. On impulse, Richard asked him what he thought of his employee, Samantha.

"Sam Martine?" the curator asked. "She's wonderful. Smartest girl I've ever met. Catches things even I miss, and I have a doctorate in this stuff. Do you know her?"

Evidently Irving Troust didn't read the *Post*. "She's a particular friend"—Richard looked up as Samantha strolled out of the bathroom, stark naked—"of mine. So I'll see you at nine tomorrow? Thank you, Dr. Troust." He hung up the phone before the man could reply. "Hello."

"He's going to come by?" she asked.

"Hm? Oh, yes. Sorry, my brain's shut down," he returned, pulling his wet shirt off over his head.

Perhaps he couldn't own her mind, but he could damned well possess her body. They inaugurated the shower, then the floor in the middle of the suite. Samantha straddled his hips, riding him and giving him a new appreciation for her fine muscle tone and control. When they were spent she draped herself on top of him, and they lay there for a long time, just listening to one another breathing. Richard could feel her heart beating against his chest.

"Rick?"

"Hm?"

"Thank you."

Not smiling would simply have killed him. "You're welcome. And thank you."

She cuffed his shoulder, her face still buried against his neck. "Not for that—though you're pretty good in the sack for a rich guy."

"*Pretty* good?"

He felt her deep, relaxed chuckle. "You're already out of control. I didn't want to make your ego even bigger." She nibbled his ear. "It's rather big already."

They were never leaving this room. "Then what were you thanking me for?"

"For wanting me to stay. For asking me to stay. I don't think anybody's ever done that before."

More moved than he could say, Richard slipped his arms around her. "If I volunteer to answer one of your questions about my sordid past, may I ask you another about yours?"

"What question?"

"Two, actually. First, are you Sam Martine at the museum?"

"Shit. Yes, I forgot. 'Jellicoe' is a pretty infamous name

around museums and other places where people keep their valuables." She placed a kiss on his chin. "Next question?"

Apparently they'd relaxed the rules for personal questions. The significance of that, though, he'd contemplate later. "Right. Were you and your father close?"

The muscles across her back stiffened, and she lifted her head to look down at him, auburn hair framing her face. "Not while I'm naked," she said, lifting slowly off him. "So if you really want to know, we have to stop this and get dressed."

"You're evil," he said, but sat up beside her. "I really want to know."

She vanished into the bedroom while he threw on a towel and practically ran to his own room to grab some dry jeans and another T-shirt. Dammit, sometimes this house was too bloody big. He wanted to get back before she changed her mind.

No woman had ever left him feeling like this—not even Patricia. For the first time he wondered whether his ex-wife had been . . . overwhelmed by Peter Wallis in the same way he'd felt when Samantha had literally exploded into his life. And he wondered what would have happened if he'd met Sam Jellicoe while he'd still been married to Patricia.

She left the bedroom just as he came back into the sitting room. "Wow," he said, slowing.

Samantha had put on a soft, ankle-length sundress of dusky blue. In her bare feet and with her still-damp hair hanging in loose waves to her shoulders, she looked like a sultry incarnation of decadent sin.

Sin tilted her head at him. "Can we at least catch the last part of *Son of Godzilla*?" she asked.

"You mean you passed up the green monster for me?" he asked, pleased again.

"You made me mad."

"I made you come. Repeatedly."

"Mm." She chuckled. "If that's the way you apologize, I guess I don't mind the being mad bit so much."

She punched the remote, and the television flickered on. Sitting on the couch beside her, he took her hand, lifting it to look at her long, delicate fingers with their short, trimmed nails. No long, painted claws for Samantha; they'd get in her way. "You have artist's hands."

"My mom played piano," she said, sinking down to lean against his shoulder. "Or so my dad said. She threw us both out when I was four."

"Threw you out?"

"Actually, I think she threw Martin out, and didn't object when he decided to take me along with him." She stopped as Godzilla came charging in to rescue his son. "As for being close, he taught me everything I know about stealing, so I could be his partner. He liked my long fingers, too. They're good for picking pockets." She flexed them.

"You must have been devastated when he was arrested."

She shrugged. "I wasn't that surprised. As he got older, he got . . . less discriminating. I think his skills were fading a little, so he compensated by going after anything that wasn't nailed down." Samantha squeezed his fingers, then relaxed her grip again. "I've never said this to anyone. Not even Stoney."

"And I won't say it to anyone else."

"I know that." She settled deeper into the couch cushions. "The last year he worked, he and I kind of . . . we didn't really work much together. We both used Stoney because we trusted him, but I didn't want to go into a place with him. And I think that made him angry, like I thought I was better than he was. And I think he was a little jealous, because I could pull jobs that he couldn't handle any longer, and I wouldn't take jobs that he *could* handle."

"You've never tried to find your mother?"

"She let us go. Why would I want to know someone like that?"

Bitterness? It sounded like it, though it could simply be more of Samantha's practicality. "You were only four, you said. Maybe your father didn't tell you the whole story."

"Stoney's never said anything different, either." She curled into him, kissing his throat. "And now for you. What sordid detail would I like to know?"

God. He could never let her know how . . . fulfilled he felt when she initiated contact. Or how dazed her touch left him. "I'm not giving you any clues," he grumbled. "Oh, look. Godzilla stepped on someone."

"He did not. He almost never steps on anyone." She chuckled. "I know. Have you ever done anything illegal? Before you met me, I mean."

He understood the reason for the question; she wanted to put them on a more even footing. Trust. She'd shown it in him, and now it was his turn. "Once. I've been on the shady side of legal a few times, but nothing that could be proven."

"Tell me."

"You could put me in jail for a very long time for this," he muttered.

"Nonsense. Donner would save you. Besides, ditto."

Richard sighed, pretending annoyance over uncertainty. That was his motto: Never let anyone think you're unsure of anything, however you might feel. It had never been as difficult to live up to as it was with Sam. "I wasn't quite . . . straight with you about my dealings with Peter and Patricia. Right after I found them together, before the divorce, I decided I wanted to get even. Peter and I were in roughly the same business, and I knew he'd risked quite a bit to acquire a computer company based in New York," he said slowly.

"As soon as I returned to the States, I cultivated the friendship of the head of the accounting firm that did his company's books. Over five months I pretended we were best friends, bought him whatever nonsense I thought would gain me his trust, and then one evening he told me in confidence that Sir Peter Wallis, the company's owner, was going to— 'lose his lunch' I believe was his term, because the figures they were going to deliver to him that Friday were awful."

"Insider trading, right? You bought the company out from under him when the stock dropped."

"I did. And then I tore it to pieces and sold off the parts."

"Did it feel good?"

"Not really. Peter lost his shirt, of course. On the downside, seventy perfectly blameless people lost their jobs because I wanted to let him and Patricia know that whatever a judge decided in court wasn't enough for me."

"I almost feel sorry for him. Did you leave him anything?"

"I'm sure he's still making a living. God knows I could have taken everything if I wanted to. I suppose hurting him once was enough to get it out of my system."

"You made your point," she commented.

"Precisely. Anyway, if I'd left him a complete pauper, I'd be paying more alimony, so all's well that ends well."

She nodded, then abruptly pushed away from him and sat up. "Okay, the movie's over. Help me dry out my kit."

"But who won?"

"Godzilla. He always wins."

Twenty-three

Dr. Irving Troust sat back, taking a swallow of iced tea and removing his glasses. "Mister Addison—Rick—I'm not quite sure how to tell you this. It is my belief that this painting is a forgery."

Richard blew out the breath he hadn't realized he was holding. Sam had been right. "I suspected that it might be, Dr. Troust. I wanted an expert to confirm that."

Troust looked from him to Samantha. "Who sold this . . . thing to you?"

"It's a bit more complicated than that, I'm afraid. The painting was an original Picasso when I purchased it." Richard approached the table and sat opposite the curator. "There are several other items I'd also like you to look at. And for the moment, I need to ask that you keep this information to yourself."

"I won't be part of a fraud," Irving said, sliding his glasses back on.

"Don't worry, Irving," Samantha said, coming forward to sit beside Richard. "He's not trying to pass them off to anyone. We would just like to know how much damage has been done."

"Of course."

Tom Donner arrived as Samantha was out selecting another item for review. "Sorry I'm late. What did I miss?"

Richard made the introductions and gave a short explanation of events. "Only the four of us know about this, so keep it quiet."

"The four of us?" Donner repeated. "That's not quite true, is it? There's at least one bad guy still out there."

"If our theory works out, I'll have a pretty good trail leading to Partino. We might be able to persuade him to help us out."

"A pretty good circumstantial trail, you mean. Shit."

Samantha returned, a small Matisse carefully held in her hands. Richard frowned, quickly stifling the expression at her stern look. The Matisse was genuine as far as he knew—but that was probably her point. It made sense. If Troust called everything a fake, then they would have to find another expert, or another theory for the files Danté had taken away.

While Irving began his examination of the Matisse, Samantha strolled to the window. Richard joined her, Tom following close behind. "It doesn't mean anything yet," she murmured.

"It damned well does. Now we have to decide what we tell Castillo."

Tom was scowling. "We tell him everything. If you're right, this has been going on for years."

"I want to know who owns the original of that Picasso right now," Samantha said, her attention apparently on her employer.

"Could you find out?"

"You two are going to get yourselves arrested for obstruction," Donner hissed. "Let the cops handle this; it's *their* job."

"If I could get hold of Stoney, I might be able to at least get a lead on it," Samantha returned, ignoring Tom's protest. "As it is now, unless Partino gives us something, I'm stumped." She faced Richard. "Of course, the idea that Danté might be facing a very long time in prison if the buck stops with him might convince him to give us another name."

"That's what I'm counting on," Rick admitted.

"I need more tea," Troust called, lifting the glass while keeping his gaze on the painting.

"I'll get it," Samantha said. "It's half my job at the museum, some days."

As soon as she left the room, Donner began growling again. "What the hell are you doing? This is not an episode of *Moonlighting*, Rick. I mean, I get that you're having fun, and that you like spending time with Jellicoe. But—"

"She's Martine, today. Don't forget."

"I will if she calls me 'Harvard' again. But you said you found twenty-seven files. That's what, fifty million dollars' worth of stolen artworks and antiques?"

"Something like that."

"That's serious shit. People have already been killed because of this, and we know they can get into this house. *Your* house, Rick."

"I know that, Tom. And that is why it's *my* call." He took a breath, forcing his hands to unclench. "I do not like giving up control."

"I'll play this however you want, my friend. But you're taking unnecessary risks, and if you're doing it to impress your girlfriend, I don't think you'll ever catch up to her on the adrenaline rush count."

He hated when Tom was right. "Let's just see what happens today," he countered. "If Troust says that Matisse is a fake, then the research Samantha and I did is either wrong, or we can't use Irving to prove anything."

"It's real?"

"Samantha thinks so, and the file was here—and up-to-date."

"Speaking of Jell—Martine—I told Kate who she is."

Oh, boy. "And?"

"And Kate likes her anyway. She's worried you'll get hurt, but she likes Sam."

"Tell her not to worry about me. I can take care of myself." Richard glanced over at the occupied curator. "Why does she think I'll get hurt?"

"She said that Sam's probably not used to staying in one place for long. Actually, she said Sam's probably more restless than you are."

"What else did she say?"

"I'm not supposed to tell you, but she doesn't see much of a future for you and a habitual cat burglar. One of you would have to change, and she knows you won't, and she doesn't think Jellicoe can."

"Well, don't tell her I said she made a lot of assumptions based on one short evening, and that people do change."

"Jeez. I feel like I'm in high school. You and Kate can just have lunch and compare notes, because I don't want to be in the middle of—"

Samantha strolled back in, a tray balanced in her capable hands. "Shut up," Richard muttered.

"Raspberry iced tea for Irving, water for Tom, a soda for me, and Hans insisted that I bring Mr. Addison a nice chilled root beer." She handed them over, then leaned against Rick's arm as she popped the tab of her Diet Coke and took a drink. "Anything yet?" she whispered.

"Not so far," Richard answered, careful not to move. Sometimes he felt like a hunter trying to lure a deer into a trap. *Don't move, or she'll remember you're there and run away.*

"I still think we need to call Castillo," Tom put in.

"Wait and see what Irving says," Samantha insisted. "And I've been thinking. If Irving gets the Matisse right, you should hire him—or someone—to examine every antique and piece of art you own. Not because they might be fakes, but to confirm to everybody that ninety-seven percent of your collection remains untouched."

"And publicize the whole fiasco?"

"If Partino goes to trial, it's going to come out, anyway," Tom put in.

Richard frowned into his root beer. "I hate the press."

"Like they're my favorite people," she countered. "Just use 'em. Otherwise, like you said, your entire collection is going to end up devalued." She sipped at her soda. "Because whether the public finds out or not, the art community will. There's no bigger bunch of gossips on the planet. Trust me on that."

Five minutes later, Dr. Troust looked up again, saw his fresh iced tea, and gulped half of it down. "Well, Rick, I may be missing something, but this one looks authentic to me. I've seen photos of it, and Matisse's style is well documented." He frowned, wiping his glasses on his tie. "What did you find, Sam?"

She smiled. "I didn't find anything, Irving. I was hoping you wouldn't, either."

"Ah, a test. And I passed."

"With flying colors, as they say, Dr. Troust. Ready for another?"

"This is rather exciting. Of course."

Richard looked over Samantha's head at Tom. "Now we can call Castillo."

By the end of the afternoon, the library was cluttered with worthless works of art. As the stacks grew larger and larger, Richard wanted to put a fist through one of them. Samantha probably would have joined him, and even Donner began to look annoyed, but Castillo showed up and told them every single fake and forgery was evidence.

"Fifteen," Samantha said, as a first-century Roman helmet went into the pile. "He's pretty clever, for an idiot. A few of those files he removed and stopped doing entries for are for genuine pieces. He could claim it was just an oversight, and that he had no idea what was going on." She glanced sideways at Richard. "He could even blame you for it."

Castillo leaned his elbows on the work table. "Or maybe he had buyers lined up for those items and just hadn't made the switch yet."

"That works." Richard passed him the plate of sandwiches

Hans had sent up, cucumber in Sam's honor. "Except that none of the fakes look like they have updated files."

Sam gave a brief smile. "That's because Partino's anal."

"This is kind of interesting," the detective said, choosing a sandwich, "but it's really out of my league and my jurisdiction. I can go after Partino for the attempted murder of Sam here, but we really need to call in the FBI if we're talking about theft on this level."

"No, no, no. We are not doing anything to Partino because of Sam," Samantha said, shaking her head and pushing back from the table. "You arrested him because of the whole tablet and messing with the security tapes and grenade thing."

"I'm a homicide detective," Castillo returned. "Murder, attempted murder, that's pretty much what I do. That leaves me with Prentiss and you. Prentiss can't testify, and you can."

Samantha looked at Richard. "No, I can't," she said unsteadily.

"We'll talk about it," Richard said.

"Why, so you can try to convince me? I *can't*." She rose and fled the library.

"Nice going, Frank," Richard grumbled, standing. He sent another glare at Donner, just for good measure. "Keep an eye on Irving."

He found her upstairs in the gallery, staring at the still-fire-blackened walls and floor. "It may not come down to your testifying, you know," he said, keeping his distance until he could gauge her mood. "We can show his attorney what we've got, and maybe he'll roll over on his accomplices."

She snorted. "You sound like Sam Spade. 'Cheese it, it's the cops.'"

"What does that mean, anyway?"

"Honestly, I have no idea." Still gazing at the mess, she put her hands on her hips. "Before I pull a job, I run through it in my head. Stop here, duck there, turn left, up the stairs."

"That makes sense," he offered, wishing she'd used the past tense.

"I can't get inside Etienne's head with this. I've tried, and it *doesn't* make sense."

"Run through it with me," Richard suggested, moving closer. "I mean, I may not have your experience, but I know what's logical."

To his surprise, she nodded. "That might help. But not with Castillo and Harvard here—and certainly not my boss."

"Tom's going to rat you out to Irving if you call him that again, by the way."

"Fine. Yale."

"We'll test your theory after dinner."

"You know," she said, coming up to him and slipping her arms around his waist, "you took me out to dinner at the Donners', so I thought I might do the same thing."

"You want to take me out to dinner." He didn't move, letting her control the level of intimacy between them.

"Yes." She leaned up to kiss him lightly.

"Will it be like a date?"

She hesitated for the briefest of moments. "Sure. And I can almost guarantee that you'll get lucky later, too."

He wanted to mark this in his calendar. It was the first time Sam had made a step to push this little relationship of theirs further in more than just a physical sense. "Before or after we run through Etienne's version of the robbery?"

Samantha chuckled, leaning forward against his chest and sliding her hands down his backside. When she straightened she had his wallet in one hand. He'd never even felt her lift it.

"Maybe both." She pulled the leather open. "I thought so," she said in a singsong voice, tossing the wallet back to him, intact as far as he could tell.

He caught it. "You thought what?"

"Most guys carry one condom," she said, breezing past him for the stairs. "One. Not three. Man, you must think you're pretty good in bed."

"So I've been told."

"We'll make it a quick dinner, then, and you can prove it to me all over again."

"Samantha?"

She stopped, turning to face him. "Mm-hm?"

"This isn't the most romantic thing to say, but since you brought up the condom thing, the last two times we haven't used . . . protection. Are you—"

"I'm clean, if that's what you're asking."

Richard flushed. "No. I meant, are you protected?"

"Jeez, you're so British," she said, chuckling. "I take the pill."

"Oh. Good. Yes, that's what I meant."

Samantha swept back up and kissed him hard on the lips. "Thanks for asking."

"Just being a gentleman."

"That reminds me. You have to wear shorts to dinner."

With a mock scowl that felt fairly real he followed her back to the library. "Shorts? What kind of dress code is that?"

She grinned as she vanished into the room. "Mine."

Twenty-four

Castillo called in three cops and a U-Haul to help cart off the fakes. After some discussion he agreed to question Partino and his attorney about the forgeries in the morning, and not to contact the FBI until after he'd called Donner with whatever information he could divulge. Samantha knew he wasn't precisely following regulations, and to her great surprise she found herself liking him.

This little jaunt of hers was becoming stranger and stranger. First she'd found friendship with someone she would have previously dismissed as a mark, then at least a respectful understanding with a lawyer, and now a similar situation with a cop. What was next, a priest?

"This had better be good," Richard said, joining her in the foyer. "I don't normally do shorts under anything less than dire circumstances."

"Those are nice," she said, grinning as he approached. He'd worn them, loose and gray and tasteful. He'd also put on the black T-shirt that made her want to jump him and forget all about dinner. And she'd intended for the attire to put *him* off-balance. She'd tried to convince herself that this had been a clever test of how far he would bend at her request, but she'd never been much for self-deception. This was about whether she could be normal, leave her world behind for a night.

"If this is your idea of a joke, you're going to be very sorry."

Sam rolled her shoulders. *Get back in the game.* "Do you have a cheesy car?"

"By cheesy I'm going to assume that you mean cheap, in which case the answer is no."

She gave an exaggerated sigh, enjoying the look of increasing trepidation on his face. "Okay, I guess we can take the Benz."

"Which one?" he asked distinctly.

"The SLK. It's a small target."

"Crikey," he muttered. "I'm driving, in case I need to make a fast getaway."

If that was the strongest demand he made all evening, she'd be surprised. "Fair enough. Let's go, then."

When they reached downtown Palm Beach she finally told him where they were going. "Harold and Chuck's," he repeated. "I've heard of that, haven't I?"

"The Fabulous Baker Boys used to play there. They have great seafood. And dancing."

"Dancing. Do we like to dance?"

She nodded. "We do."

"In shorts?"

"We have to look like tourists."

He turned up Royal Poinciana Way and slid the Mercedes up against the curb with a precision she couldn't help but admire—especially considering that he'd grown up in a country where they drove on the wrong side of the street. "Why do we have to look like tourists?" he asked, putting the retracted hard top back up.

"Because mostly tourists come here."

Rick touched her cheek. "As you've pointed out before, I don't blend very well," he murmured, stroking a strand of hair behind her ear, "but I'll try."

He didn't blend very well at all; but if he'd come wearing his rich guy shirt and slacks, they probably wouldn't have made it through the door without some paparazzi snapping their photo. This way, any interested parties would at least have to look twice. Besides, he had nice legs.

"Sidewalk or garden room?" the hostess asked as they strolled inside. Rick, of course, had her hand, and as the hordes of tourist women inside turned to look at the dark-haired god with the deep gray eyes, Sam couldn't help but feel a little smug.

"You're the date," she told him. "It's your choice."

"Garden room," he decided.

She would have preferred the sidewalk seating, so she could keep her eyes on the street. That, however, would not do anything to forward her experiment in normalcy. She followed the hostess, allowing Rick to pull her chair out for her as they arrived at their seats.

"Okay, I'll admit," he said, sitting forward to be heard over the jazz music the live band played behind them, "most everybody is wearing shorts."

"Told ya."

"Now, my dear, since you asked me out, may I assume that you'll be paying?"

"Yes, you may." One night wouldn't break her Retirement-in-Milan bank account. "Indulge yourself."

His smile deepened, warming the gray of his eyes. Her heart did a weird little flip-flop in response, and she quickly grabbed her glass of water and gulped down a swallow.

"Anything to drink, folks?" the waitress asked, her name tag proclaiming her as Candy. Sure she was.

"Do you have a wine list?" Rick asked smoothly, lifting an eyebrow at Sam, obviously hoping to make her regret the "indulge yourself" crack.

"Basically we have colors. Red and white."

Rick flashed his famous smile, and Candy nearly swallowed her gum. "What's your best red wine, then?"

She named off a French Merlot, and Rick asked for a bottle. "Sure. I'll be back in a minute to take your order."

"Humph. She didn't even ask what I wanted to drink," Sam noted.

"Well, she probably assumes that you're *my* date, and that I was ordering for both of us. Shall I snap and have her return?"

"Shut up, Brit. Merlot's fine."

With another chuckle, Rick opened the menu. "You've eaten here before, yes? What's good here?"

"The side salads are nice. And the breadsticks."

"Excuse me," a breathy female voice came from beside her, and she lifted her head. A stunning blonde in a dress cut down to her belly button and up to her crotch hovered beside the table.

"Yes?" she asked, not certain whether to scream or laugh.

"Are you Richard Addison?" the woman breathed, ignoring Sam.

Rick blinked. "Oh, me. I thought you were talking to her. Yes, I am."

"Could I have your autograph?"

"Certainly. Do you have a pen?" The woman held out a napkin and a pen, and Rick signed his name. "There you go."

"How about your phone number?" The woman gave a low giggle, but pressed the napkin back into Rick's hand.

Sam would have stood, but Rick kicked her under the table. "Ouch," she grumbled, glaring at him.

"I'm sorry, but I don't give out my phone number."

"Are you sure?" Belly Button Girl licked her lips.

"If I might make a comment," Rick continued, granting her a warm smile, though Sam noted that his eyes remained cool and untouched, "I'm a bit occupied right now, enjoying the company of a very lovely young lady with whom I enjoy spending my every spare moment." He straightened further, lowering his voice to a bare murmur. "So I thank you for your interest, but I am never in a million years going to give you my phone number. Good evening."

Her face turning scarlet under its inch of makeup, the woman turned away, departing with a sway of her perfect hips. "You're so cool," Sam breathed.

"You could at least pretend to be jealous," he said, pulling her hand across the table to kiss her knuckle.

She *had* been jealous, but no way was she going to tell him that. Not until she could figure out for herself what the hell it meant. At least she hadn't panicked and tried to belt a near-naked woman for sneaking up behind her. "She's not your type."

"And what precisely is my 'type'?" he asked.

"The kind who could have handed you a comeback instead of just stomping away."

With an uncharacteristic snort he sipped his own glass of water. "You're probably right. So what should I order?"

"Not in the mood for a side salad?" She grinned at his pained expression. A little annoyance served him right for being so gorgeous. "Okay, okay. The Alaska King Crab Claws are great. I'm getting the Macadamia Nut Encrusted Mahi."

He trusted her enough to order the crab, and she had to admit that the fish with the Merlot was much better than the beer she had been about to order. They'd retracted the garden room canopy roof, and moon and starlight shown down on the dance floor. She hadn't realized it would be so . . . romantic inside the garden room, with the jazz band playing and the couples beginning to swirl about the floor.

Finally, he set his fork and claw-cracker down on his plate. "You were right. That was great."

Sam realized she was drifting, and she lifted up her napkin. "I'm glad you liked it."

"Do you want to dance, my dear?"

"I—"

He stood, holding his hand down to her. Well, she'd suggested it first. Sighing, she took his hand and allowed him to pull her to her feet.

"I have a confession to make," he said in a low voice, sliding both hands around her waist.

"What?"

"That woman could have been naked, and I still wouldn't have been able to keep my eyes off you."

They swayed together, touching at arms, chest, hips, and thighs. "She practically was naked."

"Was she? I supposed that proves my point, then."

He'd thought Samantha meant to take him to some hole-in-the-wall restaurant in a demilitarized zone. Chuck and Harold's, however, was nice, lively, and even romantic with its open-air dance floor. He generally preferred more exclusive restaurants, because people there were less likely to approach him for autographs or investment advice, but he liked it here well enough that he would join her again.

It did feel a little silly to be slow dancing in shorts, and he didn't object when after twenty minutes or so she suggested they return to the estate to go over the gallery again. Their bill, somewhere around a hundred dollars, waited for them at the table, but Samantha wouldn't let him pay. Instead she pulled a healthy roll of cash out of her purse and put it on the table. He didn't want to know where she'd gotten the money.

"You're my date, remember?" she said, taking his arm as they went back to the SLK.

"Do you want to drive?"

"Really? I'd love to."

She put the roof back down and shifted the car into drive, then shoved it into park again.

"What is it?" he asked, noting the frown on her face.

"I just want you to know that I don't like you for this," she said, tapping the steering wheel.

"No?"

"No. I like you for . . . this." She reached over and tapped his head, drawing a strand of his hair through her fingers, and then put a hand over his chest. "And this. And because you wore shorts to a restaurant when I asked you to. Are we clear?"

He smiled at her. "We're clear."

"Good. Hang on."

As soon as they got back he threw on a pair of jeans and sneakers and met her in the gallery. She was standing at the opposite end of the hall from where she'd been the first time he saw her, her eyes closed and her hands loose at her sides. He watched her, knowing that in her mind she would be climbing down the back wall, slipping across the corner of the garden and the lawn.

"Are we in the house yet?" he asked after a moment.

Samantha jumped. "No. We're right outside." With a slight frown she turned her back, heading toward the stairs at the rear of the house. "Come on."

"How did we get in?" he asked, following her to the ground floor.

She slipped out through the back patio door, ending up in the deep shadows beneath a stand of cypress trees at the west side of the house. "The problem with this," she said, gauging the distance from the nearest camera, "is that I'm speculating based on something that might not be correct. So I'm either all right, or all wrong."

"It's worth a try," he offered, realizing for perhaps the first time what she meant when she said his security was crap. A rugby squad could have held a scrum where they were and not been noticed. "And I happen to think you have very good instincts."

"Hm. Flattery will get you whatever you want," she said with a quick grin, most of her attention still clearly on their surroundings.

A low energy ran up his spine, like the night they'd broken into Danté's. She'd mentioned the rush she got from being somewhere she wasn't supposed to be. He understood what she meant, though his focus remained on the petite figure beside him. "Shall we?"

"Okay. Here's my theory: Etienne came from this direction because it's the most protected route from where we found the footprint to the house."

"Why bother being sneaky if he's got Danté shutting down all the outside video?" Richard asked.

"I have a theory, but let's wait a minute." She slid her hand along the rough plaster wall, slipping farther into the shadows. "What's in here?" she asked, tapping on a window.

He adjusted his perspective. "That would be storage. Extra chairs and table extensions for big parties. That kind of thing."

She flicked on a flashlight he hadn't realized she carried. "There it is." With her fingertip she brushed at a faint scratch in the paint, running in toward the sill. "He slipped in a flat crow and pushed the latch open."

"So it wasn't just the outside cameras and sensors that were shut down."

"I don't think anything outside was shut down," she muttered, "or Etienne wouldn't have bothered with sneaking. If I'm right, Partino probably shut down all the internal house sensors and alarms; that's easier, especially when he might not have known exactly what kind of security you had around the door in the gallery. But we're getting ahead of ourselves. Let's go back in."

"In?"

"Through the door, unless you want to climb through the window," she said, her teeth a faint upward-curved white in the darkness.

"Let's go in."

They went back in through the patio door and headed down the maze of hallways to the storage room. The door was locked, but Samantha had it open before he could produce the key.

"The window latch is broken," she said, moving through the sheeted stacks of extra furniture. "See?" Using the back end of the flashlight, she tapped on the latch. It looked locked, but at her light touch it slipped sideways.

"DeVore broke it so he could make it look locked when he left through the same window."

"Yep."

"All right, I have a question."

"Shoot."

"Why was DeVore in the house if Danté was going to switch the tablets on his own?"

"That, my dear, is the bazillion-dollar question," she said, leaving the room again. "Okay, we're Etienne. We know where the gallery is, because we have blueprints. We also know the safe room camera won't be recording, the same way we knew it would be safe to break in through the window."

"So we go up the back stairs to the third floor," he said, as they did so, "being careful to avoid that Addison guy's crappy security until we're safely in the gallery."

She continued forward. "We get to the door, and we can be a little sloppy with cutting the secondary lock because the evidence is going to get blown up in a couple of minutes, anyway." The door hung off one hinge halfway into the room, but she went through the motions with her agile hands, then stepped inside.

"Since we know the sensor alarms are off," she continued, "we grab the tablet and slip out again, closing the door behind us."

"Why?"

"My guess would be that he wanted everything to look normal from the gallery. If Prentiss, for example, had seen the door open he might have gone in, then run back the same way, without tripping the bomb."

Richard looked at her for a long moment. "So Prentiss was the target?"

She squatted close to the wall as if setting the explosives. With a deep breath she straightened again. "You know, I don't think so."

"Tell me what you're thinking."

"This is the part I'm really not sure about." She wiped her hands on the back of her shorts, her gaze steady on the hole low in the wall where the bomb had been. "Bear with me for a minute—this is going to sound really screwy."

"I have the feeling that screwy is the only thing that'll

make any sense. And what about the security guards? Danté couldn't shut *them* down."

"They make fifteen-minute rounds. Etienne knew that, just like I did."

"So Partino and DeVore were working together."

"I don't think so. I see several indications that Etienne knew Partino was going to be shutting off the internal alarms. What I don't see is any sign that Partino knew Etienne was going to be here."

Digesting that theory, Richard lifted his head to look in the direction of the gallery entrance. "But we are sure it was Partino who turned off the camera feeds and the alarms, yes?"

"Right, because he did it when he set the grenades and planted the fake tablet on me." Abruptly she stepped forward. "Let's be Partino for a minute."

She headed downstairs, not to the estate manager's office, but to his small private room. "At after midnight, he would have spent the night here, right?"

"Yes."

"Going with the theory that he's the one who's been switching out the other art, I'm going to assume he had a fairly handy way of shutting off the alarms." Her frown of concentration deepened. "Either that, or he owns Clark. We're not talking a cut of a cut of one stolen Trojan tablet, now. We're talking fifty million dollars in stuff going out the door on a fairly steady basis."

"That's an interesting theory," Richard said darkly.

"But it's not for tonight." Opening Partino's door as easily as she'd done the storage room, she stepped inside again. "He probably had the fake in here, since you and Donner both have access to his office." She gazed around the room, a soft frown touching her face. "I meant to ask you before, why aren't there any artworks or anything in here?"

"I don't know. I really didn't supervise much of the private room decorating."

"Even the guest suites have some nice stuff in them.

Here's the guy in charge of collecting and cataloging everything, and he's got a few prints and a faux-Victorian pitcher."

Nodding, Richard finished the tour of the room with her.
"Nothing valuable can go missing in here, where he'd likely
be the prime suspect."

"According to this theory, anyway. Okay. We've switched
off the alarms and gotten hold of the fake tablet to put in
place of the real one. We've told . . . whoever our broker is
which day and time we're going to have possession of the
item, and whoever our buyer or broker was also told Etienne,
or whoever hired him."

"How do we know he did that?"

"Because from the way Etienne came into the house, he
knew the alarms would be off."

"Right. Go on."

"The tablet's expected by the broker and the buyer, and it's
going to London in a week, so whether Partino knows you're
back from Stuttgart or not, he's got to go and make the exchange. Etienne probably has no idea you're back, but he
wouldn't care. Danté starts up, has the security radio on either because he's paranoid or because that way Clark can
warn him if somebody's on to him. Maybe he overhears the
security calls like you did, that Prentiss has found an intruder.
He panics and goes back to his room, switching all the alarms
back on so nobody will be thinking it was an inside job."

"And then everything blows up, the tablet goes missing,
and he's stuck with the fake."

"Yeah. With one additional point." Samantha stopped back
upstairs where she'd originally entered the gallery. "If I
hadn't broken in, and if you hadn't been here, *he* would have
been the one to trip the wire."

Richard looked at her. The way she put the pieces together,
it made sense. "Danté was the target."

"With a lot of if's, probably's, and maybe's thrown in."

"How about a why?" he countered. "Why would someone
hire DeVore to take the tablet and kill Partino, if Partino was

going to take the tablet anyway? I mean from what you said, whoever dictated the timing of this told both of them—which would say to me that it was the same person."

"That, I'm not sure about. And there's also the question of who wanted me in here at the same time all this other shit was going on."

Someone had not just sent her in to steal something. They'd intentionally thrown her into the middle of some private little battle and not given her any idea what she was getting into. Richard swallowed. Samantha Jellicoe had been extremely lucky. And though he'd never met Sean O'Hannon, if the broker had known about any of this, Richard was glad he was dead. "Would O'Hannon have done all of this?" he asked. "Hired all three of you for the same job?"

Samantha shook her head. "He didn't have enough imagination to coordinate three different break-ins at the same time, in the same place, with no one knowing about anyone else. Besides, somebody killed him, too."

"Why you in the first place? You didn't know anything about the general sucking away of my valuables."

"My guess is that I was supposed to be the scapegoat. Whether I got killed or caught, I'd get blamed for the mess. Probably they hoped Partino and the fake would be found in the rubble. Everyone would assume it was the original, of course, and that he'd taken it back from me right before I messed something up and we were all killed."

"I admire your sangfroid, talking about your own death so calmly."

Stepping up to him, she kissed his cheek. "That's only because I'm not dead. Believe me, I'm pissed off." She cursed, kicking a charred piece of wood sideways. "And with Etienne and O'Hannon dead, I have no way of knowing who hired them. Stoney might be able to find out, but he could be anywhere right now. We can't ask Partino, since in a few hours Castillo's turning him and all your fakes over to the FBI."

"And they'll solve this," he pointed out.

"Yeah. And most of the fucking clues still kinda point in

my direction. Which means that our partnership gets dissolved, and I get the hell out of here."

His throat tightening, he caught her hand. *Jesus Christ.* What had he done? He'd known about Castillo's plan and the FBI—why hadn't he made the connection that she would still be a suspect? The answer was obvious—he couldn't conceive of her leaving, under any circumstances, and he was used to being the one in command of all aspects of a situation. Dammit. He wasn't letting her go.

"You might have said something about that before we called Castillo in," he said, using every bit of his years of hard-earned self-control to sound calm.

She squeezed his fingers. "Rick, three people are dead. I think that weighs heavier than my personal comfort." The look she gave him said a great deal more than her words, but he wasn't certain yet how to translate it—other than to realize that she didn't want to go.

How could he fix it, then, so that she could stay? Obviously, finding whoever had arranged all this would take the heat off her, but as she'd said, all of the clues had been removed from their grasp. He narrowed his eyes. Or maybe they hadn't been. "That green dress you wore to Tom's? Go put it on."

"What? Considering how little time I—"

"And heels. There're some in the closet if you didn't bring any." She continued to look stubborn, and he leaned down and kissed her. "Trust me. I'll meet you in the foyer."

Samantha had no idea what he might be thinking, but once she'd realized how much time and effort someone had gone to in order to orchestrate this long-term robbery of his estate, she'd known she would have to leave. The FBI and Interpol didn't have anything concrete enough to arrest her yet, but this would probably do it. Then they could take their time digging for more. And as her father used to say, digging always turned up worms.

The decision to go shouldn't even have been a difficult one. At most she had another twenty-four hours before the men in suits came looking for her. In the back of her mind she'd known something like this would happen; once she'd learned that Etienne had been killed she'd realized that more had to be at stake than a tablet.

If she left before dawn, she might be able to get a flight out. Once Castillo had decided not to look in her direction, the net would have loosened considerably.

Sam yanked the dress off its hanger and flung it onto the bed. Then she hurled a pair of tan shoes against the far wall. The thud they made was satisfying, but it didn't change anything. She still had to leave Solano Dorado House—leave him.

It so figured. She'd been living quietly on the outskirts of Palm Beach for nearly four years, working at a job she enjoyed and that didn't require bolt cutters or paint guns, doing the occasional work for Stoney if it piqued her interest or her curiosity. Then a week after she met . . . probably the most fascinating man she'd ever encountered, she had to leave. Fate sucked. Big-time.

Whatever Rick had in mind, he seemed to want her to look nice for it, so she took a moment to comb out her hair and refresh her makeup. As she checked her face in the mirror, she felt the unexpected urge to cry. "Buck up, Sam," she growled. She never cried. Just because she'd finally realized what it meant, how it felt, to have someone so dynamic, so important in her life, it didn't mean she got to keep it.

When she joined Rick in the foyer, she forgot her tears. She nearly forgot to breathe. He stood by the front door in a black suit with a gray shirt and a red tie. Even though she could never mistake him for anything but a confident, self-assured, and successful man, he abruptly looked . . . powerful.

"Wow," she said. "Armani really works for you."

"Thanks, and wow, back. Ready?"

"Where are we going?"

"Jail."

Twenty-five

Monday, 11:08 p.m.

The officer led them into what looked like one of the interrogation rooms from *Law and Order*, though Sam had never seen one in person until now. She stared at the wall-sized mirror, wondering who in hell was standing behind it, ready to watch and listen to their conversation.

"Relax," Rick whispered, drawing her down onto the chair beside him.

"How do we know we're alone?" she muttered back, still gazing at the glass. "What if I say something, you know, incriminating?"

He took her hand and kissed her knuckles. "You'll just have to trust me, Samantha. I won't let anything happen to you in here. I swear it."

She forced a smile. "Your shining armor is showing again."

Rick would have replied, but Danté Partino arrived in the doorway, another officer on his heels. He wore jail orange and his hands were cuffed to his belt, Sam noted with an uneasy breath. She couldn't imagine being closed into a tiny room and her hands bound.

"Could you take those off?" Rick asked, gesturing at Partino's hands.

"It's not really . . . Yeah, okay. But just for ten minutes."

As soon as the door closed, Danté slammed his chair back and stood. "Am I supposed to think you're here to help me? I have worked for you for ten years, Rick. And because this whore climbs into your bed, you believe any lie she tells you?"

"Danté, I didn't have to come here tonight," Rick said, his voice so cool and calm that Sam had to glance over at him. "Are they treating you well? I told Tom to find you the best attorney possible, at my expense."

Partino's face folded into a frown. "This is a mess," he said in a more even tone. "I have no idea what anyone is saying about me, that I stole that tablet, and that I tried to kill . . . her. Why would I do this?"

Rick nudged her under the table, and Sam jumped. That meant she was supposed to start in on Partino, she imagined. She took a breath, trying to forget where they were and that damned mirror over her shoulder.

"Money comes to mind," she drawled.

"I'm not listening to anything you say," he snapped back. "Besides, I already have money. Rick pays me well, because I do good work. You ask anyone. I had no reason to steal that tablet."

"I'm not talking about that tablet. Your cut of that would be, what, ten thousand dollars? That's chump change, even for a moron like you."

Partino leaned his fists on the table, obviously trying to intimidate her. "You are the moron, because I know that you are really the one who stole it. They found that fake in *your* bag. Not mine."

"That's because all your fakes were already up on the walls," she retorted.

He actually blanched. "I don't know what you're talking about."

"Oh, come on, Danté. The Picasso looked like it was painted by a baboon. And you're such an idiot, you even kept a record of when you took the real one."

"Nonsense!"

"June 1999," she said, mentally crossing her fingers. One wrong step, and he wouldn't cave. And in here, she wasn't precisely feeling at her best. Jesus. Her, and jail.

He glared at her with such hatred in his eyes that she steeled herself for him to come over the table at her. Instead, with a harsh breath she could feel on her face, he strode to the mirror and back again. Rick turned in his chair to keep Partino in view; evidently he didn't trust the man any further than she did.

"You can't prove anything," he hissed. "I am a good man."

"I can prove everything," she retorted, allowing disgust to creep into her voice. "Do you want me to list some more? The Remington? The blue Gauguin?"

"Shut up!"

"Sure, but it won't make any difference. The FBI will be coming to see you in the morning. I just wanted you to know that I know what you did, and that I told Rick, and that to-morrow the FBI will know, too. Can we go now?" She looked at Rick, only half-pretending.

The estate manager's face had gone gray. Seeming to lose muscle control, he sank into his chair. "The FBI. You whore."

Rick slammed his fist on the table, and both Sam and Partino jumped. "*Enough*," he growled.

"Rick, I—"

"Shut up, Danté! I want two words from you, and then I'll do what I can to help. If you don't give me those two words, I'll use every last dollar I possess to make sure you are found guilty of killing Prentiss and of trying to kill me."

"I never—"

"Those aren't the two words."

"What . . . what do you want, then?"

"The name of your buyer for the tablet. We know you had your own plans for it."

"I don't—"

"Those aren't the two words, either. Last chance, Danté." He sat back, his gaze steady on Partino's face. "Who was going to buy that tablet from you?"

His mouth opened and closed like a fish, then Danté swallowed convulsively. "Meridien," he finally rasped. "Harold Meridien."

The name sounded vaguely familiar to Samantha, but Rick's jaw clamped shut. For a second she thought she'd been worried about restraining the wrong guy when he lurched to his feet. "I'll make certain the authorities know you've cooperated," he said in a hard voice. "But for your own sake, you'd best hope you never get out of prison."

"Rick—"

Rick strode to the door and rapped on it. The officer pulled it open, and giving a stiff nod, Rick left. With a gasp Sam hurried after him.

"Give me the keys," he said, once they were in the parking lot. "I know you lifted them."

"No way. Get in, and I'll drive us back."

"I want to drive."

She cocked her head at him. "If I looked like you, would you let *me* drive?"

"Samantha—"

"You're pissed, you want to drive fast, and you want to kill this Meridien guy. I'll drive fast, and you can still be mad back at the estate. In the meantime, you can tell me who Meridien is and how you know him. And I can remind you how brave I was to walk in there, and how it's the first and last time I will ever do that again."

With a curt nod, he stepped back from the driver's door and strode around to the far side of the car. "Drive really fast," he growled.

She drove really fast. Rick sat staring out the front window, still as a statue—or more like a volcano about to erupt. Meridien. The name had something to do with big business or banking or something, but she couldn't place him any closer than that. When she'd heard the name she'd had her attention on something else, or she would have remembered. Rick would tell her, but if he didn't do it soon, she'd still have to go. Not even for Rick would she risk being hunted down by the FBI.

Frank Castillo watched as the officer put handcuffs back on Partino and escorted him from the interrogation room. He'd broken the tip of the pencil with which he'd been jotting down notes, but despite being mad enough to spit nails, he had to admit that Sam Jellicoe might have found a career as a detective, if fate and her father hadn't pushed her in another direction.

Harold Meridien. Some banker or something, he thought, but he'd check to be sure. Not local, or he would have recognized the name. At least when Addison used his influence and flirted with obstruction of justice, he got information.

Wearily he climbed to his feet. Jellicoe and Addison hadn't pushed for the name of Partino's boss in the theft and forgery business, so they definitely had something else in mind. And Addison had recognized the name. Well, it looked like he'd be making another trip to the estate in the morning. Whether they were getting results or not, there were rules to be followed. Even if Addison and Jellicoe only wanted answers, he wanted a conviction. And it was time they stopped playing games.

Samantha had barely stopped the car when Richard climbed out and strode up the front steps. He had some phone calls to make, and he didn't give a damn what time it might be where he was calling.

The front door closed behind him, none too gently. "Are you going to say anything?" Samantha demanded.

"Later," he snapped. "I need to be in Stuttgart tomorrow."

He was halfway up the first flight of stairs when he realized she wasn't following. Forcing a deep breath into his lungs, he turned around. "This just became very personal, Samantha. I'll explain later."

"Okay," she said after a moment, her face for once unreadable. "Good luck."

That sounded final. Richard frowned. "What is that supposed to mean?"

"Just what I said. Good luck."

"I don't have time for a tantrum, Samantha."

She tilted her head at him. In the dim light, he swore he saw a tear run down her cheek. "This isn't a tantrum, Rick," she returned, her voice cool and steady. "You have to go, and I have to go. That's all. It's just facts."

His heart stopped for a beat. "What? I'm just going to Stuttgart. I'll be back in a day or two, depending on what I find there." He descended a step.

Samantha sighed, her shoulders rising and falling with her heavy breath. "Tomorrow when the FBI goes after Partino, he's going to start spewing my name everywhere to try to cover his ass. I can't be here for that."

Ice shot down his spine at the thought of her in one of those tiny rooms, facing that mirror. In less than a second he made up his mind. "Come upstairs," he said. "And get packed. You're coming with me."

"You could end up being charged as an accessory," she returned, not moving. "That's not what this partnership was about."

"What this partnership *is* about," he countered, returning to the foyer and to her, "is not what it *was* about. I'm not letting you go. You don't disappear into the night, and I never hear from you again."

"Rick—"

He grabbed her shoulder, pulling her in and kissing her hard. She resisted for a bare moment, then flung her arms around his shoulders, molding her soft mouth to his. Richard held her tightly, the thought of what he'd almost allowed to happen leaving him cold.

"No," he murmured. "We're not finished, you and I." Reluctantly releasing her, he settled for taking her hand and pulling her up the stairs. "I have to call my pilot and arrange for my plane to be ready first thing in the morning. And I have to call a few people and make sure where Meridien is right now. And then we—you and I—are going to meet him for a little chat."

"Who is he to you?"

God, he even hated confessing it to her. This was three now, three people he'd known and who had tried to take from him. And it was only a small consolation that he'd never particularly liked Meridien. What mattered more, though, was that the person he chose to trust in all this happened to be a professional thief. "He was almost my partner in a banking enterprise until two weeks ago."

Twenty-six

Tuesday, 2:12 p.m.

"Change of plans," Rick said, an hour and a half into their flight. He hung up the phone at his elbow, the one he'd been on almost constantly since they took off.

"What change?" Sam had given up pretending to be too jaded to be impressed by a private jet with plush carpeting, a private cabin attendant, and a private back room with a bar, conference table, sofa bed, and a television. She turned from playing with the remote of the main cabin television to look up at him. They'd left later in the day than she'd expected, but after four hours of peering out the jet's windows and looking for cops, Interpol, FBI, and Eliot Ness, she was just glad to be airborne.

"He's not in Stuttgart. That was Tom, angry that we left without telling him."

"Neaner neaner," Sam returned. "Where are we going, then?"

"He's at the London branch." Rick sat back, sipping at the tea the attendant had wordlessly refilled every twenty minutes without prompting. "You know, I kept wondering why he wanted me to stay another day in Stuttgart, especially after the . . . extremely infeasible amount of money he wanted in exchange for controlling shares in his bank." He blew out his breath, disgust in every line of his handsome face. "He even offered to arrange a tour for the two of us at the Mercedes-Benz plant."

"Give him some credit," she returned. "He didn't want you walking into the middle of a robbery."

"Which begs the question of whether he knew about De-Vore and the explosives or not."

"If he did know, he didn't want you blown up."

"Of course not; I wouldn't be able to bail out his bloody bank if I were dead."

Sam cleared her throat. "How sure are we that Partino didn't just feed you a name to get you off his case? Can you imagine Meridien doing this to you?"

The frown he'd worn since last night deepened. "How did you describe DeVore? Larger than life, ambitious, not too squeamish about how he did business as long as the results were satisfactory?"

"Something like that."

"Well, that's pretty much Harry, too. He's tried to beat me to a deal a few times—and ended up taking some heavy losses because of it."

"Which is why he wanted you to buy shares of his bank."

He pushed to his feet. "Yes. I'll be right back. I have to tell Jack we're going to Heathrow." As he passed her he leaned down to kiss her on the forehead. "You should get some sleep. The couch in the back pulls out."

She could use some sleep. Before he could vanish into the cockpit, Sam reached up and touched his fingers, curling hers around them. "I've discovered something."

He stopped, facing her. "What?"

"I . . . like having you with me while I sleep." She scowled at his abrupt smug, arrogant expression. "It's just that you're nice and warm."

The smile curving his mouth deepened to his eyes. "Hm.

And here I am, just remembering that you promised I could have my way with you."

Damp heat started between her legs. She could certainly think of worse ways to spend a few hours. Especially when last night she'd thought the partnership had ended. "What a coincidence."

"Isn't it, though?"

When he returned from the cockpit a few minutes later she'd found a werewolf movie to watch, but not much else. She smiled at the lustful look in his eyes. It was a good thing Godzilla Week was over.

Rick knelt in front of her, sliding his hands slowly up her thighs and around her waist. "How long has it been since I've been inside you?" he murmured, gazing at her face.

"Oh, about sixteen hours, I think," she said, wishing her voice sounded a little steadier.

"Far too long." He leaned in, kissing the base of her jaw. Apparently he'd already learned that he could make her bones melt by kissing her there.

"Holy cow. I'm practically having an orgasm right now."

"Well, allow me to join you, then." He took her mouth, kissing her with lips and teeth and tongue.

"Okay, buddy, in the back room. Now," she said in as commanding a voice as she could muster.

He slid an arm under her thighs and another behind her back and lifted her up. "I can't believe how much I want you," he said. "I always want you."

He plunked her down on the conference table, returning to the door to close and lock it. "That's handy," she noted as he returned to her, yanking the buttons open on his shirt as he approached. "Are you a frequent flyer in the mile-high club?"

His mouth twitched. "I'm a member," he returned. "How can you have your own jet and not be? But as for frequent-flyer miles, no, I really haven't racked any up lately." He parted her knees, tugging her to the edge of the table and going to work on her jeans zipper. "No time like the present, I always say."

Sam reached up, pulling him down on top of her as his hand slid between the jeans and her panties. She gasped, lifting her hips. No one had ever made her feel like this, like she was floating, just by looking at her. When he touched her, time simply stopped. How was she ever going to give this up, give him up?

Rick leaned over her to push up her shirt, unfastening her bra and going to work on her nipples with his tongue and his teeth. She moaned, her hands clumsy as she unsnapped his jeans and shoved them down. He kicked them off, and slowly pulled hers down, kissing every inch of skin he exposed until she was panting for him.

"Dammit, Rick, now," she demanded, half-sitting up to grab his shoulders.

He groaned as he pulled her forward, planting himself deep inside her, the sound alone making her come. He ground into her, hard and fast, until she wrapped her legs around his hips and sat up, sliding her arms around his neck.

Still inside her, Rick lifted her in his arms, and they fell together onto the nearest couch. "God, you feel good," he panted, running his tongue along her ear. He lifted off her. "Turn over, Sam."

With a breathless laugh she complied, and with a slow slide he mounted her from behind. Rick reached beneath her to fondle her breasts, and she drew tight and shattered again.

"Rick," she groaned, feeling every inch of him as he continued his assault.

His pace increased, and with a growl he emptied himself into her. He collapsed to rest his head alongside hers, his weight warm and welcome.

Whether it was lust or safety or some kind of mutual need, for that moment together they were . . . perfect. They lay together for a long time, dozing, until Samantha finally lifted her head to look at him, then apparently gave up and let it sink back onto the couch. "Food. I need food," she grumbled.

"I think today's menu is fried chicken," he said, shifting the two of them so he was on the bottom, her agile body sprawled across his. So beautiful, she was, and in ways he didn't even think she realized. With his free hand he gently brushed hair from her temple.

"Chicken good. Me hungry," she returned, closing her eyes and resting her head on his chest.

He chuckled. "I could call Michelle and tell her we're ready to eat."

"Can't move. Dead."

"Yes, I figured it'd be up to me." Groaning, he stretched over to the end table and flicked the intercom button. "Michelle?"

"Yes, Mr. Addison?"

"Could you manage something for lunch for us?"

"Is ten minutes all right, sir?"

"That's splendid. Thanks."

He released the button, drawing his fingers along Samantha's arm. Even when he felt . . . satisfied, he still wanted to touch her, to hold her, to keep her safe.

"Rick?"

"Yes?"

"You totally rock." She curled her fingers around his as their hands met.

"Open your eyes," he whispered, looking up at her relaxed face.

Long lashes fluttered, and moss green gazed back at him. Very slowly he leaned up and kissed her, relishing the soft warmth of her mouth against his.

"Totally, totally," she added, smiling as he lowered his face from hers again.

"Samantha, promise me something."

"What?"

"Promise me that you won't leave without telling me, and without giving me a chance to change your mind."

She slid down his body. "I promise," she said.

He wanted to go straight from the airport to Harry's town house. It was still early, though, for the banker to be home.

Besides, it would mean having the limousine take them. Being driven to the kind of confrontation he anticipated wouldn't be nearly satisfying enough. His own place, just off Cadogan Square, was only a few blocks from Meridien's, anyway, so he settled for planning his attack and glaring through the bulletproof glass.

"Is this yours, too," Samantha asked from beside him, "or do you rent?"

"It's mine. Once I knew where we were headed, I had Ernest drive up from Devon to meet us."

"Devon. That's your other place, right?"

"That's my actual home, I guess you would call it. I grew up there."

"What's it like?"

He turned from his view of London to look at her. "Are you trying to distract me?"

She shrugged. "You look like you're ready to explode."

"And that's bad because . . ." he prompted.

"As Khan in *Star Trek* once said, 'revenge is a dish best served cold.' "

Richard couldn't help smiling at her. "I think someone else said it first."

"I know. But Khan's cool. He even quotes Melville."

"Do you remember everything?"

"Things that interest me, or are important to me, yes."

He wanted to ask what she remembered about him, but that sounded rather pitiful. He wanted to say something else to her, as well, had almost said it on the jet, when she couldn't run away, but that hadn't seemed fair. He wanted to tell her that he loved her. *Don't push*, he told himself. It was a large enough risk in his own mind. To include her, as possessive as he felt of her, could be . . . dangerous.

"It's not precisely revenge that I want," he said after a moment, returning to his view. "I mean it is, but first I want to know how and why and—"

The limousine slammed sideways. Metal crunched around them as Samantha hurtled against his shoulder hard enough to bruise. He grabbed her, bracing his legs on the floor and one arm against the bending sides of the car as they lurched in a sickening spin halfway into the air and smashed down to the road again.

"What—"

He caught sight of a large, heavy lorry through the broken window on Samantha's side of the car just as it hit them again, sending them across incoming traffic and toward the river. The limousine engine roared and clanked, and they lurched forward, spinning again as the truck slid with the shriek of tearing metal down toward the boot.

"Ernest!" he bellowed.

"I'm going, sir! He's trying to knock us into the Thames!"

They were grinding forward again, lurching like a broken crab, and the lorry roared up behind them. On the right, dizzyingly close, the banks of the Thames dropped steeply down to the river.

"Can we get to the trunk from here?" Samantha rasped, lurching against him again as the truck rear-ended them hard.

"Through the seats."

He didn't question as she dug into leather, looking for the latch. Instead he helped, yanking the seat forward and nearly falling to the floor as the truck rammed them from behind again.

"Open the roof," she snapped, diving into the smashed boot and reappearing with her hard-sided case.

He slammed down on the button, but after sliding open an inch, the moon roof stuck. Richard jammed his hand into the opening and shoved, his attention on Samantha as she opened her case and yanked out three pieces of what looked like a gun with a bulbous belly. She screwed them together, knees braced against his side to hold her steady.

"Grab my legs," she yelled, hefting the monstrosity and standing up through the opening in the roof.

He steadied her from below while she took aim and fired three shots in rapid succession. White paint exploded onto the windshield of the truck with enough force to crack the glass. It lurched sideways, swiping the side of a bus as it veered around blindly, windshield wipers smearing at the thick stuff.

"Get out, Ernest!" he shouted, grabbing Samantha back inside and kicking open his side door.

They tumbled out, diving behind the guardrail beside the river as the truck roared by them, smashing the limousine again, and continued on down the road. Richard stumbled around and half fell beside Samantha, who held the paint gun cradled in her arms as though her life depended on it.

"Are you all right?" he asked, pushing back her hair, trying to keep his hands from shaking.

"I'm fine. You're white as a sheet."

He kissed her, hard and deep. "That's twice I've almost lost you," he grunted, turning to find Ernest vomiting over the side of the road. "Ernest?"

The driver waved a hand at him. "Okay. Just bloody scared."

Two-toned police sirens came into hearing, and Samantha stiffened. "Shit. I can't go anywhere with you," she said, putting her finger through a hole in his light jacket.

"Give me the gun," he ordered.

"But—"

"This is my town," he said, "and my car. I can be a paint gun enthusiast if I want to. The fewer questions about you, the better."

She handed it over. "Okay. But your town sucks, so far."

With his free hand he gripped her arm and pulled her to her feet. "Very clever, by the way. I didn't know you'd brought your gear."

With a weak smile she brushed a shard of broken glass from his collar. "I never leave home without it. Rick, I think Dr. Evil knows we're here."

Sometimes you just couldn't catch a break. Sam sat in a hard-backed chair in her second police station in less than twenty-four hours while Rick gave his statement to the officer in charge. They'd believed him about the paint gun, and she hadn't had to do more than give her name—though handing over even that small amount of information gave her the willies. England was full of stuff she'd either stolen or at least been asked to relocate.

The police didn't seem that surprised that someone would want to kill Richard Addison, and she remembered what he'd said about receiving threats before. Apparently they had both found themselves in dangerous lines of work.

He walked between the glass-and-metal partitions and returned to her side. Sam had to stand up and hug him, both because she'd realized how much she'd come to rely on him over the past few days and because the only thing she'd been terrified about in the limousine had been that he might be hurt.

"I should take you to see the police more often," he said into her hair, slipping an arm around her waist as they headed for the door.

"We can go?"

"Of course. We're the victims, here. No possible explanation why someone would try to send us into the Thames."

"Yale's gonna be really mad he missed this, now."

With a quick smile he grabbed their scant luggage and led her down to the curb where a taxi waited for them. He'd already sent Ernest off in one, evidently realizing the poor guy was in no condition to drive. Giving directions to his town house off Cadogan Square, he sat back and cradled her against his shoulder, carefully, as if he thought she might break.

She felt ready to. Taking risks on her own was something she'd become used to, but she always knew where they were coming from, and she weighed the odds before she decided whether to leap or not. Grenades in doorways and rampaging trucks were new, and so was the idea that it wasn't just her own life at risk, not just herself she needed to protect. And whether it was idiotic or not, the man sitting beside her seemed determined not to let her vanish into the safety of the night.

"I'm afraid we'll be on our own in the house," he said conversationally. "The police have already been through it with bomb detectors, but I'm not sending for any of my staff until this is resolved."

"When are we going to see Meridien?"

If he noticed the "we," he didn't say anything about it. He probably expected it, by now. "No sense going now. He'll still be at the office with dozens of people I don't want overhearing our conversation. We'll go this evening. He'll be home in time to catch the football match."

"Works for me. And it's soccer."

Her case and her knapsack had crossed the Atlantic with her, and they now rode behind them in the cab's trunk with Rick's things. If he didn't own the town, as he'd claimed, he at least had some pull here. The police had even given him back the paint gun, minus the remaining pellets.

He owned the building's penthouse, and while it looked nice if nondescript from the outside, once they went in she had no trouble recognizing it as his. Expensive wood beams crossed the ceiling, and in the dining room the chandelier looked to be sixteenth century, fitted with electricity to replace the candles.

"Sorry it's so small," he said, throwing his jacket over a Louis XIV chair. "I gave Patricia the big London house and bought this one."

"Yeah, it's tiny, but it's homey," she said with a grin, gliding her fingers over the frame of the Georgian china cabinet. "Why not give this one to her and keep your house?"

He shrugged, disappearing into another room and emerging with a chilled can of soda for her. "I didn't want to live there any longer."

"Is it close by?"

"About three miles. And no, we're not going over to say hello."

"I didn't say we should. I just wanted to know." A thought occurred to her. "Did you leave any artworks there?"

His half-amused expression faded into a frown. "No. Why?"

"Just wondering whether Danté might have been busy there, too."

"Not likely. I stripped it of all my things, including the antiques. Most of them ended up over here, or in Florida. They were the only houses I wasn't . . . finished with outfitting."

"Did you leave them any furniture?"

His smile reappeared, grimmer this time. "A little. Late-model Ikea."

"Remind me never to get on your bad side," she said, not for the first time, and wandered to the windows. The view was nice, though a hundred and fifty years ago it would have been stunning. London always vaguely disappointed her; for a place with so much history crammed into it, it looked so . . . ordinary, now. And so modern. There were parts of it she liked, the museums and the historical buildings, but she'd never had much of a chance to visit those.

"Hey."

She turned around, and he flipped a British silver pound at her. She caught it reflexively, examining it in the wan remains of sunlight. "What's this for?"

"Your thoughts."

Rick would know if she lied. "My thoughts are kind of jumbled right now," she said quietly, pocketing the money. "Tonight or tomorrow, this could be over."

"I've been thinking about that, too," he returned, joining her at the window. "I'm not usually away from Devon for so long. Would you like to see the house there?"

"What are you really asking me, Rick?" she said quietly.

"I'm asking if you'd like to spend more time with me, in Devon."

She wanted to. It would be so easy just to fall into his life. After the first few days or weeks, though, she'd just be his appendage, his toy, until he got tired of her, and until she got tired of being normal. No purpose, no work, no job—

because she certainly wouldn't be able to resume her usual nighttime activities if she was living with him.

"Looks like I need to get some more money," he said, gazing at her. "Don't answer now. Just think about it."

"Okay," she answered, because she didn't want to tell him no. "I'm thinking about it."

"Any kind of hint, though?"

"Rick, don't push—"

The phone on the end table rang. They both jumped, then with a muttered curse Rick picked it up. "Addison."

As the person on the other end of the line spoke, his face closed off—but not before Sam saw the anger and the remains of a deep hurt there. Patricia, she guessed, not surprised when he said her name a moment later.

"It just happened a few hours ago," he said in a short, clipped voice. "I'm not responsible for what the BBC chooses to broadcast on the news, and no, I don't think I need to inform you when I'm going to be in town."

He listened for another moment, then drew a breath. "The woman in the car with me isn't any of your business either, Patricia. I have another call coming in. I'm hanging up now."

Sam stifled a smile. She'd never been involved in this sort of conversation before, with the ex-wife jealousy thing. Interesting. And a little flattering.

After a few seconds his expression grew more annoyed. "No, I don't want to meet for dinner. I'm here on business. Yes, with her."

Leaning back against the windowsill, Samantha found herself wishing she could hear precisely what Patricia Addison-Wallis was saying. Because from Rick's responses and the way she'd learned to read people, she had the feeling that Patricia still had a serious thing for her ex-husband.

"No, not lunch or breakfast either. I'm here with someone, and you're married. I take the vow seriously." He paused. "For God's sake, Patricia—I'd call it more than a mistake. Isn't Peter there? Good—go complain to him. I'm not in the mood for this."

Sam shook herself. As deeply interested as she found herself in the conversation, it really wasn't any of her business. "Where's the bathroom?" she asked quietly.

He gestured, and she left the room. The bathroom was all white tile and gold fixtures, and she remembered that she badly wanted a shower. Slipping out again, she headed for the sitting room and her knapsack.

"Yes, it's serious," Rick was saying, and she stopped just inside the hallway. "She's . . . she takes my breath away. No, I'm not going to compare you. Christ, Patricia, I've moved on. I've found someone else. And so have you, supposedly. So—"

Thud. Sam hurried back to the bathroom and locked the door. Breathing hard, she fought off her first-ever panic attack and leaned her forehead against the cool tile counter.

He'd found someone. He'd found *her*. In the back of her mind she'd known, but now she had to acknowledge that their partnership, this game, had changed drastically. He was serious, and so was she—or she wanted to be, but wasn't quite sure how to do it. She didn't know how much of herself she could give up to be with him, or how much of a new, improved Samantha he would even like.

"Samantha?" Rick knocked on the door. "Sam? Are you all right?"

"Fine. Just jet-lagged and truck-smashed. How's Patricia?"

"Nosy. I'm going to throw together a sandwich, then I think we'd better go. We've been on the news, so Harry will know I'm in London. Fanatical as he is about football—soccer—I'm still not sure he wouldn't leave town before the end of the match."

"Okay. I'll be out in a minute."

"Do you want something to eat?"

"I don't suppose you have peanut butter and jelly."

"No, but I have jam."

"Smart ass."

He couldn't know what she'd overheard, but that probably didn't matter. He'd asked her about Devon, and he probably knew the question had unsettled her, so he was trying to distract her. What that meant admitting, though, was that Rick was braver than she was.

"Rick?" She pulled open the door.

He reappeared in front of her. "I can send out for jelly if that's what you really want."

"You said Peter Wallis had disappointed you. What did Patricia do?"

"Other than the obvious?" For a long moment he looked at her. "Patricia had a plan. She wanted a set number of things: money, nice house, elite circle of friends, invitations to exclusive parties. I made the plan possible."

"But you asked her to marry you."

"I thought she fit into *my* plans." He shrugged. "I could claim ignorance or something I suppose, but that wouldn't be true. Plans change, Sam. After a short, happy beginning, what I needed wasn't her, and what she needed wasn't me." He touched her cheek. "Come on, and I'll make your sandwich."

"I'll be right there." Sam ducked back into the bathroom. Plans. Plans did change, didn't they? But how much, and for how long? She paced for a few minutes, then splashed cold water on her face and went to go have a sandwich.

Just after dusk Richard pulled out of his garage with Samantha beside him. The BMW had barely been driven before now, but it turned over easily enough, and he had the satisfaction of having Sam call it his "James Bond car."

Being Tuesday evening in London on a game night, traffic was fairly light. He couldn't help his abrupt impatience, even though he didn't think Meridien would bolt from a possible confrontation. In all fairness, Harry wasn't much for panicking.

He was one for being ruthless, which was why Richard had dumped a Glock 30 into his jacket pocket. He shouldn't have had a pistol in England, and if he got caught with it, much less using it, he'd be in a large amount of trouble. This, however, was not a typical business meeting with a potential partner, and he wasn't going in unprepared.

They parked around the corner from Meridien's town house. The neighborhood was quiet, occupied mostly by retired couples now, who'd grown older with the houses around them.

"Is that it?" Samantha asked, as they reached the corner.

"Yes."

"Which floor is his?"

"He has the whole bottom floor. Harry doesn't like stairs."

She continued to gaze at the tower of flats. "Bottom floor, and he might be expecting you. I say we go in through a back window."

"I'm going in through the bloody front door."

"Fine, you go in the front, and I'll go in the back. Maybe I'll find the tablet."

"Samantha, I don't want you breaking the law."

"You're breaking the law," she said, tapping his jacket pocket. "I'm helping."

"Damn, you're frightening, sometimes. You do notice everything."

She scowled. "Don't change the subject, Brit. This guy stole from you."

"What happened to serving revenge cold?"

"Forget it. A truck tried to crush me. I'm mad now."

He caught her hand as she started through the nearest hedge, her case in tow. "You were trying to steal from me, too, Samantha."

"Yes, but I never pretended to be your friend or business partner while I was doing it."

And someone had said there was no honor among thieves. He followed her around through the narrow alleyway and up to the back of the house. Lights were on, and he could faintly hear an announcer calling the match. And Chelsea was ahead, which would keep Harry's attention.

Samantha tried the back door. It was locked. "Give me two minutes," she whispered, pulling a copper wire from her pocket, "then make as much noise as you want around front."

This wasn't how he wanted to play it, but she had a point.

Sam could probably find more answers her way than he could beat out of Harry. Leaning down, he brushed his lips against hers. "Be careful."

She grinned. "You, too."

He watched until she inched open the door and slipped inside, then made his way around to the front of the house. He didn't quite wait the entire two minutes, because he didn't like the idea of Sam being in there by herself. Taking a step back, he slammed his foot into the door. It rattled and cracked open, one of the hinges breaking. Shoving it aside, he strode into the front hallway.

"What the devil is going on there?" the familiar voice of Harry Meridien bellowed. "I have a cricket bat, so you'd best get off before I call the police!"

"Call 'em!" Richard yelled back, striding forward.

He turned the corner as Harry stalked into the hallway, cricket bat raised. "Rick? What—"

"Hello, Harry. Surprised to see me?"

"What the hell are you doing? You broke my door!" Tall and thick, Meridien had been a hell of a cricket player a few years ago in college.

Richard offered him a grim smile, his blood heating. He almost hoped Harry would go after him with the bat, so he'd have an excuse to beat the shit out of him. "You stole my tablet," he replied.

"I what?"

"You wanted me to stay an extra day in Stuttgart," Richard continued, snapping his hand out to grab the cricket bat. He tossed it into a corner. "Was that to protect me, or to make sure you got what you were paying for?"

"I have no idea what—"

"Three people are dead, Harry. I suggest you consider very carefully what your story's going to be."

"Rick, you've gone mad." Harry's face darkened. "I don't know what the hell is going on, but you have no right to break into my house and threaten me! I—"

"Rick!"

At Samantha's yell he turned and sprinted down the hallway. "Samantha?"

"In here. You've got to see this."

He found her in Harry's office. The desk drawers all hung open, and from the appearance of the bent letter opener in her hand she hadn't been too careful with the woodwork. She held up a photo. "Gotcha," she said with a grim smile.

The tablet. It looked to be a duplicate of one of the insurance photos. For a brief moment, he wanted to catch her up in his arms and shout. They'd been right. And that meant Harry would know who Mr. Big—Dr. Evil—was.

Meridien loped into his office, his face red and glistening with sweat. "Get the hell out of my house, Rick. You and whoever she is. Now."

"I have a better idea," Richard snarled. "Why don't you have a seat and tell me a story?" Grabbing the photo, he waved it at Harry. "A very good story. With names and everything."

"You—she—could have put that there. It doesn't mean anything."

"Maybe not to the police, but it does to me. Now sit down, Harry, or I'll take you down."

For a moment the big man blustered, complaining about not being able to trust anyone. Then he sank into the plush chair beside the door. "I didn't do anything wrong."

"There's a chance I might not press charges if you tell me who else is involved in this." Richard sat on the edge of the desk. "And I might loan you enough money to keep your bank liquid. Maybe."

"The bank?" An almost pitiful hope widened his eyes and made his heavy chin quiver. "This . . . Partino only said he had something coming on the market, and would I be interested in having a crack at it. That's all."

"Danté called you. Directly," Richard pursued, holding back his own anger. Answers first. This didn't concern just him. Samantha still stood behind the desk, going through files as if she was completely alone in the room.

"Yes. And now I'm going to call my attorney, and the police."

"Who else besides Partino offered you the tablet?" Samantha cut in, not looking up.

"Who are you?" Harry demanded.

"I'm the one who was supposed to be the scapegoat when the other guy who contacted you sent someone in to steal Addison's property and kill Partino."

The big man's face grayed around the edges. "What?"

"That's right," Richard seconded, adopting Samantha's blunt vernacular. Hell, it worked amazingly well for her. "Didn't you know? Or were you stupid enough to let them set you up to take the blame for everything? The guy who stole the tablet is dead, the guy who hired my friend here to break in at the same time is dead, and this afternoon someone tried to shove my car into the Thames with me in it." He leaned forward. "So as you can probably guess, I'm not amused. I want names."

"He's got the Remington, too, it looks like," Samantha said, still flipping through files. "Maybe more." She glanced up, her gaze on Harry. "I'm starting to think that maybe he's the guy. The one who arranged everything."

"I am a collector," Harry said, the ruddy color of his skin darkening to the point that Richard began to wonder whether he had a history of heart problems. "I had nothing to do with anyone getting hurt."

"Prove it! Who's the other guy? Tell me now, dammit!"

Harry's round face furrowed. "Oh, for God's sake, Rick, haven't you figured it out by now?"

That stopped him for a minute. Something he should have realized already, or someone he should have suspected already, but didn't. "Pretend I'm slow and tell me, Harry. I'll give you to the count of three, then I'm going after the cricket bat. No more games. I want a bloody name!"

"Christ," Meridien mumbled, sweat beginning to pour down his face.

"How about my name?" A tall, light-haired man stepped into the room, the cricket bat in one hand and a pistol in the other.

Twenty-seven

Rick looked at him for a long moment. "You. It was you all along."

"Well, a chap's got to make a living, you know. And you provide quite a good one." The pistol stayed aimed at Rick, but the bat wavered in Sam's direction. "You must be Sam Jellicoe. Sean O'Hannon obviously thought less of you than he should have."

Meridien lurched to his feet. "Peter, I—"

The cricket bat smashed across Meridien's face, sending him into a crumpled heap on the floor. Sam held her breath until she heard the big man moaning. He wasn't dead, thank God. She returned her attention to the good-looking blond man. "Peter," she repeated aloud. "Peter Wallis."

"You *are* clever. Good. I'd hate to think it was just dumb luck keeping you ahead of me. Why don't you come over here and let me get a look at Rick's whore?"

"Don't move, Samantha," Rick ordered, shifting a little so he was between Wallis and her.

" 'Don't move, Samantha,' " Wallis mimicked. "After Patricia called you, and you didn't ask her anything special about me, I figured you'd head here to see Harry, you smug bastard."

"So now what?" Rick asked, his voice black and hard.

"Well, now I have to kill you and make it look like you and Harry did one another in."

"It doesn't do you any good," Sam broke in. The man standing before her had killed Etienne and O'Hannon. And he'd meant for Partino to be dead, and hadn't cared if the bomb took out anyone else. She couldn't think of a thing that would stop him from shooting Rick—except his own greed.

"And why is that, Miss Jellicoe?"

"All the forgeries from Palm Beach are with the FBI. Everything you took is hot, and your buffet is closed. Partino's in jail, and nothing more is coming in for you."

"Partino's a greedy little piss ant. I don't need him."

"He tried to go around you and undersell the tablet to Harry, didn't he?" Sam pursued.

"Very good," he answered. Meridien moved again, and Wallis beat him across the skull. "Down, boy."

"So what did O'Hannon and Etienne do to you?"

"Well, DeVore got angry because apparently you and he were friends, and he didn't know you'd been the one hired to go in at the same time. That was O'Hannon's fault. I just told him to send some ape to stumble in and take the blame. Instead, he sent you, clever girl, and then he panicked."

"You're pretty new to this theft thing, Wallis," she said, slipping her fingers around the bent letter opener, "just stealing from one guy and all, so I'll let you in on a secret. We thieves have quite the community. O'Hannon was a disgusting jerk, but everybody knew that. You either worked with him, or you didn't. No murders allowed. Same with Etienne. You've killed two of us. Everybody's gonna know. And somebody will talk, especially if someone's broken the code.

If there's reward money involved, we'll be standing in line to sell you out."

"Good God, I'm positively shivering. Rick, shut her up, or I will."

"Samantha," Rick said quietly.

Wallis tipped the cricket bat down to lean on it. "You know, now that I think about it, this really is the only step left. I've been stealing your oh-so-prestigious artworks for years, and you've been showing off fakes to governors and senators and heads of state."

"There is counseling available for your particular mental disorder," Rick put in. "Though I can't figure out if you have a Napoleon complex or if you're just sorry and jealous."

"Shut the fuck up," Wallis retorted. "I'm not finished. I stole your wife—which really didn't take much effort on my part—replaced your artwork with fakes and you didn't even know the difference, and now poof, I kill you. The end. I win." He chuckled, confident now. "I almost had you last week. I thought, why not? He's back in Florida early, may as well make the effort. I timed it to the minute, but your thief here moved too fast, or Danté was too slow."

"What are you—"

"Does this sound familiar? Ring, ring."

Sam saw the muscles across Rick's shoulders tighten. "The fax machine. You're the one who woke me up that night."

"Good boy. Nearly had you. Very nearly."

"But you didn't."

With a sigh, Wallis shook his head. "After your bloody divorce the newspapers all said how generous you were in letting your adulterous wife and her lover have your house in London. They didn't mention how you nearly bankrupted me with your little fun in New York, or that you stripped your lovely mansion bare and painted every wall red and threw dirty mattresses all over the floor."

"You did that?" Sam asked, forcing a chuckle. "I get it; you made your bed, now lie in it."

"I thought it was quite poetic," Rick commented.

"Nice."

Wallis shook the gun. "You thought it gave you the last word, didn't you? You were wrong. I win. Game, set, match. Now, any more questions, or shall we just get on with it? And how generous are you going to be tonight, Rick? Shall I do you first, or her?"

"Me," Rick said promptly.

"I was hoping you'd say that." He straightened his arm. From that range, he wasn't going to miss.

"By the way," Sam cut in again, desperation making her voice tight, "you did realize that the Meridien's got a video surveillance system, didn't you? You've been on candid camera since you walked in here." She slid her eyes up toward the far corner behind him and back again.

Wallis hesitated for a moment, and it was all she needed. Sweeping around Rick, Sam hurled the letter opener. Bent, its trajectory was off, but it sliced into Wallis's chest, making him flinch.

The gun went off, the roar tremendous in the small room. Samantha screamed Rick's name, but he was already moving. Hurtling off the desk, he plowed into Wallis, knocking them both over a chair and to the floor. The gun flew out of Wallis's hand, but he brought the bat around, slamming Rick across the back.

Snarling, Wallis scrambled after the gun, Rick twisting to grab his leg and slow him down. The pistol had slid under a credenza, and Sam went down after it. Wallis grabbed at her, and she elbowed him hard in the face.

"Sam, get back!" Rick bellowed, managing to climb to his knees and land a hard punch against Wallis's kidneys.

Wallis twisted like a snake, sending the cricket bat across Rick's face. Blood spurted from his lip and nose, and he stumbled backward. His attacker climbed over him, raising the bat again.

Sam jumped on his back. "No!" she shrieked, one hand on the bat and the other wrapped around Wallis's neck. She hauled back as hard as she could, and he overbalanced, going down hard with her beneath him.

The air drove out of her lungs at the impact. Gasping for breath, she tightened her grip around his neck. An elbow slammed her in the rib cage with enough force to make her eyes roll back. Her grip loosened, and he was on all fours over her, grabbing her hair and slamming her head into the floor.

Pain screamed through her head, thrumming and roaring and making sounds hollow and far away. She tried to kick, but he knelt across her legs. He'd caught her right hand and held it pinned over her head while he beat her to death, but her left was free. Through vision that blackened at the edges she reached for the cricket bat.

It slipped away from her, and then his weight lifted off. As she lost focus she caught a glimpse of Rick holding the bat like a pro, swinging it up and across Wallis's head, and then the sound of a body hitting the floor. Then everything went black.

Rick dropped the bat. Sinking to the floor, he crawled to where Samantha lay, her eyes closed and her face gray. "Samantha?" he whispered, swiping blood from his mouth. He touched her face, but she didn't move at all. "Sam?"

God, he'd killed her. When he'd stumbled upright to see Wallis slamming her head over and over into the floorboards, time had just . . . stopped. Nothing was worth this: not pride, not money, not his own life.

Shaking, he slipped a finger over her neck. A faint pulse beat against his hand, and he took in a sob of air. "Samantha? Sweetheart? Open your eyes, Sam."

Her lashes fluttered, and moss green eyes blinked groggily up at him. "Ouch," she slurred.

"Just lay still, sweetheart. Can you feel your legs, your arms?"

"Your face is bloody."

"I know. Move your toes and your fingers. Now, Samantha." A few seconds ticked by without his heart beating, then her fingers moved, first the right hand and then the left. "Good girl."

Harry's phone lay on the floor beeping at him from behind the desk, and Rick leaned sideways to grab it. Swiftly he called for an ambulance and the police, then returned his attention to Samantha. Her eyes had closed again.

"Samantha?"

"Go away. I have a concussion."

With a slight smile, he brushed hair from her face. Wallis had yanked out a handful of it, and she was definitely going to need a trip to the hairdresser's. "You can't run away now, can you?" he murmured.

"I have no legs."

"They're right here, I promise. Attached and everything. And they look very nice."

"Shut up."

"I love you, Samantha Jellicoe."

Her eyes opened again, gamely focusing on his face. He didn't expect her to answer; she'd spent too much time being alone, too long being able to depend on no one but herself. But she smiled, reaching an unsteady hand up to touch his face. He clasped it in his as her eyes rolled back, and she blacked out again.

When Sam opened her eyes, she half thought she was still in the middle of some sort of nightmare. Uniformed officers and men and women in those tan British trench coats swarmed around her, talking in a low buzz of London accents. She was off the floor, she realized, on a gurney with a needle in one arm. They'd strapped her down.

"Hey!" she grunted, fighting to sit up.

Rick appeared over her shoulder, a cold pack held to his mouth and a butterfly bandage across the bridge of his nose. "It's okay," he said, lowering the ice pack. "Just relax."

"You have a black eye," she noted. He also had a swelled lip, and a dark, scraped bruise forming on his left cheek.

"Your powers of observation remain intact," he said, smiling in a lopsided wince.

"I don't want to go to the hospital."

"Too bad."

The stretcher bumped and lifted, and then she was rolling toward the doorway. "Rick?" she said, abruptly panicking now that she couldn't see him.

"I'm here. I'm going with you. I have a broken nose."

"I win, because I have a broken head."

She heard his low, soft chuckle. "Your head's too hard to break," he returned. It's just dented."

"That's good."

"Not really, sweetheart."

She was lifted off the ground, then was inside the ambulance. A technician, then Rick climbed in after her, sitting to one side. "What about Harry and Wallis?" she asked.

Rick leaned forward to take her hand. "Harry's in another ambulance. Wallis is going to wish he was dead by the time I'm through with him."

She looked at him for a minute. "I don't think Patricia knew anything about this," she offered.

"The police are bringing her in for questioning," he returned, flexing his fingers in hers, "but I don't think she knew, either. I hope not."

"Me, too."

"I have to tell you something," he said, the smile touching his face again.

He'd already told her something; something very precious and very private, something she would keep inside her heart forever. But she didn't want him to have to say it again without her answer. "You don't have to tell me anything," she said quickly. "I know, and it's . . . I'm . . ."

His smile deepened into his eyes. "Not that. Castillo called Scotland Yard, told them he recommended they bring one Harold Meridien in for questioning regarding a series of art thefts. They charged through the door about thirty seconds after I called for the police."

"Frank was listening through the glass at the jail. I knew someone was there."

Nodding, Rick squeezed her hand. "I think I owe Frank a beer."

"I kind of like him," she agreed, surprised that she could admit to it. "He's okay, for a cop."

The technician leaned over, checking the oxygen line set into her nose and something that was monitoring her heart rate. "You need to rest, miss," he said. "No more talking."

"Okay. One more thing, though." She lifted Rick's hand as far as she could with her arm under the strap. "I want to go to Devon."

Epilogue

Tuesday, 11:15 a.m.
London Time

Two weeks later, Sam sat beside Rick as they drove past meadows and farms and groves of oak trees. She'd never seen this part of England. It seemed so peaceful and lovely, and a great deal like Rick Addison.

"Patricia agreed to testify against Wallis?" she asked, turning to look as they crossed a four-hundred-year-old bridge.

"She said she would."

"I think she wants you back."

"I'm not available."

Sam swallowed. "Will she be any help?"

He shrugged. "According to the authorities, the only thing she knows for sure is that Peter was in Florida last week for two days."

"Long enough to kill Etienne and get the tablet."

"He rented a BMW."

"The one we saw on the highway." That had been close.

Rick nodded. "Most of it's still circumstantial, but it's coming together. And they're working to make sure *you* don't have to testify. If the defense attorney gets you on the stand—"

She shuddered. "Then I go to hell for lying under oath."

He glanced at her, concern touching his eyes. He'd worn that expression a lot over the past two weeks, even after she'd managed to con her way out of the hospital and back to his London penthouse. "It won't come to that. I'm certain I have a house in a country where they don't have an extradition agreement with the States."

She made an effort to smile. "That's good to know."

They drove for another few minutes in silence. "Just up there, on the left," Rick said abruptly, gesturing in her direction.

They crested a small hill, then she saw it. "Holy crap."

A rise of green, rolling hills on two sides bordered a large lake fronted by oak and willow trees. In the middle of them, up a gentle slope of grass, stood a castle. It was the only way to describe it. A hundred windows looked out from its squared U, with spires on either corner and a rounded entryway in the front, with massive pillars that waited at the head of a wide set of granite steps.

"Nice, isn't it?" he asked, grinning.

"It's Buckingham bloody Palace," she returned.

"Hardly. It's called Rawley Park."

"You said you grew up here."

Nodding again, Rick turned off the main road, heading along a narrow, winding drive that gave glimpses of the house through sun-spattered leaves and twisting vines of ivy. "I inherited it, actually. This is where I like to spend at least a couple of months every year, if I can. It's home."

Home. She'd never really had one of those. Quiet, safe, home. It terrified her, but she wanted to try it. With him.

She craned her neck to keep it in view. "Seriously, Rick, it's magnificent. If it was mine, I'd never want to leave."

Sam frowned as soon as she finished speaking. After what he'd said to her, every time she made a statement like that, she felt self-conscious, like she was asking for something. She wasn't; not really. Spending more time with him was enough. She couldn't remember when she'd ever felt as safe, as relaxed, as she had over the past two weeks. Four, if she counted the rather interesting beginning of this odd relationship.

He only pointed out a small herd of deer in one of the clearings. "I'm glad you like it." Rick cleared his throat. "I've been meaning to run something by you, and now seems as good a time as any."

She stiffened. "I wanted to tell you something, too."

Rick glanced at her. "All right, you first."

"I've been talking with Stoney, and we're thinking of retiring."

"Really."

"Yes." She cleared her throat. If he laughed, she was either going to punch him or die of mortification. "We're going to start a business. A security installation and consulting firm."

For a long moment he drove in silence. Finally, though, a slow smile curved his mouth. "That's lucky for me, then. I was going to tell you that I'd like you to review the security at all my private properties. I've been told that it's crappy."

"Good. Then you can hire me."

He lifted an eyebrow. "I have to pay you?"

"I'll make you a good deal."

"I should hope so." He drew a breath. "There's something else you need to know."

"Rick, I—"

"Shut up. It's my turn now."

She folded her arms across her chest, pretending that intimate conversation with him didn't still leave her nervous. "Fine."

"Thank you. As I was saying, with a great deal of my collection now gone into other people's hands, and some of what remains devalued because no one can verify whether it's authentic or not, I'd like to start over." He glanced at her again. "And I'd like you to help me with that. If you think you'll have time."

"So you're trying to make sure I go legit."

"Sam—"

"I told you, I . . . don't really like things in private collections."

Rick grinned. "I know that. And I'm going to open part of Rawley Park to the public, as an art and antiques repository. That way I can showcase more works and have them accessible to everyone."

For the second time in her life, she wanted to cry. Not in sadness, this time, but in joy. It was a new experience. "Wow."

They pulled through the gates into the long, half-circular drive in front of the house. This close, it was even more massive than she'd realized. And even more beautiful.

"Samantha?"

"I'm thinking."

"Don't think. Just say yes, or say no. It's pretty simple, that way." He put the car into park and shut off the key. "And I'm giving you the Bentley, regardless."

"I told you that I didn't . . . like you for your stuff."

"My girlfriend doesn't drive stolen cars. That's where I draw the line."

Sam leaned over and kissed him, long and slow and deep. "Yes," she murmured. "I think I'll be able to work something out. In my spare time, of course."

"Good." He kissed her back. "Good." Rick smiled at her, then reached over to undo her seat belt. "Let's go. I want you to meet Sykes."

"Your butler. This is where he stays, you said."

"Yes, unless I need him elsewhere."

"Cool."

He climbed out of the car and strode around to pull her door open for her. Rick took her hand, and together they walked up the shallow black granite steps to the front door. As they reached the portico beneath the pillars, the double doors swung open, and the tallest, thinnest, oldest man in the world bowed to them.

"Welcome home, my lord," he said.

Samantha stopped. "My what?" she asked, very slowly.

They both ignored her. "It's good to be back," Rick returned. "Sykes, this is Samantha Jellicoe. She's going to be staying here with me."

"Good morning, Miss Jellicoe."

"Sykes." Sam looked back at Rick. "If I might repeat, 'my what?' "

For the first time in her recollection, Rick looked sheepish. "I suppose I forgot to tell you. I'm kind of a nobleman."

"Kind of. What kind of?"

He drew a breath, then smiled that gorgeous smile of his, the one that made her knees weak. "I'm kind of the Marquis of Rawley."

"Oh, good grief. Forget the good deal on the security consulting. Now you're paying full price."

"Hm. We can negotiate."

Author's Note

First of all, I'd like to make clear that Samantha Jellicoe and Richard Addison are fictional characters, that Solano Dorado is a fictional mansion, and that the events described in *Flirting With Danger* aren't based on any real incident—at least not intentionally, and not one that I know of.

That's the beauty of being a fiction writer—I can make all this stuff up.

On the other hand, Palm Beach, Florida, is obviously a real place, and so are Chuck and Harold's Café with its retractable roof, the Meissen Shop, Butterfly World, and the Norton Museum. In fact, at this time I'd like to offer a blanket apology to all of the real places my fictional characters have visited and will visit in the future, but the minutae of the story at times required me to bend the decor and the settings a little bit. And, of course, any damage done to these places by Sam and Rick, et al, is of the make-believe variety.

So, to get down to the nitty-gritty, I'll attempt to explain how this book came about. Those readers who've seen my name before on book covers are probably more familiar with me as a writer of historical romances. In fact, as of the publication of *Flirting* I've written two Regency romances, two novellas for anthologies, and eleven full-length historical romances. All of the previous were set in England between 1811 and 1820 during the Regency of Prince George, later to be crowned George IV.

Why does a confirmed historical romance author write a contemporary romance/mystery/comedy/adventure, then? The answer's actually pretty simple. McDonald's. The fast-food restaurant, that is.

For eleven years I had worked at the same place in Southern California—suffice it to say that it was an executive support position at a high-end automobile dealership—for a boss who was . . . difficult. On a Thursday in June, which has since become known as "freedom day," after a Wednesday that marked my second appearance on the *USA Today* best seller list and my first appearance on the *New York Times* best seller list, my boss said something typically mean, and I decided I'd had enough. I quit.

The next morning I realized that 1) I was a single home-owner with monthly mortgage payments to make, 2) I had the previous week turned in the last book of a two-book contract, and 3) I had no job. While I was fairly certain I would be offered another book contract to produce a set number of historical romances, I wasn't sure exactly how soon that would be. And so at that moment I had something I wasn't very familiar with—free time.

Amid my parents' gentle suggestions that I begin filling out applications and find another job with a steady income before I ended up at—yes—McDonald's flipping burgers, and amid my fears that I wouldn't find a position where I would both earn enough money to make my house payments and have enough energy left over actually to write a book, I reverted to my usual strategy in times of stress and popped in a DVD to watch a movie.

The movie was one of my favorites, *To Catch a Thief*, starring Cary Grant and Grace Kelly. Somewhere halfway through it, I began jotting notes to myself—what if the suave, high-rent cat burglar were a woman, and what if she tried to steal something from a rich, arrogant businessman, and what if they somehow ended up having to work together?

With that extensive outline I flipped open my Toshiba laptop computer, popped open the first of about ten thousand cans of chilled diet Dr Pepper, and started writing. I'd never written that way before, with no plot, no preconceptions, in a genre I didn't know, and with no real thought other than that I wanted to do something different and fun. And I have to say, it turned out to be a blast.

Rick Addison was a combination of Hugh Jackman, Cary Grant, and Donald Trump, while in my mind Sam Jellicoe bore a strong resemblance to Remington Steele, Ashley Judd, and me—not the cat burglar stuff, but the interest in history and art and the fondness for diet sodas and Godzilla and all things British (well, one thing British in her case, anyway).

I wanted to set the story somewhere different, too—at least for me. That precluded England, though I did end up there toward the end. And I live half an hour from Bel Aire and Rodeo Drive, settled among freeways and bad traffic and Hollywood, and I didn't want that. All the way across the country sat Palm Beach, Florida, a couple of miles from the Everglades and one of the top two or three wealthiest counties in the U.S. Heat, humidity, wilderness, wealth, alligators, a private, insulated community of the rich and famous—it seemed perfect.

Rick's Palm Beach home, Solano Dorado (Golden Sun) was loosely based on Donald Trump's Mar-a-Lago, also located in Palm Beach. While Trump's estate has been turned into a massive and exclusive country club, though, Rick's home would be designed for the privacy and comfort of one man. The two showplaces do have more in common than merely size and grandeur, however.

At the least, they share a designer in the famous Palm Beach architect Addison Mizner—the man who was basically responsible for the Mediterranean Revival style in that area of Florida. Keeping the Spanish/Mediterranean style in mind for the exterior, I wanted to stock the interior of Solano Dorado with the works of art and the antiques Rick had purchased over the years—everything from sixteenth-century tapestries to Picassos to first folios of Shakespearean plays. Sam's specialty would of course be lifting items and artifacts of precisely that value and importance. And then I would put the two of them directly at odds with one another: The unstoppable force meets the immovable object.

Since I felt comfortable with English history, I decided to make Rick both British and a lord. I did have all those tax write-off Regency era research books, and thought I might as well make use of them. It took longer to become comfortable with Sam; but after uncovering a handful of books on art fraud, high-end robberies, and burglar alarm setups, I felt like I pretty much knew where she was coming from and where I was heading with her.

Whereas I wanted Rick to be the cool, logical, confident one, I wanted Sam to be more of a hothead, a chameleon, tough and street-smart but able to sit at a table with the wealthiest, most cultured people in the world and still blend in. Neither of them is big on trust, but they find they can rely on one another.

Going from carriages and letter-writing heroines to cell phones and Mercedes-Benzes made for an interesting trip, and it was especially fun to be able to write in a character who likes *Star Wars*. If only that meant I could write off my collection of action figures. Oh, well. Here's hoping.

As it turns out, Rick and Sam will live on—their second book, *Playing With Fire*, is in the works. We'll see all the old familiar places and people, plus a few new ones—including Patricia, the ex-wife. And I haven't had to seek employment at McDonald's, which is definitely good news both for me and for the fast-food-buying public.

Do you think you know everything
about your favorite Avon authors?

Well, think again!

Because in the following pages
you are going to learn
Ten things
You never suspected about
Four of your favorite Avon writers . . .

And, of course, you'll also
be getting a sneak peek
at their upcoming
Avon Romance Superleaders!

10 Things You Don't Know About Elizabeth Bevarly

1. I will do just about anything for a slice of chess pie.
2. When I was twelve years old, I took home the blue ribbon from the Kentucky State Fair for "Best Chocolate Chip Cookies." (I will only reveal the recipe for a million dollars. Or, you know, a slice of chess pie.)
3. I secretly devour true crime books. (So I know how to kill a man a dozen different ways. Of course, I never would. Unless he tried to get between me and my chess pie.)
4. I was once almost crushed in a mosh pit at a Clash concert. (Some idiot skinhead slammed into me and made me drop my chess pie.)
5. I once kissed the singer Harry Chapin. (And he wasn't even holding a chess pie at the time.)
6. My first job was at the age of twelve, drying silverware in my aunt's restaurant. (They had fabulous chess pie.)
7. I was on the dance team at my high school the year they took first place in state competition. (There wasn't any chess pie involved, but I thought I'd mention it anyway. The pie, I mean. Not the dance team stuff.)
8. I was born on the cusp of Scorpio and Libra, which means I think a balance of emotion is extremely important, but I'm much too emotional to achieve such a thing. (But it doesn't affect my affinity for chess pie, so it's okay.)
9. My favorite color is green. (Unless it appears on a slice of chess pie, in which case I don't care for it at all.)
10. I have a fetish for china, crystal and silver serveware, especially if it's antique. (Krautheim's Millefleurs pattern, for instance, looks especially nice under a slice of chess pie.)

And now a sneak peek at Elizabeth's January 2005 Avon Romance Superleader

Just Like a Man

*B*ut even all buttoned up and battened down the way Hannah Frost had been, he'd been able to sense a barely restrained . . . something . . . simmering just beneath her surface. He hesitated to ponder exactly what that *something* might be, though, mostly because it made something equally *something* simmer inside himself. Instead of a gray crew cut, her hair had shone like pure honey in sunlight, the elegantly twisted style making him think it must be long and silky when allowed to flow free. And instead of evil eyes, she had the eyes of an angel, as blue and as big as the heavens above. And as for persimmon lips . . .

Oh, baby. Nothing could have been further from the truth. Hannah Frost's mouth had been as soft as the rest of her promised to be, full and lush and ripe. It had been way too long since Michael had kissed a mouth like that. And there were other things he could imagine that mouth doing, too. Things to him, in fact. Things *on* him, in fact. Things he *really* shouldn't be thinking about when his son was anywhere in the same ZIP code.

So instead of mentally undressing Hannah Frost, he made himself think about the way she *had* been dressed, an austere study in gray. The suit hadn't suited her at all, yet she'd seemed perfectly at ease wearing it.

Because ruminating about Hannah Frost was as far as Michael would let things go with her. And that was more than he should be doing. She was one cool customer, to be sure. Too bad she didn't have the same cooling effect on him. She made his blood run hot and wild, even after one brief, passionless exchange.

Damn. This was an unexpected development he hadn't anticipated and certainly couldn't afford.

And what the hell did she think she was doing going anywhere near Adrian Windsor? Okay, so the guy sat on the board of directors of the Emerson Academy. After all, that was the reason he'd been instructed to enroll Alex at Emerson. And to the casual observer, Adrian Windsor was a forthright, upright, do-right, citizen. But Michael knew things about the guy no one else at Emerson knew. For example, that his name wasn't really Adrian Windsor. It was Adrian Padgett. And what he knew all added up to the fact that Adrian was trouble with a capital *T*.

If Hannah Frost was involved with the guy, that was really going to cause some problems. And not just for Michael, either.

10 Things You Don't Know About Rachel Gibson

1. I got my first motorcycle in the fourth grade. It was a Honda 50—not quite a Harley.
2. My little toes are on sideways. I know that sounds freaky but is very cute.
3. I love to sing loud but can't carry a tune.
4. My name is Rachel, and I am a shoe-oholic.
5. I speak fluent pig Latin.
6. I am not crafty. I tried it once and burned my fingers with the hot glue.
7. I jumped in a pool of Jell-O and won a T-shirt.
8. I love to jetski and I'm learning to water-ski.
9. I have a terrible fear of grasshoppers.
10. I work in pajamas until noon. It's a good job.

And now a sneak peek at Rachel's February 2005 Avon Romance Superleader

The Trouble With Valentine's Day

"*W*arn me if you're going to write your name in the snow," she said to break the silence.

"Actually, I'm standing here wondering if I'm going to have to wrestle that snow shovel out of your hands." His warm breath hung in the air between them as he added, "I'm hoping you'll be nice and hand it over."

Her grasp on the handle tightened a bit more. "Why would I hand it over?"

"Because your grandfather is in there getting all worked up over you doing what he thinks is a man's job."

"Well, that's just stupid. I'm certainly capable of shoveling snow."

He shrugged and slid his hands into the hip pockets of his cargo pants. "I guess that's not the point. He thinks it's a man's job, and you've embarrassed him in front of his friends."

"What?"

"He's in there right now trying to convince everyone that you're . . ." Rob paused a moment and tilted his head to one side. "I believe his exact words were that you're 'usually a nice, sweet-tempered girl.' And then he said something about you being cranky because you don't ever get out with people your own age."

Great. Kate suspected her grandfather's nonsense was directed at Rob and not the other men. Worse, she was sure he suspected it also. The last thing she needed was for her grandfather to interfere in her nonexistent love life. Especially with Rob Sutter. "I'm not cranky."

He didn't comment, but the lift of his brow said it all.

"I'm not," she insisted. "My grandfather is just old-fashioned."

"He's a good guy."

"He's stubborn."

"If I had to guess, I'd say you're a lot alike in the stubborn department."

"Fine." She thrust the shovel toward him.

A smile touched the corners of his mouth as he withdrew his hand from the front pocket of his pants and took the shovel from her. He clamped his bare hand over hers. She tugged but his grasp tightened.

She wasn't about to get into a tug-of-war with a man built like the Terminator. "Can I have my hand back?" He relaxed his grip finger by finger, and she pulled free.

"Damn," he said, "I was kind of hoping I'd have to wrestle you for it."

10 Things You Don't Know About Suzanne Enoch

1. She used to attend science fiction conventions, but only dressed up once—as a Colonial Marine from the movie *Aliens*. Okay, she once wore a Han Solo costume, too, when her friends joined her as Luke Skywalker and Princess Leia.

2. She once appeared on national television as a romance expert on E! as part of the "Star Wars Is Back" special. She had more air time than George Lucas.

3. Her first part-time job was at Cinedome, a movie theater complex. She stayed for two weeks, until the runs of *Raiders of the Lost Ark* and *Star Trek II* ended—the ticket booth didn't have air-conditioning, and without Indy or Spock, it just wasn't worth it.

4. She won't eat anything which could potentially eat her. This includes shark, snake, and members of the squid family—and so far the karma thing has worked out, because she hasn't been devoured.

5. She mows her own lawn with a manual lawn mower. The idea was that it would be good exercise. What she didn't realize was that lawns grow so quickly.

6. She once went on a date with a guy who made props for "Pee Wee's Playhouse." He showed up wearing red-and-white nylon parachute pants and brought her a green popsicle model with a smile embossed on it. If the popsicle had been real, the relationship might have had a chance.

7. She was editor-in-chief of her high school newspaper, which together with her braces and glasses and good grades, put a crimp in her high school social life. She's since recovered, but agrees that she could still probably be considered a nerd.

8. While in college she submitted a script for "The A-Team." The script was under consideration at the time the show was canceled.

9. Her great-grandfather, Vivian Whitlock, was also a published author. His book was titled *Cowboy Life on the Llano Estacado*, and it's been rumored that he once rustled cattle and rode with Butch Cassidy and the Hole in the Wall Gang.

10. She consulted her Talking Yoda 8-Ball about whether she would be able to sell her first contemporary manuscript. The answer was "Likely, this is." Yoda's always right.

And now a sneak peek at Suzanne's March 2005 Avon Romance Superleader

Flirting With Danger

*H*e started to take another swallow of brandy, then stopped as the skylight in the middle of the ceiling rattled and opened. With a graceful flip that looked much easier than it had to be, a woman dropped into his office. *The* woman, he noted, reflexively taking a step back.

"Thank you for getting rid of your company," she said in a low voice. "I was getting a cramp up there."

"Miss Smith."

She nodded, keeping green eyes on him as she walked to the door and locked it. "Are you sure you're Richard Addison? I thought he slept in a suit, but night before last you had on nothing but jogging sweats, and tonight"—she looked him slowly up and down—"a T-shirt and jeans, and no shoes."

The muscles across his abdomen tightened, and not—he noted with some interest—in fear. "The suit's at the cleaners." Her gloved hands were empty, as they had been the other night, and this time she didn't even carry a paint gun or a pack. Again she was in black—black shoes and black tight-fitting pants and a black T-shirt that hugged her slim curves.

She pursed her lips. "Satisfied I'm not carrying a concealed weapon?"

"I have no idea where you'd keep one, if you were," he returned, sliding his gaze along the length of her.

"Thanks for noticing."

"In fact," he continued, "you seem a bit underdressed compared to the other night. I do like the baseball cap, though. Very fashionable."

She flashed him a grin. "It keeps my long blond hair out of my face."

"Duly noted for my report to the police," he said, his mind still pondering the intriguing thought of where she might carry a concealed weapon. "Unless you're here to kill me, in which case I suppose I don't really care what color your hair might be."

"If I were here to kill you," she returned in a calm, soft voice, sending a glance beyond him at his desk, "you'd be dead."

"That confident, are you?" She wasn't armed; he could rush her, grab her, and hold her for the police. Instead, Richard took a sip of brandy.

"All right, let's say I accept that you're not here to kill me," he said. "Why *are* you here then, Miss Smith?"

For the first time she hesitated, a furrow appearing between her delicate, curved brows. "To ask for your help."

And he'd thought nothing else could surprise him this evening. "Beg pardon?"

"I think you know that I didn't try to kill you the other night. I did try to take your Trojan stone tablet, and I won't apologize for that. But thievery has a statute of limitations. Murder doesn't." She cleared her throat. "I wouldn't kill anyone."

"Then turn yourself in and tell the police."

She snorted. "No fucking way. I may have missed the tablet, but not all the statutes have run out on me."

Richard folded his arms across his chest. She hadn't taken the tablet. Curiouser and curiouser—and it didn't suit him to let her know that someone else had made off with it. "So you've stolen other things. From people other than me, I presume?"

As she glanced toward the skylight, her smooth, devil-may-care countenance shifted a little. It was an act, he realized. Fearless as she seemed to be, she would have to be desperate to drop in on him here tonight. If he hadn't been so accustomed to reading people, looking for weaknesses, he never would have seen it. She was good at what she did, obviously, but that moment of vulnerability caught his attention—and his interest.

"I saved your life," she finally said, her unaffected mask dropping into place again, "so you owe me a favor. Tell them—the police, the FBI, the news—that I didn't kill that guard, and that I didn't try to kill you. I'll deal with the rest on my own."

"I see." Richard wasn't certain whether he was more intrigued by her or annoyed that she expected him to make her error go away. "You want me to fix things so you can walk away from this, without repercussions, owing to the fact that while you've been bad elsewhere, you were unsuccessful here."

"I'm bad everywhere," she returned, with a slight smile that momentarily made him wonder how far she would go in her quest to see herself cleared of any wrongdoing. "Accuse me of attempted theft. But clear me of murder."

"No." He wanted answers, but his way. And not through some sort of compromise, intriguing though she made it sound.

She met his gaze straight on for a moment, then nodded. "I had to try. You might consider, though, that if I didn't set that bomb, someone else did. Someone who's better at getting into places than I am. And I'm good. Very good."

"I'd wager you are." He watched her for another moment, wondering what she'd be like with all of that coiled energy released. She definitely knew how to push his buttons, and he wanted to push a few of hers. "I'll admit you may have something I'm interested in acquiring," he said slowly, "but it's not your theories or your request for aid."

Returning to her position beneath the skylight, she yanked her arm down. The end of a length of rope tumbled into the room. "Oh, Mr. Addison. I never give something for nothing."

He found that he wasn't quite ready for her to leave. "Perhaps we could negotiate."

She released the rope, approaching him with a walk that

looked half Catwoman and all sexy. "I already suggested that, and you turned me down. But be careful. Somebody wants you dead. And you have no idea how close somebody like me can get, without you ever knowing," she murmured, lifting her face to his.

Jesus. She practically gave off sparks. He could feel the hairs on his arms lifting. "I would know," he returned in the same low tone, taking a slow step closer, daring her to make the next move. If she did, he was going to touch her. He wanted to touch her, badly. The heat coming off her body was almost palpable.

She held where she was, her lips a breath away from his, then with another fleeting grin slid away to grab the rope again. "So you weren't surprised tonight, were you?" With a fluid coordination of arms and legs, she swarmed up through the skylight. "Watch your back, Addison. If you're not going to help me, I'm not going to help you."

"Help me?"

She vanished, then ducked her head back into the room. "I know things the cops would never have a clue how to find out. Good night, Addison." Miss Smith blew him a kiss. "Sleep tight."

Richard stepped forward to look up, but she had already disappeared. "I was surprised," he conceded, taking another swallow of brandy. "And now I need a cold shower."

10 Things You Don't Know About Karen Hawkins

1. Karen once caught her house on fire while trying to kill a large, hairy spider. Every plastic glass in her kitchen sink and the handles to two pans melted completely before the fire was extinguished. The spider was, of course, unharmed.

2. Due to an Unfortunate Meatloaf Incident in '04 that resulted in a trip to the emergency room and stitches, Karen now avoids all forms of cooking and has perfected the art of "the dial-in order." Due to the amount of tips she'd paid thus far, seven pizza delivery drivers have graduated from junior college and two have named their oldest children in her honor.

3. Karen's favorite motto: If you can't afford a housekeeper, have children. There's a reason the word "CHoREs" and "CHildREn" have not one, but FOUR of the same letters. Coincidence? I think not.

4. Karen's biggest writing challenge is ignoring her dog, Duke, a large, fluffy golden retriever who possesses the World's Saddest Stare. His Sad Stare has earned him countless table scraps, numerous pity-induced doggie treats, and thousands of consolation ear scratches. When Karen is writing, Duke will pin his penetrating Sad Stare on her until she stops what she is doing and takes him outside to play in the park.

5. When Karen sold her first book in 1998, she was working on her PhD in political science. On receiving "the call" that an editor at Avon wanted to buy her work, Karen did what all dedicated students would do—she burned her stats book on the front lawn while dancing about in crazed abandon. She has never once looked back.

6. Karen is a confirmed Anglophile and revels in All Things English, especially the hunky British Prime Minister Tony Blair. She has a T-shirt, two posters, one life-sized cutout, and a set of coasters with his picture on them. If you'd like a set of coasters for your own viewing pleasure, contact Karen Hawkins, President of the Tony Blair Fan Club, at their website *www.WeDroolforTonyB.com.*

7. To increase her writing output, Karen has developed a Reward System. One month, every time she wrote ten pages, she gave herself $10 toward the purchase of a new pair of shoes. Another month, she got to buy a dozen chocolate covered, creme-filled Krispy Kremes. This time, she rewarded herself every ten pages with a shot of tequila. Needless to say, though she met her quota every day for two weeks, she was unable to keep any work after page thirty and now attends WAA (Writers Against Alcohol) meetings twice a week.

8. Last year, Karen's daughter reached the amazing age of sixteen and now has her driver's license. After two tickets, three fender-benders, a hefty new insurance payment, and many harrowing hours waiting by the phone, Karen has hired a new hairdresser good at "covering up the white." She will report back on the results.

9. Unknown to many of her family and friends, Karen is a master-level bass fisherwoman. She's never caught anything, but she looks good in her Lucky Fishing Hat and has a lovely tan. She also has a heck of a cast and can untangle her own lines from trees, shrubs, and even an occasional goose's neck.

10. Unknown to many of her fans, Karen is a shoe addict. She is especially addicted to shoes on sale. She owns more than eighty pairs, many of which she has never worn, including a pair of thigh-high glossy black leather boots and some strappy sandals in an unlikely color combination of deep purple and orange sherbet. Like most addicts, even while standing in line at Payless, Karen refers to her ad-

diction as "a little problem" and says, "I can quit any time I want. No. Really. I can. Do you take Visa?"

For more tidbits about this author, a chance to win an autographed book, excerpts from her books, and pictures of her doing sit-ups, visit Karen on-line at *www.karenhawkins.com*!

And now a sneak peek at Karen's April 2005 Avon Romance Superleader

Lady in Red

To many people, the Marquis of Treymount seemed a cold, impersonal man, but to be perfectly honest, Honoria knew differently. Irritating and smugly sure of his own supremacy, he was far from cold. He was, in fact, a man of fierce desires and unremitting determination. Few members of the ton had faced the man when he was pursuing something he really wanted, be it an ancient tapestry or a priceless Chinese vase. When in genuine pursuit, his coldly controlled mask fell away and one was treated to the blaze of determination and cold acuity that was rather intriguing to behold.

Honoria searched his face for some glimmer of his purpose, but none came. Irritated, she dipped a slight curtsy. "My lord, welcome to my home. I daresay you've come on a matter of business . . ." She raised her brows and waited.

His deep blue eyes raked across her, lingering on her hair. Honoria had to swallow the urge to make a face at him. It was a peculiar tendency of his, to pause and measure one before engaging in conversation. She'd seen him depress the attentions of any number of toad-eating position worshippers. Under that hard stare, most people found themselves stuttering, anxious to please. Thank God she had her pride to hold her head upright, even before such an imperious gesture.

Still, she couldn't help but wish she'd worn her good morning dress, though she doubted it would make any difference other than to make her feel somewhat more confident; the man was used to the finest of the fine, and even her good morning dress could not be counted as such. She glanced at him and waited . . . but still he did not speak.

A flicker of uncertainty brushed across her. Was he silently taunting her? Or was it something else? Honoria's back stiffened. She did not like being put at such a disadvantage. Treymount's continued silence began to weight the air.

"Oh pother! Enough of this!" She crossed her arms over her chest, fighting the desire to merely order the cad out of her house. At least his rudeness freed her to speak her mind. "Treymount, what do you want?"

He bowed, an ironic smile touching his lips, his gaze still crossing over her face, to her hair and back. "I am sorry if I appeared rude but . . . did I interrupt you in something . . ." Again that flickering glance to her hair. ". . . important?"

Her face heated instantly. She was used to people staring at her hair whenever they first met—the streak of white at her right temple made a lot of people pause. Some stared. Some pointedly looked away. Some gawked as if she had two heads. But Honoria had faced Treymount more than once now. Surely he wasn't merely looking at her because of that silly streak.

She unconsciously touched her hair . . . Her fingers found something and her eyes widened. "Cobwebs!" She crossed to the mirror over the fireplace so she could see the damage, laughing when she caught sight of herself. Two frothy strands of cobwebs hung across her hair and draped dramatically to one shoulder. Worse, a faint smudge of dust lined one of her cheekbones. "Ye gods, I look as if I've been in a crypt! No wonder you were staring. I'm a complete fright."

His gaze met hers in the mirror, a surprising hint of amusement lightening the usual cool blue to something far warmer. "I was going to suggest you'd been counting linens from a dark, deep closet, but a crypt is a much more romantic location to gather cobwebs."

"Cobwebs are not romantic." Honoria whisked her hand over her head and cleaned away the sweep of misty white strands. "I am sorry to receive you while so mussed. I was assisting my little brother in locating something he's lost." That was what she got for even worrying about her appearance to begin with, she decided, shrugging at her own silliness.

The door opened and Mrs. Kemble entered, bearing a heavy tray. "Here we are, miss!" She set the tray on the small table by the sofa and then stood back, beaming. "There weren't no more apple tarts left, being as how Miss Portia visited the kitchen not ten minutes before I did and ate every last one. But Cook had some pasties a-cookin' and so I waited fer them to be ready."

"Thank you, Mrs. Kemble."

The housekeeper curtsied, though she managed to look the marquis up and down as she went. "Will ye be needing anything else?"

"No, thank you," Honoria said. "I believe this will suffice."

"Very well, miss." With one more curtsy and yet another lingering glance at the marquis, the housekeeper was gone, no doubt to regale the kitchen staff with her impressions of their lofty visitor.

Honoria went to the chair by the table and gestured to the nearby sofa. "Will you be seated, my lord?"

He hesitated, and she smoothly added, "I hope you are famished, for I am." She busied herself with the tray, adjusting the cups and putting a pastry on a plate, and all the while her mind whirled.

Perhaps he'd come about an object he wished to purchase. It was unusual, but not unheard of. Certainly other members of the ton called occasionally when looking for something specific. Not often, of course. But still . . . Mentally, she reviewed the more recent acquisitions. None of them were of the quality that he normally pursued.

If there was something good to be said for the Marquis of Treymount—and she knew of only one thing—it was that he appreciated the finest of antiquities and bought only the best. She had to admire his taste, if nothing else.

He stirred, as if making a sudden decision. "I suppose tea would not be amiss. I don't have long, but . . . why not?" He came to stand before the table, moving a loose pillow from the sofa and setting it out of the way.

To her chagrin, Honoria found herself at eye level with Treymount's thighs. It was strange, but in all of her dealings with the marquis, she had never noticed this particular part of his physique. Now that he was directly across from her, she couldn't help but admire the ripple of his muscles beneath his fitted breeches.

The man must ride often to keep such a fine figure—

He sat, his gaze catching hers. His brows rose as he caught her expression. "Yes?"

Her thoughts froze in place. Ye gods, did he know what she was thinking? Her neck prickled with heat, then her face. Hurriedly, she began pouring tea into a cup. "I—I—" She what? Admired his well-turned legs? What a horrid predicament! She could hardly admit—

His gaze dropped to the tray and he frowned. "Miss Baker-Sneed, I believe there is enough tea in that cup."

Honoria jerked back the teapot. She'd filled the cup over the brim and tea now sloshed into the saucer and tray below. "Oh dear! What was I thinking?" She reached for one of the linen napkins not soaked with tea. Just as her hand closed over it, Treymount reached over and clasped his hand about hers.

Honoria sat shock-still. His hand enveloped her, large and masculine and surprisingly warm. His fingers were long and tapered, his nails perfectly pared and trimmed, and yet that did nothing to disguise the pure strength of the man.

Her heart hammered against her chest, the unexpected touch sending the strangest heat through her body. She was going mad. She'd faced the marquis time and again at numerous auctions and never had she felt this tug of attraction. But it was more than a tug. It was a powerful wave, pure and primal. It washed over her, crashing through her thoughts and leaving her confused and disoriented.

In her bemused state, she could only stare wide-eyed as the marquis pulled her hand to him, causing her to lean forward, over the small table. His hand slid to her arm, his warm fingers encircling her wrist.

"My lord," she gasped. "What are you—"

"That's my ring." His eyes blazed into hers, accusation and anger flickering brightly in their depths. "And I came to get it back."